# SLEEPLESS KNIGHTS

## Mark H Williams

*Sleepless Knights* is, quite simply, a cracking good read. A cross between *The Remains of the Day*, *Le Morte d'Arthur* and *Harry Potter*, it's packed with charming characters, thrilling chases, intrigue and mystery. A glorious modern chapter of an age-old legend, *Sleepless Knights* introduces us to a distinctive and sympathetic new voice in fantasy writing.
— **Toby Whithouse**, writer for *Doctor Who* and creator of *Being Human*

STARRED REVIEW: Action and comedy duel for prominence in this brilliant debut novel about the knights of the Round Table. ... Williams, an experienced playwright and television writer, has created a delightful addition to the Arthurian canon.
— *Publishers Weekly*

Mark Williams' dazzling début shakes up Arthurian legend into a wildly inventive, roller coaster ride of thrills, hilarity, dark fantasy and brilliant characterisation all written with an exquisite elegance befitting the originality of the tale. Treat yourself.
— **Muriel Gray**, author of *The Trickster*, *Furnace*, and *The Ancient*

STARRED REVIEW: Written with obvious love for the Arthurian mythos, this tragic-comedy should appeal to anyone who shares a longing for the days of Camelot.
— *Library Journal*

Wonderful neo-chivalric highjinks. Williams gleefully takes the training wheels off the Arthurian cycle.
— **Mike Carey**, author of *The Unwritten* and the "Felix Castor" novels

Who would have thought that a mash-up between Jeeves and King Arthur would result in such a charmingly bonkers adventure? *Sleepless Knights* has the kind of silly energy that inspired Monty Python and *Time Bandits*, and plays out like a modern-day version of *The Sword in the Stone*. It's clearly the Arthurian epic PG Wodehouse never got around to writing. Grail-tastic fun for all ages.
— **Christopher Fowler**, author of *Film Freak*, *Hell Train*,
and the "Bryant & May Mysteries"

One of the most imaginative and original books I have read in ages. This type of out there fiction is right up my street. Give me more!
— **Darren Craske**, author of *Above His Station*, *Before His Time*,
and the "Cornelius Quaint Chronicles"

# Sleepless Knights

## Mark H Williams

METRO VANCOUVER                    DOMINION of CANADA

# Sleepless Knights

First Edition Paperback published August 2013: ISBN: 978–1–927609–01–9

First Edition eBook published August 2013, ISBN: 978–1–927609–02–6

Typeset in *Excelsior!* and Warnock

The "Atomic Fez Publishing" logo and the molecular headgear colophon is designed by, and copyright © 2009, Martin Butterworth of The Creative Partnership Pty, London, UK (www.CreativePartnership.co.uk).

## PUBLISHER'S NOTE:

ATOMIC FEZ PUBLISHING
3766 Moscrop Street
Burnaby, British Columbia
V5G 2C8, CANADA
WWW.ATOMICFEZ.COM

10    9    8    7    6    5    4    3    2

**Library and Archives Canada Cataloguing in Publication**

Williams, Mark H., 1976-, author
        Sleepless knights / Mark H. Williams.

Issued in print and electronic formats.
ISBN 978-1-927609-01-9 (pbk.).--ISBN 978-1-927609-02-6 (ebook)

        I. Title.

PR6123.I438S54 2013                    823'.92                    C2013-904336-5
                                                                   C2013-904337-3

# Table of Contents

| | |
|---|---|
| Day One | 3 |
| Day Two | 45 |
| Yesterday One | 83 |
| Day Three | 123 |
| Day Four | 163 |
| Yesterday Two | 199 |
| Day Five | 251 |
| Yesterday Three | 285 |
| The Otherday | 331 |
| The Last Day | 369 |
| Acknowledgements | 407 |
| About the Author | 409 |

For Sue, Dave and Lisa

# SLEEPLESS KNIGHTS

# Day One

# I

There was no escaping it. The Master was not where he should have been, and that was most disturbing.

Today being Ritual Day, I rose an hour earlier than usual to pay particular attention to his morning routine. Piping hot water for the daily bath. A fresh razor blade for his shave, first taking care to satisfy its appetite for bites and nicks with my own light stubble. Two rounds of toast, cut into soldiers slim enough to dip into the egg soft-boiling on the hob. Tea leaves, spooned into a dry, pre-warmed pot, allowed no more infusion than the time it takes to ascend the stairs to his chamber, set the tray upon the bedside table, and pour the first cup.

This morning, however, my knock was not answered with the customary "Enter, Lucas." Neither, after an appropriate interval, was a second, more vigorous rapping. Inclining my ear to the heavy oak door, I failed to discern any of the telltale sounds of sleep from within. With the tray growing ever more weighty in my hands and its contents in danger of crossing the perilously thin line separating brewed from stewed, I risked a peek through the keyhole.

His bed was entirely unslept in, the quilt smooth and unruffled, pillows still plumped. I calmly put the tray down on the landing and started a methodical search. *There is nothing to be gained from undue alarm,* I thought, looking under the bed and inside the wardrobe. *It is not as if this is the first time,* I told myself, scanning bathroom and airing cupboard. *I am leaping to false conclusions,* I reasoned, as I checked the cupboard under the stairs, *when in all likelihood he is exactly where I left him last night, sat in his favourite wicker chair in the conservatory.*

He was not in his favourite wicker chair in the conservatory.

The blanket I had covered him with before retiring for the night lay crumpled on the floor, a book spread-eagled beneath it. By now, my mild disquiet was threatening to blossom into moderate panic. A shrill peal cut through the morning air, and I realised that the egg had boiled dry and set off the smoke alarm. Dashing to the kitchen, I grabbed the pan and thrust it under the cold tap where it hissed at me, as if in rebuke. I opened the window to let out the acrid stench of burnt Bakelite handle and silence the alarm. It was then that I saw him.

The Master was sitting on the garden bench in his dressing gown and slippers, his vacant gaze fixed on a patch of crumbling brickwork on the cottage wall. He was chill and damp to the touch from the morning dew, but otherwise unscathed, the empty scabbard still fastened securely to his belt. A spider had spun a web between the tip of his ear and the edge of his shoulder. As I relocated the intrepid arachnid to the garden sundial, my happiness increased with the realisation that this particular episode had not been characterised by any more of the Master's wider wanderings. I lifted him up from the bench and eased his arm around my shoulder, carefully coaxing the basic motor functions that remained. In such a manner, I conveyed him to a wooden seat at the bottom of the stairs and went up into the bathroom.

As luck would have it, the level of the bathwater had just reached the overflow outlet. I pulled a lever on the side of the bath and diverted the excess water into the pipes that powered the counterweighted stair lift. The Master's chair slowly ascended to the top of the stairs, where I undressed him and conveyed him to the waters, fastening the scabbard belt carefully around his neck. I then turned my attention to the matter of his wardrobe. I had spread out the numerous pieces of the Master's ceremonial armour on his dressing table the previous day in readiness. I regarded each item of elaborate clothing in turn. Then I looked at his dressing gown, draped over my arm. I took out my pocket watch and made a few swift calculations.

I pulled a suitcase out from under the bed and packed the armour inside.

# II

My careless lack of foresight had squandered our early start, so it was late morning by the time we arrived at Hay-on-Wye. I drove the Jaguar into the yard at the side of the house, first moving the piles of junk that had accumulated there since my last visit and which prevented the access of anything wider than a bicycle. Through a series of deft manoeuvres I parked the car, before ensuring that the Master was safely secured in the back seat, his dressing gown pulled tight and the scabbard looped through the cord.

The back door was ajar. As I pushed against it, I noticed it had been forced open, and with some vigour. The door was barely attached to its hinges, its wooden panelling splintered, the glass of the upper window lying in shards on the kitchen floor. I propped the door against its battered frame as best as I could, then stopped in my tracks. Directly opposite the kitchen door, the dead body of a man sat slumped in a chair.

My heart skipped a beat. I was about to rush back to the car for the thermos flask, praying I was not too late to revive him, when a closer inspection revealed the man to be far younger than the owner of the house; in his early twenties, if that. His position made it appear as if he had simply nodded off, head lolling forward, forehead almost resting on the sword protruding from a wound in his heart. It was impossible to go any further without stepping in congealing blood. My subsequent footsteps made the sticky tearing sound one creates when walking on linoleum that has not seen a mop for some time. A recently brewed pot of coffee popped and gurgled on the counter in cheerful ignorance of the corpse. The aroma wafted away through the half-open entrance to the study, and I followed it through the gap.

The door resisted against what I assumed to be a stack of books. It felt safe to assume this, given that the room before me contained very little else. Books of every shape and size were arranged in piles, some the size of a small hedge, others as high as monumental pillars. Bulging bookcases lined every inch of wall space, their shelves coated in dust as thick as midwinter snow. The entire haphazard library formed a miniature maze that I began to navigate toward the centre of.

The layout of this literary labyrinth had changed entirely since my last visit, and my progress was little helped by the few rays of sunlight strong enough to push through the grime-coated bay window. Gingerly, I extended my fingers into the gloom, only to find a dead end of heavy tomes. I was about to move the topmost of these volumes, when a voice sounded from somewhere within the warren.

"Leave it, Lucas," it said. "It's bad enough being so late. For pity's sake don't compound matters by rearranging my entire library." By this verbal marker I found my way to the desk, where the speaker was engaged in his daily toil.

"I would not dream of it, Sir Kay."

"Well just don't, is all I'm saying." I paused for him to continue. When it became clear he was not about to address the unconventional scene in his kitchen, I considered it prudent to broach the subject myself.

"Forgive me if I am stating the obvious, Sir Kay, but there appears to be a dead body in your kitchen."

"Hm? Oh yes, that little bastard. He's ransacked three houses in the last month alone. Battered the old dear over the road black and blue for fifty quid and a TV set. Been watching me come and go all week, biding his time. Had the shock of his life when he ran into me last night, biding mine. See to the usual routine, would you Lucas?"

"Excuse me, Sir Kay?"

"Get rid of the body. Like you did last time."

"Last time, Sir Kay, was just over a hundred years ago."

"So?"

"Such matters are not as... straightforward as they once were."

"It's straightforward enough to me. Direct application of the Eternal Quest! Protect the weak and fight evil-doers. Elsie over the road is your 'weak.' That witless whelp cluttering up my kitchen is the 'evil doer.' "

"I understand what you are saying, Sir Kay. But I doubt the representatives of law enforcement will see it that way."

"Then you'd better dig a bloody deep hole. Spade's in the shed. And next time, phone ahead before you turn up, will you?"

"I did consider it, but decided against interrupting your labours."

"Well it didn't work. I couldn't settle on a single thing all morning for looking at my watch, wondering when you'd decide to roll on up." He picked up a book and quickly placed it over a newspaper crossword.

"And how is your work, Sir Kay?"

"Don't ask."

"Very well, Sir Kay."

"I'm fed up with the lot of it, Lucas. Fed up with looking at it. Fed up with thinking about it. And certainly fed up with talking about it."

"In that case, I shall —"

"Sometimes I wonder why I ever bothered putting pen to parchment in the first place. All it's ever brought me is anonymity, failure, penury and disappointment."

"Come now, Sir Kay. I am not much of a reader myself —"

"Ha, you said it there."

"— but I have always held your *History* in the highest esteem. As has the Master."

"Yes, he would, wouldn't he? But what's the good of writing something so, so..."

"Clever?"

"It *is* clever, but that's not the word I'm after. So, so..."

"Influential?"

"Just let me think for a moment!" He clicked his fingers. "Seminal! What's the point of writing something so *seminal* as my *History*, when I'm never allowed to claim any credit for my, erm... seminality..."

"Seminalitude?"

"Damn it man, are you a butler or a thesaurus?"

"Sorry, Sir Kay."

"Well, I suppose I should pack."

"You have not already done so?"

"Of course I haven't! I've been too busy working. What kept you, anyway? You haven't been this late since — oh. Oh no. He isn't, is he?"

"If you are referring to one of the Master's delicate spells, then I am afraid you are correct."

"Oh dear me, no. He could be gone for days. Weeks. Years! What are we going to do about tonight?"

"I am sure we will manage, Sir Kay."

"But it's hardly ideal, is it?"

"No, it is not, Sir Kay. Which is why I would be most grateful if you would prepare for departure, and with a degree of haste." I had taken out my pocket watch, and did not care for the expression on its face.

"Yes, yes, don't fuss, I was just about to." Sir Kay began to select certain volumes from the library, carefully placing them into a large leather hold-all.

While he continued with his packing I set to work in the kitchen. I reattached and boarded up the back door, swept up the glass, and washed the worst of the blood from the floor. By the time Sir Kay was staggering to the car with the first of several suitcases, I had buried the body of the intruder and the murder weapon, the shallow grave easy to obscure thanks to a thick tangle of weeds in the untended vegetable patch.

"Are you quite sure you will need so many books, Sir Kay?" I said, returning the spade to the shed. "We shall have you back by this time tomorrow."

"Once again, Lucas," he puffed, shoving in a large box on top of the cases, "you demonstrate your complete ignorance of the creative life. We writers thrive on books. They are our lifeblood. Speaking of which, you'll want to give the kitchen floor another clean. You missed a spot."

# III

According to my updated itinerary we remained within the margins of an acceptable time frame. Nevertheless, it was still something of a relief to leave Hay behind and head for the hills, the vintage car's suspension making only the mildest of complaints at the weight of Sir Kay's books. Their owner sat beside me in the passenger seat, absorbed in an ancient tome. The Master remained strapped into the back seat and gave no outward sign of waking in the immediate future. Sir Kay was correct in anticipating that this would make the evening's ritual difficult, but it was by no means impossible. What concerned me far more, as it always did, was the safe conveyance of all seven participants to our destination in plenty of time for the appointed hour. But, even the grandest banquet is served one course at a time, so I focused my attention upon the hills and forests ahead.

When we reached the right spot I pulled the Jaguar into a lay-by and switched off the engine. "I am going to get Sir Pellinore, Sir Kay," I said. He did not look up from his book, but I took a barely audible grunt to indicate comprehension. "I anticipate I shall be no more than half an hour. Please pause in your reading from time to time, and check on the Master. His seatbelt is secure, but it is no substitute for a wary spirit and a watchful eye." Another mumble came forth. "Should you require refreshment, you will find a selection of ham sandwiches in a Tupperware box on the back seat. Those with mustard are wrapped in tin foil; those without, in cling film." I paused until I received a final low murmur in the affirmative, and opened the boot of the car to retrieve the items essential for the summoning of Sir Pellinore.

First a large mouldering headdress, upon which the antlers of a stag were secured, like two frozen flashes of forked lightning. Next, a grey cloak, threadbare cousin to the headdress, which I wrapped about my shoulders. Finally, a walking staff, gnarled and stout, and a hunting horn small enough to fit in my trouser pocket. Thus equipped, I stepped over a low ditch, through a gap in the hedge, and into the forest.

I did not venture far before the cheerful brightness of the summer day vanished, with only an occasional dappling of sunlight penetrating the canopy of leaves. Unlike Sir Kay's study, however, this landscape was reassuringly consistent in its geography, and I had no fear of losing my way. Between the gathering of tall oaks; across the narrow trickle of a stream. Past the log stump that resembles Queen Victoria. Up a muddy embankment, along the moss-hugged ruins of a stone wall, and into a glade, agreed upon long ago as a suitable summoning spot. I took a moment to prepare myself, under the inquisitive eye of a local pheasant. With the horn ready in my hand I cleared my throat, tipped back my head and, in a faltering tenor, sang out

> *Questing Beast, Yelping Beast,*
> *Yell Hound, Yelper, Hound of Doom!*

I followed this with two long blows on the hunting horn. I allowed a full minute to pass, during which the only response was the coo of a distant dove and a bewildered tilting of the head from the pheasant. So I sang again, in a more forceful tone,

> *Questing Beast!*
> *Yelping Beast!*
> *Yell Hound!*
> *Yelper!*
> *Hound of Doom!*

Two further horn blasts were more than enough for the pheasant, who gave me a pitying look and returned to his foraging. But this time, I was answered by a faint yet clearly discernible baritone.

> *Beware the sword of Pellinore,*
> *That seeks for thee by sun and moon!*

I gave another blow on the horn. Into the prevailing stillness came the sound of a large form galumphing through the undergrowth. The baritone now took up the complete chorus by itself, as well as a verse I could not quite make out. I scanned the flora in front of me. Judging by the direction the sound seemed to be coming from, I calculated he would arrive through the bush to my left. I steadied myself in front of it. I trained my eyes upon it. I braced myself.

The bush to my right exploded in a flurry of foliage, to reveal the bounding form of Sir Pellinore. As usual, a misjudgement in momentum carried him into the centre of the glade and straight into me. As usual, he was dressed in full armour and greatcoat, all but obscured by a covering of bags, ropes, traps, weaponry and camping equipment. And, as usual, we tumbled to the ground in a seething jumble, from which I attempted to disentangle us.

"Herne the Hunter, as I live and breathe!" he cried, clasping me about the shoulders as we got to our feet.

"Greetings, Sir Pellinore," I replied, steadying my antlers and trying to stay in character, "how goes the quest?"

He patted a dozen pockets, handing me a clump of moss, a catapult, and a dozing field mouse before he found what he was looking for. "Feast your eyes!" A handful of pungent droppings were thrust under my nose. "From the Wild Boar of Wales."

"Indeed, Sir Pellinore?" I said, holding my breath.

"Indeed 'indeed,' Herne boy bach. And you know what *that* means!"

"I am sure I do, Sir Pellinore," I said, turning aside for a gulp of air. "But in the event that I am mistaken, I would be grateful if you could remind me."

He leaned in, close enough for me to remove several of the twigs stuck in his hair. "The Beast is abroad, Herne." A brisk movement beneath the layers surrounding his legs suggested a hop of glee. "Wherever the Wild Boar is found, the Questing Beast is never far behind! Mortal enemies, the pair of 'em. Destined to hunt each other down to the bitter bloody end, or 'til time itself runs dry." He drew closer. "Caught the trail just once, this twelvemonth. Last Boxing Day, it was. I was snatching a nap under a tree when I was woken by its sound — that yapping and baying of sixty hounds, coming from the belly of the Beast. Then I saw it, through the morning mist! Just a glimpse, mind, but long enough to hold each other, eye to eye. Head of a snake. Body of a leopard. Feet of a stag, and a lion's arse. Or was it the feet of a lion, and a stag's arse? It was dashed foggy...

"But, here's the thing, Herne — I was not alone in the hunt! A gang of brigands on horseback joined the chase, hullabalooing and dressed in red like a pack of sore thumbs. Spoiling the quest, damn their eyes! *My* quest, the quest of Pellinore or his next of kin! I told them as much. At least, I tried to. They galloped screaming for the hills at the first sight of me. Tch! Amateurs. I picked up the trail, but the Beast had long since scarpered. Too fast for Pellinore. But not too fast for Pellinore *and* Herne! The kill is mine, of course. But I could use a nose like yours. Not to mention that magic stuff you do so well. What say you, Herne? Will you join me on the gallivant?"

Sir Pellinore sneezed ferociously and a shower of droplets flew from his moustache. Quite how it had got so waterlogged on a dry summer's day was a mystery, though it probably had something to do with the fronds of pondweed that I brushed from his shoulders.

"It is a tempting offer, Sir Pellinore," I said, choosing Herne's words with care, for lengthening shadows in the glade told me the sun was entering its afternoon wane. "But before we discuss terms and conditions, I have a message from the Master. He summons you to the ritual."

"Flying Squids of Atlantis! Is it that time already?"

"It is, Sir Pellinore."

"It can't have been a year since the last one?"

"It has, Sir Pellinore."

"Well I'll be a badger's aunt."

"If you must, Sir Pellinore."

"Right-o. Point me at my horse."

"Transport will have to be on foot, Sir Pellinore," I said, recalling his last encounter with a car. "Sir Lucas the butler awaits you on the path."

"Lucas! That old cove! Mind you, Herne," he said with a series of exaggerated winks, "not a word to him about the Questing Beast. Not exactly official business, if you catch my drift?"

"As ever, your secret is safe with me, Sir Pellinore."

"That's m'Herne."

"This way, Sir Pellinore."

I guided him out of the glade, gathering up his rope as we walked and liberating several small animals caught in its coils. We had almost reached the forest path when he insisted on checking some traps he had set outside a rabbit burrow. I took advantage of the interlude to remove my antlers, and not without relief, for prolonged wearing of the headdress produces a chafing about my forehead.

"Ah, Lucas! There you are."

"Good afternoon, Sir Pellinore."

"You were right, Herne — Herne?" He swung around, goggling. "Funny. He was here a second ago. You haven't seen a huntsman mooching about, Lucas? About your height? Antlers? Answers to the name of Herne?"

"I have not had the pleasure," I said, holding the headdress firmly behind my back.

"Pity. Think you two would get on."

"I am sure we would."

"Well, I'd best be off. Westerly direction, isn't it?"

"East, Sir Pellinore," I said, turning him around and watching him walk off down the narrow track, a fox cub trotting at his heels.

I returned to the car to find Sir Kay exactly as I had left him, a clump of tin foil and a few crusts on the dashboard the only sign of movement. Unfortunately, it was not the only thing that had changed during my absence. I opened the back door. I checked on the floor. I looked under the car. I even opened the boot, just in case. But there was no mistaking it.

The Master had gone.

# IV

"I'm telling you, Lucas, the first I knew of it was when you returned," said Sir Kay, "and if you hadn't spent so long nymphing around in the woods with Pellinore, he'd still be here." I drove along the forest road at a snail's pace, scrutinising the trees for any sign of the Master. "What's more, I'm not a bloody detective. I was engrossed in my work. He could've quietly opened the door at any time and slipped away without me noticing."

"In any case, Sir Kay, perhaps you might look for him now, while I keep my eyes on the road ahead?"

Sir Kay closed his book with a reluctant thud. "There he is!" he said, pointing through the windscreen. "Look, up there!" We screeched to a halt.

"Where?" I said, craning forwards.

"Behind that tree," said Sir Kay. "Not there — *there!* No... my mistake. That's another tree. Sorry."

I engaged the handbrake and took stock of the situation. If the Master was suffering the sleepwalking variant of his condition, he could not have ventured far during the time I was away from the car. Additionally, there was a chance that instinct would lead him to our ultimate destination. If, on the other hand, he did not reach it of his own accord, then at the very least there would be more people available to form a search party. Cheered by this prospect, I drove with all legal speed to The Once & Future Inn.

†

For a supposedly quiet pub, the main bar was remarkably busy. Unfortunately, the Master did not number among its many patrons. Neither did the member of our party who should have arrived at his regular table several hours ago. I left Sir Kay nursing a whisky on a bar stool next to where Sir Pellinore was already on his second pint. The landlord caught my eye as I approached the far end of the bar.

"Lucas!" he beamed, punching me in the shoulder. "Pull up a pew. Will you join me in a nip of something?"

"Thank you, Sir Perceval, but no."

"A bite, then?" Sir Perceval hollered over his shoulder towards the kitchen. "How are those chickens doing?"

Through a gap in the door I caught a glimpse of the Grail, that curious Celtic cauldron. It hovered along a line of small baskets in which a succession of sizzling chicken quarters appeared from out of thin air. I decided to overlook the security breach posed by this misuse of the Master's property, not to mention by the increasingly bustling bar, for more pressing concerns. "I have urgent need of your assistance, Sir Perceval. The Master is experiencing his old complaint."

"Oh Lordy. What set him off this time?"

"It may have been a spot of crumbling brickwork on the cottage wall that bears a passing similarity to a certain someone."

"But we checked the wall last time I was over! There was nothing that looked even remotely like her."

"Apparently, we failed to account for the highly subjective influence of the Master's imagination in these matters. It is a lesson I should have learnt after the cloud formations of 1976."

"Yes, you should."

"Unfortunately, while I was summoning Sir Pellinore this afternoon, the condition took a turn for the worse. He is now suffering from the wandering variation."

"But he hasn't had one of those since the Middle Ages!"

"Indeed, Sir Perceval. It is long overdue, and I should have been expecting it."

"Well, he can't have got very far; there is that, I suppose."

"That was also my reasoning. I must depart immediately for De Troyes Manor. Before you prepare the Lower Room, perhaps you might assist Sir Kay and Sir Pellinore in a thorough search of the surrounding region?"

"Consider it done." Sir Perceval started to drain his tankard, before pausing mid-gulp. "Sorry, but you said something about preparing...?"

"The Lower Room, Sir Perceval."

"No Luc, you've lost me now. Say again?"

"Preparing the Lower Room. The basement. For tonight."

We had been talking loudly to compete with the general hullabaloo, and I was reluctant to raise my voice any higher. I cast a careful look over both shoulders and leaned in closer. "For the ritual," I hissed.

"The ritual!" Sir Perceval roared. "By the Giant's cloak of beards, that's never tonight?"

I winced at the patch of sudden silence that always follows a loud and indiscrete public utterance. "Sir Perceval! A little delicacy, if you please."

"Sorry, of course, of course," he said, tapping his nose conspiratorially and failing to lower his voice to anywhere near the level I would have preferred. "It's not like me to forget. Wrote it down and everything." He gestured at the wall behind him. On my last visit I had given him a calendar to prevent just such an eventuality as this. I could only suppose that beneath the patchwork quilt of iou-s, recipes torn from magazines, and ribald messages from pub regulars, it was still there.

"Surely you were reminded by Sir Gawain?" I said, glancing again at his empty table.

"I promise you Lucas, he made no mention of the ritual when he was in earlier."

"Forgive me, Sir Perceval. By your use of the word 'earlier,' am I to take it the aforementioned knight is no longer on the premises?"

"Well, er…" Sir Perceval's already ruddy face deepened to dark scarlet.

"Then, where is he?"

"He, er… um… That's a good question." Perspiration beaded his brow. "Do you know, I feel a funny turn coming on. I think it's my heart."

I cleared my throat.

"It being the weekend, he has gone south, naturally," said Sir Perceval.

"Not so 'naturally,' given that we are under orders not to stray from the immediate vicinity," I said.

Sir Perceval polished off his pint and swallowed hard, but the ale did little to diminish the fire in his cheeks. "Well, when I say *south*, what I really mean is —"

"Sir Perceval. You need not temper your words. *If* Sir Gawain has ventured further than is strictly permissible, the Master does not need to be informed. Provided I can find our comrade in time for the ritual."

"He went to Cardiff for the night," said Sir Perceval, with a sigh of relief. "But you didn't hear that from me, Lucas."

"Of course, Sir Perceval."

# V

De Troyes Manor was situated *en route* to the city of Cardiff; no small blessing, for after picking up its owner I could enlist his help in the retrieval of Sir Gawain. But, as I noted the large number of vehicles parked along the length of the tree-lined drive, I began to suspect that the attention of Lance De Troyes might be otherwise engaged.

Mr Crossley, Mr De Troyes' head butler, confirmed as much when he met me at the door. "Tonight is the presentation dinner for the De Troyes Foundation's Active Life Achiever of the Year, Mr Lucas," said that fine footman, handing my coat to a subordinate. I glanced into the main hall, thronged with the county's great and good. "The final course has just been cleared, but I could bring you a selection of cold cuts while you wait?"

"Thank you, Mr Crossley, but time is in short supply. Please inform your master of my arrival, and the need for a swift departure, as soon as he has performed his duties."

"Forgive me, Mr Lucas, but he made no mention of leaving the Manor this evening."

"That is curious, Mr Crossley."

"That was my sentiment. He has set aside this night for yourself and the Old Boys every year that I have been in his service. However, perhaps the following message will illuminate his intentions. He wishes you to know that he is feeling 'far from hale and hearty' this evening. Are you quite alright, Mr Lucas? Your face has taken on a sudden anaemic hue."

"I wonder if you would be so kind as to fetch me a glass of water?"

He did so. I drained it in one draught.

"Thank you. Those were his exact words?" I said.

"To the letter. Master De Troyes was adamant I convey the message just so."

"The message is well delivered, Mr Crossley," I said. He nodded and returned to his duties. I positioned myself at the back of the main hall, centre to the stage where the man of the hour was preparing to make his speech.

Lance De Troyes adjusted his microphone, observing his mature and immaculate audience until every eye was fixed on him alone. A crackle of anticipation charged the air, raising gooseflesh on the arms of every woman and several of the men. The chatter of the crowd dropped to a low susurrus.

"Ladies and gentlemen. Welcome to De Troyes Manor. Now, you all know I'm not one for long speeches. Not when the night is young and the wine is vintage." He paused in a warm wash of laughter. "But of all the work undertaken by the De Troyes Foundation, the Active Life Achiever of the Year is closest to my heart. This year's winner is an example to us all. I fully intend to follow her example — when I finally retire, that is." He ran a hand through his lightly silvered hair. "But I digress. Tonight is not my night. Tonight belongs to a lady who sits on no less than *five* of the charity committees supported by the De Troyes Foundation. A lady who, when not sharing her expertise on the bowling green with disadvantaged teenagers, is keeping her fellow pensioners as fit as she is with her aqua yoga classes. A lady who considers any spare time to be wasted, if it is not spent at her sanctuary for abandoned dogs. And so, without further ado, it gives me enormous pleasure to present the Active Life Achiever of the Year award to... Mrs Kathleen Bliss!"

A twinkling septuagenarian took to the stage, to a round of envious applause. Lance kissed her on both cheeks, and presented her with a gold envelope and a magnum of champagne. "Ladies and gentlemen. Charge your glasses, and join me in a toast. To... er... To..." He patted his breast pocket absently. The audience fell silent, save for a solitary cough.

This was it, then.

"Join me, in raising your glasses to..." A murmur of concern passed through the crowd. I swiftly made my way to the front of the hall.

"In raising a toast, to the charming and deserving..." Lance De Troyes loosened his tie. "Forgive me, friends," he said, "but I feel far from hale and hearty this evening."

With that, he tottered on his feet and keeled forwards.

The crowd's murmur exploded into a full-blown gasp. The lectern was upturned — knocking over a side table and a jug of water — as Lance De Troyes fell like a cut oak. I caught him by the shoulders, mere inches before he hit the ground, and gently lowered him the rest of the way to the floor. Kathleen Bliss let out a curdling scream. The horror-struck crowd were about to press in upon us when Mr Crossley intervened. "Please, stand back, give us some room," he said, crouching beside the body of his master and feeling for a pulse. "Mr Lucas. Is he —?"

"Help me convey him to the drawing room," I replied. His sentence was best finished behind closed doors. I wished to avoid the pandemonium that would undoubtedly ensue, should the crowd get wind of the fact that Lance De Troyes was dead.

It is to Mr Crossley's eternal credit that, following his master's sudden demise, decorum defined the hour. A doctor attending the dinner was brought to the body, confirmed the death, cause as yet unknown, and was assured by myself that the necessary arrangements would be made. The distraught yet diligent house staff calmed the guests with the temporary cover story that their host had collapsed from exhaustion, before clearing the premises. Then they too were dismissed, having been informed of the sad news, and that their employer, mindful of a congenital heart condition, had made ample provision for their welfare. Only when the last of them had gone did Mr Crossley's shoulders droop by so much as a fraction.

"Well, Mr Lucas," he said, brushing away some dust from his master's jacket, "I shall contact the ambulance service."

"Thank you, Mr Crossley, but I will see to things from here. Go and get some rest."

"Thank you, Mr Lucas, but I would rather attend to it personally. There will be statements to make, documents to sign."

"All of that is to be undertaken by myself as executor, as stipulated in Mr De Troyes' last will and testament," I said, moving to the drawing room safe and producing the document for his perusal. "It was his desire that you be spared any of the unpleasant but necessary matters that would follow his untimely demise." Mr Crossley's eyes passed along each page until they reached the signature at the end.

"I see," he said, folding the will and handing it back. "Then I have little choice but to bid you goodnight."

"Goodnight, Mr Crossley. You will be notified of the funeral arrangements. My deepest condolences."

"Thank you, Mr Lucas. Farewell, sir."

✝

The moment the mansion was out of sight I turned the Jaguar into a secluded lane and regarded the body of the deceased, propped up on the back seat and hastily covered with a picnic blanket. With mounting trepidation, I removed the thermos flask kept in the glove compartment for emergency scenarios such as this. I dispensed a measure of liquid which gently steamed like hot tea. I turned so that I was kneeling in the driver's seat. With one hand, I drew back the makeshift shroud and lowered Lance De Troyes' chin. With the other hand, I carefully poured the cup's contents into his open mouth. I closed his mouth again and took out my pocket watch.

For twenty eight seconds, nothing happened.

At thirty five seconds, his lips and chin glistened with a faint gleam where some of the liquid had spilled.

After forty two seconds, Lance De Troyes coughed, spluttered, and took in a gasping lungful of air, like a half-drowned man breaking the surface of the sea. He opened his eyes and blinked hard. "That went rather well, don't you think Lucas?" he said.

"There were no technical hitches to speak of, Sir Lancelot," I replied, somewhat relieved. Sir Lancelot flexed his muscles and stretched his arms. He picked up a suitcase from the floor of the car, opening it on the seat beside him.

"A pretty commonplace death. Slow-acting poison. Almost makes me nostalgic for all those arrows," he said.

"I really am sorry about that —"

"Relax, Lucas, I'm pulling your leg. They can't all be showstoppers, especially these days. It had to be done. Lance De Troyes was getting a reputation as something of a Dorian Gray. Some of the old dears were asking awkward questions about where their investment money was going. Still, onwards and upwards. Scotland next. Been working on a character called Connor MacRitchie. A laird. Ginger.

You'll like him. Same plan as before. Set up a charity, under the guise of building a hedgehog sanctuary or some such rubbish. Charm dotty millionaires out of their cash and give it to the people who really need it.

"I take it I can rely on you to find a suitable house and get the staff up and running, Lucas? Once my funeral's over and the dust has settled." Sir Lancelot pulled out a tie from the suitcase and held it against his collar.

"Excuse me for saying so, Sir Lancelot, but Scotland is…"

"Yes?"

"Scotland strikes me as…"

"Go on."

"Somewhat removed from our base of operations."

"So was France."

"Indeed, but that was some time ago."

"I follow the Eternal Quest how I choose, Lucas. You know that. *He* knows that." The hoot of an owl broke a silence that was seconds away from becoming uncomfortable.

"Forgive me, Sir Lancelot. I shall assist in any way I can."

"Good." A second hoot followed, as if to clear the air. "Shame I can't bring old Crossley with me. How did he take it, at the end?"

"Stoically, but not without an appropriate measure of sorrow."

"Yes. Yes, of course. Good old Crossley." Sir Lancelot seemed to be having great difficulty deciding which jacket to wear, for his eyes were downcast, as if mesmerised by the contents of the suitcase. I was about to suggest charcoal grey, when he made his choice and plumped for black. I started the car and returned to the road.

"Tell me, Lucas. And be honest. How was I tonight, performance-wise?"

"I have no notes to give, save your choice of day, Sir Lancelot."

"Don't flap, I haven't forgotten what night it is. We have plenty of time. Besides, I thought it was rather fitting. Death and rebirth, the circle of life?"

"I appreciate the dramatic irony. But today has seen a more demanding timetable than usual."

"Oh?"

"The Master is suffering from his recurring condition."

We had reached the turning that led back to the Once & Future Inn. I stopped at the crossroads and regarded Sir Lancelot in the rear view mirror. The light cast by the full moon gave his face the appearance of being hewn from stone.

"Then he'll just have to drink it through a straw," he said.

"He is also in the grip of a wandering variation," I said. A deep sigh wafted over my shoulder.

"Grant me mercy... I suppose you want me to help search for him?"

"It is not that straightforward. There is also the matter of Sir Gawain. He has ventured unaccompanied into the metropolis."

"God's teeth!" A fist struck leather upholstery.

"I am inclined to agree, Sir Lancelot," I replied.

# VI

I confess I was unprepared for the panorama presenting itself as we entered the heart of Cardiff. The streets teemed with revellers in advanced states of inebriation. Females, dressed in the flimsiest of attire, staggered past lurid neon signs, or lurched on unsuitable shoes into the path of the taxis they were attempting to hail. Their male counterparts, though more sturdily shod, yielded nothing to the women when it came to intoxication. When not swaggering and preening for the attention of potential mates, they rutted with rivals in periodic bouts of violence. So territorial were these clashes that I half expected them to start marking their turf. Sure enough, I had scarcely formed the thought when one of them unzipped his flies and did exactly that. The ill tidings of the dashboard clock returned me to my senses.

"What manner of feast day is this?" I said, when we had located suitable parking down a side street.

"Saturday night. Perhaps you should stay with the car, Lucas. The capital on a weekend is no place for a butler."

"Thank you for your concern, Sir Lancelot. But I think it would be better, given our tight schedule, that I accompany you in the retrieval of Sir Gawain."

"Stay close to me, then. And watch your step. There are pitfalls aplenty for the unwary traveller."

As indeed there were, even during our short journey to Jennifer's Nightclub, a favourite haunt of our companion according to Sir Lancelot. A man stumbled towards me, a bottle of lager slipping from each hand; these I caught before they could shatter on the pavement, placing the empty one in a litter bin and the full one in my trouser pocket. I pulled back a girl who was teetering on the edge of the kerb, so that she might find herself inside the bus she was waiting for, rather than spread across the front of it. The tramp intent on following her aboard found his hand clasping not the bag he had been grabbing for, but the full bottle of lager from my pocket, and was still thanking his lucky stars when the doors closed and the bus drove the girl safely away.

All the while, Sir Lancelot forged ahead with the kind of stride that informed anyone blocking his path of the folly of their ways. Including the stocky guardsmen stationed at the nightclub doorway, who simply nodded him through as if he owned the place. For all I knew of his numerous business interests, he probably did. Upon entering, a monstrous sound assailed my ears, as of the rumbling and growling of a cornered animal. This dreadful racket was interspersed with a female wailing, like a lady confronted by the desperate creature, screaming for her very life. But apparently I was the only one disturbed by the din, for the occupants of Jennifer's moved happily to its rhythm. At the centre of a sea of bodies I espied Sir Gawain, nimble of foot and brimful of ale, oblivious to Sir Lancelot wading steadily towards him. I hesitated at the edge of the dancing area, partly because I was still taking it all in, and partly because the young man entering the club behind me, assuming me for some kind of attendant, had just handed me his coat. I placed it around the shoulders of a scantily clad girl who was on her way out, and followed in Sir Lancelot's wake.

Sir Gawain was dancing at the centre of a group of women fitted out in a variety of costumes, including several in a style favoured by the French serving classes during the last century. Their approval of Sir Gawain's dancing was in inverse proportion to the disapproval of a gang of men surveying the scene from a table to our right with skirmish-hungry stares. Upon seeing Sir Lancelot, Sir Gawain merely rolled his eyes and continued to dance. "What do you want, Lancey? Can't yer see I'm busy?" he shouted above the noise.

"No you're not, Gawain. You're coming with me."

"I like your friend, Gawain," said a girl in black, with plastic feline ears and smudged whiskers on her cheeks. "What's his name?"

"Buggering Off," said Sir Gawain, moving between Sir Lancelot and the cat-woman.

"Aw come on, share it with the hen!" said one in a bridal veil, a red letter 'L' pinned to her back. She draped her arm around Sir Lancelot's neck, her head lolling on his shoulder. He looked towards the table of observers, just as a collective jolt of anger spurred them up out of their seats. Sir Gawain noted it too, and smiled thinly.

"Ach, don't bother with him, Sandra," said Sir Gawain, putting his arm around the bride. "I'm your last request, remember?"

"You've exceeded your limits, Gawain," said Sir Lancelot.

"Oh I'm just getting warmed up," replied Sir Gawain, taking a long swig at a champagne bottle.

"It's Ritual Night," said Sir Lancelot through gritted teeth. From the corner of my eye, I marked our observers' swift approach. Sir Gawain released the bride.

"Then I'll get a taxi."

"To the Inn? Talk sense, man!"

"You're not the only one with money, Lance DeWhatnot."

"We're running out of time. We need to leave."

"*This* is my Ritual Night, right here. So why don't you run back to your wee mansion?"

"You fool, Gawain! You'll die —"

"You're dead, you Scottish bastard." Our observers, all six of them, now had us surrounded. Their leader pushed Sir Gawain in the shoulder. "You're old enough to be their dad," he said.

"Grandddad," chimed a henchman. Physically, this was true, though inaccurate on a point of technicality by some years. Over one thousand, four hundred years, to be more precise.

"Barry? What the hell are you doing here? Just go, will you!" said Sandra.

"Shut up and stay out of this, I ain't even started on you yet," replied this 'Barry.'

Sir Lancelot inclined his head towards Barry, as if he were about to share an intimate secret. "One: You do not address a lady in that tone and manner. Ever. Two: Kindly remove your hand from my companion's shoulder. Now."

Barry's hand stayed exactly where it was. At his side, the fingers of the other hand squeezed the neck of a beer bottle. His mouth twisted into in a grim sneer. Green eyes flashed fire. With a flick of his wrist he smashed the bottle on the side of a pillar.

"Or what?" he said.

"Or I promise you, you will not leave this place without suffering blows most dolorous."

"You what?"

Sir Gawain took a step closer to Sir Lancelot and Barry. "He means *come an have a go if ye think yer hard enough, ya manky wee goat scrote.*"

Barry's jagged bottle swung for Sir Lancelot in a wide arc. Sir Lancelot stepped neatly to one side, upsetting Barry's balance, not to mention his pride, as he found himself floored by his own momentum. The bottle flew out of his hand and towards the unflinching Sir Gawain, nicking his neck. Sir Gawain touched the skin, looked at the blood on his fingers, and smiled. "Been there, done that," he said, and head-butted Barry's chief henchman, sending him sprawling back towards his fellows.

As if a stone had been dropped into the centre of an ant hill, the patrons surrounding us scattered in alarm. Furious now, Barry's gang attacked. One flew for Sir Lancelot's waist, only to meet the knight's foot, sending him into the path of another, who was charging for Sir Gawain with a chair raised above his head. The chair fell towards the cat-woman, who proved decidedly less nimble than her namesake; I caught the chair by the leg and threw it to Sir Gawain, who made good use of it to brain a man about to strangle him from behind.

From the farthest corners of the nightclub, a battalion of Barry clones flocked to his flag. The mere existence of the fight was enough to secure their allegiance to his cause; no sooner was one man dispatched to the heap of casualties on the dance floor, than another sprang up to take his place. Thus assailed from all directions, Sir Lancelot and Sir Gawain found themselves marooned in the centre of an ever-growing Barry island. Retreating to a vantage point outside the sphere of conflict, I could see that chaos reigned within. Flying bottles filled the air, smashing against mirrored walls. Bystanders took advantage of the *mêlée* to settle old scores and create new ones especially for the occasion. Staff ran pell-mell in all directions, shouting for the authorities who would not be long in arriving.

And when they did, what then?

A pint glass hit the clock behind the bar. The clock face read a quarter to eleven. Panic seized my heart. But not, as you might think, at the realisation that we were running out of time. It was more that, unless I was very much mistaken, *time itself* had suddenly ground to a standstill. The shards of the pint glass, far from exploding in every direction as one would expect, had frozen at the moment of impact. To my left, a man's fist rested in front of his victim's face, from which a line of blood hung suspended, as if he were pulling a red ribbon out of his nose. A chair sat serenely in the air to my right. A beer bottle hovered above my head, its contents arrested mid-spill in a long, globular arc. I flexed my fingers, and was highly relieved to find them functioning at normal speed. Whatever the explanation for this bizarre and alarming occurrence, I alone remained unaffected. I swallowed my fear as best I could, and did the only thing I could think of, under the circumstances.

I set to work.

I vaulted over the bar and took two carbon dioxide fire extinguishers from the wall. Jumping up onto the bar, I ran down its length, ducking a drinks tray and hopping over the sprawling body of a bouncer. At the end of the bar I leaped into the air and, using floating chairs as stepping stones, landed on the heads and shoulders of the men surrounding Sirs Lancelot and Gawain. By running the circumference of this circle, I came level with a fire alarm panel fixed at the top of a pillar, and broke the emergency glass with my elbow. I landed alongside my comrades and gave them an extinguisher each, removing the safety hooks and squeezing their hands around the trigger so that the first puff of gas oozed from the nozzle. Finally, I rearranged the poses of their immediate attackers, directing their blows away from the intended targets and back towards themselves.

I dusted my hands, just as time resumed its normal flow. The alarm rang out and engaged the sprinkler system. Our immediate vicinity was filled with smoke, water, and the violent cries of men startled to discover they were punching themselves in the face. I grabbed the flummoxed knights and ran with them through the nearest fire exit, out into an alleyway, and back to the Jaguar, sirens wailing ominously through the sultry night air.

# VII

An uneasy silence characterised our return journey to the Once & Future Inn. Sir Lancelot glowered in the passenger seat. Sir Gawain sulked in the back, taking frequent gulps from a hip flask. I was grateful for the time to gather my wits and soothe my senses, as my curious experience had left me feeling drained and confused. I gripped the steering wheel tightly to stop my hands from shaking, and by forcing myself to concentrate on the road ahead, returned to a satisfactory state of self-control. Nothing mattered now, save finding the Master and returning to the Inn before midnight.

"Do you intend to continue looking for him?" said Sir Lancelot, as if reading my thoughts.

"Yes, Sir Lancelot: Sir Kay, Sir Perceval, and Sir Pellinore are combing the vicinity for the Master as we speak."

"Doesn't he know what night it is?" exclaimed Sir Gawain.

"In such matters he has no control over himself," I replied.

"Unlike the rest of us, Gawain," said Sir Lancelot.

"Oh belt up."

"Lucas," said Sir Lancelot, ignoring him, "are you saying you'll search for him until midnight and beyond? Even if it means forfeiting our lives?"

"Heavens, no. Only my own. Everybody else I will convey to the table beforehand."

"Yes, I believe you would... You said he's suffering from the wandering variety of his condition. Where did you leave him last?"

"By the woodland, where Sir Pellinore makes his quest."

"What time did he disappear?"

"I could not say precisely, but I would estimate between two and three o'clock this afternoon."

Sir Lancelot ruminated awhile. "Tell me, Lucas. Do you ever wonder what would happen if any of us failed to drink from the Grail on Ritual Day?"

"On occasion, Sir Lancelot. Today being a good example of such an occasion."

"And...?"

"I foresee a number of possible outcomes, should that unfortunate scenario come to pass. All of them are highly undesirable."

"Hm." Sir Lancelot ruminated a further while. "I think I know where we'll find him. An old road, now a fallow field. It's far enough for him to have exceeded the range of your search party, but close enough for him to stray there these past hours, if he had a mind to it."

"Forgive me Sir Lancelot, but time *is* pressing hard — can you be sure?"

"Pretty sure. He's been there before, Lucas. We all have."

I was sure that Sir Lancelot was mistaken, for there was nothing to distinguish this field from any of its neighbours, apart from a forest that bordered its easterly edge, stretching up and away over the hills. Indeed, so little did this neglected spot impress itself upon me that I hesitated as I straddled the wooden gate, looking back towards the car. Sir Lancelot merely flapped an exasperated hand towards the field, so I climbed down to make a closer inspection of the waist-high weeds.

The cloudless sky and a full moon provided ample illumination, and my spirits rose when I saw a stretch of flattened grass in front of me, made by one who had recently shuffled their way up the field's incline towards the forest. Treading softly and scarcely daring to hope, I followed the track into a small clearing.

There, to my blessed relief, was the silhouette of the Master. He sat cross-legged and facing a tree trunk, his knife in his lap, surrounded by wood shavings. He had started to carve a picture in the bark, and sat in deep contemplation of his craftsmanship, tracing the outline of a woman's face with his finger. I rested my hand lightly upon the Master's shoulder.

"Sire?"

King Arthur looked startled, as if he were being addressed by a complete stranger. Then recognition spread across his face, banishing all bemusement. He yawned. "Lucas. There you are."

"Yes, sire. Today is Midsummer's Day —"

"I know what day it is. You do not need to remind me of my own terms and conditions."

"No, sire. But you had wandered, and went missing —"

"And now you have found me. And we have plenty of time. Come. Let us go." I helped him to his feet, brushing off the shavings and supporting him as we walked down the flattened path back to the car.

†

The Once & Future Inn had rung last orders, but there was no sign of the landlord and his search party. I checked the basement to find it fully, if a little hastily, prepared. A table had been created from several catering packs of mayonnaise, with seven beer barrels serving as chairs. Something in the corner moved at the sound of my feet on the cellar steps — the Grail, covered with an old sack. My pocket watch read ten minutes to midnight.

"Where are the rest of my knights?" said the Master from behind me. Sir Lancelot and Sir Gawain followed him, closing the door.

"They formed a search party to find you earlier this evening, sire," I said.

"Must we now venture out to seek *them*?"

"That's not the royal 'we,' I'll bet," muttered Sir Gawain.

"A few more minutes and we shall have to commence without them," said the Master. Heavy footfalls sounded on the floorboards above, sending small showers of dust sprinkling down upon us. The cellar door swung open to admit the breathless and bedraggled trio.

"Sire! Saints be praised!" said Sir Perceval. "And Sir Lancelot! Oh, and Sir Gawain! Alive; alive and unscathed! A miracle."

"Had you reason to think otherwise?" said the Master, giving Sir Lancelot a quizzical look.

"Why, yes!" said Sir Perceval. "The televisual tidings, of course! Such carnage! Er, that is to say..." In response to the Master's darkening expression, Sir Perceval's face began to take on the crimson complexion I recognised from earlier in the evening.

"Sit down and catch your breath," commanded the Master. "Kay. What are these 'televisual tidings' of which he speaks?"

"Sire," I said, "perhaps this particular tale would be better told *after* the ritual, given that we have less than eight minutes remaining?"

"Sir Kay? Now, if you please."

Sir Kay glanced at me for assistance, but I could give none, for the Master had spoken. "Well, sire. Picture the scene. The moon is high in the velvet black sky; as round and full as a well-turned cheese. Sir Perceval, his voice ringing as clear as a smithy's hammer on anvil, strides out 'pon the bracken-strewn forest floor, proclaiming —"

"Cut to the meat," growled Sir Gawain.

"I can hardly do the tale justice without setting the scene."

"Consider it set," said the Master. "This is not the time for *Chronicles*."

"Oh, very well. We divided ourselves in two, myself to search the immediate area, while Perceval and Pellinore made a foray into the next valley."

"I'm on good terms with the landlord of the Horse & Hound," said Sir Perceval. "I hoped one of his patrons might have seen you on your wanderings, sire, and could provide me with information."

"By the time I arrived, the only thing he'd provided you with was half his cellar," said Sir Kay.

"Information harvesting is thirsty work. I noticed *you* wasted no time getting a drink."

"What was left of it, after you'd finished."

The Master cleared his throat sharply and Sir Kay continued. "While partaking of a small, well-earned measure of fortifying spirit, sire, I chanced to view the pub's television set. There we saw a sight most doleful. A picture of Sir Lancelot, struck stone dead!" The Master's expression had taken on the colour of burnt toast, but Sir Lancelot did not bat an eyelid. "It seemed that he expired in front of a large audience of onlookers at a charity dinner, and was pronounced deceased at the scene. Quite, quite dead." Sir Kay paused to look at Sir Lancelot, as if to verify his status among the living.

"Get to the skirmish!" said Sir Perceval.

"I'm coming to that. The news programme went on to say, in so many words, that it was curious how Lancelot — though they called him by some other name, Lance somebody —"

"De Troyes," said Sir Lancelot.

"That it was curious how this 'Lance De Troyes' was dead, given that corpses are not usually in the habit of starting large scale brawls. Someone matching his exact description had been identified at the scene of a violent quarrel in the city centre, at a popular nightclub —"

"This being a cross between a tavern and a banqueting hall, for dancing, assorted revelry and suchlike," said Sir Perceval.

"Yes, thank you, Perceval. The scale of this conflict, sire, was conveyed via some hazy black and white pictures of Sir Lancelot engaged in combat against tremendous odds —"

"Oh aye," said Sir Gawain, sitting up. "Hog the glory, why don't yer!"

"— and emphasised by a roving newsman, reporting from the scene, which was one of great devastation, with many wounded. This herald implored witnesses to come forward, offering a reward for information that might aid the authorities in pursuing the perpetrator and his accomplices, and bringing them to justice."

My watch read four minutes to midnight.

"The very existence of the Eternal Quest has been placed in jeopardy," said the Master.

"The fault was mine, sire," I began.

"No, Lucas," said Sir Lancelot. "If there is any blame, it's mine to bear."

"Ours," said Sir Gawain.

"As you wish, Gawain. Ours."

"There's no cause for panic," said Sir Perceval. "We'll just do what we always do. Move on and lay low, until all this blows over."

Suddenly, from somewhere outside the pub there came the sound of a high-pitched wailing. Sir Pellinore shot bolt upright, wide-eyed. "Banshees!" he cried.

"No," said Sir Kay. "Those are sirens."

"Mermaidens? On land? Never!"

"*Police* sirens, Pellinore," said Sir Kay.

"Kay, please tell me you remembered to switch the lights off," said Sir Perceval.

"It's *your* pub!"

"But you were the last one down —"

"Quiet!" said the Master. Having reached a crescendo, however, the caterwauling quickly subsided into the night, and each knight breathed a sigh of relief.

"Did you hear that, Lancelot?" said the Master. "They will not rest until they have found you. Until they have found me."

"Let them come," said Sir Lancelot. "I am ready for the spin of Fortune's wheel."

"Your confidence is misplaced."

"We'll see."

"No, Sir Lancelot. We shall not. First, we partake of the Grail. Then, I will decide how to preserve the Eternal Quest, which you are so willing to sacrifice to feed your lust for fame and glory."

My watch read two minutes to midnight, as each knight took his place around the small table. By small increments I squeezed between the Master and Sir Perceval's ample girth. At a word from King Arthur, the Grail rose up from under the sacking and moved towards him, filled with a dark foaming liquid that bubbled and smoked like a broth. The Master held the Grail and drank deeply, then passed it along to Sir Lancelot. In this manner did each knight sup in his turn — Sir Gawain, Sir Pellinore, Sir Kay, Sir Perceval and myself. Each man yawned and stretched, feeling his life renewed to his very bones. Sir Kay once described the experience of drinking from the Grail as "like rubbing sleep from the corners of your soul," but to me it has always tasted like medicine of the bitterest kind.

When all had partaken, we stood at the Master's command to recite the vow, the tallest stooping to avoid hitting their heads on the low rafters.

"I, Knight of the Round Table, swear loyalty to my fellow Knights, and to uphold the code of our glorious and Eternal Quest. An eye for unrest. A sword to the tyrant. A shield for the weak. To never lack in courage, mercy, generosity and grace. In the name of Almighty God and the King."

My pocket watch reached the stroke of midnight.

# Day Two

# I

There was much to be done once the Master's decision had been made. Indeed, I was so absorbed in preparing for our departure, Sir Lancelot may have interpreted my industrious manner as somewhat brusque. He approached me as I was seeking appropriate clothing in which to dress the Master and Sir Pellinore for contact with the wider world. The latter's full hunting garb would act as something of a beacon, while the former would be no less conspicuous if he remained in his nightwear and dressing gown. A return to the cottage, however brief, was out of the question. So was the ceremonial armour I had hastily packed for the ritual. I therefore had to content myself with the items in Sir Perceval's lost property box.

"Slim pickings there Luc," he remarked, as I inspected a mouse-bitten travelling cape in the dawn light. "Unless you want them to look like they're off to a fancy dress party with a very broad theme."

"I was hoping for a more muted effect," I said, discarding a tunic of faded Lincoln green. Sir Lancelot picked it up and rubbed the material between his thumb and fingers, before tossing it back in the box.

"Lucas; a word," he said. Sir Perceval, who had been on the point of leaving the room, suddenly found much to interest him in the woodwork of the door frame. "In private," added Sir Lancelot.

"Don't mind me, I've got no interest in your little schemes. Got stacks to do," said Sir Perceval, and made a great show of bustling out of the room. Sir Lancelot closed the door firmly behind him. Whatever it was he had to say, I hoped it would not take long, for I had just discovered a jacket with leather patches on the elbows in the Master's size, and I was eager to match it with a pair of trousers. "Well? What do you think?" said Sir Lancelot.

"The collar has seen better days, but it will fit him well enough," I replied.

Sir Lancelot made an impatient tutting sound. "Of his decision."

"It is not my place to offer such an opinion, Sir Lancelot." A grey cotton shirt had caught my eye, and I scrutinised it for moth bites.

"So you do *have* an opinion, at least?"

"The Master's decision is the Master's decision. That is the beginning and the end of it."

"Oh come off it, Lucas; this is me you're talking to. It's a crazy idea! Even by his standards."

"This conversation does not appear to be heading in a constructive direction."

"And what's so constructive about what he's proposing? The only way to deal with this problem is face it, head on. You know that, Lucas. The question is, what are you going to do about it?"

"I am going to support the Master fully in his decision. A decision that was not taken lightly."

That much, at least, I could say with confidence. After the ritual, we had retired to the main bar to discuss our options while the Master sat in deep deliberation. Throughout the long debate he remained silent. Only when our chatter burned as low as the dwindling fire in the grate did he finally speak.

"We shall seek Merlin," he said, rising from his chair. I stood up alongside him. "Only he can help us now. Lucas: attend to the matter of our departure."

The five who remained seated looked at each other in amazement.

"Forgive me, sire, I'm tired," said Sir Lancelot, "but I could have sworn I just heard you say 'We shall seek Merlin.' "

"He is the only one who can offer counsel on this matter. The only one who can, by his magical arts, protect the Eternal Quest from all that threatens to destroy it. We leave at first light."

"But Merlin's dead," said Sir Gawain.

"Merlin passed out of history. But he did not die. Did he, Sir Kay?"

"Well, I don't think so. Not exactly. That is to say, not technically, if the history is correct, but —"

"Your *History*, Kay?" said Sir Perceval.

"In part, yes. My book has a brief section concerning wizards. But there are other books in my collection, some of them attributed to Merlin himself, that speak in more detail of his final destiny."

"So consult your books, and tell us exactly where to find him," said the Master.

"It's not that straightforward," said Sir Kay with mounting alarm. "These are not primary historical records. They're scraps of legend; rumour and hearsay. A patchwork quilt of prophecy and poetry, stitched together by bargain-basement bards."

"Then you will simply have to unstitch them," said the Master.

"But it's been so long, sire! Take my own *History*, for example. Even *I* find it hard these days to remember what is true, and what was written to, well…" Sir Kay swallowed and twitched his cheeks, "…conceal the truth."

"Calm down, Kay. It won't come to that," said Sir Lancelot. The side of his mouth twisted upwards in a lopsided smile. "We won't be seeking Merlin, because that means going back west. And that is no easy journey. Isn't that right, sire?"

"Petty practicalities are not my concern, Lancelot!" shouted the Master. His hands gripped the back of his chair so tightly that it trembled audibly on the stone floor. "Merlin is my decision, and that is the end of it. Sir Kay, you have until dawn."

"As you wish, sire," said Sir Kay, and left to commence his research.

"Perceval. Is my bed here made up?" said the Master, letting go of the chair.

"Always, sire."

"Then I shall retire."

"What a brilliant idea," said Sir Lancelot.

The Master turned to look at him for a moment. There was that smile again; Sir Lancelot's dark amusement at a private joke.

"Wake me when we are ready to depart, Lucas," said the Master, and went to his room.

✝

My fingers alighted on a black, clip-on tie in the bottom of the lost property box. "I believe that the Master has the best interests of the Eternal Quest at heart," I said, fumbling with the rusty clasp.

"And that's your final word on the matter?" said Sir Lancelot. The mechanism was stuck tight, but it came loose with some cajoling.

"A crude invention, but it serves its purpose well enough," I said, holding the tie against the shirt so he could see the match. But Sir Lancelot was already at the door. He opened it with some force, disturbing Sir Perceval, who just happened to be passing at keyhole level in a low crouch and straightened up suddenly, pulling a muscle in his back.

# II

The question of transportation was, at heart, one of mathematics. On one side of the equation: seven knights, plus luggage and one cauldron of the approximate height and circumference of a well-fed middle-aged stomach. On the other side: two means of transportation. The Jaguar would take five of us. Another two would have to use the only other vehicle in Sir Perceval's garage: a motorbike and sidecar, left to the landlord in the will of an eccentric regular to settle a thirty year bar tab.

The finer details were sorted out by means of a little logic, and a lot of cajoling. As to the logic, the Jaguar would lead, with myself as the most experienced driver taking the wheel. Sir Kay, bag-eyed and belligerent from his nocturnal studies, insisted he could only navigate from the passenger seat; however, there was no question of the Master agreeing to travel in the back. Sir Perceval's cauldron-like proportions ruled him out as far as the bike was concerned, and the very thought of Sir Pellinore travelling in such an unsupervised manner made my mouth dry up like a stale biscuit.

This left Sir Lancelot and Sir Gawain as the bike party; an arrangement which provided the additional benefit of helmet and goggles to disguise the two of us who were, thanks to their recent television appearance, the most recognisable of our company. Of these two, Sir Lancelot was the more experienced rider, and had spent decidedly less time than Sir Gawain in Sir Perceval's wine cellar over the past twelve hours. Thus, he was given the task of driving the bike and dealing with Sir Gawain's many objections. I left him to it, and turned my attention to the matter of the cajoling.

"Books be buggered, Kay! The Grail takes priority!" said Sir Perceval.

"Fine. We'll see if that perishing pot can find Merlin. Perhaps it will conjure us a compass from a crouton?"

"May I suggest, Sir Kay," I attempted, "that you leave behind those volumes you have already consulted these past few hours?"

"Out of the question! I need to cross-reference *en route*. Besides, I've already agreed to give up the front seat. Maybe I should give up the back seat too, hm? Cram myself in the boot? How would you like that?"

"Very much indeed," said Sir Perceval.

"Fine. I'll just stay here and rot with Sir Hosis of the liver." Sir Kay strode over to where Sir Gawain was resisting Sir Lancelot's attempt to exchange his tankard for a mug of black coffee.

"Sorry, Lucas," said Sir Perceval, folding his arms and resting them on his belly. "But if the Grail's not going, then neither am I."

At that moment the Grail, which had been resting on top of a toolbox, floated up into the air and hovered above the car, whereupon it conjured a protective rubber mat and several ropes from within its interior, tying itself securely into place on the roof through the open windows. As it did so, I could have sworn I heard it utter a weary sigh.

If only Sir Pellinore had been so compliant. From the moment we had gathered in the garage he had been jittery and aloof, as if he were afraid the car might rear up on its hind wheels and attack him. He sat in the corner of the garage furthest from the Jaguar, clad in the T-shirt, jeans and leather jacket I had selected, muttering to himself and drawing patterns with his hunting knife in a patch of oil on the floor. On closer inspection these revealed themselves to be anatomical sketches of the car, complete with notes speculating about its diet, behaviour and habits.

"That beast, Lucas. I have seen one before," he said. I watched him warily, having witnessed the occasion in question. It had taken a large amount of sweet-talking and an even larger cheque to persuade the owner of the vehicle not to involve the police. "At night, their eyes light up like dragons, and they roam the highways for prey. Wasteful, too. Once they've killed they barely eat a morsel, leaving the carcass for the crows and flies. Hedgehog they go for mostly, sometimes fox, or a bit of dog. Occasionally... a human."

Unfortunately, Sir Perceval chose this moment to begin his lengthy manoeuvre into the back seat. His preferred angle of rear-end first, and his red-faced, reluctant demeanour, gave him the appearance of a forest creature being swallowed by a substantial serpent. Sir Pellinore sprang forward with a yelp of alarm, knife aloft, and was inches away from slashing the front tyres when he was grabbed by Sir Lancelot.

"Bloody hell!" said Sir Perceval. "What's bitten Pellinore?"

"You're the one being bitten! Eaten alive, dammit! Unhand me, yellow knight!" he shouted, thrashing to remove Sir Lancelot and continue his rescue. I glanced at his anatomical drawing, and a solution occurred.

"It is a form of symbiosis, Sir Pellinore," I said.

"Foul Symbiosis! Have at thee, and be gone!" said Sir Pellinore, still struggling.

"No, Sir Pellinore, we knights, and the car, we —"

"We live together in intimate association, to our mutual benefit," said Sir Kay, cottoning on in spirit, if not in brevity.

"You scratch my back, I'll scratch yours," added Sir Lancelot.

"G-n-will-you-let-go-of — Ah! Aha. Now then." He stopped squirming. "You mean, like the Kraken and the Merfolk, who pick fish bones out of its mighty teeth in exchange for safe passage to warm seas?"

"It is almost exactly like that," I said. This seemed to allay his fears, and Sir Lancelot released him. Sir Pellinore took one last look at his drawing as if committing it to memory, then approached the car cautiously, keeping his hand on the hilt of his hunting knife in case the Jaguar decided to go back on its part of the bargain.

# III

My heart was in my mouth as our little convoy set out along the narrow roads surrounding the Once & Future Inn. The tension came partly from the importance of not attracting any undue attention to our progress. But it was more than that. The simple act of sitting behind the steering wheel was an unpleasant reminder of the unsettling occurrence in the nightclub.

Now that some time had elapsed, I was plagued by a nagging sensation of *déjà vu*. The explanation for it, however, lay beyond my grasp, and in reaching even tentatively for the memory I experienced intense waves of nausea, so I resolved to focus on the more tangible concerns of the present.

I decided it would be safer to drive slowly along the back roads as much as possible. As well as making us less conspicuous, this would give Sir Kay more time to research our final destination, for although I knew we had to head west, we would soon have to commit to a more specific direction.

We had scarcely gone five miles, however, when a police vehicle pulled out from a junction, separating us from Sir Lancelot and Sir Gawain, who had been keeping a close but cautious distance behind the Jaguar. As alarming as this was, I tried to remain calm. In the event of any separation, we had arranged that the forward party would continue west, pulling in at the nearest suitable spot to wait for the others to catch up. Besides, we were doing nothing wrong, and there was no reason to think that the police car's presence on such a quiet country road was anything other than a coincidence.

Until, that is, the driver switched on his lights and siren.

"Lucas? What's going on? What does he want?" said Sir Perceval.

"At this moment, your guess is as good as mine, Sir Perceval," I said, praying that the Jaguar had not been identified leaving Cardiff city centre, or that the body of Sir Kay's intruder had not been discovered in his back garden.

"Well, this is just fantastic," said Sir Kay as I pulled over onto a grass verge. Sir Lancelot gave me a barely perceptible nod as he and Sir Gawain passed us on the bike. This made me feel slightly better, but there was still the unfortunate matter of Sir Pellinore, wriggling with delight at the prospect of quizzing the officer on the science of automobile biology.

"This flashing, wailing species disgorges its passenger with ease," he said, squinting through the back window at the officer getting out of his car. "I'll ask him what manner of symbiosis he shares with *his* host, and see if it compares with our —"

Sir Perceval leaned over and hit him squarely across the head with a hefty book. "I stand corrected," he said, as Sir Pellinore slumped unconscious into Sir Kay's lap. "Your library is proving its worth after all." Sir Kay grimaced and hastily obscured Sir Pellinore with a blanket.

"What is it, Lucas, why have we stopped?" said the Master, waking from a doze.

"The police, sire."

"What?"

"A routine check, I am sure."

The Master went as white as a washday sheet, opened the car door, and proceeded to vomit on the grass, just as the officer reached the driver's window.

"What's up with him?" the policeman asked.

"Car sickness, officer. It will soon pass," I said. The officer regarded the Master with a smirk, and I was struck by an overwhelming, but blessedly brief, impulse to reach for one of Sir Kay's books and wipe it from his face. He took out his notebook and shifted his attention to the Grail lashed to the roof.

"Bit precarious, that."

"It is tied securely, I can assure you. Classic cars and roof racks do not good bedfellows make."

"No, suppose not. Lovely vehicle. Nice colour. Cream and... maroon, is it?"

"Plum," I said.

He inspected the protective rubber sheet beneath the Grail. "Play havoc with your paintwork."

"Needs must, officer."

"Where you taking it, then? Antique fair?"

"Yes," I replied, grasping the unwitting lifeline with both hands. "That is indeed where we are heading, officer."

"Should fetch a fair bit, I reckon." He rapped the Grail with a knuckle, eliciting a hollow clang. I felt Sir Perceval tense up behind me and prayed for his continued restraint.

"Old, is it?"

"I am no expert, but I believe so."

"Iron age?"

"Ancient Celtic, certainly."

"Smashing piece. Tempted to make you an offer myself. You can read in the car then, can you?" This was directed at Sir Kay, who was attempting to obscure both his own face and the blanket-covered Sir Pellinore with a large leather-bound book.

"Sir — er, Kay," I said. "The officer asked you a question."

"Mmm," replied Sir Kay.

"Don't know how you do it. I'd be chucking up my breakfast, like your mate here. What're you reading, then?"

With enormous reluctance Sir Kay lowered the tome to nose-level. "Research," he said, and raised it again.

"Oh, I get it." The officer winked. "Don't let them so-called antique experts put one over on you. Knowledge is power, like."

"Never a truer word spoken, officer," I said. "Will that be all?"

"Almost. 'Fraid I'm going to have to be a bit of a pest first, though. Ask you gents to step out of the car, so I can have a good look at you."

"Is there a problem, officer?"

"No, no. No problem. Only, we're on the look out for a couple of men in connection with an incident in Cardiff last night. Quite a big fight, it was. Lot of damage to property, a lot of injuries. Two men were identified at the scene, maybe a third. Older men, like. About your age. One eyewitness put them leaving in a classic car. We're especially keen to speak to one in particular, name of De Troyes. You probably saw his picture on the news."

"We do not have a television," said the Master.

"Fair do's. Would you mind stepping outside the car anyway, sir? And you gents in the back? Won't take a minute."

"This is ridiculous," said the Master. "We've never heard of Lance De Troyes, so why can't we be on our way?"

The policeman paused, pencil poised above his notepad. "Now that's funny. Because I never said anything about his name being Lance, and yet there's you, saying you've got no telly…"

A bumble bee flew in through my window and out through the passenger door. Its buzzing sounded unnaturally loud to my ears, perhaps because all five of us were holding our breath at the same time. The policeman fixed me with a penetrating stare. I held his gaze and stared back. Deep into his eyes.

"I think you will find that you did mention his full name," I said, calmly and quietly. "You said you were keen to speak to a man by the name of Lance. Lance De Troyes."

The officer opened his mouth to speak, and then closed it again, as if he were unsure of even the smallest syllable. "Did I?" he said at last.

"Yes, you did. But I am sorry to say we have never heard of him."

"Oh. I... see," he said, more confidently.

"In fact, none of the gentlemen in this car know who he is. So, you can inform your colleagues to mark our vehicle off their lists, and not to stop us if we are seen again."

"I'll do that, sir. Yes. I'll be sure to do that."

"What is more, if they should see two gentlemen riding a 1940s motorbike and sidecar, there is no need to stop them, either. They cannot help with your enquiries."

"Right you are. I understand," he said.

"We should probably be going," I said, a little faster and a little louder.

"Of course." The officer seemed to perk up. "Don't let me keep you." He checked the rooftop ropes again with a brisk tug. "Seems secure enough. Just drive careful mind. Keep her under thirty, I would."

"Thank you, officer."

"No worries. All the best."

"And to you."

I watched him walk back to his car, scarcely believing my own powers of persuasion, and fully expecting the others to express equal amazement at what had transpired, as soon as the policeman was out of earshot. But they merely sat waiting for the off, as if nothing untoward had occurred, and so I put the car into gear and drove back onto the road.

# IV

The bike party were not too far ahead, and our little convoy reformed in a lay-by half a mile away. Once I had informed Sir Lancelot of the reason for the delay, we resumed our westerly progress. Before long our route necessitated more substantial highways, and thus we would soon require a more specific destination. After several miles I bowed to the inevitable, handling my words with the degree of care one would reserve for a nest of hibernating hornets found in one's attic.

"Sir Kay... I wonder if you have decided on our final destination?" I said.

"As a matter of fact, yes," he replied, closing his book and removing his spectacles.

"Oh. Have you?"

"Yes, I have."

"Splendid. So where in the west are we heading?"

"Carmarthen."

"Carmarthen it is," I said.

"Or, Cardigan," he added.

"I see. Well —"

"With an outside bet on Haverfordwest."

"Forgive me, Sir Kay, but is that not *three* possible destinations?"

"Yes, and it's three more than anyone else has come up with. So unless they have any better ideas, I suggest they keep their big fat mouth shut," he said, for the benefit of the smirking Sir Perceval.

"I am not criticising your efforts, Sir Kay," I said. "But searching three separate locations is highly impractical, not to mention unwise, given our recent brush with the law. Is there any way you could narrow it down?"

Sir Kay sighed. He opened his book, and pushed his glasses back onto his nose.

"I wish I could. When considering Merlin's last resting place, it's a hellish job remembering what's truth and what's fiction. See, here. One book, based on my original *History*, says it's Carmarthen, the town of his birth, where Merlin rests beneath a hawthorn tree. Another, claiming to pre-date my *History*, says 'Merlin's Bridge' is so-called because the wizard sleeps there in the stone. A third book, a collection of prophecies *attributed* to Merlin, suggests Cardigan, as that's the name men now give to —" Sir Kay dropped his voice to a low whisper "— *you-know-where*. But precisely where at *you-know-where*, it doesn't say."

A thought surfaced, like a bubble in a drink.

"He is at Cardigan," I said.

"Maybe he is, yes, but —"

"I know it," I said. And somehow, I did. "That is where we will find him."

"It's as good a place as any, I suppose. But *where* in Cardigan?" said Sir Kay.

"Perhaps, in this matter, we should do what everybody else does," I said.

The Tourist Information kiosk was part of a motorway service station, which also provided fuel for the petrol-hungry bike. Sir Lancelot steered into the petrol station on the lower forecourt, while I parked the Jaguar on the upper level. The Master immediately made for the conveniences and I followed at a discreet distance, lest he remain inside too long and lapse into another reverie. Sir Kay began a grudging search for a guidebook to Cardigan, and Sir Perceval was entrusted with Sir Pellinore in case he awoke from his enforced sleep.

My hunch proved its worth. Sir Kay was not long in finding exactly what we needed, and read aloud from the appropriate page of *Warren's Guide to West Wales Wanderings* as the Master and I rejoined him in the glass-fronted kiosk.

" 'The landscape of Cardigan Bay is rife with myth and mystery, and is rumoured to be one of the locations of the legendary court of' — well, I don't need to read that bit, er, let me see now... ah yes. 'The cliffs of Merlin's Bay (pictured) are said to be the last resting place of the famous wizard, imprisoned in the rock by Viviane, the Lady of the Lake. If they listen carefully, visitors to the cave known as Merlin's Tomb (below, inset) might be able to hear the magician snoring in his eternal sleep.' " Sir Kay snapped the book shut. "Hackwork of the deepest dye. I say we check Carmarthen first, just to be on the safe side."

"I feel it prudent that we make for Cardigan immediately. We have been blessed thus far with a relatively uneventful journey. It would not do to tempt fate, Sir Kay. Sir Kay? What is it? What is wrong?"

I followed the direction of his appalled gaze; a look I had previously only ever seen him use in bookshops, when witnessing a purchase he did not approve of.

The scene that presented itself through the window of the Tourist Information kiosk was, indeed, stupefying in the extreme. It ran as follows. Sir Perceval's stomach had overruled my request to stay in the car with Sir Pellinore. He was queuing at a nearby burger stand, and so absorbed in the menu that he failed to see what we did — a bleary-eyed Sir Pellinore stepping out of the car and walking the life back into his legs, wobbling like a fawn.

At the same time, in the parking space directly opposite the Jaguar, an elderly couple had returned to their vehicle and were placing their pet poodle into the caravan hitched behind it. The animal was voicing loud protests at the travel arrangement, struggling wildly under the old woman's arm. To Sir Pellinore's befuddled senses, an innocent canine was being sacrificed to appease the caravan's blood lust and buy the humans' safe passage in its interior. We were standing well out of earshot, but I suspect the gist of his resultant cry involved a pledge to rescue the pup from its pagan captors, or die in the trying. To that end, he drew his knife and made a successful running jump at the back of the departing caravan, which then sped away with Sir Pellinore dangling from its rear roof ladder.

Sir Pellinore's exodus did not go unnoticed by Sir Gawain on the lower forecourt. Sir Lancelot had refuelled the bike and was waiting to pay for his petrol inside the shop. Sir Gawain, conducting his own refuelling *via* his ever-present hipflask, quickly transferred himself from the sidecar and onto the saddle. He kick-started the bike, and zig-zagged off towards the dual carriageway roundabout in hot pursuit of the caravan.

Sir Lancelot returned to the empty space where the bike had been only moments before. His response was as immediate as it was awe-inspiring. Scrambling up the grassy bank separating the service station from the carriageway, he sprinted along the verge, carefully judged his moment, and took a flying somersault onto the main road, falling beyond our sight and into the arms of a fate unknown.

†

"Sir Kay. Under the passenger seat you will find a pair of binoculars. I would be grateful if you would assume the role of look-out."

"At least we're still heading west," said Sir Perceval between mouthfuls of hamburger. "We should look on the bright side."

"Bright side?" said Sir Kay, removing his spectacles and focusing the binoculars. "This is a total debacle!"

"At least it's a debacle going in the right direction."

"Can't this museum piece go any faster?"

"It is a classic car, Sir Kay, and a severely overloaded one at that."

"And we know who to blame for that, don't we, Perceval."

"No, we don't. Perhaps you can look it up in your new guidebook, Mr I Need To Pack My Entire Bloody Library?"

"Sir Kay, please, the binoculars," I tried again.

The Master stirred in the passenger seat next to me. He had responded to the recent spectacle and its implications with a remarkable degree of composure. A magazine was open on his lap at a picture of a fetching female film star, and his gaze had taken on the rheumy-eyed appearance that characterised the onset of another trance.

"Where are we? What are we doing?" he asked.

"We are *en route* to our destination, sire, attempting to retrieve Sir Pellinore."

"Ah, Pellinore! That good knight! Forged on ahead, has he?"

"In a manner of speaking, sire."

The Master smiled like a wistful uncle. "Pellinore the beast slayer. Did I ever tell you about the time we fought the Wild Boar of Wales?"

"Perhaps later, sire. Sir Kay, can you see anything?"

The road started to rise into a gradual incline, the dual carriageway full of traffic moving in both directions.

"No. Hang on... yes. Got them," said Sir Kay.

With my naked eye, I too could just make out the caravan on the horizon, the bike gaining on it by a series of reckless manoeuvres.

"Pellinore's up on the caravan roof," said Sir Kay. "Looks like he's trying to hack it open with his knife. Gawain's overtaking vehicles at quite a lick on the bike... and... hmm. That's weird. There appear to be two serpents fighting each other in the sidecar."

"Give me those." Sir Perceval snatched the binoculars from Sir Kay and refocused. "Those are Lancelot's legs, you dolt. He must have landed in the sidecar upside down."

Several cars had pulled over on the hard shoulder to avoid the bike. Angry drivers shouted into their mobile phones. "Can't see the caravan anymore," Sir Perceval continued. "Gawain's almost at the top of the hill. He's in the fast lane, but the traffic's slowing him down. No, he's gone."

By this time, Sir Lancelot had managed to right himself in the sidecar, and was later able to fill in the gaps in our version of events. Sir Gawain, frustrated by their lack of progress in the crowded fast lane, decided to cross the central reservation *via* a turning junction, driving directly into the face of the oncoming traffic on the other side of the carriageway. As we cleared the brow of the hill, it became immediately apparent that there would be little need for the binoculars. Firstly, because most of the cars ahead had pulled over to let the bike pass, leaving the downhill road open to our view. Secondly, there are some pictures that have a way of searing themselves instantly and permanently onto the retina. A bike speeding towards an oncoming oil tanker I would place firmly into this category.

Sir Gawain spurred on his steed, hell-bent on his wild shortcut, hunched forwards over the handlebars, while Sir Lancelot tried to wrestle back control of the vehicle. At the last possible second, the bike swerved to the left to avoid the tanker, knocking over some traffic cones in another central turning junction, but otherwise returning back to the correct side of the carriageway unscathed.

The oil tanker did not do so well out of the confrontation.

The driver swerved into the slow lane, applying the brakes hard to avoid the car in front of him. This sent the tanker into a sliding skid, from which it might have recovered, had it not been hit by a lorry travelling behind. The extra force of this impact sent the tanker careering over onto the wheels of its right-hand side towards the aforementioned turning junction in the centre of the carriageway, which it took at an angle of forty-five degrees before falling over.

It swung around on its side with a howl of screeching metal and came to a juddering halt, completely blocking the road ahead of us. Petrol poured from a gash in the tanker like blood from a wound. The dazed driver climbed down from his cab and staggered over to the side of the road, where he attempted to flag me down.

My instinctive response was to stop, convey him a safe distance from the stricken tanker and await the arrival of the emergency services. But I also knew that this would mean the sure and certain end of our quest. I therefore did the only other thing I could think of. I increased my speed and drove onto the hard shoulder, pushing the car as fast as it could go.

"Lucas! Have you lost your mind?" said Sir Kay.

"Sire, Lucas has gone mad! Tell him to stop the car!" said Sir Perceval.

But the Master had slipped into a catatonic state, his head lolling on his shoulder.

"I suggest you find something to hold on to," I said. "I fancy this will be somewhat unorthodox."

I edged the car onto the embankment at the side of the road, which got progressively steeper the closer we got to the tanker. Realising that I was not about to stop for him, or indeed his vehicle, the driver ran for the safety of the surrounding fields. Between the cab of the tanker and the side of the road there was a gap exactly half the width of the Jaguar. I took the last few metres of the embankment at top speed.

The car swung up onto its right side. The wheels left the ground, and we shot up and clear through the gap. The weight of the Grail on the roof turned us upside down in mid-air, and the momentum of the jump flipped us back round again in a perfect side roll. We landed upright on the road, on the other side of the tanker, just as its engine caught fire.

The world exploded.

The Jaguar was engulfed by the fireball. I kept my foot pressed firmly to the floor. The sheer force of the blast carried us through the inferno and out the other side. Naturally, as soon as we were safely clear of the blast zone, I reduced my speed to the legal limit.

In the rear view mirror I could see Sir Kay and Sir Perceval staring at each other, open mouthed. They quickly let go of each other's hands and transferred their astonished gazes to the back of my head.

"How did you... did we... just...?" said Sir Kay.

"Nice driving, Lucas. I think," said Sir Perceval.

The Master remained in his reverie, head slumped forwards. The magazine on his lap slid to the floor with a gentle flop.

✝

Once again the bike party waited for us, this time in the car park of a fast food outlet just outside Carmarthen. Sir Lancelot had regained control of the vehicle. A black eye, thick lip and sullen silence from Sir Gawain testified to the struggle. To my enormous relief Sir Pellinore was in their custody, having been recovered from the caravan when it stopped at a roundabout, the owners continuing on their way blissfully unaware of the entire affair. A battalion of emergency vehicles sped past us towards the horizon, where black smoke besmirched the clear blue sky.

"How bad?" said Sir Lancelot.

"There was an incident, involving the fuel tanker Sir Gawain almost collided with. We emerged unscathed, but the damage in our wake is substantial." I omitted the matter of my manoeuvres with the Jaguar, for in truth I was not at all sure what I had done, much less how I had managed to do it.

"And what about him? Is he still committed to this fool's quest?"

"I have received no alternative orders. Although, much of the Master's recent attention has been absorbed by a mild recurrence of his complaint."

Sir Lancelot shook his head. "First, the police stop you. And now this." He sighed and ran a hand through his hair. "I'm hardly one to talk given recent events, but we aren't doing a very good job of concealing our presence. I'm worried, Lucas."

"Do not fear, Sir Lancelot. Once the Master has consulted Merlin, everything will be back to normal."

"That's what worries me most of all. Come on, then. We'd better get going, and just pray that we haven't used up all our luck."

"Very well, Sir Lancelot," I said, and tried not to think about how much this whole matter of Merlin was worrying me, too.

# V

The route to Cardigan was the kind of drive the Jaguar took to like a duck to water. Both the car and its driver relished the respite of wood-lined roads and tree-formed tunnels that filtered the midday heat down to a cool evergreen. So peaceful was the overall effect that our recent tribulations almost seemed to belong to the distant past.

"Through arteries of time, we flow back to the heart of things," said Sir Kay, as if reading my thoughts.

"That's not bad, Kay. You should write it down," said Sir Perceval.

"Not one of mine. Merlin, from his book of *Prophecies.*" He held up a very old volume, no more than a bundle of tied parchment, thick and brittle.

"I thought we were using the guidebook to find Merlin," Sir Perceval said.

"The guidebook tells us where we might *find* his last resting place. But funnily enough, it's very quiet on the subject of ancient summoning spells. And that means magic." Sir Kay thumped the book. I jumped at the wheel. The car wavered slightly on the road.

"Is it wise to cast such a spell?" I said. "Even you, Sir Kay, with your great reading, cannot claim to be well versed in the literature of enchantment."

"How else do you suggest we recall Merlin? Dig through the cliffs with our bare hands, then shout down the hole and hope he pops out to tell us to keep the noise down?"

I confess I had been more concerned with where we seven were going to spend the night, and had given little thought to such matters. "Might there not be some form of written instruction on the cliff? Runes, perhaps?" I said.

"Yes, and a stone lever with a great big sign saying 'In Case of Emergency, Release Wizard,' " said Sir Kay. "This is magic, Lucas, not some tawdry seaside attraction."

"Lucas. Are we there yet?" said the Master, roused from his deep slumber. Sir Pellinore, who had been somewhat sedate since the unsuccessful rescue of the dog, perked up at the sound of the Master's voice and pressed his nose against the window.

"We are going the wrong way!" he cried.

"At ease, Pellinore," said Sir Kay.

"But this is not the best route." His hands fumbled uselessly with the locked door handle, and he started to scrabble at the window-winder.

"Pellinore!" said Sir Perceval, trying to pull his hand away and getting an elbow in the cheek. "Kay, help me, he's going for his knife again, I think he wants to stab the seat."

"This is not the fastest way to Camelot!" Sir Pellinore wailed.

At the mention of this word in front of the Master, all fell silent. I slowed the car and looked over at him, prepared for the worst. "Hush, Pellinore," said the Master. "This is the right road. It has merely been a long time since any of us have travelled it." Sir Pellinore relaxed into peaceable silence. But as for the Master, it was as if by speaking the words he had performed an incantation of his own and transferred Sir Pellinore's anxiety to himself. He shifted in his seat and stared out of the window as we passed over a small bridge, scratching absently at his chin.

The route to Merlin's Bay took us through the town that was now called Cardigan. We passed over the river Teifi, and there before us, on the edge of the town and commanding a view of the estuary, stood the remnants of the latest incarnation of the castle. Back then, this had merely been the Camelot gatehouse. Now, it was all that remained of our once glorious home. This was the part of the journey I had been most dreading on the Master's behalf, for I was not sure what the sight of it would do to him. For the moment, however, my fears were allayed, for he gave no indication of recognising our surroundings. This was hardly surprising. So reduced was it from its former state of magnificence, that I was only able to identify it myself when road works slowed our progress to a stand-still, and I was immensely relieved when the cars in front of us began to move again.

# VI

The car park overlooking the small sandy beach of Merlin's Bay was almost full, but we managed to find a place in the top corner. The Master and Sir Pellinore remained in the car. Sir Lancelot and Sir Gawain pulled up alongside us on the bike as we attempted in vain to remove the Grail from the roof.

"Are all the ropes loose?" said Sir Perceval.

"Yes, I just checked them," said Sir Kay.

"Well check them again!"

"I don't believe this. We're being delayed by kitchenware," said Sir Kay.

"It definitely won't move now."

"Oh, have I hurt the medieval microwave's feelings?"

"If the pair of you don't stop performing, I'll knock your heads together and pitch you over the cliff," said Sir Gawain, taking off his helmet and goggles. Mercifully, the drive seemed to have sobered him up a little.

"Do you hear that, Perceval? I think we should apologise," said Sir Kay. "When it comes to 'performing' we've offended Sir Gawain's sense of scale. Perhaps I should set some cars on fire?"

"Good idea, Kay. And I could run down to the beach and start a fight with some families."

"You'd get battered by the bairns before you set foot on the sand," said Sir Gawain, and spat on the grass.

"What's the problem, Lucas?" said Sir Lancelot, stepping between Sir Gawain and Sir Perceval.

"The Grail, Sir Lancelot. It is highly reluctant to move." Sir Lancelot placed both of his arms around the Grail and tried to lift it, but it remained clamped to the car roof like a limpet.

I considered our options. Merlin's Bay lay below us like a picture postcard. Our progress through the weekend traffic had been slow and sporadic, and it was now mid-afternoon. Sun-bathers still colonised the sand, and the rocks towards the inlet known as Merlin's Tomb were taken up by children with buckets and shrimping nets, as well as a couple of fishermen.

"Perhaps it is best to leave the Grail where it is for now, Sir Lancelot," I said. "It is my belief that we should do nothing until the beach has cleared for the day."

"I'm not so sure. The tide will be coming in by then. Kay, how long will this magic spell take?"

"I've found what I believe to be the incantation, and it's simple enough to perform," Sir Kay replied.

"If there should be any magical fanfare, so to speak, it would be better if we were the only ones to witness it," I said.

"Oh, it'll only be something minor if there is," said Sir Kay.

"Are you quite certain, Sir Kay?" I said. "In my limited experience, the only thing one can successfully predict when it comes to magical matters is their unpredictability."

There was that feeling again, the nausea that accompanied the incident in the nightclub and its aftermath. My palms were hot and itchy, and I wiped a sheen of sweat from my forehead.

"Relax, Lucas. As long as we go by the book, everything will be fine." Sir Kay patted the *Prophecies of Merlin* under his arm.

"Very well," said Sir Lancelot. "We wait here until the tide turns."

✝

Merlin's Tomb was more of a hollow than a cave, a grotto in the cliff-side carved by the relentless wash of the sea. To the right of the narrow inlet as we faced the cave, a pebbly shore led onto jagged rocks, and beyond that nothing but the sheer face of the cliffs until the open water. To our left lay the way back over rock pools to the sandy beach and up to the car park. The Grail's dogged refusal to move had not lessened at the end of the afternoon, and so Sir Perceval opted to stay with it and the vehicles, as well as Sir Pellinore, a responsibility he assured me no amount of distractions would divert him from this time. The cave was only wide enough to comfortably admit one person, so the Master went in alone, clutching an electric torch and a copy of the incantation made from the original. Sir Kay and I stood guard directly outside, while Sir Lancelot and Sir Gawain remained on the shore to rebuff any curious stragglers. But most of the visitors had retired for the day shortly after the tide had turned, the sea now steadily making its way up the beach.

Within the cave I could hear the Master scuffling on the damp rocks, and with each foot-slip I cursed the cave's cramped dimensions for preventing me being at his side. To take my mind off it, I picked up Sir Kay's copy of *The Prophecies of Merlin* and read the relevant passage for myself, at first idly skimming over the words of the summoning spell, but my interest growing as something caught my eye.

"Sir Kay," I said, "I wonder if you might share with me your interpretation of the incantation's opening line?"

"What, *Dark is the hour and dire the deed*? It's obvious. Whoever recalls Merlin is only doing it because they face a dark hour of some sort, or because they've committed a dire deed. That sums up our current situation pretty well, wouldn't you say?"

"Without a doubt, Sir Kay." I read the passage again, for my curiosity had not subsided. I risked further inquiry. "It is only that — and I feel foolish for voicing the thought, especially to one as well-read as yourself, but —"

"Lucas..."

"Do you think it is possible that the 'dark hour' and 'dire deed' —"

"Go on..."

"— might refer to the *act* of summoning Merlin, and not to the circumstances that inspire the summoning?" Sir Kay took the book from my hands. "Sir Kay?"

"Sssh!" he said, and read to himself, mumbling through his lips. Inside the cave, the shuffling sounds had ceased. "Dark is the... dire..." muttered Sir Kay.

*"Dark is the hour, and dire the deed!"* shouted the Master within the cave.

"Hmm," said Sir Kay, furrowing his brow. He turned over several brittle pages.

*"But the need is great! T'is great indeed!"* the Master continued.

"Ah," said Sir Kay, scanning some text towards the back of the book. "You know, it might be a good idea to postpone this for a minute, Lucas."

*"Merlin from your slumber, cross the wide green sea!"*

A gust of wind whipped along the shore and riffled the pages of parchment. "Sire!" I called into the grotto. "Sir Kay feels it prudent that we pause the incantation!"

*"For I, King Arthur, do wake and summon thee!"* said the Master.

The setting sun disappeared behind a bank of black clouds. The beach was plunged into sudden night. The sea, moments ago as smooth as pressed linen, became rough and squally. "Is there additional information?" I said.

"You could say that, yes," said Sir Kay.

There was a sound like a loud clap of thunder, followed by a hot blast of air. The Master was thrown backwards out of the cave and landed at our feet.

# VII

I stood over the fallen body of the Master, and once again time seemed to slow to a standstill. For a terrifying moment I thought the anomaly from the nightclub had caught up with me, but when I shook my head the sensation passed. I checked his pulse; he had been knocked unconscious by the blast, but was otherwise intact. "Attend to him," I said to Sir Kay, and ran inside the cave.

The interior was illuminated by a point of purple light on the floor, no wider than a two pence piece, yet dazzling in its intensity. As I watched, the point widened and extended up into a column, as if someone under the ground had switched on a very powerful torch. As soon as this beam of light struck the cave roof, the entire cliff-side shook and the floor rumbled beneath my feet as if from an earthquake. Forked tongues of violet lightning sparked off the beam, licking the cave walls hungrily. I ran back outside, partly from fear of electrocution, and partly to see how far the shaft of light extended. Sir Kay was shouting something. Further down the beach, Sir Lancelot and Sir Gawain were running towards us, all of them transfixed by the top of the cliff.

Turning and looking up, I saw that the beam of light had sliced clean through the top of the cliff, quadrupling in width and lashing wildly into the sky like water from a giant hose. With sickening accuracy the beam whipped down to the car park, towards the form of the Grail upon the car roof. For an instant I saw Sir Perceval attempting to pull the cauldron clear, attended by a howling Sir Pellinore. Then the giant beam of light connected with the Grail, and the car and everything surrounding it exploded.

"Perceval!" cried Sir Kay, and started to run back to the fire-ball.

I grabbed his arm. "You must stop this, Sir Kay!" I shouted above the rumbling.

"I can't," he said hoarsely. "It doesn't say how!"

I ran back inside the cave, where the beam had grown to the width of a serving platter, its wild carvings sending rubble raining down from above. I could hear Sir Lancelot calling my name from outside the cave mouth, but I pressed forwards. Shielding my head as best as I could with one arm, I squinted into the blinding light. A hooded head was sticking out of the hole in the floor. I could see nothing of the face beneath the cowl, but it could only belong to the wizard.

"Merlin!" I shouted, over the escalating din. "Close the portal!" The hooded head shook from side to side and the figure rose up through the hole to mid-torso. "We have made a mistake!" I cried. "Go back!" The wizard was now out as far as his waist. A bolt of lightning sent another shower of rubble down on my head. With a loud thooming rush, Merlin shot clear out of the ground and up through the hole in the roof. The cave mouth was nearly blocked by debris and, as I squeezed out through the remaining gap, another rock fall closed it up behind me. I scrambled to my feet on the shore just in time to see the body of the cloaked and hooded wizard flying into the air through the violet beam, which now flowed up over the fields and towards the eastern horizon in a rainbow-like arc. As soon as Merlin had gone the sky cleared and the sea fell calm. The beam of light lost its roaming intensity and streamed vertically up into the heavens with the steady pulse of a geyser.

But there was still the aftershock to contend with. The cliff above us convulsed violently. With the help of Sir Lancelot, I dragged the Master clear of the inlet as the remaining part of the cliff-side collapsed into the sea, cutting us off from the beach and the smouldering car park, and stranding us on the jagged rocks. On our precarious perch, Sir Lancelot, Sir Gawain, Sir Kay and I stood around the body of the unconscious Master, while the rising tide lapped at our feet.

# Yesterday One

# I

There was no escaping it. The Master was not where he should have been, and that was most disturbing.

Today being the first day of the Winter Feast, I had risen an hour earlier than usual to pay particular attention to the King and Queen on their anniversary. This morning, however, my knock was not answered with the customary "Enter, Lucas." Neither, after an appropriate interval, was a second, more vigorous rapping. Inclining my ear to the heavy oak door of the Royal Chambers, I could hear the sound of only one person sleeping within. Sure enough, a cautious look revealed the Queen alone and deep in slumber, the King having already risen and no doubt attending to some thoughtful surprise for when his beloved awoke.

I closed the door softly and crept back along the landing, where my silent exit was compromised by a sudden collision with a woman at the top of the stairs. The goblet and tray I was carrying flew out of my hands. I was quick enough to recover the tray in mid-air, but missed the goblet, which was on the point of hitting the flagstones when the interloper caught it.

"Oh, my goodness, you frightened the life out of me!" the stranger said. My natural instinct upon discovering a trespasser in the Royal Tower was to reach for my sword, but I was so impressed with her reflexes with the goblet that I stayed my hand. "Are you alright? Can I help you?" she asked. Lost for words at such impertinence, I took a moment to note her uncommonly striking eyes, gleaming like burnished bronze. I quickly recovered my composure. "It is I who should be asking that of you," I replied, perhaps more curtly than I intended. "This is the Royal Tower. Only my most senior staff and I have free access."

"But I *am* staff."

It was all I could do to restrict my response to an indignant cough. "Forgive me, but you are certainly not. I am Sir Lucas, Royal Butler. There is not a single person working at Camelot above my jurisdiction. If you *were* a member of staff, I would certainly know of it."

"Sir Lucas! But it is you I am looking for. I am Beaumains. Your new deputy."

A pale hand was put forward in greeting, and I shook it. A kitchen worker's hand, rough and worn yet strong and supple. Immediately I understood the source of our confusion, and felt rather foolish. "Of course. I should have realised from the accent. Forgive my surprise, but you were not expected for several days," I said.

"My ship was blessed with a fair wind from France, and I took little rest on the road to get here in time for the Royal Anniversary. I bring a gift, from King Ban." A shoulder bag was opened to reveal a gold plate studded with gems.

"Sir Lancelot's father is most generous," I said. "Still, you really should have waited for me at the Gatehouse instead of entering the Royal Tower."

"Pardon me, Sir Lucas. But I am eager to meet them," she smiled.

"So are all who come to Camelot. But they, at least, find the patience to wait until the King and Queen are washed and dressed."

Beaumains' smile waned. "I was keen to get started in my work. That is all," she said.

I began to feel the same sense of self-reproach I get whenever I am a touch too severe with my apprentice, Gwion. "Enthusiasm is, of course, highly commendable. But enthusiasm without discipline is like a sword without a scabbard. Sooner or later, you will cut yourself."

"I will try to remember that," she said.

"Good." A rather uncomfortable silence ensued. "The goblet. It was... well caught," I said at last.

"Thank you," said Beaumains.

"Your reflexes do you credit. As do your references. I understand your family served King Leir?"

"My grandfather."

"And Sir Lancelot speaks of you in the most favourable terms." At this Beaumains glowed, and it was such a pleasing sight that I resolved there and then never to consciously diminish it.

"But where is Lancelot? I have missed him so much," she said.

"At present, Sir Lancelot is away questing. We are expecting his return any day now. It would be a noble adventure indeed to keep him away from the Winter Feast. But please," I said, moving to the spiral staircase, "this way. There is much to be done. We will not have time for a leisurely tour. Yours will have to be of the working variety."

"They are the best kind," said Beaumains.

"I could not have put it better myself," I said.

†

From the Royal Tower we walked out along the castle's eastern wall. To our right lay the inner courtyard and the staff quarters, where bleary-eyed night workers mumbled greetings to their fresh-faced daytime counterparts. Below us, to the left of the castle wall, lay the sleeping town of Camelot, and past that the fortified enclosure of the town's outer wall. The world beyond was still shrouded in pre-dawn darkness, save for the roadside torches lighting the bridge over the river. By this illumination, the vague outlines of men on horseback could be seen approaching the main gates in close procession.

"They arrive in droves," said Beaumains.

"It has been like this for days," I replied. "Thanks to Sir Lancelot, this year's Christmastide will see record attendance levels."

"No man can best him in combat," said Beaumains. "It is a sight to see."

"Sir Lancelot is a knight of the highest skill," I agreed, "and his custom of sending vanquished foes to pay tribute to the Queen is testament to his nobility. However, it is a year since he first went out to extend the King's justice. I confess that even I was not prepared for the sheer scale of his vanquishings. Do not forget, Beaumains, once these knights have paid their tribute, they all require food and lodging. Then there are the guests arriving for the Royal Anniversary, and the attraction of the Knighting ceremony. Add to their number the usual volume of challengers and questers approaching the Round Table, not to mention those seeking the renowned hospitality of the King's winter hearth, plus the population of the town and castle, and we have a Camelot that is stretched to the seams."

"Bursting with life," she said with a smile.

"I would not have it any other way," I agreed, liking her even more. "It's taken many years, but King Arthur has finally brought light to this dark land. Providing a fine, fierce feasting is the least we can do. Although, it would be enormously helpful if they did not all arrive at once. Perhaps

I will speak to Sir Lancelot and see if we can arrange some sort of vanquishing timetable, to spread the burden over the feasting year. If even a hundred vanquishees could be forwarded to Whitsuntide, it would do much to lighten the load."

We had reached the end of the wall and the steps leading down into the Great Hall. Beaumains was about to start down the first of these, when I held out a restraining hand. "Not that way," I said. "Let me show you how Camelot is able to take any strain its guests care to place upon it." I walked towards the end of the wall, and turned to see a suitably surprised expression on Beaumains' face as I stepped between the turrets and disappeared.

# II

We descended the steep winding staircase and into the clanking, hissing, bustling realm of Lower Camelot. All along the main corridor, numerous pages zipped by, conveying service apparatus, running errands and delivering messages.

"I was involved in the construction of Camelot from the design stages," I said, stepping aside to allow a platter of fruit to pass by. "As a result, I was able to ensure the domestic realm was constructed first — directly on top of the foundations, and beneath ground level. The hidden entrance we just came through on the turret wall is one of hundreds situated throughout the town and castle, providing staff with hands-on access points between Upper and Lower Camelot. My plan was to maximise service, efficiency and guest satisfaction, whilst providing as little disruption as possible and remaining out of sight to the untrained eye. Over the years this has, I am pleased to say, become something of a staff philosophy."

"Ingenious," said Beaumains, peering into the kitchens and jumping back as a waiter appeared under a teetering pile of plates. "But I will get lost down here for a hundred years."

"I based the overall design on a series of concentric ovals. The outer circles support the town and grounds, while the inner serve the castle. If you lose your bearings, simply follow the blue line on the wall, and you will eventually get back here: the centre point of the Lower Great Hall."

This area now stretched ahead of us, a vast room containing a network of lifts and pulleys, pipes and troughs, crossbeams and timber scaffolding, illuminated by torches set deep in the walls.

"Even our biggest castles have nothing on such a scale. What is this?" Beaumains had stopped by the central conveyor belt.

"A swift way of sending items from one end of the Lower Great Hall to the other."

"Magic?"

"Nothing of the sort! It is powered by a diverted underground stream which also provides Camelot with a constant supply of fresh water."

I guided us into an alcove and stepped up onto a wooden platform — one of many situated along the walls — and adjusted the balance of the counterweight for two. "You may find the following sensation takes a while to get used to," I said, and released the control lever. The lift winched us swiftly into the air. Beaumains gasped and gripped my arm, only letting go when we came to a smooth halt facing the back of a tapestry that hid the lift from view. I moved it aside for her to step shakily into the light and space of the Upper Great Hall.

I was pleased to see that my three Heads of Staff had already arrived for the morning meeting. Eric's eagle eye observed two kitchen hands staggering beneath the weight of a freshly-spiced boar, skewered on a spit as long as a lance. Bedwyr called out instructions to a page stacking wood in the eastern fireplace, concerning the best arrangement for maximising burning time. On the upper dais of the Round Table, Enid swept the walkways clear of any mice unwise enough to linger in her path. I gave a discrete cough to notify all three of the start of the meeting.

"A very good morning to you all. I would like to begin by introducing my new deputy Beaumains, with whom you will all be working closely. Beaumains, this is Bedwyr, Head Waiter; Enid, Head of Housekeeping; and Eric, Head Chef." All three nodded and smiled in greeting. "Now then, Bedwyr. The seating plan."

"Filling up fast. Twenty or so left on the lower tables, but I've not checked with Geraint yet for overnight arrivals."

"Then we will have to find more dining space outside the Hall, and prioritise accordingly. Enid, did you speak to Mordred about volunteering some rooms in the West Wing?"

"Tried yesterday," said Enid, folding her arms. "But he says he needs the space for all the guests he's invited to see him get knighted."

"He'll be lucky. The smart money's on Gawain, not that midden mouth," said Eric.

"All the same, he won't budge," said Enid. "Reckons it's the very least the Master can do, when by rights he should have his own rooms in the Royal Tower. Then he told me to mind my own business and bail out his bedpan."

"He should thank his lucky stars he's not bunking up with the horses," said Eric.

"Please, Eric. I understand that Mordred can be a demanding, not to say difficult, guest —"

"Guest? Ha! Guests leave." said Enid.

"But he is first and foremost the King's brother, and I would remind you to keep that in mind at all times. Enid, tell Mordred that the West Wing will be cleared for emergency accommodation, whether he likes it or not. Any guests he has invited himself will have to take their turn on a first come, first served basis like everybody else. If he has any quarrel with you this time, then point him in my direction."

"Yes, Sir Lucas."

"Eric, any dietary requirements Bedwyr should be aware of?"

"Only Sir Marrok. His curse hasn't been lifted, so he can't eat nuts or drink any mead which may contain traces of nuts."

"Thank you. Finally, has anyone seen the King this morning? He was not in the Royal Chamber."

"Owen left breakfast early to meet him at the armoury," said Bedwyr.

This was of modest concern. Upon leaving the King the previous evening, he had made no mention of departing Camelot, and certainly not on any business that would require a trip to the armoury.

"Very well. I may have cause to leave Camelot temporarily this morning. I will entrust Beaumains to your capable hands, to get better acquainted with your respective areas of expertise. Eric, perhaps you would start with a tour of the kitchens?" The three Heads moved to go about their work, Eric waiting to accompany Beaumains. "Beaumains will catch up with you in a moment, Eric."

I waited until the Great Hall was clear, and took her to one side. "A quiet word, concerning Mordred. Be sure that his appearance is made known to you, and keep an eye on him. The King has asked that his needs are met, within reason. But as you just heard, reason to Mordred is often a grey area."

"Do not worry. I know his type and how to handle them."

"All the same, there is some delicate family history you should be aware of. You have heard, I take it, about the business with the sword in the stone?"

"Of course. Our minstrels never tire of singing of how Arthur pulled Merlin's sword out of the stone, proving his royal birth."

"But what minstrels are not permitted to sing of — by strict Royal decree — is how humiliated Mordred was by the affair. For this, I blame no one so much as Merlin himself. Not that he is around anymore to take responsibility for his actions."

At the mention of the wizard, predictably enough Beaumains' jaw had dropped. "You knew Merlin?"

"My first job was serving in the Court of King Arthur's father, Uther Pendragon, to whom Merlin gave counsel, such as it was. At that time, Arthur's mother, Igraine, was married to the Duke of Cornwall. Self-control was never one of Uther's virtues. Desiring Igraine for his lover, Uther waged a petty war on the Duke. While the Duke was away fighting Uther's forces, Uther had Merlin transform him into the exact physical likeness of the Duke, so that he might, er... with Igraine. That is to say, so that he could, um..."

"Know her intimately."

"Yes, thank you. Merlin's one condition was that the result of this adultery — namely, Arthur — would be given over to his care, until the boy came of age."

"But why?"

"Because Merlin did what Merlin did, regardless of the consequences."

"Surely there was a reason? He was a magician, he was wise."

"That is a matter of opinion. Suffice to say that the Duke of Cornwall died in battle on the very night Arthur was conceived, widowing Igraine. Uther, to his debatable credit, took Igraine as his Queen and her only other child, Morgan, as his adopted daughter. Nine months later Igraine gave birth to Arthur, who was taken away to be raised in secret. Shortly after that, the Queen had another son by Uther — Mordred — but sadly, Igraine did not survive childbirth. If only she had, it would have been better for Morgan. Lacking her mother's guidance and detesting her stepfather, she left home, swearing vengeance on Arthur for the sins of his father. It is said that she took to the dark arts and made her home in the depths of the Otherworld.

"As for Mordred, he spent his formative years believing himself to be the rightful heir to the throne, little realising that the first born was, in fact, Arthur. When Uther died and the sword in the stone appeared, Mordred was convinced he would be the one to pull it out, and was not deterred by his total inability to do so. For seven days and seven nights, without food or rest, he tried to remove that sword. He became a laughing stock, and his efforts were in danger of creating an even bigger spectacle than the sword itself. Until, of course, Arthur turned up and removed it without so much as breaking a sweat."

"Poor man. To suffer so publicly. I feel quite sorry for him."

"Your pity is admirable, Beaumains, but misplaced. The King has bent over backwards to make amends to him ever since, and Mordred has wasted every opportunity that has come his way. If he could hear your kind words, rest assured he would think them the very least he deserves for being so hard done by."

"I understand. I will be watchful and wary, Sir Lucas," said Beaumains, and she followed after Eric to the kitchens.

# III

I strode through the Gatehouse door, and stopped in my tracks when I almost walked into a tree. I was about to ask Geraint why a major walkway was so obstructed, when the offending foliage spoke and revealed itself to be a man. A giant, to be precise; and no ordinary giant at that. From tunic to jerkin and face to feet, he was entirely green. Geraint the Gatekeeper stood his ground in front of him, like a sapling struggling for sunlight in the shadow of a mighty oak.

"Goad me not, Gatekeeper! My patience wears thinner than a beggar's blanket," bellowed the giant.

"Come on, sir, be reasonable. It's not a matter of goading, it's simply a question of formality."

"I — demand — an — audience — with — King — Arthur!" A branch-like finger prodded Geraint in the chest with every word.

"There really is no need for that. Let me get you some ale from the Reception Pavilion — oh, Mr L, thank the blessed beard of Merlin!"

"Good morning, Geraint. And who might this be?"

"This gentleman here is the Green Knight."

"Welcome to Camelot, Sir Green Knight," I said. With a loud creak the giant bent down to scrutinise me with an emerald glare.

"And who are you?"

"Sir Lucas, Royal Butler. At your service," I said, giving a small bow.

"Then buttle me to the Knights of the Round Table! Much chatter have I heard of their splendid skill, and wish to put it to the test — *with a challenge*."

"I am afraid that will not be possible."

"Ho! So! You dare to stand in my way?"

"Not at all, Sir Green Knight. My team and I provide a full and comprehensive support package for every quest, challenge and adventure to arrive at the gates of Camelot. There will be ample opportunity for you to present yourself to the Round Table during the course of the feasting period. Please give full details of your challenge, including terms, conditions and expiry date, to Geraint here, and we will fit you in — Geraint, when is the first available time slot?"

"Day after tomorrow, between the indoor falconry and the love poems of Sir Tristram," said Geraint, consulting his notice board.

The Green Knight reached behind his massive back and produced a double-bladed axe, which he hefted from hand to hand. "If this be a jest, butler, then it is a feeble one, and may prove to be your last. Do you expect *me* to *wait*?"

"No, not at all."

"Good."

"You misunderstand me, Sir Green Knight."

"That's more like it."

"I do not *expect* you to wait," I said. "You *will* wait."

A growl started to rumble in the depths of his throat. The Green Knight raised himself up to full height. He swung the axe back over his shoulder. The weapon whistled through the air and halted a sword's width from my neck. I knew the distance to be the width of a sword, because that was precisely what had stopped the Green Knight's axe in its path. My sword. The Green Knight gave a startled cry at the sudden appearance of the blade. He lowered his weapon.

"Ha!" he cried, and clapped me on the shoulder. "This is no mere butler, eh Gatekeeper? Then wait I shall. But not for long, mark you. Now, where is this ale?"

"The Reception Pavilion is located in the second courtyard to your left," I said. "Ask for Granville the Brewer. I highly recommend the cask honey beer."

The Green Knight stomped out and Geraint fairly shook with relief. "Phe-eew. Thanks for that, Mr L! I tell you what, I've seen it all this morning. One woman was in here earlier, convinced her baby boy's gonna find a magic cauldron that'll bring eternal glory to Camelot. Insisted she present him and his so-called 'Grail Quest' before the King."

"I hope you set her straight, Geraint."

"Certainly did. Told her to wait until he could walk, at least. She didn't like that. Kept going on about how it was her precious Perceval's destiny, written in the stars. If you ask me, there's so much written in the stars you could pretty much read anything in 'em. I've just started omens in my magic studies, bad ones and good ones, and how to tell the difference, like."

"What you do in your own time is none of my business, Geraint. I would appreciate it if we could stick to professional matters."

"Right you are, Mr L."

"Has there been any reduction in the number of arrivals since yesterday?"

"An increase, if anything! Already this morning we've had Sir Uwaine, Baron Sagramour, Sir Meliot, Baron Bagdemagus and Sir Partridge from the Kingdom of Pear Tree. No, I made that last one up. But here's the thing — Sagramour and Bagdemagus both said they were here to see Mordred knighted. That'll be the day, I said! That Red Knight vanquishing was a set-up if ever there was one, and if they had any sense they'd bet their family gold on Gawain being a Sir before sundown. Well, we had a few words over that, but it ended with them insisting point blank to be put straight into the West Wing."

"I see. Where are they now?"

"With Mordred. I was all for letting them wait outside until I'd squared it with you, but he said he was dealing with it on the King's behalf. But I thought Sags and Bags were on the list of Banned Barons?"

"You thought correctly, Geraint. The West Wing is being cleared this morning for emergency accommodation, but priority will be given to those who got here before them. Make a list of all the guests so far and give me a copy by noon."

"Will do. But now, what about the horses? We're having a hell of a time finding room, it's nose to tail out there. If only Merlin were still knocking around! He'd sort it out."

"Perhaps, Geraint. Unfortunately, Merlin considers it more important to dote on the enchantress Viviane, allowing her to seal him under the earth."

"He'd do one of them space-making spells, like when he conjured up that stable with all those different levels, remember?"

"Yes, I do. I also remember spending three days trying to return the horses to their rightful owners, after it transpired that Merlin made no provision for their identification or efficient retrieval."

"Still, it made the King laugh."

"Speaking of the King, did he pass through the gates this morning?"

"Aye, he did as a matter of fact. Went out before dawn, on his own. Said something about hunting, and to tell you not to worry, he'd be back for breakfast."

"Forgive me, Geraint, but that cannot be so. The King's sword is in a state of severe disrepair."

"Yes, I did wonder about that, but he took it anyway. Reckoned it was good for a few more quests yet."

"I see. Still, I suppose if there is nothing enchanted involved, it is not so bad. I will send a squire out to him with a new sword from the armoury. Did he happen to say where he would be hunting?"

"He mentioned something about the Enchanted Glade in the Enchanted Forest."

"Thank you, Geraint. I will catch up with you later."

"Hang on, who shall I send out with the sword?"

"Only a magic blade will suffice in the Enchanted Forest. I will go myself."

"But where you gonna find one of those? I mean, it's not as if they grow on trees, is it?"

# IV

The snow-topped trees of the Enchanted Forest spread out below me as Plum trotted out of the Camelot rear gates. It had been no small task to locate my steed, pushed as he was to the back of his stall and squashed between a piebald colt and an asthmatic old mare. But, with the kind of skilful hoof-work that made me bless the day I chose him, he extricated himself from the stable and we were soon on our way.

Once I was confident he had hit his stride on the hill, I clicked my tongue and he sped up to a medium canter. The forest path levelled out ahead of us. My limited and never pleasant experiences of the Enchanted Forest had taught me to hold Plum back for a high gallop until it was absolutely necessary. Nevertheless, time was of the essence.

The morning mists were starting to clear, and the King had at least an hour's head start. I was not at all confident that his sword would survive even one encounter with a magical opponent, and the very thought filled my heart with dread. This dread was useful, in that it overwhelmed my apprehension at venturing into such unpredictable territory, where even the most meticulously planned routine could be thwarted in a heartbeat. Geraint was correct in his assumption that magic swords do not grow on trees. I was instead pinning my hopes on their existence under water.

No-one forged a finer magic sword than the faerie folk, and their nearest known habitat was the Enchanted Lake. I pulled my hood tighter over my head and urged Plum into the forest, steeling myself for whatever it might throw in our path.

The griffins were hibernating, so their nesting grounds were easy to negotiate for a horse as nimble as Plum. Their deep snores were disturbed by not so much as a single twig snap, and once safely through I rewarded him with a handful of oats. The Enchanted Marsh stretching ahead of us might have posed more of an obstacle, but thanks to a particularly bitter winter, the surface was almost entirely solid. A lone Marsh Wisp poked a spectral head out of a rare patch of unfrozen ooze, made a half-hearted attempt to point me in the wrong direction, then sank shivering back to his foul bed. Our progress was slow and slippery on the icy ground, but clumps of marsh grass provided traction, and we reached the other side without mishap.

We emerged from the trees onto the shore of the Enchanted Lake and I took down my hood. Immediately I pulled it back up again as clouds of sprites swarmed into my face, pulling at the short hairs of my beard and making obscene gestures. I swatted them away and dismounted by the misty waters. Not a single sound of fish or fowl came from that bewitched place. I felt a queer sensation passing down my spine and swatted my back; several sprites yelped in pain and dropped to the ground. A peculiar music filled the air. I tried to block it out, fearing its purpose was to bedazzle the unwary listener, and started to hum a boyhood ditty to counteract any malign influence.

My fears were confirmed by the appearance of a ghostly arm in the centre of the lake. The arm started to beckon me forwards in time to the music. I hummed louder. When it could see, or rather sense, that I was not about to move as instructed, the arm was followed by the rest of the body. There before me stood a lady and, to my great relief, in her non-beckoning arm she held a sword.

"Who approaches the Lady of the Lake?" she said.

"Sir Lucas, madam, of King Arthur's Court."

"Why do you approach me, Sir Lucas of King Arthur's Court?"

"I seek a magic sword, faerie-forged and fit for a King."

"Why does King Arthur not seek such a sword himself?"

"He is otherwise engaged, but I come as his envoy."

"You are his greatest champion?"

"No, madam."

"A powerful magician?"

"Certainly not, madam."

"A bard?"

"Not I, madam."

"Then, who are you?"

"I am the King's butler."

"Ah," she said. For some reason, I cared even less for that "ah" than for the peculiar music. "Then, step into the barge," she said.

Before I could ask "what barge?" a small boat silently and smoothly parted the mists of the lake and came to rest at my feet. I carefully stepped into it, and slowly — much too slowly for my liking — it conveyed me to where the lady stood on the water, cradling the sword like a beloved child.

"Behold — Excalibur," she said. As she did not immediately offer it to me, I beheld it for what I hoped was an appropriate interval. "This sword cannot be broken while it is wielded by the hand of the just," she said, eventually.

"That is good to know, madam," I replied, and made to take it. But she was not finished.

"Far more precious than the sword is the scabbard. It will protect the wearer from shedding blood and cause his wounds to heal. "

"Understood, madam," I said.

"Know also that Excalibur cannot be used against another who has wielded it. If it is, then the sword will shatter and a curse fall upon he who struck the unjust blow. He will be doomed to wear the scabbard for the rest of his days, or else suffer all the wounds from which it has ever saved him!"

"I fully comprehend the terms and conditions."

She nodded and gave me the sword in the scabbard, which I tied securely around my waist. The peculiar music faded away and the Lady of the Lake sank beneath the misty waters.

If anything, the boat's return passage was even slower. Although it would have been the height of stupidity to jump out and wade through the enchanted shallows, the temptation to do so was almost unbearable. At last I was back on the shore, where Plum was trying to shake off a posse of sprites who were making imprudent use of his saddle. I brushed them away, placed my foot into the stirrup and fell backwards to the ground as the untied saddle came loose in my hands. Accompanied by much spritely laughter, I re-fastened the saddle girth and tried again. In the corner of my eye I saw one particularly amused culprit, doubled up with mirth at my fall. I shot out my hand and grabbed him before he could fly away, tying him into a cloth purse in my saddlebag. "Plum," I said, "it is time for a high gallop."

# V

The Enchanted Glade was a favourite spot of the King's. Most of my previous excursions into the Enchanted Forest had taken me there, and it was the one place I knew I could find in a hurry. Even if this were not the case, there were no shortage of signs leading me in the right direction. Most of the trees surrounding the glade had been uprooted and lay splintered on the path, requiring several athletic jumps from Plum. The ground had been churned up as if by a giant plough, and from ahead came the sounds of a frantic skirmish, interspersed with the loud bellows and squeals of a cornered animal. Plum galloped into the clearing and instinctively reared back at the sight before us.

The glade was dominated by a large wild boar, which I estimated to be twice the size of a cow. Its tusks were long and sharp, its hairs coarse and brittle, its eyes bloodshot and angry. Half of this anger was directed at the figure of King Arthur, who stood before it, the hilt of his broken sword in one hand, his red hunting cape in the other. The other half of the boar's anger was focused on a knight attempting to scale its bristled back by gaining a foothold on the remains of the King's broken blade sticking out of the animal's rump. This knight clung on for a few moments, bucking and bouncing around, before being thrown off by a spasmodic kick from the boar's hind legs, the front pair continuing their complicated dance of retreat and advance with the King.

Clearly, the hunt had reached something of a stalemate. Victory would be decided by whoever tired first. Of the two hunters, the King sported the more extensive injuries, bleeding copiously from his forehead, his heavily-bandaged left leg looking like it might buckle any moment. In contrast, the knight who had climbed onto the boar's back appeared as if he could happily continue the fight no matter how long it took, or how slim his chances of eventual success. As for the boar, its entire countenance spoke of a beast who was not about to give up the ghost without a fight. I felt it was wise to give the animal a wide berth, so as not to further enrage it with the presence of a third aggressor, and so I geed Plum around the outskirts of the clearing, positioning us behind the boar's rear-end.

I untied Excalibur from my waist, and drew the sword from the scabbard. For a second I heard a chime of the Enchanted Lake music, which excited the sprite I had trapped in my cloth purse. Grabbing him tightly in my fist, I pulled down the bag. "Freedom is yours if you perform this one task," I said. "Fly this sword to that man on the ground. Go!" I opened my fist and, as the lore of his kind obliged him, he obeyed my command. Excalibur was snatched up into the air, flew in a smooth arc over the boar's head, and hovered in front of the King's sword hand. Startled but pleased, King Arthur dropped his broken blade and clasped his fingers around the new hilt. Immediately it was as if the strength of a hundred men flowed through his veins, and he attacked the boar with renewed vigour.

His wounds were still a cause for concern, however. I clicked Plum back over to the King's corner of the fight and dismounted out of sight in the trees. As unobtrusively as I could, I moved directly behind the Master, crouching low and attempting to disguise my approach from the boar by shadowing the King's every step, feint and parry. Whilst maintaining my crouching shadow movement, I reached in front of the King and untied his old sword belt and scabbard. With one hand I held up the King's stockings and chain mail trouser; with the other, I threaded the new sword belt and scabbard around his waist. The buckle firmly tied, I retreated to a safe distance to observe the results.

They were, to say the least, impressive. As soon as the buckle was tied, the gash on his forehead began to heal, blood pouring back up his face and into the wound, skin closing behind it, smooth and unblemished. His left leg straightened up, strong and firm. The boar backed off in alarm at an opponent so suddenly revitalised. The other knight sprang onto the boar's back again and stabbed his sword between its shoulder blades. The boar's legs gave way and it uttered a long, curdling squeal. King Arthur cut off its head with one clean stroke of Excalibur. Then he sat down to rest, and suddenly noticed me behind him.

"Ah, Lucas! Meet King Pellinore."

"Pleasure, boyo," said King Pellinore, slapping my back, hard.

"Lucas is my butler, Pellinore."

"Well, someone has to be."

"Sire, a word about your wounds," I said. "They have healed only thanks to the scabbard of your new sword. It would be wise not to rely too much on the enchantment, and get them looked at on your return to Camelot."

"Yes, yes, Lucas, don't fuss. You can blame Pellinore here for my cuts and bruises. He challenged me to a duel, and put up quite a fight."

"Perhaps you might tell me the rest of the story *en route* to Camelot, sire. The Queen will be concerned for your safety," I said.

"We'd been fighting for half an hour or so," the King continued, "when Pellinore recognised me, and told me to yield to the rightful ruler of this land. I told him I'm the King around here, and if there's any yielding to be done, it will be by him."

"Then he fought me like a weasel possessed."

"Pellinore's pledged allegiance to Camelot, Lucas. He says he'll give up his Kingship and join the Round Table, as a knight. How about that?"

"Splendid, sire —"

"Better than splendid! Pellinore is an expert in all manner of beast lore."

"It's a good life, butler. Mind you, some in the trade get a bit obsessive. The man is master of the quest, the quest is not master of the man. Never forget that."

"I shall endeavour to remember it, King Pellinore."

"Pellinore's going to help us with the dragon problem in the east," said the King.

"Ever find yourself facing a dragon, footman? Don't suppose you do. Still, if you discover one nesting in your laundry room, remember this: *Dracontias*. The dragon stone. Lodged in its brain. Cut that out with a blade to the top of the head, and Uther's your uncle — one slayed dragon, yours to take away."

"Anyway, we'd just shook on our deal when — crash! Out of the trees thunders this boar, snorting and charging," said the King.

"Big as a griffin and twice as mean."

"So we set upon it and, well, you saw the rest. Tie up the carcass, will you, Lucas? I thought we could add it to tonight's menu."

"Don't waste any of it, mind," said King Pellinore. "The beast died bravely and should be honoured. And the tusks make fine drinking horns."

"Might I suggest, sire, that such an item would make a suitable present?" I said.

"Who for?"

"The Queen, sire. For your wedding anniversary."

"That's never today?"

"It is indeed, sire."

"In that case, yes, you'd better see to it."

"I will instruct the butcher accordingly," I said, trussing up the boar carcass and tying it behind the King's horse.

"Well, what are we waiting for?" said King Arthur. "To Camelot! Lucas, go on ahead and prepare Pellinore the best of lodgings."

"Yes, sire."

"And set a place for the newly knighted Sir Pellinore on the Round Table!" shouted Arthur, as Plum galloped back to Camelot.

# VI

On returning to the Great Hall, I was gratified to see my staff had excelled themselves in my absence. Save for a few finishing touches, it would soon be time to open the main doors and admit the guests for the first sitting. Fires roared in the three main hearths. Meat hissed and crackled on spits, and assorted beverages stood in plentiful jugs. I tasted some wine at random, and was trying to ascertain the vintage when my apprentice appeared by my side out of thin air, carrying a serving plate and preceded by a soft, low popping sound.

"Gwion?" I said, choking slightly on the wine. "What is the meaning of this?"

"Nothing, Sir Lucas, sir," he said, quickly crossing his arms to hide something tied around his neck.

"Give it to me," I said. Reluctantly, Gwion took off a thin silver necklace with an amber jewel strung upon it. "What is this?" I said, taking it from him.

"An amulet, Sir Lucas."

"No. It is one of Merlin's amulets. A magic amulet of teleportation. And what have I always said about magic amulets?"

"We're not to use them."

"Wrong again. We are not even to *touch* them. Thus we never, *ever*, use them. So why do I find you are not only in possession of such an amulet, but brazenly disobeying my instructions and using it to perform your duties?"

"Because I said he could."

I turned to see Beaumains holding a basket of bread.

"*You* did?"

"Yes. Is there a problem?"

"Gwion, I shall deal with you later. Get out of my sight and get back to work. Are there any more of them?" I said, when he had scurried off.

"Not that I could find. Gwion was testing the range for me. I was intending to give it to you, when you returned."

"I see. Well, it is your first day, so I will let it go this time. But if I ever see one of these things in Upper or Lower Camelot again, you will be instantly dismissed. Do I make myself clear?" I started to take loaves from the basket, placing them onto serving plates.

"Not really, no," said Beaumains.

A loaf slipped out of my hands. "I beg your pardon?"

"I mean, what is your problem? We've been working flat out all morning. I happen to hear about these amulets that used to belong to Merlin, and I think to myself: what is Sir Lucas' philosophy? 'Maximise service, efficiency and guest satisfaction. Provide as little disruption as possible and remain out of sight to the untrained eye.' And what better way of doing that, than with one of these? But no, that's not good enough for your dizzyingly high standards, so you bully poor Gwion and then start on me. So no, Sir Lucas. You do not make yourself clear. Not at all."

"I see," was all I could manage at first. My head and face burned, with anger, yes, but something else, something I had never felt before and could not immediately fathom. "Then I should have made my instructions more explicit. I have always maintained, as a matter of the strictest policy, that magic is never a substitute for getting the job done oneself.

It makes one sloppy, prone to cut corners, neglect duties and forget basic skills. In short, it is a cheat."

"I had no idea you held such strong feelings on the matter."

"Well, I do." I swung the amulet on its chain and threw it to the back of the east wall fireplace, making a mental note to retrieve and dispose of it after the feasting. There was a pause, during which Beaumains looked directly into my eyes, with a searching intensity that bordered on the insubordinate. What shocked me most about the look, however, was not its impertinence, but the fact that for some reason it did not bother me anywhere near as much as it should have done.

"Then I owe you an apology," said Beaumains, though it sounded more like a rhetorical question than an admission of guilt.

"Apologies are superfluous when a lesson has been learned. Now please, let us consider the matter dropped."

Beaumains nodded curtly, and we went back to work.

✝

"Presenting Sir Aliduke and Sir Menaduke!" said Sir Kay. The two knights started on the long way forward to pledge themselves to the Queen, and the Great Hall applauded half-heartedly. I contented myself that their lack of enthusiasm sprang from the number of arrivals having reached triple figures, and not from anything amiss on the catering front. The whole of Lower Camelot was running at maximum efficiency. Not a meat bone fell to the ground that was not cleared away and replaced with a fresh serving; no goblet was emptied before the drinker found it to be replenished.

Upon the dais of the Round Table at the northern end of the Hall, the King divided his time between his best Knights, introducing Sir Pellinore, and — if I interpreted the latter's actions correctly — getting him to recount their skirmish with the boar. The Queen sat on the High Table behind them, next to her husband's empty seat, appearing somewhat overwhelmed. As well she should, for she had just spent the past hour receiving tributes from the first batch of Sir Lancelot's vanquishees.

"My throat is about to expire, Lucas," said Sir Kay, stepping down from his podium. He took the hot drink of honey I had prepared for him. "Not to mention my patience," he added, taking a sip. "Oh, that's better. If I have to sit through another tedious, drawn-out quest anecdote, I will tear my hair out. Every knight who's so much as picnicked in the Enchanted Forest thinks they've got an epic trilogy in them, and that they're entitled to take up several hours recounting every last detail. Something needs to be done."

We were positioned at the south end of the Hall by the main doors, where Sir Kay was effecting his duties as Master of Ceremonies. Gawain, the promising young warrior from the Orkneys, came over from his family table, wringing his hands nervously. "Where do I stand, Lucas? I don't wanna look too keen, you know?"

"You are fine where you are, master Gawain," I said.

"Aye, if you say so. Can we have a drop more wine on our table?"

I signalled to a drinks page. "I'd water that down if I were you, Lucas," said Sir Kay through the side of his mouth. "He's been drinking since sundown."

"I am sure it is just nerves, Sir Kay," I said, although I was also concerned for Gawain's sobriety, and how it would mix with the potential loss of face, should the knighting not go his way. I looked over to his table. The Orkney clan were all present, including Father and Mother and young brother Gareth, who followed his older sibling's every word and gesture with adoring eyes. A page approached from the Round Table and whispered at length into Sir Kay's ear. His face betrayed no emotion to the casual observer, but there was a slight flicker about his left nostril that did not bode well. Sir Kay nodded, dismissed the page, and cleared his throat.

"Knights, ladies, people of Camelot! The nominations for promotion to the Round Table are as follows. Gawain of the Orkneys, for *The Quest of the White Hart and the Maiden*." The Great Hall applauded, and the Orkney table got to their feet, stamping and cheering. "Mordred, for *The Vanquishing of the Red Knight*." There was decidedly less applause for this, except for some oafish noise from Mordred's direction.

Beaumains appeared at my side. "Not a popular choice?" she whispered.

"I have no time for gossip," I replied, "but it was widely rumoured Mordred set the whole thing up himself, and that the Red Knight was none other than Sir Sagramour — the one with the scar, sat on his left."

"And finally," said Sir Kay, "Bors, for his part in *The Adventure of the Magic Ring*." Bors received a muted smattering of polite applause. "That one was more of a team effort," I explained to Beaumains, "A fine, epic one at that, but considered less knightworthy than a solo quest."

"And the winner is..." Sir Kay paused to allow the maximum build up of tension. "Mordred, for *The Vanquishing of the Red Knight*."

The sense of disappointment in the Great Hall was palpable. Even Sir Kay did not disguise his surprise at the result. From the Orkney table there came the sound of scraping chairs and raised, angry voices. Gawain was being simultaneously calmed down by his mother and goaded on by his father. Matters were not soothed by the strutting, preening manner in which the new Sir Mordred took his place on the Round Table.

"Uh oh," said Sir Kay. Gawain's father was now pushing his son to his feet, backed up by the increasingly fractious clan.

"What can we do?" said Beaumains.

"In my experience, the only thing that can extinguish the fire of a man so battle-minded is a new challenge, to divert his energies in a more constructive direction," I said.

"All well and good, Lucas," said Sir Kay, "but such challenges do not grow on trees."

"Beaumains," I said, "walk with me."

# VII

The Lower Camelot route was only a shade less congested than the upper level, but even the slightest time advantage would make all the difference. We had left Sir Kay with instructions to keep Gawain away from Sir Mordred and the Round Table for as long as possible. By my conservative calculations, this meant we would have to be jolly quick about it.

We passed down through the Lower Great Hall and along the main service corridor. Like hardy salmon battling upstream, Beaumains and I dodged waiters, side-stepped pages and ducked beneath platters until we arrived at the staircase beneath the Reception Pavilion. Emerging into a loud carnival of vibrant festivities, I scanned the area for my target. Ordinarily, he would be a spectacle difficult to miss, but today the pavilion was somewhat oversubscribed in the spectacle department. "Who are we looking for?" Beaumains shouted.

"The Green Knight," I said. "A giant. Entirely green."

"There!" Beaumains pointed to the bar, where Granville the Brewer was siphoning wine into the Green Knight's barrel-sized goblet. Judging by the reddish tint to his green cheeks, it was by no means his first.

"Ah!" said the Green Knight, crushing my shoulders, " 'tis my butler of iron, come to join me in a bumper!"

"Thank you, Sir Green Knight, but I am on duty."

"Then I shall sink one for us both," he said, emptying the barrel with a noise like a river in flood.

"I bring good news, Sir Green Knight. We have an unexpected window in our Great Hall schedule."

He finished with a gurgling belch and wiped his hand across his beard. "Glad tidings indeed, good butler! But, far be it for me to deny a fellow challenger his place. He might then challenge me, before I had put my challenge. Then I would have to answer his new challenge, instead of putting my first challenge! Afore we knew it, we would be knee deep in challenges, and not able to fathom where one challenge ended and the other challenge began."

"Not at all, Sir Green Knight. This challenge is yours alone to offer."

"Come on, man! Join me in a brew!"

"Perhaps later, Sir Green Knight."

"Then once more, I shall quaff for two." He nudged Granville, who shrugged at me and began to refill the barrel.

I fancied that a less delicate approach was required, but before I could formulate one, Beaumains spoke. "Gawain of the Orkneys seeks to answer your challenge, Sir Green Knight. But says he doubts if it will test him, any more than the mewling of a newborn babe." Something seemed to have stuck in her eye, for it twitched several times in my direction.

"Really, Beaumains," I began, but then realisation dawned.

"Ho, does he now?" said the Green Knight.

"Indeed he does," I added. "What is more, I distinctly heard him say something about there being no knight alive he could not get the better of, and…" I looked to Beaumains.

"…still be home in time for supper," she finished.

"Ha! I would sore like to meet this cocksure stripling."

"He awaits you in the Great Hall," I said.

"Then lead on, good butler!"

The Green Knight picked up his axe, steadied himself, and followed us out of the pavilion. Immediately we came up against a courtyard packed with revellers of every shape and size. I attempted to pass two dancing giants but thought better of it.

"It is no use, we will have to go back the way we came," said Beaumains, failing to move a battalion of raucous knights.

"Out of the question," I said. "Even if he stooped, the Green Knight would never fit down the service corridor."

"We could carry him lengthways?"

"With the help of twenty, perhaps."

"What is the delay, butler?" boomed the Green Knight. "My axe hand grows twitchy."

"This gathered throng is something of an obstruction, Sir Green Knight, between us and the Great Hall."

The Green Knight focused on the seething masses ahead of us. He drew in a breath so long and deep that the torches on the walls began to flicker. "moooooooooooooooooove!" bellowed the Green Knight. He marched forwards and the crowd parted like water before a mighty prow.

In an instant we were at the Inner Courtyard leading to the Great Hall. This would be decidedly more difficult to negotiate, even for our green pathfinder. In addition to the feasters, temporary accommodation tents had been erected throughout the courtyard. Any space not so used was taken up by makeshift stables, refreshment cabins and stalls selling a range of dubious merchandise. An image of the increasingly hostile Orkney faction flitted through my mind. "If you have any inspired ideas, now is the time to share them," I said to Beaumains. She glanced up at the walls of the Inner Courtyard and across to where they passed close to the roof of the Great Hall. "I do have one idea, Sir Lucas. But I suspect you will think it somewhat unorthodox."

I listened to her plan. It was indeed unorthodox. But we had little choice.

"Do it," I said, "I will see you in the Hall." Beaumains gave her instructions to the Green Knight. She climbed up onto his back and he began to scale the wall. I ran to the nearest access point, and dashed back down to the lower levels.

In the Great Hall, my worst fears were confirmed. The Orkney faction were on their feet, led by Gawain's father, the seething King Lot. The disturbance had yet to command King Arthur's attention, but several knights on the Round Table cast inquisitive glances towards the back of the Hall, and it would not be long before the boldest of them came to investigate. The new Sir Mordred, having taken his place among their number, kept smiling and waving in Gawain's direction, which further fanned the flames of Orkney discontent.

"Please, Gawain. I am sure your Knighthood will be forthcoming at Whitsuntide —" said Sir Kay, putting out a consoling arm.

"Whitsun! I'll be dead by Whitsun. And so will *Sir* Mordred if he carries on."

"King Arthur's decision is final."

"I know his kind of decision. It's not what you do. It's who you know."

"That's not true."

"You would say that. You poxy knights are thick as thieves."

"I will give you the benefit of the doubt, Gawain, and put that down to the wine talking," said Sir Kay.

"You wouldn't know a decent day's questing if it bit you on your overfed arse."

"Would you like to put that to the test?"

"Aye, I would at that. But first things first." Gawain pushed Sir Kay out of the way and barged past the surrounding tables.

*Yesterday One* / **119**

"It's a disgrace, it's a fix, and no mistake," King Lot was saying to me. "No-one humiliates my lad like that. I want to speak to Arthur about this, King to King. Butler, get me an audience with him, or I shall get one myself."

"There will be no need for that, sire. If I might entreat you all to sit back down," I said.

"Lucas…" said Sir Kay in alarm.

"I see him, Sir Kay," I said, and followed after Gawain.

"That's ma boy!" said King Lot. "Give 'em hell!"

Gawain was striding down the central walkway leading up to the dais. His hand was on the hilt of his sword. If he drew it, this would be the beginning of the end, for baring a weapon in the Great Hall was tantamount to a battle cry. Sir Mordred noted his approach and began to laugh loudly, encouraging his neighbours to do likewise.

"Gawain," I hissed, still several paces behind him. "You are making a scene."

"You ain't seen nothing yet," he said, not turning around. His sword hand started to pull out his blade, provoking a murmur of interest on the Round Table.

"Please, sit back down."

"Stay out of this, Lucas." Gawain drew his sword full out from the scabbard, still walking forwards.

All of the noise and chatter in the Great Hall ceased as every pair of eyes focused upon him. The Knights of the Round Table got to their feet, their own swords drawn, ready to use them at the slightest nod from the King.

"Oy! Arthur!" Gawain shouted. "I want a word with you."

The King's face cracked into a wide smile. "Ah, Gawain! Sorry about the knighting. It was a close call, and you put in a very strong application. But when you hear about Mordred's experience, I'm sure you'll understand."

"Well said, sire," said Sir Mordred, clapping. "I look forward to the day when we Knights of the Round Table welcome the little laddie into our hallowed ranks."

I had finally caught up with Gawain at the centre of the Hall. From directly above our heads there came a low knocking sound. A few chunks of roofing debris, no bigger than hailstones, fell to the floor in front of me.

"Gawain?" said King Arthur, seeing the drawn sword as if for the first time. "What is the meaning of this?"

"Sire," I said, stepping forwards. "I can explain."

"No he can't," said Gawain. "Shut it, Lucas."

"Forgive me, but I most certainly can," I said. "I have a challenge for you, Sir Gawain."

"You? You're challenging me?"

"*You* are challenging Gawain, Lucas?" echoed the King, scratching his head.

"No, sire, not I," I said. "But I know a man who is."

With impeccable timing, the ceiling above us collapsed in an explosive shower of wattle, slate and clay, and a mighty figure plummeted to the ground like a fallen angel. In the midst of the dust cloud the Green Knight rose to his feet, axe in hand and terrible in bearing. "Where is the one called Gawain?" he roared.

"Right here," said Sir Gawain. "Who wants to know?"

"I am the Green Knight," said the Green Knight. "I bring you a challenge, if you are man enough to take it, which I doubt to my very bones."

"Bring it on, big man. I'll knock yer mossy block off!"

The Green Knight took his axe and lopped off his own head, which fell to the floor with a squelch at Gawain's feet, splattering him with green blood. The Great Hall gave a sharp gasp of shock, followed by a second exclamation when the headless body stooped down, picked up the head, and offered it to Gawain.

"There is more to my noggin than meets the eye," said the severed head of the Green Knight. "But what say we settle our terms over a bumper of ale?"

Gawain wiped the blood from his face, and took the head by the hair. "Why not?" he said. "But you're buying."

"Oh bravo!" said the King, getting to his feet and applauding loudly, whereupon the entire hall followed suit. "Well played, Gawain!"

Gawain passed the head back to the Green Knight and they returned to the Orkney table, now glowing with clan pride, to arrange the conditions of the challenge.

†

"That," I said to Beaumains as we swept away the last of the debris, "was exceedingly well met." The Hall had emptied to prepare for the next feast, which gave us precious little time to repair the roof and reset the tables. But at that moment I felt as if I could have performed every domestic duty at Camelot single-handed.

Beaumains blushed a little. "It was nothing, really. I noticed the roof construction of the Great Hall when we passed it this morning, but I admit that it was something of a risk."

"Never in a thousand years would I have taken such a chance myself," I said. "But I am glad that you did." Beaumains gave me a somewhat disconcerting look. "As I say," I said, feeling my own cheeks colour, "a first class first day, Beaumains, first class. You will be a great asset to Camelot."

She smiled. And as she did so, the first of the new guests poured in, and the Great Hall was replenished with laughter, life and legend.

# Day Three

# I

As daylight faded, the five of us had remained a cluster of cliff-side castaways. The Master was still unconscious, but breathing steadily. Sir Lancelot paced back and forth between the rock pools that marked the ever-decreasing perimeter of our prison. Sir Gawain tried to move some of the smaller boulders blocking the way back to the beach, but only succeeded in sending more loose stones rattling down upon us.

"For God's sake leave it alone, Gawain, before you bury us alive," said Sir Lancelot.

"And scuttlin' about like a crab will do us the world of good, I suppose?"

"Shut up."

"I will not shut up."

"No, just *listen* for a minute." Sir Lancelot stopped in his tracks. "What's that sound?"

"The emergency services?" I ventured. "Or else the armed services. Or both."

"No, it was something else. A sort of... growling."

Slowly, we turned to look at the magical light behind us, still streaming upwards in a vertical, steady beacon. With no cave — or indeed much of the cliff — remaining around it, the beam was clearly visible to its base, where it disappeared to an unseen source underground. Perhaps it was my imagination or a trick of the dwindling light, but it seemed to have increased in circumference since Merlin's release. And there was indeed a growling noise coming from within it; clearly audible above the sound of the beam itself, which gave off a low electrical hum. I stepped as close as I dared towards the purple-pink light — and quickly stepped back again.

A snout was poking tentatively through the hole in the ground. It disappeared as soon as I had seen it, then reappeared, followed by a long pair of jaws and the talon-tip of a claw that scratched at the rocks in an attempt to gain leverage.

"There's a dragon down there," confirmed Sir Gawain. "Look."

"Dragons are extinct," said Sir Lancelot.

"Aye, so was Merlin 'til half an hour ago."

"It does indeed resemble a dragon," I agreed.

"Oh, it's a dragon alright," said Sir Kay. "And it won't be the only one."

Since the collapse of the cliff-side, Sir Kay had fallen into a similar state of subsidence. He sat as far apart from the rest of us as possible, hunched over *The Prophecies of Merlin*. I was greatly alarmed by the expression on his face. It was the look of someone who has not merely bitten off more than he can chew, but has just realised that what he is eating is decidedly unfit for human consumption. "Oh, Lucas," he said, "we've done a very bad thing."

"What's all this 'we' business?" said Sir Gawain.

Sir Lancelot took the old book from Sir Kay's trembling hands and read aloud. "*...and ye who summon me, be swift in all that ye demand, for my return will open a gateway unto the Otherworld.*"

"Bloody hell," said Sir Gawain. He stooped down by the unconscious Master and shouted in his ear. "Didn't see that one coming, did yer?"

"Sir Gawain, please," I said.

"Well, I mean! A fine plan this turned out to be."

A few feet away from us, the dragon, having found a foothold, had squeezed the upper half of its body through the hole and was craning its neck beyond the confines of the magic beam, sniffing cautiously at the evening air.

"The Master formulated the best plan he could, to preserve the Eternal Quest," I said. "Now that circumstances have changed, we simply need a new plan."

"We need to clear up this mess, that's for sure," said Sir Lancelot. "Everything else is secondary."

"Whatever we do," said Sir Kay, "I suggest we do it quickly."

The dragon had caught our scent and was now frantically clawing at the rock, intent on pulling the remaining half of its body up through the gap. A gust of wind ruffled my hair as two leathery wings unfolded and gave an experimental flap.

"First, I suggest we remove the Master to a safe distance," I said, keenly aware of the boiler-room gurgles coming from the dragon's stomach.

"Agreed," said Sir Lancelot.

"Then, we attempt to find Merlin and send him back, and hope that doing so will close up the Otherworld portal."

"No arguments there," said Sir Lancelot, not taking his eyes off the dragon. "Any ideas how to get us out of here, before our new friend claims an easy supper?"

"How about a boat?" said Sir Kay.

"A boat would be ideal, Sir Kay," I said, "but failing that —"

"How about *that* boat?" Sir Kay added.

I looked out to sea. Clearing the headland was no less a sight than King Arthur's old ship, its unfurled sails and dragon-head prow silhouetted against the setting sun. Even more remarkably, its small landing boat was floating rapidly towards us on the rising tide.

"Holy nuns o' Glastonbury," said Sir Gawain. "The Prydwen!"

"But how on earth did it get here?" said Sir Kay.

"Aye, the last thing I remember, we sailed her to bits," said Sir Gawain.

"Who cares how it got here?" said Sir Lancelot. "Lucas, you and Kay grab the landing boat and get the King over to the ship." The air temperature around us rose by several degrees, as if someone had suddenly opened an oven door.

"But what of Sir Pellinore and Sir Perceval? And the Grail?" I said. "We cannot abandon them."

"We won't. I'm staying here."

"No, Sir Lancelot —"

"If we all get in that boat, it'll be a floating funeral pyre before it's halfway to the ship. Go, Lucas. Get the King away. I'll follow as soon as I've dealt with the dragon and found Pell and Percy."

"Lancey's right, for once."

"Thank you, Gawain."

"In fact he's so right, I'm staying with him."

"Gawain —"

"You're not taking all the glory this time, big man, so think again."

"If I might interrupt this tournament of testosterone, and draw your attention to the rapidly filling lungs of the dragon behind us?" said Sir Kay, struggling to lift the Master by the arms. I quickly took up the Master's legs, and together we placed him and ourselves into the landing boat and pushed off from the shore. The miraculous little vessel seemed to be already moving on a homing course for the mother ship, and so I threw the superfluous oars to Sir Lancelot and Sir Gawain. The two knights caught them just as the dragon pulled its hind legs out of the hole.

"Ah, it's been a while," said Sir Gawain, twirling his oar in one hand like a baton. He ran straight at the beast, dodged a jet of flame, and used the oar to pole-vault up onto its back.

With a loud roar the dragon took to the air, swiftly followed by Sir Lancelot, who jumped and grabbed its departing tail. Up over the cliff and out of sight they flew, towards the lights and sirens of the emergency services approaching on the main road, as I had predicted.

From within the portal to the Otherworld, a second dragon had already started to emerge, claws scrabbling in its haste to join its companion. Reluctantly Sir Kay and I turned our gaze out to sea and the fast-approaching outline of the Prydwen.

# II

*

"Calm down, Sir Kay. Take your time."

"That's just it! There is no time left. Hours, perhaps! Days, if we're lucky!"

"Left before what?"

"The end of the world."

The Prydwen was heading out to sea. When we had first boarded her, I was filled with a horrible feeling that the ship was setting out on the exact same voyage she had made when we last set sail in her, all those years ago. In vain I wrestled with the ship's wheel, while my trembling companion sat hunched up against the mast. "It's all here, in the *Prophecies*," said Sir Kay. "Everything that happens after you open a gateway to the Otherworld. The first stage: creatures fanged and foul, winged and woeful. Stage two: the dead shall rise. And as for the third and final stage? The Dark Queen of Annwn shall return. Morgan Le Fay, Lucas! She's going to bloody kill us. We never should have left Lancelot. We're on a ghost ship, on a one way trip to Hell!"

"In which case, perhaps you might help me to change our course, by taking down the sail," I said, for the ship's wheel still refused to budge.

"Save your energy. You'll need it for the end of the world."

"Try to remain calm, Sir Kay. It will not come to that. Even now, Sir Lancelot and Sir Gawain will be attending to the matter of the dragons. By this time tomorrow, we will have found Merlin and closed the Otherworld portal."

I abandoned my struggle with the wheel. Clearly, whatever forces had guided the Prydwen to us also had a very clear idea of where we were going. A jet of dragon fire lit up the cliffs behind us like an infernal lighthouse beacon. I turned my attention back to the Master, lying flat upon the deck. If only the ship *were* taking us back into the past, I thought. Then we might return to Camelot as it was in its glory days; a shining refuge, not the moss-covered ruin it had become.

The boat creaked and strained. The sails turned. I tried to see what had caused the change in direction, and gasped as a dark shape loomed up out of the water ahead. At first I fancied it a sea monster loosed from the Otherworld depths; then I realised it was only the shape of the headland. We were not sailing out to sea any more, but up to the mouth of the estuary where the river Teifi met the ocean. On reflection, this seemed like a wholly sensible destination. Nobody would be looking for us in Cardigan; by now all attention would surely be focused on the cataclysmic events unfolding on the coast. Granted, our ship made a strange sight, but with a bit of luck perhaps it would take us up to the town bridge without attracting attention. The old walls of Camelot might once more provide sanctuary to their lord and master.

But it was not until we approached the upper reaches of the estuary and the outskirts of the town that I realised how literal such protection would be. From within the town itself there came a sound like a small earthquake, which whipped up the water around us and set the boat rocking from side-to-side. Sir Kay stood up in the prow. "Oh my sweet Heaven, what is it now? Some kind of aftershock?"

"I doubt it," I said, for this noise had an entirely different tone to the cliff-side eruption. For one thing, it was nowhere near as sudden or violent. It sounded as if the earth had taken on an aquatic quality and was gurgling like a gentle brook. I joined Sir Kay in the prow and stepped up onto the carved wooden dragon-head to get a better view.

The streetlights of Cardigan illuminated a most curious sight. The very structure of the modern town was changing even as we approached the quayside, in front of our very eyes. A house was being dismantled by some unseen force. A pub was demolished from the roof down, slate by slate and brick by brick. In the empty plot created by this strange resettlement, a new construction was being built. Or perhaps it would be more accurate to say that an old construction was being re-built. For, out of the very depths of the earth, there began a steady bubbling up — a rubbling up, one might say — of a vast walled town and castle.

"Camelot," whispered Sir Kay. "Lucas. What dream is this?"

†

The Master's chamber in the Royal Tower was exactly as we had left it. From the well-made bed to the fire burning cheerfully in the grate, all was as I remembered it to be, as was everything else in Camelot. Not that memory could be wholly trusted after so long an absence, especially given my state of mind at that moment, which was, to put it mildly, a babbling bedlam of questions. I waited until they died down and picked the two most prominent conundrums. One: where were the people who lived and worked in the town of Cardigan that had, only moments ago, occupied this very spot? And two: had the former citizens of Camelot — its knights, staff and citizens — also returned along with the buildings, to take up their places in their home of old? This second question filled me with a sense of anticipation that was half excitement, half fear. I wasted no time in putting the Master to bed and leaving him to the care of a reluctant Sir Kay, while I made a thorough exploration of the premises.

A walk along the outer town walls answered the first question. All of the modern town of Cardigan lay just outside the Camelot walls. It was as if a giant child playing with bricks had pushed aside the town to make way for his Camelot construction, but still cared enough about his old models to leave them intact. My relief at this sight was quickly overwhelmed by the thought of an angry mob of locals seeking an explanation, but a thorough scan of the reconstructed streets of Cardigan outside showed them to be as deserted as Camelot within.

The view from the Gatehouse was slightly more informative. Here, several men and women had attempted to gain access to Camelot, but had barely got within three feet of the main gates before collapsing in a deep sleep, their snoring the only sound to be heard in the unnatural stillness of the night. And so it was that, when a high and desperate cry came from the direction of the Royal Tower, I heard it with a dreadful clarity, and ran with all haste to the source.

# III

The Master was sitting up in bed and clutching the scabbard around his waist, as he tended to do at moments of high stress. Sir Kay's relief when I ran through the door was palpable.

"Lucas, there you are! I've tried explaining, but he won't listen."

"Sire?" I said, attempting to remove the Master's hands from the scabbard. "Sire, it is Sir Lucas."

"What is this trickery? Is it Merlin's work?"

"It is no trick, sire. This is very much Camelot."

The Master took in the room in its entirety, ending with the empty space beside him on the double bed. "If this is Camelot, then where is..." He swallowed hard. "Where are all the people?"

"The old population do not seem to have returned along with the town and castle. As far as I can gather from my investigations, the three of us are the only ones here."

At this, the Master released his grip on the scabbard and a little colour returned to his cheeks. "Sire, it is my belief that Camelot's return is a side effect of summoning Merlin from the Otherworld," I said.

"Then do not trouble me with details," said the Master. "Bring Merlin to me at once."

I glanced at Sir Kay for assistance, but he was busy looking in every direction save mine, whistling a tuneless melody. I cleared my throat. "I am afraid that will not be immediately possible, sire. Merlin was expelled from the gateway to the Otherworld with some degree of force."

"Then, what are we doing here? Why were you not immediately on his trail?"

"Because Camelot's return was not the only side effect of summoning Merlin, sire."

"The end of the world is nigh!" said Sir Kay. "The creatures of the Otherworld have been unleashed! Morgan Le Fay will return to lay waste to the earth!"

"Morgan?" said the Master, turning pale again. "She will want the Grail! She will want revenge."

"We are doomed!"

"No... Take heart, Sir Kay," said the Master. "The power of my half-sister is nothing compared to the magic of Merlin. He will reverse this mishap, and make everything right again."

Sir Kay opened and closed his mouth several times before he spoke. "That is commendably optimistic, sire —"

"Three of us?" said the Master, suddenly.

"Sire?"

"You said the three of us are the only ones here, Lucas. We should be seven." The Master's eyes narrowed to slits. "Where is Lancelot?"

"I was coming to that, sire," I said. "I regret to inform you that Sir Pellinore and Sir Perceval are missing. When the portal was opened there was something of an explosion —"

"It blew them to bits, and the Grail too!"

"We do not know that for certain, Sir Kay. It is true that they suffered a most dolorous blow from the blast. But we were separated from them by the landslide following the explosion, and do not yet know how they fared."

"Where is Lancelot?" repeated the Master.

"Sir Lancelot and Sir Gawain stayed at the cliff-side," I said.

"There was a dragon," said Sir Kay.

"They remained behind to ensure our escape from this dragon, and to see if they could bring aid to our fallen comrades."

"I see," said the Master, swinging his legs out of bed. "Yes. I see it all now."

"In which case, sire," I said, "perhaps you might turn your mind to our next course of action. This new Camelot seems to be protected by some kind of sleeping enchantment, but we cannot stay here for long. Soon the envoys of the modern world will be at our door."

"Treachery," said the Master. He began to pace back and forth in front of the hearth. "I knew this day would come. I have been lenient, yes, I have been very lenient with Sir Lancelot, allowing him to pursue the Eternal Quest with a certain degree of freedom. And this is how he repays me."

"Forgive me, sire, but Sir Lancelot's actions enabled us to escape. Even as we speak, I am sure he will be searching for Sir Perceval and Sir Pellinore."

"Yet again, Sir Lancelot's actions have endangered the Eternal Quest. You want my orders, Lucas? Go and find Merlin, so that by his arts he might close up this portal, and return the Eternal Quest to its previous state of secrecy. Well? What are you waiting for?"

"But what about the others, and the Grail?"

"The power of Merlin will see to all that. You are forbidden to contact the traitor Lancelot. Let him flounder in the wilderness and pay for his duplicity. Now go."

"Yes, sire," I said, and left the Royal Chambers. Sir Kay made to follow me, but the Master raised his hand. "Not you, Kay. You stay with me at Camelot."

Sir Kay hesitated, and then nodded curtly. "Of course. But with your leave, I would like to pay a visit to my old scriptorium."

"Very well. But remain on the premises."

Sir Kay followed me out of the Master's chamber. He waited until we were out of earshot, then drew me aside. "He doesn't give two hoots for the fate of Perceval and Pellinore. It's like they never existed."

"I am sure that is not the case, Sir Kay. The Master has a lot on his mind, that is all."

"So what are you going to do?"

"What else can I do, but follow my orders? I trust that the Master will soon see for himself that he is wrong about Sir Lancelot."

"Is he, though? Lancelot's no stranger to the limelight, after all. In which case..." Sir Kay's eyes glittered strangely.

"Sir Kay?"

"Never mind. Of course, *you* could always find out what Lancelot's intentions are."

"Out of the question. That would mean disobeying the Master."

"But you wouldn't be disobeying him. Not technically. You would still be finding Merlin."

"I fail to see how, Sir Kay."

"Think about it. You've got more chance of finding Merlin with the help of the others than you have on your own, haven't you?"

"Yes, but —"

"So, by finding Lancelot, you will still be finding Merlin, and serving the Eternal Quest. Which is what Arthur wants, after all."

I was beginning to concede that Sir Kay had a point. "Then again," he added, "you've got enough on your plate just getting out of Camelot in the first place. How on earth are you going to cover any distance, with no transport, and with the entire world alerted to our presence? You'll be arrested in five minutes flat. Of course, I could have told Arthur that, if he'd bothered to ask. But oh no, I'm nothing more than a glorified typewriter. Anyway. Best of luck," Sir Kay patted me on the shoulder and headed for the scriptorium, leaving me alone on the landing.

Sir Kay was not overstating the difficulties presented by the Master's orders, whichever way I chose to interpret them. It was then that the glimmer of an idea came to me. I cannot say that I cared for it. In fact, as soon as the idea started to take shape, my entire mind rebelled against it. But the more I tried to wipe it out, the more ground the thought gained, like a stubborn stain that grows in prominence for all one's efforts to remove it. I yielded to its logic, and resolved to make my way to the Great Hall at first light.

# IV

Early next morning, I peered into an empty fireplace with no small amount of trepidation. The hearth was stone cold but, even if a roaring fire had burned within the grate, I could not have been more reluctant to put my hand inside. I kneeled by an inglenook and inspected the wide expanse of the chimney. Nothing. I breathed a sigh of relief. But suddenly a finger of sunlight poked through the window, illuminating the back of the fireplace with such brightness that I recoiled as if burned. Regaining my wits, I noticed that this dazzling intensity was caused by the very object I was reluctantly seeking.

At the back of the chimney, suspended on a protruding stone, hung a thin silver necklace with an amber jewel strung upon it. I carefully reached in, minding not to touch the gem with my hands, and held it before me. The rising sun caught the ornament again, sending splashes of golden light dancing about the tapestries on the wall like hungry moths. There was no mistaking it. Against all odds, the amulet of teleportation had remained where I had left it, confiscated from young Gwion and cast in anger to the back of the fireplace at that long ago Winter Feast, never to be retrieved. Until now.

With a ceremonial slowness I lowered the chain over my head. The amulet itself was the size of a small fist. It hung between my ribcage, and the unfamiliar weight caused my head to lean forwards, as if the jewel were demanding my attention physically as well as mentally. This was just as well, as I had completely forgotten how to work the thing. I tried to cast my mind back through the centuries. I seemed to recall that they operated by control of thought; that the amulet-wearer simply had to visualise the person or place he wanted to go to, and he would be taken there in a heartbeat. If that were so, then I quailed at the mental diligence required to use it effectively. But I had to test it nonetheless.

My first impulse was to see how matters fared with my fellow knights. I was sorely tempted to go straight to Sir Lancelot, but it would be highly unwise to start my teleportation experiments on such a scale. I decided instead to picture somewhere in the immediate vicinity; a safe environment where my sudden appearance would be less obtrusive. I settled on the scriptorium. I closed my eyes and thought of the word 'scriptorium.' I opened one eye. There was a slight blurring at the corner of my vision, but other than that I was still very much in the Great Hall. Perhaps, then, one had to touch the amulet at the same time? I placed my right hand onto its cool, smooth surface. I took the first in a series of increasingly deep breaths. This time, as well as thinking of the word 'scriptorium,' I tried to picture something of the room as I remembered it. The high wooden shelves. The neat rows of rolled parchments. Scores of archived vellum tomes, the accumulated wisdom of the ancient world.

As I did so, I became conscious of a sea change in my thoughts. Although my memory of the scriptorium was weak and inaccurate, the very act of thinking about it brought the place vividly to life. My ears experienced an alteration in pressure, as of a sudden difference in altitude, accompanied by a soft, low popping sound. All at once the shelves of the scriptorium appeared, and I realised that I was standing directly in front of them. Unfortunately, so was Sir Kay, gathering materials from a writing bench. He turned towards me, and only the large stack of parchments piled up in his arms prevented him from seeing me quickly disappear again.

I opened my eyes back in the Great Hall and sat down to catch my breath, for I was weak at the knees and shaking all over. I was overwhelmed by a conflicting series of emotions: elation at the feat I had just accomplished, guilt at betraying an old principle, and relief at not being caught in the act. One thing I knew for certain; I had been entirely correct in banning their use. Such an experience could very easily become habit-forming.

Disobeying the Master's orders, on the other hand, could certainly not, and yet that was precisely what I had to do next. I reminded myself that I was serving the Eternal Quest by doing so, and attempted to gather the necessary resolve. I was on the point of touching the amulet, when I stopped myself. How could I have been so stupid? There I was, about to attend to my fellow knights, without anything in the way of weaponry to bring to their aid!

I teleported to the armoury, surprised but also pleased at how much easier it was the second time. I selected a sword each for Sir Lancelot and Sir Gawain, and, on reflection, one for Sir Pellinore and Sir Perceval, in the happy event of their being found overnight. These I packed in a long hessian drawstring bag, designed for carrying two or more swords comfortably about one's person, which hung behind my back with the reassuring ballast of a knapsack. It would have felt all the better for the addition of a thermos of tea and a packet of sandwiches, for they were sure to be in need of refreshment, but I thought it best to be on my way. This small act of preparation had settled my nerves, and was enough to help me muster the confidence required to close my eyes, touch the amulet, and picture Sir Lancelot in my mind.

There was a soft, low popping sound.

Immediately followed by a loud, high, roaring sound.

I opened my eyes to find myself several thousand feet up in the air, plummeting to earth with all the grace of a man with four swords tied to his back.

# V

My first thought was that the amulet had been bewitched by some ill enchantment and delivered me to my doom, and that this was what happened when one compromised the hard-earned principles of a lifetime. In fact, I reflected as the wind thundered in my ears, I jolly well deserved it, and should think myself lucky it was nothing worse. This bout of self-pity was fleeting, and I tried to focus my mind on teleporting back to the Great Hall. This was rather difficult, as that portion of my mind not concerned with my imminent appointment with the ground was trying to figure out how to stop myself from performing a series of sickening somersaults. I pictured the Hall as best as I could, and reached for the amulet.

It was not there.

I tore frantically at my neck and torso, only to see the amulet falling just below me, down towards the shape of a large white cloud. A white, dragon-shaped cloud, the size of a single-decker bus from head to tail, with a man clinging to its neck and repeatedly punching it. Either I was hallucinating cloud formations as I approached certain death, or the amulet had indeed transported me to the vicinity of Sir Lancelot. I turned my body upside down, the better to reduce wind resistance and sky-dive down to my target. I came level with the white dragon in time to see the amulet hook around its tail and fall towards the point where it joined the beast's hide.

With both hands I grabbed the tail, as thick as a human thigh and thrashing at the air like an angry serpent, and hung on with all my strength. I reached along the tail to where the amulet was wedged around the scaly skin. The necklace had no clasp, and I pulled uselessly at the chain. Clearly it could only be removed by pulling it back the way it came.

The dragon presumably employed its tail as a sort of rudder, for the addition of my weight caused it to rear up in flight, sending Sir Lancelot falling backwards. The dragon turned its head to determine the source of the de-stabilising influence, then flicked its tail sharply upwards. The tail buckled beneath my hands, sending me flying forwards onto its back; a not unwelcome development, as the dragon then sent a jet of flame at the spot I had recently occupied. The flame singed the dragon's own tail, and it uttered a screech of pain that tore at my ears. From my new perch on the beast's haunches I crawled, using its sparse tufts of spiny hair as handholds, to where Sir Lancelot had once again reached the dragon's neck. *En route* I was able to build up a more complete picture of the situation.

Our white dragon was the middle one of three of its kind, flying in a diagonal formation — a green one ahead and above us, a red one behind and below. From the snatches of ripe Caledonian curses coming from ahead and above, I identified the figure on the back of the green dragon to be Sir Gawain. The red dragon behind and below us seemed to be the only one not carrying a knightly passenger. When I dared to glance over the white dragon's flanks, the patchy view of the ground showed us to be approaching a major habitation, shortly revealing itself, by several recognisable landmarks, as the city of Cardiff. From the little I knew of dragons, this made perfect sense. As a species they were instinctively drawn to major populations, those being the best places to satisfy their basic needs of flesh, riches and ruin. The denial of such simple dragon pleasures was presumably the work upon which Sir Lancelot and Sir Gawain were engaged; work in which a sword would prove an essential tool.

There was also the matter of the red dragon to contend with; a task which, by process of elimination, fell to me. As clearly as if I had heard them only yesterday, the words of Sir Pellinore came back to me. *Dracontias. The dragon stone. Lodged in its brain. Cut that out with a blade to the top of the head.*

And so to work.

Now that it had removed me from its rudder, the white dragon was flying relatively straight and steady. The amulet was still lodged around its tail. Well, it would just have to remain there for the time being. Releasing my handhold, I drew myself into a crouching position, loosened the drawstrings of my bag, and took one of the four swords from its scabbard. I did not dare throw the sword directly to Sir Lancelot. But perhaps there was a way of simultaneously securing it for him to retrieve, and of conveying me to the red dragon?

"Sir Lancelot!" I shouted. He turned from his position at the dragon's neck and almost let go of it, so startled was he by my inexplicable presence.

"Lucas? What the hell?!"

"I shall explain at a more convenient time!" I yelled. "I have brought you a sword! Hold on tight!" Sir Lancelot nodded, and redoubled his grip.

The red dragon held its position behind and below the white. A jump would not be enough to cover the distance without some form of propulsion. I turned again towards Sir Lancelot and took aim for the centre spot on our white dragon's back, where the flesh was slightly softer. I threw the sword as hard as I could. It struck home like a javelin, embedding itself by several inches. The beast howled in fury.

Its entire back convulsed like a trampoline, catapulting me backwards past its tail, through the air, and directly down into the flight path of the red dragon.

This was when I detected the first flaw in my plan. The part of the red dragon to which I was flying head first was its jaws; jaws that were quick to open wide in anticipation of the airborne fast food heading in their direction. In one fluid movement, I pulled another sword from my pack and, just as the jaws closed around me, thrust the point up into the roof of the dragon's mouth and wedged the hilt behind its lower teeth. I pulled myself up out of the mouth by using its nostrils as a handhold, a jet of flame shooting past my escaping feet, and took up position behind its mighty neck.

Naturally the red dragon took great umbrage at being denied a meal in such a brazen manner, and started upon a series of dives, ducks and rolls to try and dislodge me, not to mention the sword stuck in its mouth. I dug another sword into its neck for purchase, which did nothing to improve its mood. I realised with satisfaction that by dint of similar sword-work, Sir Lancelot's white dragon had lost altitude and was now flying level and within jumping distance of my red one. Pulling out the sword from the neck in front of me, I cut open the top of the red dragon's head and prised out the Dracontias stone in a shower of blood and brain.

The bat-like wings stopped beating. The red dragon let out a gasping groan somewhere between a roar and a sigh. The carcass dropped away beneath my feet. I let go of the sword, and jumped up for the white dragon as the red plummeted down to earth above the river Taff. The amulet had now slipped to the very tip of the white dragon's tail, and was on the point of being flung off into the air when I grabbed it and pulled it back over my head. I touched it with my hand and teleported over to Sir Gawain.

In contrast to Sir Lancelot, he was not the least bit surprised at my sudden manifestation. "About bloody time an' all," he shouted, and stopped boxing the green dragon's ears to take the final sword from me. Before I could counsel caution, Sir Gawain sliced open the head and removed the dragon stone. We immediately pitched forwards as the dead beast fell through the sky.

Below us lay a sports ground, the centre circle of the field marked out like a target. A football match was taking place, and sounds of pandemonium rose up to greet our imminent arrival. "Watch out below!" cried Sir Gawain in response. "Happy landings, Lucas!"

I was not sure if the amulet would work for two, but this seemed like the ideal time to find out. I took hold of Sir Gawain's shoulder and touched the jewel, thinking of Sir Lancelot and the white dragon. Immediately we were beside him at the neck of the beast. This time, Sir Gawain had the good grace to be mildly taken aback.

"What happened there?" he said, as we took up hasty handholds.

"An amulet of teleportation," I said. "I am sure it will work for three of us if we link hands."

"Not an option, Lucas," said Sir Lancelot. "Look." He pointed below. We were following the course of the river Taff over green parkland, the city centre of Cardiff fast approaching ahead of us. The white dragon, wounded and exhausted, was flying low, its belly skimming the tops of the tallest trees, turning its head to roast them as we passed.

"I can't let it reach the city," said Sir Lancelot.

"Then scunner the beastie now and be done with it!" said Sir Gawain.

"There are too many people in the park, I won't risk bringing it down here."

"Where, then?" I said.

"The river. It's the safest place."

"And how are you gonna persuade it to do that?" said Sir Gawain. "I dunno about you, but I'm fresh out of sugar lumps."

Sir Lancelot smiled. At me.

# VI

'The benefit of hindsight' has always struck me as an inadequate turn of phrase. In my experience, whenever one considers events from a hind-sighted position, such a perspective rarely provides one with anything resembling benefit. An example: with hindsight, Sir Lancelot's plan, though it sprang from the purest motives and was sound enough in theory, was a decidedly different matter when put into practice. At the time, however, while the widespread destruction that followed was as far from our minds as a worst case scenario could have been, it did seem the most practical option.

For argument's sake, I am willing to concede that it *just might* be possible to steer a dragon by interfering with the movement of its tail. After all, I had recently witnessed this first hand when I had landed on the rudder-like appendage. *That* tail, however, had belonged to a decidedly different dragon. For one thing, it had been carrying the weight of two knights intent on reducing its lifespan, not three. For another, it had yet to endure the strategic sword strokes of Sir Lancelot, delivered with the express purpose of bringing it closer to ground level.

And so, far from yielding to my attempts to twist his tail to the left, in order to steer right and downwards to the proposed landing in the river Taff, the dragon made it clear that he would not co-operate with such a manoeuvre. He uttered a deep rumbling bellow like an iron table leg being scraped across a tiled floor, banking left towards the city centre, focusing all his remaining strength on shaking off his stubborn parasites.

My hands were still clasped around the tail. This sudden movement threw me off his hind-quarters and into space. So it was that I once more found myself clinging on to the very tip of the white dragon's tail with both hands, and thus unable to reach for either Sir Gawain's outstretched hand, or the amulet around my neck. "Sir Lancelot!" I shouted, "The dragon is proving somewhat un-steerable!"

"I'm going to bring him down, now!" he replied, from the creature's neck. "Hold on, you two!"

The dragon, for all the world as if he understood our plans, chose that moment to start rolling from side-to-side. Such displacement mattered little to me in my already disorientated position, but it was enough to send the sword flying out of Sir Lancelot's hands and almost dislodge Sir Gawain from the dragon's haunches. My weight pulled the dragon's tail down almost vertically, so that my line of sight was clear. This proved to be a mixed blessing, as it allowed me to see that the dragon was flying straight towards a clutch of trees. Branches whipped past me in a flurry of foliage, to reveal the walls of Cardiff Castle dead ahead.

The dragon's altitude rose to a level only slightly higher than those walls. Unfortunately for me, it was slightly *less* than a tail-length higher. I waited until I was close enough to smell the moss on the stones, then tucked my legs up into a swinging crouch. The dragon cleared the walls and, by the seat of my trousers, so did I. The castle grounds were packed with tourists, many of whom were gathered around a guide, his back turned to our rapid approach. At the sudden appearance of this unadvertised vision of the mythic past, the crowd screamed and scattered, to the initial bemusement of the guide, until he turned and gazed with horror upon the storybook spectacle bearing down upon him. The dragon did not disappoint. It sent a roaring jet of flame running along the ground towards the hapless fellow, who closed his eyes and prayed, possibly for a timely rescue by a knight of old. I did the best that I could, pulling hard on the tail and diverting the dragon's line of fire at the last second, leaving the guide un-scorched.

The dragon was not flying high enough to clear the further castle wall so it simply went through the top of it, charging head first into the stonework. I closed my eyes as the world turned to a maelstrom of rubble around me, but still I clung on, hoping that my fellow knights had managed to do likewise. But when I opened my eyes, it was to see Sir Gawain tumbling past me, landing spread-eagled on the grass of the outer castle lawn. The shadow of the white dragon passed over cars and buses, which screeched and smashed to a horn-honking standstill.

Energised by lightening its load, the dragon increased its speed, flying towards the glass-fronted façade of a large hotel. The glass smashed and the dragon half flew, half hopped through the restaurant, squashing a table of diners and setting fire to the bar. With another explosion of glass we emerged from the other side — now minus Sir Lancelot.

The dragon flew down a side street and out into the main pedestrianised shopping centre, exhausted and blind with rage. It bounced from one side of the street to the other, gouging out great chunks from the side of buildings. Glass and masonry showered down on the people below, while I clutched the dragon's tail for dear life. The pedestrianised area came to an end mere yards away. After that, running along the front of the castle was more traffic, more panicked masses fleeing for cover. Tackling the dragon down here would only add to the sum total of chaos and casualties. The river was still the best place for it. Somehow, I had to lure it there.

I released my grip on the dragon's tail and let myself fall to the street below. Finally unburdened, the dragon roared with triumph and landed several yards ahead of me, where it wasted no time in ransacking a hamburger outlet on the corner of the street, feasting on the terrified customers within. I got painfully to my feet to scan the skyline, and found the very vantage point I was looking for. A double decker bus, of the open-topped tourist variety, stood on the nearest side of the bridge where the river passed through the city. This bus, like the cars stopped at haphazard intervals in the intervening stretch of road, had been hastily abandoned.

The distance between dragon and bus was too great to rely wholly on the amulet. If I was to successfully use myself as bait, the dragon would have to see me, and give chase. Quite what I would do when it caught up with me, given that I was fresh out of swords by now, was a problem that would have to wait in line.

Now that the dragon had started to feed, distracting it from its dinner would be no easy task. But if there is one thing a dragon loves more than food, it is money. To my left stood a bank, so I touched the amulet, and concentrated on the vault that would surely lie within. Immediately I was surrounded by shelves containing tightly wrapped bundles of notes, and despaired. The currency of the modern age would mean nothing to the dragon's primeval eye. Then my foot nudged a pile of small sacks. I untied one and smiled, picking up the bag of pound coins and teleporting to an area of road several metres away from the feasting beast.

I dipped my hand into the bag of coins. My fingers closed around a cool, heavy handful. The dragon's head was stuck through the hole it had made in the burger bar window. "Excuse me!" I shouted at its rear. When there was no response, I followed this with a "Dragon!" The dragon reversed on its hind legs. I was not at all sure of the correct tone, so I resorted to one I had often heard dog owners employ in the retrieval of a puppy. "Here boy!" I whistled. "Come on! Over here!" The dragon pulled its head out of the window, munching on a leg. "I have some nice, shiny riches for you. See?" I let the coins trickle through my fingers. The dragon made a few darting steps towards me, and I threw the rest of the handful into the air like a careless sower. The dragon twitched in delight at the clinking *pitter patter* of the coins as they fell. It snorted and pawed at the tarmac, sizing me up with a lizard stare. Then with a roar it bounded towards me.

I tarried not. I ran up the street with all my might, clutching the bag, while a sound like the unfolding of a giant umbrella behind me told me the dragon had taken to its wings. The hairs on the back of my neck prickled with heat. I jumped to the left as a spear of flame passed over my right shoulder. I leaped onto the bonnet of a car and ran across its roof. The bridge and the bus were still several hundred yards away. My plan was working, in that the dragon was building up a good head of speed, but it would all be for nothing if it caught up with me too soon. I still did not dare to use the amulet, for fear that my sudden disappearance would cause the dragon to slow down, and squander the momentum I was hoping to use to my advantage.

My neck hairs tingled again. This time I ducked and could not stop myself from falling forwards, losing my balance and sprawling onto my hands and knees. I twisted around with desperate haste and reached for the amulet, even as a jet of red hot flame poured towards my face.

It froze an inch from my nose, harmless as a carnival streamer.

Once again, the bizarre time dilation was upon me. Once again, only I seemed to be unaffected by it. The dragon hung mute and still above me, its gaping jaws ablaze, like an exhibit in a particularly well-funded museum. This time I did not allow myself the luxury of bewilderment. But as I got to my feet to run, something in a window display to my right caught my eye. The shop specialised in Celtic crafts and souvenirs, and in amongst an ironic arrangement of cuddly stuffed dragons, an object flashed where it caught the sun. A sword. A sword standing in — I almost laughed aloud at the sight — a wooden replica of an ancient stone. I hurried inside, took the sword by the handle, and pulled it out of the stone. I sprinted the rest of the way to the bus, half-stumbled up the steps, and on to the front of the top deck.

Time flowed true around me once more, the dragon's fire turning the spot where I had fallen into a bubbling tarmac stew. I held the sword aloft and waved it for good measure. Still flying, the dragon raised its head and, thankfully, spotted me on top of the bus. With two more wing beats the dragon bore down upon me and opened its mouth. I teleported. The dragon snapped its jaws around thin air. It had just enough time to register surprise at my sudden appearance on the top of its head before I cut through the skin and expelled its *Dracontias*. The dragon's amassed speed sent it sailing over the bridge. By means of a directional thrust to its head with my feet as I jumped off it and into the air, I sent it crashing down through the side of the bridge and into the river below. I teleported safely to the river bank as the white dragon plunged beneath the surface with an almighty splash followed by a hiss of steam.

For a moment, all was peace and quiet. Then a thrumming, thumping sound filled the air, accompanied by a voice, brittle and tinny. I looked up to see a police helicopter, a voice loud-hailing me from within. The helicopter was one of hundreds of approaching objects. At first I marvelled that they deemed such force necessary to apprehend one old and weary knight.

Then I became aware of a darkening of the sky. Day turned to dusk, and I realised that those shapes I had taken to be other helicopters were, in fact, more dragons. Hundreds more, of every size, shape and species; an endless plague procession from the west.

"Put down your weapon!" cried the loud-hailing voice; but his instruction was superfluous. As if it weighed a hundred tonnes, the souvenir sword, bent to an L shape and thick with blood-matted dragon hair, dropped from my hand. I touched the amulet, and my mind turned to the only person in the world qualified to deal with such a carnival of monsters. With a soft, low popping sound, I disappeared.

# VII

I opened my eyes to find myself beneath a canopy of trees. There was no immediate sign of Sir Pellinore, but I trusted that he would not be far away in what I strongly suspected was the place we used to call the Enchanted Forest. After a few seconds I realised, aside from my own laboured breathing, that everything was uncomfortably silent. Not a bird stirred in the trees, not a creature rustled through the scrub. Nevertheless, I was conscious of another presence around and about me, as if someone or something was following me very closely. Following; or perhaps hunting. I walked for some way in what I trusted to be the right direction, tracing the flow of a brook for lack of any other guide. Just ahead of me the stream widened into a small pool, and I knelt to drink.

Dust and debris fell from my clothes and hair, and on seeing my reflection I noticed that the day's exertions had left me looking far from presentable. I washed my face and cleaned my cuts and grazes as best I could, placing my bloodied hands under the soothing water. My reflection broke as the surface rippled. Over my shoulder, I thought I had seen the distorted form of a hooded figure. I stood up, but the figure vanished, and the rotten stench of a stagnant pond filled my nostrils. My reflection reformed and a hideous apparition was revealed at my shoulder, as if I had suddenly grown a sinister Siamese twin. Its neck and head were that of a cockerel, but its face was human, set in an expression of pure loathing. It tilted back its head like a snake preparing to strike, and would surely have done so, had a pair of hands not clamped around its throat and broken its neck with one twist. In the same movement, those hands scooped up the dreadful creature and hurled it into the bushes where it landed out of sight.

"Cockatrice," said Sir Pellinore. Turning to thank him, I realised he had performed the entire motion with his back turned to the beast. "Never look at one. Give it a glance, just one, and you're finished." The bushes rustled, presumably the cockatrice in its final throes. Sir Pellinore plucked a wooden stake from inside his jacket and hurled it at the sound, cutting the movement dead. Immediately he snapped a branch from a tree and began to whittle a new weapon with his knife, his eyes roving ceaselessly at the forest around us.

"I am glad to have caught up with you, Sir Pellinore. There is much to convey. I am in urgent need of your assistance in matters of beast lore —"

Sir Pellinore stopped carving and grabbed me by the shoulders. "Herne?" His eyes were red raw and ringed with shadows, his voice thickened as if by a heavy cold.

"It is Sir Lucas, Sir Pellinore."

"I call for Herne but he does not heed me." A twig snapped to our right and Sir Pellinore whirled around, brandishing the half-finished spear.

"We need your help, Sir Pellinore. You and Sir Perceval —"

"The forces of Hell took Perceval. Took him and the Grail, when the thunderbolt struck; off to Annwn they went. I was thrown clear by the boom. When I awoke, I tried to follow, but the critters had me surrounded. Fearsome critters, butler, the likes of which I've never seen. Lobster Cats and Cricket Bats. Tweezer-stealers and Grockle-grabbers. The Lesser-spotted

Karantamagentis. Wolf Gulls. Sand Witches." Sir Pellinore gripped me by the lapels. Large tears rolled down his cheeks. "The Dancing Dogs of Denby!" he rasped.

He let me go and began to pace the ground with his now-finished spear. "Never clapped eyes on any of 'em before, yet their names fill my head. And they knew me. Oh they knew me, alright. They were driven after me! Chivvied, I was, by the Beast itself. Yes, the Questing Beast is abroad, butler. It bays for my soul, sending forth its heralds to run me to ground." The wind moved the trees to our left, accompanied by the distant sound of barking dogs. "But I will achieve that quest, or bleed the best blood of my body!" The yapping grew louder. With a pitiful howl, Sir Pellinore ran off through the undergrowth. Something shook the tops of the trees and a shadow seemed to flit over my head and follow after him, but with its passing the yelping faded.

I hesitated to give chase, unsure of what to do next. Remembering what Sir Pellinore had said of the fate of Sir Perceval and the Grail, I wondered if I might now teleport to them. But when I touched the amulet, I was unable to picture them in my mind's eye, their physical reality obscured as if by an impenetrable mist. They had passed out of range; or perhaps into a realm where such concepts ceased to have any meaning. I shuddered at the thought; and then had an idea. Might the amulet work on Merlin? After all, he was now in the physical world.

I closed my eyes and tried to picture him. At first it was the same as with Sir Perceval and the Grail. But slowly, an image began to form, the outline of a dark cowled head. I felt my fingers tingle and my ears block up as if I were on the verge of teleporting — and for the briefest moment I felt as if I had — but then I hit an obstruction, as if I had run into the mental equivalent of a brick wall. I concentrated my entire mind to the task, but it was like trying to break through the wall using a teaspoon. Eventually I gave up and opened my eyes, disappointed, but not surprised, to find that I was still in the forest. I resolved to lay the matter of locating Merlin, as well as the rest of the day's transpirations, before the Master. To that end, I teleported back to Camelot.

†

I materialised in the infirmary, where I heated some water and applied herbs and salves to my wounds, before gathering together such items, along with a stock of fresh linen, into a first aid kit that we could take with us to assist our comrades in the field. I had decided to first seek Sir Kay, hoping to receive his advice on how best to place my considerable burden of information before the Master.

As I was bandaging my right arm, I noticed an envelope addressed to myself, propped in front of one of the infirmary's examining mirrors. Even before I broke the wax seal, the ornate calligraphy announced the penmanship as Sir Kay's. I unfolded the parchment within, and read the following.

> *Dear Lucas,*
>
> *If you are reading this, I can only assume you have returned to Camelot in one piece (though how you managed it is quite beyond me). I have therefore left this note in the infirmary as, if indeed you can still walk, you will certainly be making it your first port of call.*
>
> *After you left, the King's mood darkened to pitch black. My suggestion that we sally forth to seek news of Perceval and Pellinore, whose fates lay heavy on my heart, was not well received. Neither was my more moderate compromise, that we at least take a look at our immediate surroundings beyond the Camelot walls. Finally,*

*when I proposed that our time would be well spent in drafting an official speech announcing his return to the world, Arthur picked up my inkwell and flung it into the fireplace, stating that he would condescend to a brief look at our surroundings, in disguise, if it would put an end to my 'ceaseless prattle.' We made our way across the battlements. From there we could see the reconstructed town of Cardigan, fenced in, as it were, by a line of sleeping bodies under the enchantment you had previously observed, Lucas. This spell did not affect us, however, as we discovered when the King forced me to test it. And so we passed its invisible boundary and proceeded into the town.*

*Save for those fifty or so who slept outside Camelot, not a soul did we find in the whole place. It was most eerie, Lucas. The citizens' departure had been made in haste, for in several of the houses we entered, the doors had been left wide open, and television sets remained switched on. You should know, Lucas, that it was by such means that the King discovered what he later described as your 'vile treason.'*

*Every channel was given over to news of the breach of the Otherworld, though they did not know it as such, preferring such grandiloquent terms as 'Armageddon' and 'The Apocalypse.' The most prevalent pictures consisted of footage taken from a helicopter at a distance, of Lancelot and Gawain grappling with dragons in the sky, and then an image of you alone, Lucas, taken from ground level, clinging to a beast as it flew through the streets of Cardiff. I did not see any more, for the King exploded into a high rage because you had not sought Merlin as he commanded. He threw a chair at the television set and stormed back to Camelot, locking himself within the Royal Tower, where he presumably still resides.*

*Well, for all I care, he can stay there. These past few hours have stretched my patience to the limit, and I have decided to throw in my lot with Sir Lancelot etc., for better or worse. If I should, as a result of this, receive a little of the attention due to me as the author of* The History of King Arthur and His Noble Knights, *the most influential work of Arthurian literature ever committed to paper, then that is all by the by.*

*I remain yours,*
*Sir Kay*

I refolded the letter, a half-tied bandage dangling like a cobweb from my arm. I walked behind the examining mirror and down a hidden staircase into Lower Camelot, then through its passageways to the foundations of the Royal Tower. I stepped into the lift that would take me up to the Master's chambers on the top floor. Sir Kay's tidings had given me cause for great self reproach, and I severely regretted my recent actions. However, I was certain that once I had fully explained the events of the past few hours to the Master, he would see that I had only been acting in his best interests, as well as those of the Eternal Quest. The lift came to a stop behind a tapestry, and I stepped into the room.

The Master sat with his back to me, in a chair in front of the fire. I cleared my throat, but he did not stir, and so I started to walk towards him.

"Stay where you are, Lucas."

"Sire. I bring much news —"

"News of Merlin?"

"Not of Merlin as yet, sire, but —"

"Then why do you return?"

"Events have progressed, and not altogether for the best. But with your leadership, I am sure that the Eternal Quest —"

"Leadership? I gave you my leadership when I asked you to seek Merlin."

"I did try, sire, but a wizard abroad runs to his own itinerary."

"You did not try. Instead, you chose to give aid to those knights who have abandoned the Eternal Quest to meet their destiny alone."

"With respect, sire —"

"Do not sully the word, Lucas. Your actions prove you know nothing of respect. I saw it with my own eyes. You have made our troubles a thousand times worse."

"I am sorry, sire."

"You are dismissed."

"Very good, sire. Should you require anything, I will be in my quarters."

"No, Lucas. You are dismissed from my service. Perhaps the word 'banished' might make more sense to you? Very well then. You are henceforth banished from Camelot."

"Sire?"

"There is no place on the Eternal Quest for the disloyal."

"But sire —"

"Just go. Go, and join your fellow traitor knights."

I stepped back into the alcove and pulled the lever.

"As you wish, sire," I said, and descended to the lower levels.

# Day Four

# I

It is often said that charity begins at home, and the very same rule applies to housekeeping. That is not meant to be a joke; nor do I think it is stating the obvious. On the contrary, it is surprising the number of times this basic principle is ignored by those who should know better. Even I, with the experience of an exceedingly long lifetime under my belt, am occasionally guilty of failing to measure up to the mother of all domestic maxims.

Upon leaving the Master, the counterweighted lift had conveyed me down into the bedrock at the central heart of the lower levels, where my old living quarters had been situated. My first thought on entering was that a gang of thieves had somehow managed to get past the sleeping enchantment and ransacked my room. The bed was a bombsite, devoid of pillows, quilt halfway to a stone floor whose existence could only be guessed at, obscured beneath clothes cascading like a waterfall over the side of the laundry basket. My few personal effects were apparently of little interest to the burglars, as these had been left in random piles, small islands in a wide sartorial sea.

A moment's reflection yielded a more rational explanation. From everything I had seen thus far, Camelot had been reconstructed exactly as we had left it. There was no reason to doubt that this same principle also applied to the lower levels. It was not the state of my quarters that was in question, so much as my own memory of them. For, now that I came to think of it, we *had* left in rather a hurry. There had been so much to organise before we set off on the Grail Quest, and at such short notice, that it had been necessary to entrust run-of-the-mill domestic tasks to other hands. My belongings were arranged in such a higgledy piggledy manner because I had been forced to decide what to take and what to leave in great haste, my own packing needs coming second to that of the expedition. I realised that I was now being presented with an opportunity rarely found in the domestic realm — to finish a task which necessity had dictated I abandon. A thorough spring clean of my old quarters would do much to clear my head and help me decide how best to proceed.

When it comes to the whole matter of spring-cleaning, the first thing to be thrown out should be one's sentimentality. So-called keepsakes are, indeed, items kept merely for the sake of it, clung onto out of a misplaced affection for what is really only worthless junk. With this dictum as my guide, I had soon filled the lift with the miscellaneous clutter of yesteryear. Overalls that were several sizes too small. Aprons re-patched so many times that no scrap of the original garment remained. An old glass and sand egg timer, cracked and useless. All this I transferred by the armful via the lift to the Upper Courtyard, where I arranged it in orderly piles against the base of the Royal Tower.

After several hours' work I stood up and stretched. To the west, the sun was setting. I became suddenly aware of a tremendous weariness in my bones. It had been days now since I had experienced anything like a substantial sleep. Although the Grail's regeneration was most invigorating, it was no substitute for a good night's rest. And now that the Grail had gone, who could say what the effect on our physical frame might be? I pushed the unsettling thought aside. I would be of little use to my fellow knights as an exhausted husk, whatever fate had befallen them. Moreover, a new day might also bring about a cooling of the Master's temper. And so I left the pile of rubbish neatly stacked against the tower, and returned to my quarters.

But rest proved to be elusive. I am not the sort of person who usually remembers their dreams. I certainly have them, for I often wake to find myself tangled up in my sheets as if I had been fighting off some phantom assailant. This time, however, my imaginings were as clear as day. Indeed, so vivid was the nightmare, that if I were a more fanciful man I would describe it more as a waking vision.

As soon as I got into bed I slipped into a delirium. I have occasionally experienced such a state after a particularly strenuous day, when my physically exhausted body craves sleep, but my overactive mind is having none of it. Usually, this involves the playing back of select events as if on a cinema screen, as a prelude to the blessed release of unconsciousness. But on this occasion my mind was positively teeming with sights and sounds. Flights and fist fights. Dragon flames and fireballs. Ships and castles, magic spells and peculiar wonders.

At the same time, a second film flickered beneath it all, like an old black-and-white movie struggling for my attention behind the Technicolor bombast of a modern blockbuster. Try as I might, I could make out nothing of the obscured classic, as every time I was on the verge of seeing something, the entire picture would freeze, before vanishing like a lost memory.

After several of these scenes had gone by, I realised with a jolt that the motion picture was not taking place in my mind at all. It was playing out around my bed, in three-dimensional life. The entire story was being manipulated by a cloaked

*Day Four* / **167**

figure that stood in the corner of my room. At times this mysterious director would glide around, picking up images like picture frames and slotting them into place around me according to his secret artistic vision. Or he would pile up a series of scenes in his hands like a deck of cards, shuffle them in a blur of light, and spread them out in a fan before gleefully dealing them into the air. His face was hidden by a large hood, and it was some time before I realised that this was Merlin himself.

Despite my reservations concerning the wizard and his ways, I was overjoyed at the prospect of bringing him to the Master and restoring my standing in his eyes. I sat up in bed and attempted to ask him if he knew anything of the nature of our dire need and the circumstances of his summoning. But when I opened my mouth, the wizard simply plucked the questions out of me, inserting my words into the procession of pictures like the framed speech captions in a silent film. At last the intensity of the images subsided, and I seemed to wake up, though the hooded director was still with me, standing at the foot of my bed. Not daring to speak again, I leaned forwards and pulled back the hood. I caught only the briefest glimpse of the wizard's chin before the entire face turned into the spiteful snarling features of the cockatrice. I awoke with a startled yell, falling sideways out of bed.

By rights I should have been more exhausted than ever. But though I was far from fully refreshed, I did not feel significantly worse for my phantasmagorical fever. The question was, had a night's rest made any improvement to the Master's temperament? I decided it was a little too early to risk finding out, and that it was better for me to seek his forgiveness with something to show for myself. In all the activity of my first teleportation, I had been denied the opportunity to reunite the company, that we might stand as one body and repair the damage to the Eternal Quest. The mere thought of success in this venture was enough to lift my spirits. I buffed my shoes to a serviceable shine. Then I took the amulet from the bedside picture hook on which I had hung it, and marshalled my mind towards Sir Lancelot and Sir Gawain.

# II

I found myself looking down on a large field, surrounded on all sides by rows of tiered seating. The arrangement bore such a strong resemblance to the tournament grounds to the rear of the Royal Tower that I wondered if the amulet had merely transported me to a different part of Camelot. But as my eyes took in everything else around me, several details confirmed this to be a different place entirely. A broad canopy extended over the field, forming an unnatural metallic sky. Floodlights served as the sun, illuminating a turf that was not divided into standard jousting lanes, but set up to accommodate sport of a more modern variety.

The field itself was the site of frantic activity. Men and women carrying bags and clipboards scurried back and forth between a podium at the centre of the field and a tunnel leading directly beneath the tiered seating where I stood. This podium was occupied by several official-looking figures standing in clusters, as technicians weaved around them setting up microphones on a lectern and attaching cables to television cameras. In front of the podium, a hundred or so chairs had been set up in rows, rapidly filling as more and more people emerged from the tunnel below me. The chairs and the podium were hemmed in by lines of uniformed guards bearing weapons, surveying the scene with the watchful air of the soldier on stand-by.

I had just started to make my way down the steps towards the seating area when Sir Lancelot suddenly appeared from out of the tunnel. He was not accompanied by Sir Gawain, but rather by more armed guards, including one whose uniform denoted him as The Man in Charge. It was then that I realised this entire set-up was for Sir Lancelot's benefit. As he strode towards the podium the crowd got to their feet, shouting questions and thrusting their flashing cameras past the soldiers surrounding him. One of the guards made a threatening motion with his rifle and the audience reluctantly parted. This gesture, combined with the clamorous nature of the crowd, told me it would be wise to wait before drawing attention to myself. Fortunately, all eyes were now on the podium, so I walked down to the ground level unobserved and stood at the back of the gathering to observe what transpired.

After a hasty consultation with the podium's occupants, The Man in Charge stepped forward to the microphone. The amplified sound of his throat-clearing rang out like a call to order. A big screen behind him flickered into life, displaying an enlarged view of his head and torso. "Ladies and gentlemen of the media, my name is General Richard Barber," he began. "Thank you for your patience. I'm sure you have many questions, but I'd ask that you hold back until I've finished. Although what I am about to say will raise more questions than it answers.

"First, the facts. I can officially confirm that Great Britain is under attack from forces beyond this world. Approximately five hundred of what I can only describe as... 'dragons'..." The General paused, as if he was finding it difficult to acknowledge the reality of the name, "...have emerged from Ground Zero, on the West Wales coast."

The General's face was replaced by a map showing Cardigan, then blurred footage, taken in the air from out to sea, of the energy beam shooting up from the Otherworld portal on the cliff-side. The beam was now as wide as a house. Myriad monstrous forms swarmed up out of the earth, provoking gasps of amazement from the crowd. General Barber raised his voice. "Our helicopters could only get so far before they were overcome by the sheer number of hostiles." He allowed himself a small appreciative nod at this more appetising term, as the screen depicted one of the 'hostiles' engulfing the helicopter in a fireball before the image went fuzzy. Several people cried out in alarm. "Ground Zero has been evacuated within a fifty mile radius. The cause of the blast will shortly become clearer to you. I can also confirm the appearance of some kind of fortified town and castle, on the site formerly known as Cardigan." More wobbly footage, this time taken from above the reconstructed Cardigan, showed Camelot at a distance.

Sir Lancelot watched this with interest. I realised that Camelot's return would be news to him, too, and this was undoubtedly the first information he had received concerning the events that followed the parting of our company on the cliff-side.

"Cardigan itself has been moved aside by unidentified forces, to make way for this fortress. At the moment, we're proceeding on the assumption that Ground Zero and this unexplained phenomenon are linked. Our soldiers came up against an invisible force field surrounding the fortress, causing them to instantly lose consciousness. Miraculously, that same force field also brought five fighter jets and three helicopter gunships to the ground, without so much as a scratch on anyone or anything.

"As you can see, this force field affects anyone approaching the fortification at ground level." The screen cut to a camera-man approaching the outer walls of Camelot on foot, several sleeping bodies piled up on the ground ahead of him.

As soon as he drew level with them, he too slumped to the floor, the camera arching backwards to give a sudden brief shot of the sky.

"Finally, as you will be aware, yesterday Cardiff suffered a heavy attack from a number of airborne hostiles, resulting in high civilian casualties and wide-spread damage to property. Soldiers apprehended two men in the city centre. A third man was picked up by the police while attempting to hitchhike his way from Cardigan to Cardiff, and is currently being held in connection with a body found at his residence in Hay-on-Wye. These three men are also wanted in connection with several other recent incidents, but as far as we're concerned today, all of that is frankly irrelevant. Because when it comes to these men," the General straightened his cap, as if to reassert the authority of all he once held dear, "we step into the unknown. We're still awaiting the final results, but every test, reference, and cross-check over the past few hours, has drawn a blank. We therefore have no choice but to accept that these men are who they claim to be. I have authorisation from the highest level to facilitate their full co-operation in this national crisis, in what will henceforth be known as 'Operation: Hostile Takedown.'"

The General took a deep breath and braced himself. "Ladies and gentlemen, I now hand you over to..." He groped for the remainder of the introduction, but seemed to feel, in light of his recent dragon difficulties, that it was beyond his grasp. "Perhaps it's better if he introduces himself." The General stepped down and the man in question stepped up. He raised his hand and every last drop of audience murmur evaporated as a legend addressed them with quiet authority.

"Good morning," he said. "I am Sir Lancelot."

# III

From my position at the side of the pitch, I had a most unsatisfactory view. I would have preferred to be closer, but for the time being there was not much I could do about that. From the remainder of the press conference, I learned that Sir Lancelot (and presumably also Sir Gawain) had taken up residence in the stadium, requisitioned as the headquarters of 'Operation: Hostile Takedown.' The venue's retractable roof provided temporary protection from the dragon hordes. This was reinforced by heavy artillery, stationed immediately outside. However, the frequent ricochet of gunfire from the stadium walls highlighted the first problem to address — namely, the unsuitability of modern weapons in dealing with dragons. Put simply, the solution was in danger of creating far more destruction than the problem. Sadly, this lesson was not learnt quickly enough to prevent Cardiff suffering a level of bombardment it had not seen since the Second World War.

One over-enthusiastic platoon had destroyed the front of the museum. In Cardiff Bay, the drawback of deploying heat-seeking missiles was brought vividly to life with the levelling of several blocks of flats and a world class opera house. And all this was accompanied by a dragon casualty rate that stubbornly refused to rise from zero. Fortunately, this sobering statistic strengthened the case of the two men arrested at a scene of similar destruction earlier in the day, who insisted that far from being responsible for such carnage, they were actually attempting to put a stop to it. *Why should we believe you?* was the gist of the official response. *Because you have nothing to lose,* was the unanswerable reply.

And so it was that several hours and one press conference later, Sir Lancelot was engaged in the task of instructing the modern military in the lost art of dragon slaying. From the central podium he issued instructions through a loud-hailer, while all around him, troops wielded swords of every description. These appeared to have been scavenged in great haste, and I sympathised with the hapless lackey given the task of assembling an arsenal from such odds and ends. Tourist replicas, much like the one I had utilised for my own recent dragon bout, were swung alongside flimsy foils never used outside a fencing class. Some soldiers considered themselves lucky to get their hands on antique broadswords, until they tried unsuccessfully to lift them up, while others brandished blades that were little more than crowbars crudely sharpened to a point and wrapped in a hilt of cloth.

The soldiers were divided into units of ten, each unit allocated a fake dragon on which to practice. These not-to-scale models consisted of a gymnasium horse body with a cardboard box head taped to the front, into which a football *Dracontias* had been lodged beneath several towels. Small trampolines were positioned at the rear, and from these each soldier would jump onto the dragon's back, attempt to dislodge the stone, and jump down again in swift succession.

They were learning fast, which was just as well. According to a screen displaying their itinerary, 'Operation: Hostile Takedown' would commence with the retracting of the stadium roof at six o'clock that evening. Sir Lancelot surveyed the scene, correcting technique and apportioning praise or criticism as he saw fit. "Cut, thrust, lever! Cut, thrust, lever!"

he said, his amplified voice high and clear, "Remember the principle!"

One principle unlikely to apply to battle conditions was a dragon choosing to land in front of a conveniently-placed trampoline. But this had not escaped the tutor's expert eye. "Let the dragon come to you. Show no fear, they can smell it, like a dog. When he's upon you, it's dodge or die. Then, quick as you can, get on the dragon's back. Don't let him fly too high, or you have another problem." Sir Lancelot illustrated this understatement by pointing at a computer-generated diagram on a display screen, showing the best way to exit a plummeting dragon. This boiled down to a strategy of staying with the beast after the fatal blow, and relying on its carcass to break one's fall. I imagined Sir Gawain would have something sharp to say on this optimistic tactic, but I had yet to spot him. He was not on the platform; neither was he to be seen moving among the recruits, offering pithy advice. This was a shame, as I was hoping to have a quiet word. The high level of activity on the pitch made it impossible for me to reach Sir Lancelot on the podium without attracting the kind of attention I was still keen to avoid. Thus I remained at the ringside, cursing my uncharacteristic tardiness.

If I had only arrived an hour earlier, I could have furnished Sir Lancelot with information that would have made his recent press conference even more effective. Of course, I am talking about mere icing on the cake, for Sir Lancelot's address had been note-perfect. It was, he said, placing hand on heart, "true that several of the Knights of the Round Table have walked among you for many years. The matter of our mission has been necessarily secret, but trust me when I tell you that our work has only ever been for good."

As to the next inevitable point, he answered the question of our immortality without revealing the existence of the Grail by a simple catch-all phrase. We had, he said, been sustained by 'magical means.' The persistent questioner asked him to provide a more specific definition of magic, but Sir Lancelot simply replied, to much laughter, "are dragons in the sky not magical enough for you?" This deflection provided a neat link to the Otherworld portal, which was, he said, an unfortunate side effect of our presence in the modern world, but easily dealt with. 'Operation: Hostile Takedown' would soon have the crisis under control, thanks to the simple process of swapping guns for swords and giving the military a crash course in hand-to-claw combat.

If I was being hypercritical, the speech was deficient not in what it *did* state, but in terms of what it *did not*. As I say, Sir Lancelot could not be blamed for this. There were factors he was simply unaware of. It was, however, most unfortunate that all of these factors concerned the Master. Here I confess that my account is incomplete. Had I related the content of the press conference word-for-word, it would have rendered the above information unintelligible — for not a moment went by without yet another question about the Master: *Why is King Arthur really here? Who is he? Where is he? What is he doing in his country's hour of need? What has he done with himself all these years? Is the castle in Cardigan the legendary Camelot? If so, will we find him there? Is he intending on claiming the throne? What does he think of the current Royal Family?*

If the barrage was relentless, then so was the unchangeable reply. To these questions and a hundred more like them, Sir Lancelot gave the same flat response: "No comment." Only when he drew the proceedings to a close did he offer any elaboration. "I can't answer for King Arthur. All I will say is that I intend to put everything right. Now if you'll excuse me, I have work to do. Thank you and good day."

Of course, I understood his reluctance to speak on the Master's behalf. He undoubtedly felt it was the Master's right alone to address the world on the matter of his return. However, the effect of his refusal to comment was to paint the Master in a light that was far from flattering, especially when compared with Sir Lancelot's active stance. This was proved at the end of the conference, when I heard several comments to the effect that King Arthur had better show his face soon, and it was just as well one of his knights was willing to do something about all this mess. I was certain that when Sir Lancelot was brought up to speed, he would use the first available opportunity to redress the balance from the Master's perspective. But in addition to this, another matter concerned me. One that arose from the contents of his speech, and made it imperative that I talk to him as soon as possible.

I was craning my neck and searching for a way to reach him, when I happened to notice a large glass-fronted room, on the opposite side of the stadium to where I stood. Several figures were busy within, attending to a seated red-headed man. I was too far away to confirm his identity as that of Sir Gawain, but the odds were in his favour. I walked into the shadowy tunnel leading back to the lower levels, and, when I was confident nobody was watching, teleported over.

# IV

The people in the glass-fronted room were so wrapped up in their own activities that I was able to enter unchallenged. The room was a studio, of the kind where interviews are conducted with sporting stars and relayed by television cameras to the viewing public. These cameras were in operation now, and in a smaller ante-room off to the back, a group of men and women attended to a bank of monitors, shouting instructions into microphones as various images appeared on their screens. Most of these pictures featured the figure in the main studio, who was indeed Sir Gawain.

At present he was engaged in a tussle with a young man attempting to replace his hip flask with a bottle of water, while a girl applied powder to his forehead with darting dabs of her brush. Another man was directing the cameras, which were all trained upon the seated knight. "Positions, everybody," said this fellow. The attendants stepped away from Sir Gawain. A screen lit up directly in front of him, displaying a script that moved from the bottom to the top.

I stepped into the ante-room, the better to observe Sir Gawain, as from my current position I could only see him in profile. He shifted uncomfortably under the bright studio lights, peering at the scrolling words.

"Quiet please," said the director. "We're live in five, four, three..."

Music blared from the speakers, and an unseen voice spoke in solemn tones. "Emergency Broadcast, live on all channels!" The words were accompanied by a sequence of images, and I saw that the problem had already spread beyond Wales. One picture showed dragons against the London skyline, picking up cars in their talons and flinging them at the face of Big Ben like bowling balls. No doubt there would soon be similar scenes in towns and cities all over the world.

Sir Gawain was also captivated by these images, and it came as something of a shock to him when his own face appeared on the screen. He jumped, then saw himself jump, and realised that he was staring at the wrong camera. He quickly gathered his wits, clearing his throat with a violent cough. His obvious nerves, coupled with the fact that he was not a natural reader, gave his voice the parrot-fashion of a child forced to recite poetry against his will. "Good. Evening. Ahm Sir Gawain. Of King. Arthur's court in this time of notional — *national* crisis, we... need men of courage to step..." The camera zoomed in on his face. Drops of sweat beaded his brow. He licked his lips, took a swig of what was now mineral water, grimaced and spat it out. "Step forward, and, ah, answer their..." Panic filled the booth as the technicians considered cutting to more footage. The director made it clear by means of several wild hand gestures that they should do no such thing.

It pained me to see Sir Gawain such a prisoner of his nerves, and I was considering what I could do about it when he suddenly got to his feet. "Ah, sod this Churchill shite. Listen up, and listen good! Think you got what it takes to take down a dragon? With nothing but your bare hands and a sword to stop your head getting snapped off?" At this, the screen showed the dragon I had disposed of in the River Taff, with Sir Gawain stood on top of its floating corpse, waving his sword triumphantly at the cameras. The film cut back to the studio. "Well, do yer? Then shift your arse to Cardiff's Millennium Stadium, and we'll see if yer balls are up to the job, won't we just?" With that, he tore off his microphone and stomped off-camera. The screen then filled with pictures of Sir Lancelot training his troops, and the relevant contact details. "Lancelot Needs You!" said the voice over.

"Eh?" cut in Sir Gawain, returning to position. But the cameras had stopped rolling. Sir Gawain grabbed the director by the lapels. "What's the deal? You told me you wanted *me* for this!"

"We do, we do," stammered the director. "You're perfect! If you'd just put me down a moment —"

"Then why're you plastering his squashy nose all over the shop?"

I deemed this an opportune moment to make my presence known.

"Ah, Lucas! Did you see all that, then?"

"I did, Sir Gawain." He put down the director and pulled me to one side in conspiratorial conference.

"I thought of telling 'em you killed that dragon, but I figured it'd be less confusing to let 'em think it was me, y'know? Save you the bother."

"Most considerate of you, Sir Gawain."

"Who are *you*?" said the director. If he was grateful for my timely intervention, he hid it well.

"Sir Lucas the butler, at your service," I replied, with perhaps a smidgeon less sincerity than is my custom.

"*Sir*? You mean you're one of them? Why didn't you say so! Megan! We've got another one!"

This Megan was a striking woman in early middle age with long black hair, a pale complexion and an air of self-importance. "Megan Carter, Media-Military Liaison." She extended a hand.

Sir Gawain turned to her with a snarl. "Lucsy's goin' nowhere with you lot." He manoeuvred me out of the studio and into the stadium, over to a row of seats some distance away from the booth. I held down one of the folding chairs for Sir Gawain, and sat beside him.

"I am glad of the chance to finally talk with you, Sir Gawain. Sir Lancelot seems highly preoccupied."

"Yeah, right. It's a full time job, poncing around."

"I am afraid I bring bad tidings of Sir Perceval and Sir Pellinore."

"Feared as much. We had no time for a look-see on the cliffs when we took after them dragons."

"Sir Perceval and the Grail appear to have passed into the Otherworld, but that is not to say they are beyond hope. Sir Perceval has returned from there twice before, after all. I have every confidence that with the Grail by his side, he will do so again. Sir Pellinore's fate, however, is less rosy. The Questing Beast has turned his mind."

"When has it ever not?"

"Indeed, but this time I fear for his welfare."

"I'd love to help, Luc, I really would, but —"

"There is more, Sir Gawain. I have urgent information for you and Sir Lancelot, concerning the Otherworld portal. If Merlin's prophecies are correct, what we have seen so far is just the beginning."

"How d'ya mean?"

"Opening the portal and summoning Merlin has set in motion a train of events that will progressively worsen as time goes by."

"How much worse?"

"The next stage is characterised by the ominous description that 'the dead will rise.'"

Sir Gawain whistled. "And what then?"

"The return of Morgan Le Fay and the end of the world. But with your help, it will not come to that. We all need to reunite and combine our efforts. We need to find Merlin."

"Fat chance of that."

"Be that as it may, we must try. To that end I was hoping you and Sir Lancelot would accompany me back to Camelot to join the Master."

"No can do. I'm needed here. You just saw my recruitment speech."

"Yes, and I must say I am surprised the modern military think it wise to enlist civilians."

"Dunno about wise, but they reckon they're gonna need 'em. They're suffering losses to dragons all over the shop. There's chaos on the streets since it all kicked off, lootin' and shootin' left, right and centre. The TV people are happy to help, as long as they can broadcast the whole thing. I'm fronting it; or at least I *was*, 'til Sir Posealot stuck his lance in."

"Is there any way I can talk to Sir Lancelot?"

Sir Gawain considered the matter. "You leave all that with me."

"Thank you, Sir Gawain, but I would rather convey the details concerning the Merlin prophecy myself."

"No, no, no, you don't wanna worry him with that while he's training. He'll get the message alright. I'll make sure of it."

"Very well. Find me as soon as you have spoken to him," I said.

"Aye, I will. Look out," said Sir Gawain. The woman called Megan, not to be deterred, was heading towards us from the direction of the booth. "I've had a gut-full of that lot. Stall her, Lucas," he said, and before I could protest Sir Gawain had made a swift escape down to the pitch.

# V

My initial wariness around this Megan was soon outweighed by the sheer depth and intensity of her concern. I had merely thought to ask if she knew of the whereabouts of Sir Kay, but she expressed such heartfelt interest in every aspect of our predicament that it was all I could do to keep up with her questions.

"Is it true what they're saying, in that castle, it's really him? The legendary King Arthur has returned? Along with his brave knights, of course?" She had taken me back inside the glass-fronted studio booth, where she made me a most welcome cup of tea.

"Indeed, madam," I said.

"Call me Megan," said Megan.

"The Master has sent us forth as his envoys, but I can assure you he is alive and well, and considering the best way to proceed."

"And you're, what — time travellers? Immortals?"

"Immortal... after a fashion."

"I'm sorry, that was unfair. The last thing I want to do is put you in a compromising position."

"Not at all, madam. It is merely that events have moved so swiftly, and in such a short space of time. I am finding it difficult to maintain what you might call a party line. Forgive me if I seem over cautious."

"No, no, not at all. I really admire you all. Living legends! Walking among us! It's just, there are so many things people are crying out to know about King Arthur. If only they could hear it from the man himself, then maybe they'd stop making things up."

"Really? They are doing that?"

"Oh, the usual culprits in the press and online, saying the same old stuff: *Is he straight or gay? Messiah or anti-Christ* —"

"But Sir Lancelot —"

"Did a terrific job, didn't he? A natural born crowd-pleaser! But the thing is, it's no substitute for the real deal. 'King Arthur speaks!', that kind of thing."

"I see the good sense in what you are saying, madam," I began.

"Megan."

"But, as I said, the world will hear from the Master in due course."

"The thing is... in a way, they already have. Unless he strikes while the iron's hot, he'll be yesterday's news. But of course, all this is a moot point. We'd never get past that sleeping force field thing."

It was then that I saw, as clear as a well-buffed wine glass, exactly what needed to be done. A solution that would enable the Master to see for himself the trouble Sir Lancelot was taking to rectify the crisis in our affairs. One that would also provide King Arthur with a platform to represent himself, so that the world might see him as he truly was. Then, with our company reunited, we could find Merlin and restore the Eternal Quest.

"This 'force field,' as you call it, may not be so much of a barrier as you fear," I said.

"Really?" Megan's eyes glittered.

"We knights are able to pass through it unaffected. I am not one hundred per cent certain, but perhaps those accompanying us may do likewise."

"That would be just brilliant. And we'd provide everything — cameras, portable studio, the works."

"I will need to speak to the Master first, you understand. His disposition can be rather delicate."

"Don't worry." She clasped my hand in hers and gave it a squeeze. "We'll take good care of him. Well, what are we waiting for? Let's go."

"I should like to speak to Sir Kay before we leave, if that is possible. I understand he is currently being held by the police."

"Afraid not. If we're going to get a military helicopter, we have to leave now."

"Very well," I said, and did my best to keep pace with her step, which was surprisingly fleet of foot.

✝

The helicopter flew over a ruined city. Dragons swarmed above streets shrouded in smoke, swooping down to stoke up the numerous fires they had started, or ransack those few shops untouched by human looters. Only the stadium remained dragon-free. The beasts circled the protective military barrier, kept at bay by intermittent bursts of gunfire, but maintaining their orbit with a leisurely air, like sharks waiting for a water-treading swimmer to tire.

The helicopter gunship assigned to Megan and her colleagues was flanked by six others, three on either side, and we flew in a tight V formation. I assumed that our westerly progress would be hampered by dragon attacks. But aside from a few near misses they were content to leave us alone, drawn to the city by their instinct towards chaos and ruin.

This was just as well, as the closer we got to our destination, the thicker the air became with tooth and claw. Dark clouds massed on the western horizon. A flash of violet lightning burst from the cliff-side portal, a lurid cloth flicking at the dust-clumps of the clouds, the beam itself still pulsing steadily upwards into the sky. Eventually we saw Camelot, the solid outline of the fortified town standing in stark contrast to the Otherworldly light. Even from a distance of several miles it was a truly magnificent sight; a fairy tale ripped from the pages of a picture book and plastered onto the surface of the modern world.

For some time, my fingers had been worrying at the amulet's chain like a string of rosary beads. I stopped abruptly when I realised Megan was staring at me intently, her gaze only broken when the helicopter made a sudden dip in altitude. "The pilot won't risk flying any closer because of the force field," she shouted to me. "But I've told him you'll come back when you've confirmed that you can get us safely inside."

"Give me half an hour," I said.

# VI

I materialised at the far side of the courtyard containing the Royal Tower, to discover that the Master had been nothing if not busy. He appeared to be engaged in a spring clean, similar to the one I had recently undertaken in my own quarters. But where my intention had been a methodical clearing of the deck, the contents of the Master's chambers at the top of the Royal Tower had been haphazardly thrown out of the window and into the courtyard below. This was an area of considerable size, yet barely an inch of it was not covered by his old possessions. I concealed myself in the shadow of a pillar at the opposite side of the courtyard to the tower. This was partly due to a degree of anxiety concerning the reception I would get, given my recent banishment. But it was also to see if closer observation would reveal any kind of logic in the Master's methods.

If there was any to be found, it was beyond my comprehension. Several more bundles rained down from the top window onto the sprawling pile on the ground below — the same spot where I had carefully stacked the fruits of my recent labours, now completely obscured by the Master's belongings. Winter cloaks of rare design were squashed beneath his carved oak dressing table. Ornate chests from his personal treasury formed a careless tower, emeralds, rubies and sapphires spilling from their splintered sides.

Several minutes later, the Master himself appeared in the doorway, arms filled with yet more items which he deposited on the landslide. He surveyed the cluttered courtyard, pointing at certain patches — a pile of boots here, a rusty lance there — all the time mumbling and scratching his head as if he were making a complex calculation. Then he looked up at the sun, nodded his head, and, with the satisfied air of a man suddenly remembering exactly what he came into a room to look for, carefully selected a broken picture frame and a bag of jewels from the junk pile.

I suddenly realised he was heading in my direction and was sure to see me. I was struck by the irresistible urge to hide; not so much to prevent him from seeing me, but so he would not know that I had seen him. But if the Master did notice me, he made no outward sign, merely dropping his burden on the grass and arranging it next to a heap of torn curtains. I stood for a time, paralysed by indecision.

"Pass me that chair leg would you, Lucas?" said the Master.

"Sire?" I said.

"The broken chair leg. By the tapestry, there."

"Sire?" was all I could manage by way of a follow-up.

"Look, are you going to stand there sire-ing all day, or are you going to help?"

"Forgive me, sire. My hesitation is on account of my recent banishment."

"Who's been banished?"

"I have, sire."

"Who on earth banished you?"

"You did, sire."

"Did I? No, that doesn't sound like the sort of thing I'd do. Especially after you gave me such a brilliant idea."

"Sire?"

"I presume it was you who stacked those things against the Royal Tower?"

"Indeed it was, but that was part of an orderly spring clean. This, if I may be so bold, is something else entirely."

"Isn't it just," said the Master, beaming bountifully. "I'm so glad you like it. A fitting monument, don't you agree?"

Again, I found myself lost for words. Here I must make a confession. To my shame, I had not been entirely honest with Megan. I knew full well that the helicopters would pass through the force field unscathed so long as I, as a representative of Camelot, remained with them. I could not say exactly how I knew this; only that the certainty came from the same instinctive place in one's mind that deals with such routine matters as blinking and sneezing. No, what really concerned me — my reason for wanting this advance audience with the Master — was to ascertain the state in which I would find him, and how it spoke of his potential reaction to uninvited guests.

Seeing him now, my conclusions were twofold. Firstly, given the full range of possibilities, his current condition of erratic cleaner was by no means the worst. Secondly, even if unexpected visitors were a bitter pill to swallow, it would do his spirits the power of good, once he knew of their good intentions. "I will return shortly, sire," I said, passing him the chair leg he had asked me for.

"Splendid," said the Master. He dropped the chair leg at a random angle on the ground, looking enormously pleased with himself.

✝

It was my intention to direct the helicopters to the main outer courtyard, so as not to disturb the Master unduly, making a subtle approach on foot. But Megan was adamant we land as close to him as possible, time being of the essence, and so despite my better judgement we made a beeline for the Royal Tower. Only when we passed over the inner walls did I realise the true nature of the Master's work.

Those domestic sundries which I assumed to be haphazardly scattered were in fact painstakingly arranged to create a picture; one that was only properly visible from the aerial vantage point afforded by our descending helicopter. A line of torn robes formed the curve of a cheek. Apparently random piles of dark rubies became glittering eyes. Like the hillside etchings of some anonymous Neanderthal worshipper, the Master had carefully sculpted a tribute to his lost deity. The female face was visible for only a few seconds, before the helicopter rotor blades whipped away the long black hair and broke an oaken nose beneath its landing gear.

All the while the Master had stood on the balcony outside his chamber window. I expected him to come rushing down in alarm, waving his arms in a futile attempt to redirect our landing. But he simply stood there and watched, mute and powerless, as the portrait disintegrated before his eyes.

Entirely unaware of their desecration, the passengers disembarked and began to unload equipment, trampling back and forth until every last nuance of the Master's subtle design was covered by cameras, cables and monitor screens. I was momentarily taken aback to see General Barber and several other high ranking officials, for I had presumed they would be back at the stadium for the imminent start of 'Operation: Hostile Takedown.' But then, given the content of his press conference, it was only natural that the General would want to inspect 'Ground Zero' for himself.

Up on the balcony, the Master stepped back inside his room. His movement did not go unobserved by Megan, who was directing her team, sending them scurrying into every nook and cranny. "Unit One, find a base to set up the studio.

Unit Two, locate the nearest electrical outlet, run cables from the town if you have to. I want to be broadcast-ready in one hour."

"Excuse me, Megan — I think it is best that I speak to the Master first," I said.

"Haven't you just done that?"

"Yes, but —"

"We'll handle it from here. Unit Three, you're with me." Accompanied by two men and another woman, and followed by General Barber and his troops, Megan marched towards the Royal Tower.

It would have been a simple matter for me to reach the Master ahead of them, even without the amulet. I could have passed through the hidden doorway in the tower wall, stepped into the lift, and been in his room and at his side before they had got even half way up the stairs. But perhaps they could get through to the Master in a way that I had so far failed to do. Besides, a consultation of my pocket watch told me there were less than ten minutes remaining until six o'clock, the appointed hour for the start of 'Operation: Hostile Takedown.' I muttered up a quick prayer to providence and took my leave of Camelot.

# VII

I had been away from the stadium for a matter of hours, but in my absence it had undergone a considerable transformation. Various elements had been fused together to create a strange hybrid of sports ground and military compound. Advertising hoardings, many featuring Sir Lancelot, lined the bottom of the spectator stands. The seats were rapidly filling with an enthusiastic audience, and I was appalled nobody had informed the spectators of the life-threatening scenes that would shortly take place in front of them. Then I realised that this, of course, was exactly what *had* brought them here.

Transparent protective barriers, presumably fire resistant, enclosed the stands. At either end of the pitch, large screens counted down the minutes until the retracting of the stadium roof. Below the screens were anti-aircraft guns and several battalions armed in the modern manner. The message they spelled out was clear: Sir Lancelot's traditional methods might result in less collateral damage, but it couldn't hurt to have a little back up, should those methods prove less effective in reality.

I had materialised in the mouth of the tunnel leading from the backstage dressing rooms onto the pitch. The sound of quick-marching feet filled the corridor behind me, and I jumped aside as Sir Lancelot sprinted past and out into the stadium's floodlit brightness, followed by a squadron of soldiers. Curiously, there was no sign of Sir Gawain among their number. It was unlike him to miss out on such a spectacle. No doubt his hands were full with the demands of training up the new civilian recruits.

However, if Sir Lancelot's confidence was anything to go by, such back-up would be unnecessary. He took to the pitch with a jaunty jog, leading his men on a lap of honour, smiling and waving to the crowd. The military were clad in their regular camouflage augmented with helmets, as well as shoulder, shin, and knee-pads. Sir Lancelot had acquired various items of light armour, presumably from the same place as the assortment of swords which, for want of enough scabbards, each soldier held aloft in his right hand. Upon completing their lap the men, at least a hundred in total, assembled in close formation, performing warm-up exercises and practising sword moves.

The clock counted down the final minute. A great stillness filled the air, a calm so intense it verged on hysteria. At last, the mechanism controlling the roof clanked into life. The great halves of the metal covering parted, revealing an unnaturally cloudy sky. I wondered if, in all the excitement, anybody had thought to make provision for luring the dragons inside. After all, out there in the city they were enjoying the dragon equivalent of a free festival. They were hardly likely to be attracted to the stadium by a mere sense of occasion. A ripple of restless disappointment passed through the audience. Even the troops appeared crestfallen, nervously shifting beneath their makeshift armour, like party guests who had misread an invitation and turned up in fancy dress.

A tiny green speck appeared against the grey gloom. With alarming swiftness, the first dragon increased in size as it began its spiralling descent. Soon it was joined by another, then another, circling like a gathering cyclone. Sir Lancelot walked out to the centre of the pitch and stood in the eye of the storm, chin set, sword drawn. The lowest of the dragons skimmed the still-retracting roof, its trailing talons screeching on the metal like nails on a blackboard. Several troops fell cowering to their knees. "On your feet!" urged Sir Lancelot. "Remember, fear is like meat to them."

As if on cue, the lead dragon uttered a sound that made audience and troops alike gasp in revulsion. It was a sound scooped from your worst nightmare; a noise that cut like a scalpel through every atom of your existence. To the ears of everyone else it sounded like a howl of the purest pain. Only Sir Lancelot and I recognised it for what it was: a dragon's laugh. One man bolted for the tunnel. The first dragon swooped down and, with one light snap of its jaws, bit off his torso like a jelly baby. The severed legs fell to the pitch and a stupefied hush filled the stadium. With a roar, the dragons broke formation and set upon the gathered soldiers.

'Operation: Hostile Takedown' had begun.

Despite the unpromising start, these men had been trained by the best. Galvanised by the sight of their fallen comrade, they sprang into action. To their undoubted surprise, the hostiles found themselves the subject of a thoroughly comprehensive take-down. Certainly, they flamed and chomped and roared as much as ever. But Sir Lancelot's tactics worked like a dream. A dragon would be within an inch of vaporising a knight, only to find its target jumping up onto its back and relieving it of its *Dracontias*. By the time the beasts got wise to this strategy, covering fire from the machine guns prevented them from gaining height, and the metal roof closed again, trapping them inside the stadium.

From here on, the audience were not short changed in terms of spectacle. If anything, Sir Lancelot was surpassed by his pupils, who treated the crowd to a feast of aerial acrobatics. With every blow struck they visibly grew in confidence. Dead dragons flumped down onto the pitch with heavy slaps, like giant leather jackets. One soldier flew a dragon like a bucking bronco, steering it on loops around the stadium before killing it off with a flourish and alighting on the ground to rapturous applause. Another agile fellow waited until his steed flew over another dragon before cutting out the *Dracontias*. Then he used the stone like a catapulted boulder to brain the beast below him, jumping from the dead dragon onto the dazed one and repeating the trick all over again.

It was lucky for Sir Lancelot that the soldier developed this tactic. On one occasion he found himself backed into a corner and without his sword, and it was only the intervention of one such 'boulder' that saved him from a severe singeing. At last, perched precariously on a pile of their prey, the winners stood victorious, basking in the crowd's adoration. Sir Lancelot — shaky, but smiling — waved and nodded. But it was his young rescuer who got the biggest cheer of the day, his delighted face filling the monitor screens.

For the first time since setting out from the Once & Future Inn, I felt a sense of relief sweep over me. The carnival atmosphere, the sense of triumph and a job well done — in the light of all this, Merlin's prophecies seemed decidedly alarmist. Here was Sir Lancelot, mopping up the dragon menace, even without the aid of Sir Gawain and his civilian recruits! Should the so-called armies of the dead unwisely decide to put in an appearance, they would simply send them packing, too. The Master was in safe hands, and thanks to Megan and her team, the world would shortly know and love him again. Our fellowship would be reunited, and everything else rectified and restored as soon as we found Merlin.

Even as I had this thought, up on the opposite side of the stadium I could have sworn I saw a familiar cloaked figure sitting in the midst of the cheering crowd. But I must have been mistaken, for when I blinked and looked again, the hooded man was no longer there.

# Yesterday Two

# I

I returned to my quarters intending to blurt out the news of the impending quest to Beaumains the moment I got in through the door. But no sooner did I reach the threshold than I came to a faltering halt. With a sense of weary resignation I bowed to the inevitable, and was just about to start on my System when I realised that my recent complaint was not the reason for the pause. Nevertheless, there I was, gazing at the scene before me as if I were seeing it all for the first time.

I could not for the life of me say why. The tasks my deputy was performing — banking up the fire, keeping an eye on the eggs boiling in the pot — were no more earth-shattering than the preparations for our evening meeting, things I had witnessed a thousand times over the past thirty years. Sensing my presence, she turned and smiled, breaking the spell. As she did so, the momentous decision of the past hour fell into perspective. Gladly I stepped into a routine more welcome to me at that moment than a hot bath.

"Good evening," I said.

"Don't you mean morning?"

The last few grains of sand in the glass egg timer had run dry. I removed the pot from the fire and picked up a plate of bread. Scooping an egg from the bubbling water with a wooden spoon, I tapped it smartly against the plate and felt the shell give way against a perfect white.

"That egg timer," I began.

"Is the best present you ever had," finished Beaumains.

"Well, it is."

"I know. I count it among my life's greatest achievements to have given you at least one gift that gets used."

"So, how was your day?" I sat down by the fire and handed her the plate of food.

"It would end a lot better than it started if I could see you eat something," she said.

"I am fine."

"I can't remember the last time I saw you take a meal."

"I have been grazing all day."

"Grazing like a mouse."

"I will have mine later. Tell me how your day went."

She rolled her eyes. "How do you think it went? He is getting worse." I sighed from my depths. "But you are tense," she said, putting aside her plate. Her fingers were on my neck and shoulders before I could protest.

"Beaumains, this is hardly the proper way for — oh. Oh my." Knots of tension tied some time before breakfast and drawn ever tighter as the day wore on unravelled at her touch.

"Did I hit the spot?" she said.

My body responded with an involuntary twitch, like a dreaming hound. "Yes."

"Sorry Lucas, you were saying?"

"Mmm? Nothing. Please, carry on. Your fingers read my back like Braille."

"Like what?"

"Braille," I repeated, although it was as if the word came from somebody else, speaking from a great distance. "It is... I am not sure what it is. I suppose I am just tired. Please, continue. What were you saying?"

"Mordred. Even before he is out of bed, he is a bother," said Beaumains.

I closed my eyes, and focused on her voice:

# II

I tell you Lucas, I am glad to see the back of this Tournament for another year. It is hard to say who has been groaning more — the knights battered half to death, or the staff working 'round the clock to patch them up in the infirmary, just so they can go out and kill themselves all over again. Those few kitchen staff not boiling herbs or running to the scriptorium to check recipes for salves and ointments, are at the beck and call of the bedridden, who seem to forget they have squires of their own to empty bedpans or fetch them a 'medicinal snifter.' So where *are* these squires, you ask? Out on the field watching the sport, that's where; or in the Great Hall, demolishing the Queen's birthday feast faster than my team can make it. As for Bedwyr, he may as well start his quest now, for all the good he is in the kitchen. This Grail fever is contagious; my staff are dropping with it like flies.

Anyway, there I was, up to my arms in blood and bruises, when Mordred swaggered in, demanding that Sir Sagramour be discharged into his care.

"No," I said. "Certainly not. His wounds had not healed when you took him out yesterday. And now they are ten times worse."

"Tough," he said, "I need Saggy on the field, Beaumains. Today's the day we teach this so-called 'Knight X' the lesson of a lifetime and remove his coward's mask."

"That is not my concern," I replied. "If Sir Sagramour gets on a horse today, his side will split and his guts fall out, *splat*, simple as that."

"Then get your precious Lucas to do the stitches. I hear he's a dab hand at knitting." I looked at the full bedpan at my feet and considered my options. But I have held my tongue so many times around this imbecile that I have worn a special groove in it to fit my teeth.

"I'll be back in an hour. He'd better be ready to joust," said Mordred.

My tongue slipped from its groove, just a bit. "A joust is a test of skill. What you do is fuss and feathers, the brawling of children."

Mordred's mouth shrank to a thin dash. "My brother doesn't think so. I hope you aren't being so treasonous as to criticise the King's plans for the Queen's birthday. You and your butler are not as indispensable as you like to think. Which reminds me. My gift for the Queen. See that she is given it at the High Table, before the toasts are made in her honour. And I want Saggy out of here by noon for the first round, or the King shall hear of it. Step to it! His sores are weeping." And out he went, quickly followed by my one-fingered salute.

Now, this gift of his had been bothering me, Lucas. As I told you yesterday, Mordred has mentioned it every day since it arrived last week. So, after putting in a full morning with Enid in the infirmary and then making a vain attempt to talk to a Grail-eyed Bedwyr about seating plans for the feast, I went to see Geraint.

I arrived just in time to see him being burned alive. Smoke poured from the Gatehouse door and a great clamour came from within. I was about to raise the alarm when Geraint burst out, wearing what appeared to be a cloak of fire. "Flames to ice!" he yelled, rolling on the ground at my feet, "flames to ice!" I was wondering exactly how I was supposed to achieve this, when the fire around him changed colour and shape, and I realised of course that he was casting a spell. Instead of forming into icicles, however, the tongues of flame were transformed into a hundred blue mice who scurried for cover as fast as they could.

"Ah well, close enough," he said. I helped him to his feet and removed a stray mouse from his ear.

"What happened, Geraint, are you hurt?"

"I've had worse, Miss B," he said, flashing me a gap-toothed grin and tapping his eye patch with a singed finger. "I've got something inside for magical burns, that'll see me right." He limped away and I followed him inside the Gatehouse.

This was not as easy as it sounds, for the room was packed floor-to-ceiling with deliveries for the Queen. "Careful where you step. I'm only half way through this lot," he said, peeling off the smouldering tatters of the cloak and placing them into a large chest. "Another one for the Hazard Box. I tell you, it's filling up fast. That last one was particularly nasty. What we wizards call a 'catch-all curse.' Anyway, what can I do you for?" He took a jar of foul-smelling green paste down from a shelf, applying liberal dollops to his scorched skin.

"I have a question, concerning gifts," I said, wrinkling my nose against the pong of the stuff.

"Fire away. So to speak."

"How easy would it be for a cursed item to reach the King or Queen?"

"Ho, well, you've asked a question there, Miss B. I try to check every one of them myself, but with the best will in the world, I won't make it through this lot by tonight. What I could really do with is an apprentice. But nobody wants the work, not when so many people are having a pop at the King. Not that you can find many suitable candidates anyway.

It's all jousting and questing with young people nowadays. Which reminds me — Sir Perceval and Sir Gareth are back."

"Ah, that is good news! Lucas will be pleased."

"Aye, they've gone off to find him. *Tch*, those kids! Full of it, they were. Wouldn't go into details, said I'd have to wait for tonight's *Chronicles*." Geraint put the ointment back on the shelf with a wistful look in his eye. "Always wanted to have a go at that myself. Some of the things that've happened to me would make blinding stories, the wife is always saying I should —"

"Geraint."

"Hm?"

"The curses."

"Oh right; yes, sorry. My own tests are as rigorous as I can make them, but they're not foolproof. Thing is, before he left us — way back before your time, Miss B — Merlin installed a load of enchantments, to protect Camelot from all manner of curses, jinxes and hexed objects. And for a while, they worked a treat. But magic's moved on so much since then. Practically all of the spells are out of date now, easily beaten by new magicians trying to make a name for themselves. And that's just the young 'uns, never mind the old pros — believe me, the hexmanship on some of these is out of this world. Take that Scorch Cape just now. That kind of fire-power could only come from a very powerful sorcerer indeed. Not to mention all this lot." He pointed at the items in the Hazard Box. "Already this morning I've turned up three bags of Coughy Apples, a set of Paperback Dragons, and a hand-held Mirror of Madness and Maelstroms."

My attention drifted at this point, for my eye had been caught by a set of ladies' undergarments of exquisite design and delicate weave, and I reached out to pick them up. "Don't touch those!" shouted Geraint, slamming the box lid shut. "Underwear of Doom. Very nasty. Believe me." The few un-scorched patches on his skin turned as red as the rest of him. "Er, moving on, about that question of yours — why do you ask?"

"I am concerned about Mordred."

"Aren't we all. I was meaning to have a word with you and Mr L about that Tribe of his."

"Tribe?"

"Aye, that gaggle of young knights who follow him around like sheep. Hanging around the Gatehouse, mocking everyone who turns up, doing impressions of the older knights as they walk by. Behind their back, of course. Time was, they'd be taken down a peg by one of the old guard. The Tribe would keep their cheek in check, if Sir Lancelot was around more often! No respect, the lot of them. Mind you, to be fair, one of them's got Sir Gawain down to a T." He chuckled, briefly. "But that's not the point."

"Has Mordred submitted anything for testing?"

"He has, as a matter of fact. This." Geraint handed me a non-descript toasting goblet. "With specific instructions that it's presented to Her Majesty for the toasts after the feast."

"And have you checked it for hexes?"

"I should say! It was top of my list. But so far I've come up with nothing, and I subjected it to the full works, believe me. I've no choice but to give it the all clear and let him have it back."

"Hmm." I turned the goblet over in my hands. It seemed perfectly normal; tasteful, unostentatious, refined. In short, *nothing* like Mordred.

"I do have one theory, as it happens, Miss B. Only, it's a bit, er... delicate."

"You can speak freely with me, Geraint."

"Well... it's like this. They do tell of a goblet hex called The Cup of Shame. You curse a goblet so that it spills the wine of an unfaithful lover. My cousin Will knows a man who knows a man who saw it used once, on the bride-to-be of a baron up North. She took one sip and copped a face full of red, all down her white dress. Hilarious, it was; not for her, mind, she was burnt at the stake. You don't think Mordred's got his hands on one of those?"

†

At this point, I was compelled to interrupt my deputy's story.

"Come now, Beaumains! The King has nothing to fear concerning the Queen's fidelity. I would not have expected you to lend credence to the millers of rumour."

"Excuse me, Lucas, I do no such thing!"

"Well, then. *You* had nothing to fear from such a trinket."

"But tonight we have seen that I *did* have something to fear, and from bigger things than spilt wine."

"That was a full-blown assassination attempt, on a different scale entirely. Why were you so concerned about a cursed toasting goblet?"

"You know I would never do anything based on idle gossip alone. I told Geraint as much, and I was about to tell you, if you had not butted in."

"Sorry."

"I was concerned about what this goblet *represented*. Something that smelled bad, and yet another in an increasingly wide variety of odours coming from Mordred."

"Of course."

"Good. So I can continue with my story?"

"Please."

"Thank you. Now, where was I?"

# III

Geraint took the goblet back from me and held it up to the light.

"Trouble is, Miss B, there's no way of telling a Cup of Shame from an ordinary goblet until an unfaithful lover drinks from it. And by that time, well, it's all academic, isn't it? But listen, you know the Queen better than anyone, apart from the King. She's got nothing to worry about on that score, has she? I mean, granted, that time the King was away sorting out the Giant business, she and Sir Lancelot did seem to be getting, well, closer, but —"

"If it is cursed then it has no place in Camelot, Geraint. That is my bottom line. It should also be yours."

"Miss B, if I've ever said so much as a *hint* of a bad word against the Queen, then you can kick my arse from here to Annwn. But that doesn't change the fact that people talk. If Mordred's looking to ignite a scandal, then something like this goblet could do more harm than any Scorch Cloak. Point is, you've got to be careful. Alright, let's say for argument's sake it *is* a Cup of Shame, and we confiscate it. All Mordred will do is put it about that the Queen's got something to hide, then the rumours just get worse, and then — well, I don't want to go there, truth be told. No, I can't see any way around it, except to let things take their course. The Queen's got nothing to be ashamed of, so what's the worst that can happen?"

"It is a potential security breach, Geraint, and I do not want it near the Queen, full stop. What if we were to swap it for another, identical goblet?"

"No, I don't reckon that'd work. Mordred seemed to hint that he'd know if it was tampered with; made a big deal about its 'unique ancient craftsmanship.' At the time I thought it was just more wind, but that must've been what he was getting at — warning me, like, in case I decided to switch it."

"OK then... What if I swap it *after* it is given it to the Queen, but *before* it is filled with wine for the toasts?"

"That might work. The toasts won't be 'til later... You'd be serving at the High Table anyway, and Mordred will be on the Round Table. If the old switcheroo was made fast enough... You'll have to be *very* quick, mind, he'll be expecting something like that."

"Can you make me a copy by this evening?"

"Aye, I reckon I could. It won't pass muster close up, but it should fool him at a distance."

"Then I will call in for it later."

"Righto. Leave it with me, Miss B. If I'm not here, I'll stash it in the bottom drawer of my worktable, out of sight."

†

Even before leaving Geraint and the Gatehouse, I could hear the noise of the crowd. I made my way along the outer walls, past the Castle and down towards the tournament ground, chants and cheers rising and falling on the summer breeze. There was still half an hour to go before the games began. It was obvious from the noise and from the multitudes filling the streets below that the final day of the contest would be a fitting way to commemorate the Queen's fiftieth year.

But if Her Majesty was pleased or flattered in any way, she did not show it: I found her in the awning at the back of the Royal Box, in the state of mind which I call 'shield up.' I have encountered this barrier enough times not to take it personally, and to know it can only be lowered by careful indifference. Show too much concern too soon, and the shield will be pulled all the closer. Show too little, and you risk causing offence. Today, however, I did not need to be as attentive as usual to its shifting tones and textures, for I knew that the instant Knight X appeared, her mood would change. So I went through the motions of our daily lesson in swordsmanship in silence. Besides, the only time I had dared to ask her what use she might find for such martial arts, her reply was as sharp as her blade. "There's nothing else to do around here," she had said, and attacked me with such vigour that I resolved never to ask again. The Queen is a fast learner, and there are few moves left in my repertoire that she does not know. Before long she will be a warrior equal to any Knight of the Round Table. So, for an hour we practised, hidden from view, as the tournament grounds filled up to capacity.

A creaking from the wooden steps leading up to the Royal Box spoke of King Arthur's approach. The Queen passed me her sword, and I hid it with my own in a place under the floorboards. I had collected her midday meal *en route*, so I busied myself transferring bread and meat from platter to plate while she reclined on the divan, surrounded on all sides by her many presents. She picked up her needlepoint, and made a great show of being absorbed in embroidering a neat border of crosses on a quilt. On the table in front of her, a magic chess set played itself.

King Arthur entered with a spring in his step. He leaned over to kiss her on the cheek, but she made no move towards him, forcing him to lean over the divan at an awkward angle in order to make his greeting.

"Happy birthday, darling," he said.

"Thank you."

"You like the gifts?"

"Love them."

"I'm so glad," said the King, and sat beside her, brimming with glee. "You deserve no less than the very best." The Queen sat up straight on the couch and continued with her stitching. "And, who knows, there may be more to come later in the day," he added. The Queen smiled and nodded. The King tapped the side of his nose. "But my lips are sealed."

"ок, then."

"Ask me no questions and I'll tell you no lies, Ginny."

"I won't."

"You will just have to wait and —"

"Please, Arthur. I'm trying to work."

"Sorry, sorry." The King smiled and winked at me as if I were his co-conspirator, though I had no idea what he was talking about. The pattern on the quilt then caught his eye, and some of the bounce left him. "It seems no-one is immune from the charms of Knight X," he said. The Queen's needle halted mid-stitch. She looked down at her work and the border of crosses.

"Kisses," she said.

"Ah."

"It's for our chamber."

"You're such a romantic."

He leaned over for her cheek again, but at that moment a horn sounded from outside and the Queen jumped up like a startled deer. The King found himself puckering at thin air. He smacked his lips loudly, as if that had been his intention all along. "Time for lunch," he said, and made a hasty exit. The Queen moved to her seat out on the balcony to observe the competitors emerging from the entranceway beneath our feet.

As the undefeated victor, Knight X was obliged to take a lap of honour before his opponents were allowed onto the field. He performed this without relish, and I found myself musing once more on the sombre note this champion struck. From boots to helmet he was dressed in black, giving him the appearance of one in mourning, a fashion that extended to his black stallion, saddled with the bare minimum of accessories. His helmet was without a visor, but his face was masked with scarves wrapped around his head, with only a blank strip for the eyes. Sword and lance were dark and dull, as was his shield, except for a large 'X' painted in silver grey. He led his horse at a funeral pace without a scrap of flamboyance, as if even the briefest wave would be the height of self-indulgence.

All this was in total contrast to the reaction of the crowd. Every man, woman and child were united in praising his name. Knight X banners dominated all four stands. Silver Xs were painted on faces and tunics. Knight X flags and half-scale models of his famous black sword were snapped up faster than the delighted vendors could make them. Only once did the object of all this adoration acknowledge his surroundings. Passing by the Royal Box, he turned and inclined his head in respect to the Queen, before taking up position at the end of the field, his lance at rest.

The first challenger took to the pitch. Sir Mordred and his cronies in the knights' enclosure stamped and brayed for Sir Bagdemagus as loud as they could, but their cheers were drowned out by the jeers of the crowd. Another horn sounded. Knight X and Sir Bagdemagus lowered their lances and readied their steeds. Although the appearance of Knight X had animated the Queen, it seemed to have done little to raise her spirits. I decided to attempt conversation while I moved around behind the balcony seat, tidying up gifts and clearing away the untouched food. A mound of crumbs moved under the table, revealing a blue mouse, presumably one of Geraint's creations.

"Fancy, Sir Bagdemagus being booed. I never thought such a poor reception would be given to a Knight of the Round Table," I said.

"That accolade fades with every Baron my husband lets his brother sneak in through the back door."

"The King has his reasons, I am sure," I said.

"Oh, I'm sure of that, too. I just wish they were good ones."

A final bugle blast signalled the start of the bout. From my half-stoop behind the Queen's seat, I could see the top row of the opposite stand settle down in anticipation.

"Perhaps you should say something to him, ma'am."

"Perhaps I should. Perhaps I should also ask the sun not to shine."

There was a drumming of hooves as the two knights spurred their horses into the first pass. An intake of breath from the crowd. A splintering crack. A roar of disapproval. I peered over the rail in time to see Sir Bagdemagus throw aside a broken lance and shift a fresh one to his duelling hand. At the opposite end of the pitch Knight X threw away the remains of his shield. "Two lances?" I said. "Surely that should be disallowed?"

"By whom, exactly?"

"Your Majesty could intervene."

"You've seen Knight X joust. A hundred lances won't help Bagdemagus." The Queen smiled for the first time. The second pass began. I returned to my work and attempted to change tack.

"People love this Knight X," I said.

"They do," said the Queen.

More thundering of hooves. A twang, a prang, and this time a sharp exclamation of delight from the crowd. When next I looked, Sir Bagdemagus's second lance was stuck handle-down into the ground, the knight hanging from the tip and flailing about like an armoured trout. The Queen clapped her hands loudly.

"A mask captures the imagination, I suppose," I said. "People want to know what it hides."

The Queen stopped clapping abruptly. "We all have something to hide," she said. I looked at her, and immediately wished I had not. "Well? Isn't that what you want me to say? 'We all wear masks, we all have secrets, *blah blah blah*.' Why don't you take whatever you want from that, and share the scraps among the staff as you see fit? I'm sure they drool over your every morsel of gossip like dogs under the dinner table."

*You are wrong*, I said to myself, and thought of the goblet.

"I'm sorry, my lady —"

"Oh, just get me some wine," she said, returning to the divan and her needlework.

Knight X retired until the next round. I made to leave, colliding with the King in the doorway. His previous deflated look had swollen with so much optimism that I worried he might go pop at any moment.

"It's time, it's time," he said, grabbing me by the hand as he called to his wife, "Ginny, get up, look!" The Queen sighed, put down her embroidery, and allowed herself to be dragged back to the balcony.

Up in the sky, standing bold against the clear blue, letters and words were writing themselves in coloured smoke. The audience on our side saw them too, and started to point, and then to laugh. The spectators on the other side followed their gaze, enjoying the unexpected visual treat, turning the words into a chant that was taken up by the entire ground, the baffling nature of the message only adding to its festive appeal. The Queen tutted and shook her head.

"You really shouldn't have. Forget the wine, Beaumains, I'll get it myself," she said, and left.

"Ginny, wait," said the King, as if there was still a chance that the plumes of red, white and green in the sky could spell out something other than 'DEATH BY VINEGAR'.

# IV

I had been unloading barrels of mead from a lift behind a tapestry in the Great Hall, when I saw Mordred place his goblet among the other gift items on the High Table. Then he left, at the prompting of Enid, following the rule that only serving staff are allowed in the Hall for the hour preceding any feast. Mordred did not go without some reluctance, but Enid's broom brooked no argument. For a second he looked as if he might change his mind and take the goblet back. But, presumably not wanting to draw Enid's attention to it, he made his exit.

As soon as the door was barred behind him, I took a closer look at this goblet, scarcely daring to believe my luck. What was to stop me from switching it *now*, before any guests arrived? Then I could relax and attend to my duties, without having to worry about making the swap under Mordred's watchful eye. However, my most pressing concern was not to arouse any suspicion. There was nothing to stop Mordred from taking a last peek at his gift, and noticing it had been swapped for a duplicate. Everything would depend on the quality of Geraint's copy, so I decided to check this first, before I moved the real one. I made my way to the Gatehouse and, finding no Geraint within, took the liberty of entering the small back room that served as his workshop.

As promised, the copy was in the bottom drawer of his worktable. And not just any copy. Geraint had surpassed himself. To my untrained eye, this goblet could have been the other's twin in every respect, save its lack of cursedness. That settled it. I picked up the fake one from the drawer, returned to the Great Hall, and in one move made the swap, stuffing the real goblet into the wide front pocket of my tunic.

But I was not in the clear yet, for there was now the matter of what to do with the cursed object. It would be highly unwise, I thought, to keep it upon my person. And so I went back to the Gatehouse for a second time, hoping that Geraint might have returned, so that I could entrust the cup to his care.

"Geraint. It's Beaumains," I whispered, "Geraint, are you back?" The door creaked open and a ray of evening sun lit up the empty room, every gift having now been transferred to the Great Hall. I weighed the Cup of Shame in my hands and ran my mind back over recent events, to check if there was any flaw in my plan. I was standing by the empty worktable drawer, absorbed in my thoughts, when I heard the Gatehouse door creak open and close abruptly. Like a cornered thief I shoved the cursed goblet into the bottom drawer and slammed it shut, spinning around on my heel to see the panic-stricken face of Enid.

"Oh Beaumains, there you are, thank Merlin I've found you! It's the Round Table, it's ruined, all ruined!" she wailed.

"Please, just calm down," I said, although in truth I was talking to my own wildly thumping heart. I closed the workshop door and left the Gatehouse, following Enid's flustered path back to the Hall.

✝

Well, from her tone you would have thought the Round Table was on fire. Of course, I understood where her alarmist nature came from. To lose her beloved Eric to a poisoned apple meant for the King's table would put anyone on edge. But for the sake of my own nerves I have made it my custom to always divide Enid's panic by a factor of four, to get a more accurate sense of the scale of the problem. What vexed her on this occasion was only the usual rigmarole of the seating plan. I would have preferred to spend my time finding Geraint to tell him of the success of the 'switcheroo' and congratulate him on his workmanship, but it would not be long before the first guests arrived. Besides, one glance at the place names on the Round Table told me it required serious reordering. Enid wrung her hands and kept looking at the door.

"Enid? What kind of order is this?"

"Bedwyr's. He's sat them all according to Grail experience."

"This will not do. Did you get my instructions?"

"Yes, but the seating plan makes my head swim at the best of times. I was finally getting there, when I left to get some more cushions for Sir Aliduke on account of his bad back, and by the time I'd returned, Bedwyr had mixed them all up again. And now there's no time left, and the knights will be here any minute, and —"

"Enid. We have time. Now hush, and let me see." I made a swift circle of the table's fifty seats, reading off the wooden place-names slotted into the back of each chair.

Enid's alarm was more justified than I had given her credit for. If the knights remained in this order, bones would be broken with bread, and blood would flow with wine. It is a shame that a seating system invented to ensure equality among knights now has to be ordered according to a list of squabbles that only gets longer with every passing feast. But it is a challenge that I relish, for all its frustrations, and I set about rearranging the table according to my initial plan, un-slotting and re-slotting place names as I made a second circuit.

"Sir Agravain apart from Sir Balin, on account of the blood feud. Sir Balin out of earshot of Sir Lamorak, who is still making allegations about Balin's relations with his lady. Likewise Sir Balan, who will fight to the death in his twin brother's name. Lamorak suffers with heat rage, so cannot go too near the fire, so... yes... here. No. No, no, no... that puts Lamorak in eye contact with Sir Menaduke, lest we forget their duel over the Maiden of the Apple Trees... But if I swap *him* with Sir Agravain... fine. Now, after the debacle of the Quest of the Fountain, there should be at least a knight's width between Sir Agravain, Sir Bors and Sir Accolon. But that puts Bors in a better seat than Menaduke, who was knighted before him. So, I put him here, next to Sir Marhalt, who — saints be praised — has no quarrels to speak of, now that Sir Mador is no longer with us. So we shall put him here, as a buffer between Sir Mordred and his ilk, and the rest of the knights. Oh, and no carving knives to be left unattended here, here, here... here, and here. We do not want a repeat of the many stabbings of Sir Mador. *Voila*." I stood back and surveyed my handiwork. The doors at the end of the Hall creaked open and the first guests poured in, and Enid and I returned to Lower Camelot.

The demands of the kitchen were such that my moments in the Hall during the feast were few and far between. On the few occasions I was out there helping the waiters, I made eye contact with Geraint only once. He gave me a discreet thumbs-up with his good hand, which put me at ease somewhat. I also observed Mordred as I passed the Round

Table. He was fast approaching his usual obnoxious level of drunkenness, casting sly, satisfied glances at the High Table.

At last the final course was cleared. I put aside my tray and stood at the side of the stage. This was the moment that you appeared, Lucas, through the curtain covering the entrance to the Green Room, to hastily confer with the King. Geraint was talking with the Queen, who was indulging his horseplay, but as soon as you returned to the Green Room, a signal from the King prompted Geraint to hobble down from the dais, and I motioned for him to stand next to me. "A quiet word, Miss B," he began. But the King had risen to his feet and was clearing his throat.

"Good people of Camelot. You are most welcome on this special day. My Guinevere is fifty years young." The Hall clapped and laughed, raising their goblets in salute. The Queen put on the indulgent smile she reserved for her husband's lengthy tributes. But this year there was something different about the King. His manner had completely changed from the doting husband of the Tournament, to someone who was now simply going through the motions; his voice hurried, his tone preoccupied. "Well, time's getting on, we have a lot of old favourites in tonight's *Chronicles*, and many toasts to follow. But first, there is the matter of the winner of the Tournament. Knight X, would you step forward."

Knight X rose from the table where he had dined alone. He made his way down the centre aisle and up the steps to the dais of the Round and High Tables, to a burst of loud applause, marred only by ungracious booing as he passed several of his defeated opponents. Mordred, however, cheered with boisterous enthusiasm, and his round of applause lasted several claps longer than everybody else's.

"This tournament has been yours alone," said the King. "We respect your right to keep your face hidden, but hope you will one day feel your true self to be welcome here at Camelot.

Accept your prize, as a small token of our admiration." The Queen held out his trophy, a bronze dagger. Knight X stood before her. He removed the bottom section of his face scarf and lowered his head, as was his right, to kiss her hand. Queen Guinevere held out her arm. Only from where I was standing could one see that her hand trembled slightly at his touch. The King raised his goblet. "To Knight X!" he cried.

"Knight X!" came the rejoinder. All got to their feet and raised their cups, all drank, all sat back down again. All except Mordred, that is. He remained standing, a smile playing upon his thin lips.

"Now, without further ado," said the King, "the *Chronicles*! The following knight needs no introduction —"

"If I may be so bold, sire," said Mordred. "I would like to add something to the festivities. In honour of the Queen's special day."

Geraint leaned on his walking stick and whispered in my ear. "Don't worry about him," he said, patting me on the arm. "I've sorted it all out."

"Yes I saw, and thank you, Geraint; you did an excellent job."

"Cheers Miss B. I'll admit, I was a bit concerned."

"No need, it was perfect."

The King looked at his brother with a mixture of indulgence and distrust. "Well, what is it, Mordred?" he said.

"I wouldn't say it was *perfect*," whispered Geraint. "It's been a while since I've done any close-up magic, but I covered it with a classic bit of misdirection, where I plucked a flower from the Queen's soup bowl with my other hand."

"Sorry Geraint, you've lost me," I said.

"A gift, sire" proclaimed Mordred. "A gift, followed by an early toast."

"The old switcheroo," whispered Geraint. "I saw the fake was still in my drawer, and assumed you didn't have time to pick it up. So I made the swap myself, just now. Don't look so worried. No-one saw a thing. See?" He pulled aside his cloak. The fake goblet was tucked under his arm. "The hand is faster than the eye. Ah, I've still got it, fair play."

"Geraint," I hissed. "That was not the real Cup of Shame up there. That was the fake. I had already made the switcheroo!"

"Oh, buggeroo," said Geraint.

All eyes were now on Mordred, walking over to the High Table, including those of Knight X, who had paused on his way back down the dais steps. "It's nothing, really," said Mordred, picking up a pitcher of red wine. "Just a simple little goblet. But I would count it the greatest honour if the Queen would drink a toast from the gift of a humble knight such as I." Mordred took the Cup of Shame from among the many presents in front of the Queen. He filled it to the brim and offered it to her. She looked to the King, who simply shrugged, and so she accepted it warily, holding it at half an arm's length.

"Correct me if I'm wrong," said Mordred, filling his own cup, "but I don't think anyone has congratulated the Queen on the wonderful job she did while the King was away fighting Giants? To keep the Court going single-handed! Well, I say single-handed. She had a lot of help from Lancelot. Good old Sir Lancelot. Have you," Mordred turned to face Knight X, "have *you* heard of Sir Lancelot, Knight X? Terribly good knight, he was. The King's best friend. You wouldn't have had such an easy time of it on the field if *he'd* been around. He always loved a joust. I wonder what kept him from the Tournament? Other things on his mind, I suppose. Still, I digress. I would like to propose a toast to Queen Guinevere. To her loyalty and fidelity." He held up his goblet.

The people in the Great Hall had started to echo the words of the toast with an uncertain murmur, when Mordred spoke again. "Oh, by the way, before we all drink. There is *one* thing

I should say about that toasting goblet. There's a funny little legend attached to it that caught my interest."

A deathly hush filled the Hall.

"A silly bit of folklore. Embarrassed to mention it, really. But apparently..." Mordred shook his head and laughed mirthlessly. "Apparently, it spills the wine of an unfaithful lover. They call it the Cup of Shame." My blood ran cold as ice. "I don't know, those yokels, they'll believe anything. Obviously, I thought there was no harm giving it to the Queen. And so. To Queen Guinevere! Her loyalty and fidelity." Mordred drained his cup in one and placed it down on the Round Table.

The Queen looked again at the King, but his head was bowed above his own cup. Several people around the room chose not to wait for his lead and started to drink. As for Knight X, he had not moved from the steps. His eyes remained on the Queen throughout Mordred's speech, and she looked back at him now. Something in his look caused her own gaze to harden. She turned this expression to meet Mordred's insolent face, and raised the cup to her lips.

"To my loyalty and fidelity," she said.

At that precise moment the wall behind King Arthur exploded and a werewolf sank its teeth deep into his neck.

"Which is where my day becomes your day," said Beaumains, standing up to stretch her legs. "So, tell me Lucas, how did it go for *you*?"

# V

As much as I loathed holding anything back from my deputy, I felt it wise not to tell Beaumains about the state of mind in which I started the day. She was aware that I had been feeling out of sorts for some time now, and the last thing I wanted was to cause her needless worry. In truth, until this morning I had not been unduly concerned about it myself, and had put it down to nothing more than the symptoms of a full workload.

It first happened in the stables' food store, when I stopped off to get some oats for Plum's breakfast. There I was, surrounded by sacks of the stuff, without the foggiest notion of what I was looking for. The very act of recall induced in me a feeling of being rooted to the spot, unable to move a muscle until I could remember why I went in there. The paralysis was accompanied by an acute awareness of the time I was frittering away, not to mention the guilt that such a feeling produces in any serving man worth his salt. So I started, as I always did, to employ my System — a conversation with myself, by which I would attempt to break the deadlock. Today however, my System provided perils of its own. My inner dialogue went like this:

"What did I come in here for?"

"You of all people should know that."

"All the same, I have not the first clue."

"That is alarming."

"I know."

"What if you were doing something important?"

"I am well aware of the gravity of the situation. Worrying about possible implications is hardly going to improve matters."

"Neither is standing here talking to yourself. What you need is a Filofax."

"What's a Filofax?"

"A diary, in which one makes a note of one's daily tasks, to avoid forgetting them. Although, it would be more accurate to call it a personal organiser, as the word Filofax is a brand name, and is more synonymous with the yuppie culture of the 1980s."

At this point, terrified by the plunge into madness that my mind was taking, I brought the inner conversation to an abrupt end. Thankfully I remembered the bag of feed, and turned my attention to shooing away the strange blue mice who were attempting to gnaw through the sacking.

As I say, there was no sense in bothering Beaumains with any of this, so I started the account of my day an hour or so later, with my encounter with a highly animated Gwion in the top room of the Hawk Tower. He moved to a table covered in jesses, lures and wound lengths of creance, and pulled out a large piece of parchment hidden beneath. "I'm as ready as I'll ever be, Master Lucas. My strongest birds are doing most of the work. I've given the older ones the less demanding moves." Gwion pointed at the parchment, on which he had sketched a detailed plan of flight. Each bird had been assigned a separate letter, which it had been trained to spell out in the air, in the correct order, to form the complete message 'Happy Birthday Guinevere.'

"But there are two main problems, Master. One: getting them to keep to the correct formation. All it takes is one tiny distraction, or for two of them to collide mid-air, and the message will turn into complete gibberish. Two: releasing the powder." He picked up a small object like a carrot, attached to a jess. "I've found plenty of it in Merlin's old stores — I've got red, white and green — but everything depends on each hawk releasing their powder at the right time. But, I think I've fixed it. Here, I'll show you with Pickford."

Gwion approached a goshawk on its perch, whispering and clicking to put the bird at ease. Stroking Pickford under the chin, he took the carrot-shaped object and gently tied the jess around his leg. Pickford's wings flapped reflexively and he clawed once at the carrot before settling down. "Now," said Gwion, moving back to the table, "watch this." He took a small wooden whistle out of his tunic pocket and spread out the flight plan on a table. "Pickford's flying the first letter 'H'. As soon as he gets into position, I give the first signal." Gwion blew the whistle. In response to a pitch inaudible to our ears, Pickford hooked a talon through the bottom of the carrot. A thin stream of powder poured from the base. Gwion blew the second signal, and Pickford clawed it shut again.

Not for the first time, the awe in which I held Gwion's ingenuity was mingled with a teacher's guilt that the domestic realm was failing to fully utilise the considerable skills of my apprentice. "I've had to train each bird to respond to a different frequency, which means a lot of whistles," he said, indicating a rack of carved instruments in various sizes. "But, all things considered..."

"You have done an excellent job, as ever, Gwion," I said.

He grinned and looked at his feet, embarrassed I sensed not so much by my praise, as by his own desire to hear it. A beam of sunlight fell through the narrow high window, catching the motes of dust in the air. "I love it when that happens," he said, alighting on a change of subject. "It always makes me wonder how many specks of dust are in a shaft of light."

"One hundred million, seven thousand five hundred and twelve," I said automatically. Gwion laughed, uncertainly, and was about to reply when the air was filled with the rapid pounding of footsteps on stone, and Sir Perceval and Sir Gareth burst into the room.

✝

From the rooftop of the Hawk Tower, the knights in the tournament ground were no bigger than crumbs of bread scattered across a table cloth. I could just about make out Knight X, a dot of darkness surrounded by an encroaching circle of silver specks. It appeared as if the tournament had moved to the hand-to-hand combat stage, and would soon be drawing to a close. The formation on the field changed suddenly, as if an invisible hand had shaken the table cloth, and everyone piled on top of Knight X in a frantic mêlée.

I was attempting to focus my eyes on the ever-growing heap of legs, swords and armour to discover the fortunes of Knight X, when I saw him strolling across the rear wall of the North stand, looking down as the scrum below pummelled each other senseless in their attempt to grind him into the grass. As usual, I could only look over the side of the tower for a few minutes before experiencing a lurching sensation in my stomach, made all the more disturbing as I never normally suffer any fear of heights.

I leaned back from the edge and held onto the stonework with both hands, but the eccentric architecture of the rooftop only made the feeling worse. Everything about the tower top seemed designed to disorient and bamboozle, from the slant of the floor that made one feel in constant risk of sliding off the edge, to the stone-carved beasts perched in the four corners like malevolent sentinels. This tower was not as high as the Royal Tower, yet from here it appeared through an optical illusion to be a good deal taller.

None of this seemed to bother Sir Perceval and Sir Gareth; from the lengthy account of their adventures, they had recently received a thorough grounding in the subject of the uncanny.

"...And then there were the warriors, made of glass," said Sir Gareth.

"Only with the heads of dogs," said Sir Perceval.

"Glass dogs, mind, not real ones."

"I never said they were real dogs."

"No, but it was sort of implied."

"Well, glass dog heads is what I meant."

"That may be what you *meant*, but it's not what you *said*."

"Only an idiot would think I meant a real dog."

"Are you calling me an idiot?"

"If the cap fits."

"Is that a glass cap, or a real cap?"

"It all sounds most *Chronicle*-worthy," I said hastily, fearing that the demands of questing had taken their toll on their friendship. "I am sure Sir Kay will give you priority billing this evening."

I did not want to appear rude, but it was high time for me to be in Lower Camelot, though I hesitated to leave Gwion on his own. After the 'DEATH BY VINEGAR' sky-writing debacle, he had wedged himself into an archway in the tower's western ramparts. He sat with his head in his hands, mumbling bitter curses against the blue mice who had distracted his less committed hawks and thrown the rest of them into disarray.

"But here's the thing, Lucas," said Sir Perceval. "*I've actually seen the Grail.*" He shone with the radiance that infused him whenever he mentioned the word. Until now, I had put this fervour down to an upbringing which instilled in him the unshakable notion that this quest was his and his alone. Ever since his presentation at Court, Sir Perceval's name had been synonymous with the Grail. Even these past few years, when it had come to obsess the greater part of all knighthood, the unspoken assumption was that Sir Perceval would, as the legend required, ask the right question and possess this magical wonder. This time, even I could see that his zeal had a different hue, as of one who has not merely seen the light, but taken part of it away with him.

"I almost had it; I was *this* close in the Glass Fortress." Sir Perceval held his fingers up to my face in an almost-pinch. "If not for the guard dogs with the heads-and-bodies-of-glass, I'd have it by now. We must go back with more men. The Grail can be won, Lucas. The most powerful treasure in the Otherworld! Who knows what it can do?" said Sir Perceval.

"We will go and see Sir Kay," I said, for his enthusiasm had deeply impressed me. "When he has listened to what you have to say, I am sure he will have no objection to putting your story in tonight's *Chronicles*."

# VI

"Well, I've listened to what you have to say," said Sir Kay, "and there's no way I'm putting your story in tonight's *Chronicles*."

"Sorry?" said Sir Perceval.

"Did we miss something?" said Sir Gareth.

"What part of 'I've seen the Grail' don't you understand?"

Sir Kay's Green Room was filling up with the usual mixture of the great and the garrulous, tall tale tellers and yarn spinners, experienced climbers all on the peaks of high adventure. There was Sir Ector, propping up Granville's backstage bar, mead-eloquent on the time he fought the blue hounds of the Black Baron and left both hounds and Baron black-and-blue. By the fireplace, Sir Lanval slackened male jaws with vivid boasts of his night with a faerie woman, whose beauty — not to mention athleticism — improved with every telling. Next to him, Sir Dagonet gave his highly selective account of assisting King Arthur against a race of Giants who made cloaks from the beards of their defeated foes. No blade had touched Sir Dagonet's beard since the victory, and for this evening's rendition he had augmented it with a false extension tucked into his tunic, which he unfurled at the story's climax to hoots of delight.

All these tales would shortly be presented in the Great Hall as part of the customary *Chronicles*. In addition, of course, to the story that gave the backstage room its name,

Sir Gawain requiring little persuasion to tell the story of the Green Knight 'just one more time.' Sir Perceval and Sir Gareth's request for a last-minute billing was therefore no small matter, but I was disappointed to see that the passion they had effortlessly conveyed to me fell on deaf ears.

"Oh, you've seen the Grail. How *wonderfully* original," said Sir Kay, folding his arms. "As if I haven't heard five hundred Grail stories today already."

"This one is different," said Sir Gareth.

"This one is *real*." Sir Perceval gripped Sir Kay's arm. For a moment, I thought he was convinced.

"Aren't they all," he said, pulling his arm away. "This very morning I had a knight in here who's convinced the Grail is not a cauldron at all, but an actual person, still living, who just happens to be the bloodline descendant of the original Tooth Faerie."

"But these are all old stories," said Sir Gareth, gesturing around the room. "They've been told a hundred times before."

"That's because they're tried and tested. Finely honed crowd-pleasers, that's what the people want. You go out there with yet another Grail story, I give you half a minute before the first flagon hits your head."

"Not with *this* Grail story," said Sir Perceval. "It's got everything. Death-defying deeds!"

"The evillest of evils!" said Sir Gareth.

"Temptation!"

"Virtue!"

"Triumph!"

"Adversity!"

"A talking horse!"

Sir Kay mimed a yawn. "Sorry. No can do. Now, if you don't mind, I've got important things to be getting on with." Sir Kay walked over to the fireplace to help Sir Dagonet re-tuck his beard. The two knights looked at me beseechingly.

"I am sorry, but Sir Kay's word is final," I said.

"No, it's not," said Sir Perceval. "King Arthur's is."

I had feared he might say that, for the thought had occurred to me, too. Ordinarily I would never go behind Sir Kay's back. But this news was, at the very least, something the King should know about. "Very well. Wait here," I said, and slipped through the thick curtains covering the Green Room door.

The *Chronicles* stage was situated to the left of the dais of the Royal High Table, on a separate platform along the back wall of the Great Hall. I made my way across it unobserved by the feasting masses, and engaged the King in a hushed aside. At first, the mention of the Grail had little effect on him, but when I spoke of Sir Perceval, his eyes gleamed with something of that knight's inner light.

"Sir Perceval? Then, Merlin's prophecy is true…"

"Indeed, sire? And to which of the esteemed wizard's numerous prophecies might you be referring?"

"Before he left, Merlin spoke of the coming of a knight to Camelot whose sole purpose would be to point the way to the Grail, so that it might be claimed by its rightful achiever."

"So I can tell Sir Kay to give them priority billing?"

"Hmm?"

"In tonight's *Chronicles*, sire. So that Sir Perceval and Sir Gareth can tell their story."

"Certainly not," said the King, and the light left his eyes.

"Sire?"

"This tale is not yet ready for the *Chronicles*. After all, it is only half a quest until the Grail has been achieved. Who else knows of this?"

"Thus far, only myself and Sir Kay."

"Good. Keep it that way. Call a meeting of the inner circle in my study in the Royal Tower, as soon as the feast is over. Inner circle *only*, Lucas. This is a matter for the utmost discretion."

"Very good, sire," I said.

The King pondered for a moment, then rose to his feet to bring the Hall to order. "Good people of Camelot. You are most welcome on this special day," he began, and I left him to make his birthday speech.

✝

I found Sir Perceval standing directly behind the curtain separating the Green Room from the Great Hall, wringing his hands and pacing the floor. "Lucas! Well? What did he say? Are we on?"

"No —"

"Damnation!"

"But I bring good news, Sir Perceval. In fact, better news than we hoped for. Whilst not the immediately desired outcome, it is, nevertheless, one which provides grounds for optimism —"

"Lucas, get to the flaming point!"

"The King has called an emergency meeting of the inner circle of the Round Table, at which you will both be present." I indicated Sir Gareth propping up the bar, surrounded by a crowd of maidens who frequented the Green Room in the hope of attentively listening their way into a prestigious marriage.

"The inner circle?" said Sir Perceval. "My God, Lucas, that's outstanding. You know what this means? We're going on another Grail Quest!" He positively danced at the thought.

"It would not do to raise your hopes too highly," I said, but again his infectious glee caught me and I smiled in spite of myself.

"So Gareth's allowed to come, too?"

"I presume so. After all, you will both be needed to navigate to the Otherworld. Was Sir Gareth with you, when you saw the Grail?"

"No, he was escaping from a Castle in the realm of Annwn at the time."

"Good gracious. Is there no end to the stories your journey provided?"

"Oh, that one's hardly worth telling, to be honest. Gareth filled me in on the way back. He was captured, interrogated by the Queen in a very half-hearted manner, and then escaped." At the bar, Sir Gareth's anecdotes were provoking over-enthusiastic gasps of wonder from the maidens.

"Which Queen was this, Sir Perceval?" I asked.

"Hmm? Oh, Morgan, naturally."

"Morgan Le Fay?" I pressed him. "The Dark Queen of Annwn?"

"Yes, and if you ask me, her reputation is based on severe exaggeration. I mean, how bad can she be, if Gareth escaped so easily and without a single scratch?"

"That is unusual indeed, Sir Perceval," I said, aware of an unpleasant sensation in my stomach. "I am no expert, but I believe that to date, no-one captured by the Dark Queen has ever escaped to tell of it."

"Yes, I did think it a bit strange. But then, standards are dropping everywhere these days."

Over at the bar, Sir Gareth had just ordered another round of drinks. He had his back to us, and was staring up at the thin slit of a window. A cloud moved to uncover the face of the moon outside, and a single shaft of its light fell upon Sir Gareth's head. I made my way over to him, followed by Sir Perceval. "Hey, Gareth," he said. "I was just telling Lucas how you fluked it out of Morgan's castle."

Sir Gareth slowly turned to look at us. He looked far from hale and hearty. His face had turned paler than the moonlight that still streamed in behind him. His eyes were stretched open, wide and bloodshot. And since I had last seen him, he had grown a bristly beard.

"Morgan? Morrrgan? Morrrrrrrgan."

"Yes, Morgan Le Fay. Gareth, what's got into you?" The maidens moved away in alarm. Sir Perceval and I took an instinctive step backwards.

"I don't know, Percy," said Sir Gareth. "But it's something... bad." He doubled over as if struck by a sudden stomach cramp, and looked up at us with a face full of pure, primal fear, not to mention even more hair. "Perceval... Help... Me?"

"Lucas," said Sir Perceval, pulling my sleeve. "What should I do, should I get Arthur?" Sir Gareth fell to his knees, clutching a head that was sprouting shaggy black hair at an alarming rate. He tore open his tunic to reveal a hirsute layer beneath, and started to pull off the rest of his clothes with hands that had lengthened into sharp claws. Several knights, attracted by the ruckus, rushed to our side and drew their swords.

"Put your swords away! It's Sir Gareth!" said Sir Perceval. But the creature that rose before us was no longer any such knight. A werewolf stood in front of the backstage bar, eyes red, jaws slavering.

"ARRRTHUR! GET ARRRTHUR! WOLF KILL KING, KILL KING ARRRTHURRROOOAARRGH!"

The werewolf lashed out with a claw. He caught hold of Granville, who was sneaking up behind him with a chair, and threw him behind the bar.

"Form a circle!" I shouted, "Keep him away from the Great Hall!"

Sir Ector and Sir Lanval joined us, swords drawn, but with one leap the wolf cleared our heads and bounded up to the Green Room curtain. It stopped, sniffed and growled with demonic delight, priming its haunches. Before it could move, the way was blocked by Sir Dagonet and Sir Kay. The wolf growled. It sniffed again and turned its gaze on the wall directly in front of it. With one mighty spring the werewolf hurled its body like a battering ram, smashing through the stone wall. Amidst clouds of dust I saw the astonished face of the King as the beast sank its teeth into his neck.

As fast as I could, I turned and ran in the opposite direction, to the very back of the Green Room.

†

Sir Pellinore's Corner was a separate area of the Green Room, a tent constructed from thick drapes and embroidered hangings acquired on his many travels. It was highly probable, given his non-appearance at the scene, that the occupant remained entirely oblivious to the rumpus without. Sure enough, pulling back a heavy curtain decorated with a hideously-faced cockerel creature, I found him perched on a cushion, sharing a long pipe with Sir Palomides the Mapmaker. A large drawing of the Kingdom was spread out in front of them. Sir Pellinore was making energetic markings on the parchment with a quill, while Sir Palomides looked on in despair.

"Pelly old boy," he said, attempting to stop the pen with his own in a half-hearted parry, "I think you'll find there's a ravine there."

"Where?"

"Where you've written 'Here Be Dragons.' Again."

"But *here* they most certainly *be*. Tracked 'em, seen 'em, got the spores. No sense telling a knight about a ravine, when he needs to know about dragons. They love the forest. Plenty of kindling."

"It's a wonder they find the time to visit the forest, what with them also being spotted here, here, here, here, and here."

"That's the problem with dragon maps — *they're never to scale!* Eh? Pally? Get it? Scale? You can have that one."

"Can't I just write 'Everywhere Be Dragons' at the top of the map, and be done with it?"

"Are you stark raving mad, man?"

You will scarcely believe it possible, but their talk of maps and beasts was enough to completely dispel the chaos in the Green Room from my mind. All I could say for certain was that there was something very important I needed Sir Pellinore for. Other than that, all was silence.

"Ah, footman, just the fellow! Talk some sense into Palomides."

"What he proposes sounds like a suitable compromise, Sir Pellinore," I said.

"Oh. Does it? Righto, if you say so. We'll start again with a fresh one."

Sir Pellinore crumpled the map into a ball, then froze as a long, high wolf howl filled the air.

"Killer Toads of Cemais! A werewolf! Where?"

"In the Great Hall, Sir Pellinore," I said. "I was hoping to solicit your advice on the matter."

"Take one enchanted sword. Plunge into the heart. Twist to the left. Twist to the right. Leave it in until the death rattle, then pull it straight out again."

"The werewolf is Sir Gareth."

Sir Pellinore propelled me out of the tent and before I knew it I was jogging alongside him through the Green Room.

"Bite or curse?" he said, rolling up his sleeves.

"From the nature of the transformation, I would say curse."

"Curse history?"

"His surprised reaction would indicate this is the first transformation. It started a few minutes ago, at most."

"Then a hunk of hope remains." Sir Pellinore was sprinting now, and I struggled to keep up with his pace. "Hexmanship?"

"Morgan Le Fay."

"Did I say hunk?" He ran up the steps to the wolf-made hole in the wall, two at a time. " 'Tis more like a morsel." Sir Pellinore somersaulted through the hole and out into the Great Hall.

✝

"And, well. The rest of it you saw for yourself," I said to Beaumains.

"If I had not, I would scarcely have believed it," she replied. "All in all, it has been one of those days. Well… if that will be all, Sir Lucas. I think I will bid you *adieu*."

"Wait. There is more." I turned and stoked the dying embers of the fire. My deputy looked at me with a quizzical expression. "I am afraid you do not know the half of it, Beaumains," I said.

# VII

So much had been decided at the meeting of the inner circle, that it is difficult to know where to begin. As soon as I had satisfied myself that Sir Gareth was receiving the very best medical care in the infirmary, I prised Sir Gawain away from his brother and we made our way to the King's study in the Royal Tower, to make the necessary preparations for the meeting. The Master was in his chambers attempting to console the Queen, and had left orders for me to summon him only when everyone had arrived. Despite protesting that she was none the worse for her recent ordeal, the Queen remained visibly shaken, and I agreed that he was wise to stay with her for as long as possible.

Sir Perceval was the first to arrive, his face a tournament ground of competing emotions. There was excitement at being included in the hallowed inner circle, and pride at the prestige of such a meeting being held at his instigation. But such feelings were tempered by the grave confirmation his story had recently received. Next came Sir Pellinore, almost knocked off his feet by another wave of thanks, Sir Perceval shaking his hand fit to drop off, Sir Gawain slapping him on the back and swearing promises of eternal fealty and everlasting ale. Then came Sir Kay, laden with maps and scrolls and saying *how sorry he was for not believing Sir Perceval's Grail story, even though he really had nothing to*

*apologise for, given that he was hardly to know how things
were to turn out, and was only trying to do a job which was
difficult enough at the best of times, not that anyone ever
realised, much less cared.*

Sir Lancelot followed shortly after. His arrival coincided
with that of the King through the door leading off to the
Royal Chambers. The two regarded each other from opposite
sides of the table.

"The Queen sends her deepest thanks, Lancelot. As do I,"
said the King, indicating for him to sit. Sir Lancelot did so.

"Anyone would have done it."

"But not anyone *could* have done it."

"There was only one sword for the job."

"And only one swordsman."

"Your Majesty is too kind."

I found Sir Lancelot's reluctance to accept the Master's
praise strange. The manner in which he had earned it was so
extraordinary, that even now I can scarcely take it in. Having
made his somersault through the gap in the wall, Sir Pellinore
wasted no time in subjecting the werewolf to a procedure
he later described to me as the Manticore Manoeuvre. Thus,
when I emerged from the Green Room some moments after
him, I was greeted by a most uncommon sight. Sir Pellinore
had clamped himself piggy-back fashion onto the werewolf,
his arms looped around the beast's shoulders, his legs
crossed about the hairy stomach. This tactic was not without
its drawbacks. Firstly, as Sir Pellinore's huffing and puffing
testified, an enormous amount of pressure was required
on behalf of the immobiliser. Secondly, as the werewolf's
howling and growling proved, it had a decidedly aggravating
effect on the immobilisee. It was a temporary solution,
and one that was not helped by the reaction of those in the
immediate vicinity.

Most of the feasters had fled the Hall. The Knights of the Round Table remained behind. Half of them had rushed to the aid of the fallen, bleeding King and hysterical Queen. But as they surged around the Master, I saw that Excalibur's enchanted scabbard had already started its usual work, the blood from his wound pouring back up his neck and into the gaping bite marks that healed into smooth skin. The rest of the knights surrounded the stationary werewolf, but were prevented from advancing by Sir Gawain.

"Keep back! Keep back the lot of yer!" he said. "Death to the man who touches a hair on my brother's head! Or anywhere else on him, for that matter!"

"KILL KING ARTHURRR! KILL! KILL!" said the werewolf, and jumped a step forwards as Sir Pellinore involuntarily relaxed his grip.

"Don't be a fool Gawain, Gareth's as good as dead," said Sir Bors.

"No," said Sir Gawain. "Not if we cut out the lupine gland. Right, Pell?"

"Gnnnn-uh-huh." Sir Pellinore nodded as best he could. "Need... sword. Faerie-forged."

"Excalibur!" said Sir Gawain.

Everyone looked to the King, who was still down on the floor. His wounds were healing fast, but not fast enough. Even if he had enough strength to stand after such a mauling, it was doubtful he could perform the necessary operation.

"King Arthur's the only one who can wield an enchanted blade with the required skill," said Sir Bors.

"Not the only one," said Sir Gawain. "Lancelot can. I've seen him use one before. Not Excalibur, but a faerie-forged sword nonetheless." Sir Gawain turned to where Knight X stood among the group who had rushed to the High Table.

"But Sir Lancelot is away questing," I said.

"Is he now?" said Sir Gawain.

Sir Pellinore's grip slackened further. The werewolf lurched towards the fallen King. The Queen placed herself directly in its path.

"Don't you dare touch him!"

"ɢʀʀʀᴜɪɴᴇᴠᴇʀʀʀᴇ!" said the werewolf. Sir Pellinore dropped from its back. A claw swung for the Queen's face. Knight X blocked it with his left arm and fetched a right hook to the wolf's jaw that sent it whimpering to the floor. "Quickly, hold him!" he said, his mask falling from his face, and I gasped in amazement to see Sir Lancelot beneath. In the blink of an eye he was at the King's side, taking up Excalibur.

The werewolf struggled against the combined efforts of Sirs Bors, Menaduke, Agravain and Accolon to pin it down. Knight X — that is to say, Sir Lancelot — extended the sword so that the point touched the space between the werewolf's neck and left shoulder blade. The wolf shrank from Excalibur, as if perceiving a light obscured to the rest of us. "Whatever happens, keep your grip," said Sir Lancelot to the restraining knights. As if he were signing his alias, he made a deep incision in the shape of an X. The werewolf writhed and yowled in pain. The knights held him fast as the sword sliced through to uncover the lupine gland: a hairy black lump the size of a crab apple, malignant and mocking.

Everything of Sir Lancelot was concentrated upon the sword point. Excalibur danced in his hands in an absurdly dainty manner. The werewolf bucked and thrashed and foamed at the mouth. Sir Lancelot cut around the remainder of the gland and thrust beneath it. This time, the wolf's howl had an undertone that was reassuringly human. Sir Lancelot bent Excalibur in a lever-like motion. The gland was expelled with a wet pop and flipped up in the air like a tossed coin. I caught it in a bowl and passed it to Sir Pellinore, who threw it into the fire where it sizzled and writhed and seemed to shriek with a woman's voice, before vanishing in a puff of blue smoke. The werewolf looked at Sir Lancelot with a hangdog expression, panting feebly, its tongue lolling and receding to human shape and size. The rest of its features did likewise, until Sir Gareth lay naked in a pool of blood, twitching and shivering in a grim parody of childbirth.

✝

"That witch queen filth will pay for cursing an Orkney!" said Sir Gawain, slamming his empty cup down so hard it cracked in his hand.

"I propose something more than simple revenge," said the King.

"Oh, there'll be nowt simple about it. I'll give her a curse alright. I'll give her a curse where the sun don't shine."

"Peace, Gawain."

"Don't give me 'peace' after all she's done! And all to get to *you*."

"I did not call this meeting to discuss my sister's desire to make me pay for the sins of my father," said the King.

"How can you say that, sire? Every attempt on your life so far has been relatively manageable," Sir Kay said. "But tonight — tonight was on another level! The people will demand we strike back."

"And strike we shall. But if what happened to Sir Gareth is to have any positive effect, we must learn from it. The curse was not intended merely to kill me, although I do not doubt that was Morgan's preferred outcome. It was a warning."

"Warning against what? Women with more loose upstairs than a rat-ridden hovel?" said Sir Gawain.

"A warning against questing for the Grail. Sir Perceval has seen it."

Those who had not heard Sir Perceval's story now turned to him with undisguised awe. "It's true," he said, his fervour subdued but no less potent. "I almost got it, but it was too well protected."

"So Morgan likes her trinkets and she guards 'em well. Big deal," said Sir Gawain.

"The Grail is more than a trinket," said Sir Perceval.

"Much more," said the King. "Merlin spoke to me of it once. The Grail has the power to do whatever the achiever wants it to. The ultimate treasure. I understand what you are all saying. The attacks on Camelot, on the kingdom, have been getting steadily worse, and yes, I am partly to blame for that. There have been... other things on my mind, besides wayward Giants and marauding dragons." The King looked at Sir Lancelot.

"Your biggest problem is not from any beast, but from man," said Sir Lancelot, unfazed. "I've been out there, I've seen it. The lawlessness. The mockery of Camelot justice. It would make you all weep. I do what I can, but I'm just one knight. The tide of violence is rising, and soon it will be lapping at the foot of your Royal Tower."

"Then this is exactly the opportunity we need," said the King, "to rouse us from our slumber! Perceval has shown us the way. We go to the Otherworld. We bring the fight into the realm of Annwn — right to Morgan's doorstep, Gawain — and we take away the Grail, her greatest treasure, for the glory of Camelot. *Now* do you see?"

"Ha! Let the brigands challenge Camelot justice when we have the Grail!" said Sir Pellinore.

"Just hang on a minute," said Sir Lancelot. "Who exactly do you propose to send on this quest?"

"The inner circle; we seven," said the King.

"And leave Camelot unguarded? No. I will stay."

"I need my best knights by my side. There are many who are capable of keeping Camelot safe in our absence."

"And many more again who would be delighted to see it fall. Some of them even sit on the Round Table."

"We will only be gone for weeks, Lancelot; a month at most," said the King. "And when we return triumphant with the Grail —"

"Which we will!" said Sir Perceval.

"— it will be the start of a new Golden Age!"

"Like the old days, eh Artie?" said Sir Pellinore.

"That's the spirit, Pellinore. Just think of all the new *Chronicles* you can tell, Kay."

"Lord knows, the bottom of the barrel won't take much more scraping," Sir Kay smiled.

"Then it's decided. We leave at first light," said the King, getting to his feet. "Pack lightly. Lucas, prepare the Prydwen."

✝

"And that is my dilemma," I said to Beaumains. "After everything we have both seen today, how can I leave Camelot?"

Beaumains chewed her lip. "King Arthur suspects nothing of Mordred's schemes?"

"What he does notice, he sees with the same short-sighted eyes he always turns to his brother's activities. As for the things the Master does *not* see, I have always chosen to keep them from him, knowing the guilt he feels where his brother is concerned. Now, I wish that I had not."

"It does not seem like the best time for Arthur to be going anywhere."

"The Master's mind is made up. But I cannot go gallivanting off on a quest! My place is here."

"Lucas. What is it, what's wrong?" she said.

"Nothing. It is just the dilemma. You know how I hate things being unresolved."

"There is something else. Tell me."

"I am fine," I said, avoiding her eyes.

"You are not. You have not been yourself for months."

"Please, Beaumains, it is late. I would prefer to talk about it some other time."

"Ah, so you admit there *is* an 'it.' "

"An 'it' I insist you drop."

"I am not going anywhere until you tell me." She pulled a chair over to the doorway and sat down. "And neither are you." She crossed her legs and folded her arms.

"You really are the most exasperating woman on the good green earth."

"On it, under it, above it, beyond it."

Defeated, I sat back down again. "It is hard to explain in words. At least, it is hard to explain it in plain words. To be a good butler here, to serve someone as great as the Master, one cannot lose one's head, even if — no, *especially* if — everything around one is magic and pageant. What this has always boiled down to for me is a domestic common sense — service sense, if you like. I have always maintained that such a quality is essential to the successful running of Camelot. Ideally, this means that one should be here, but also *not* here. A part of things, yes, but never too close to anything. It follows that I, above all people, do not merely set this standard, but exemplify it with every fibre of my being."

"And you do it very well," she said, but it did not sound entirely like a compliment.

"But recently, I have been feeling... like I did when I was a boy, waking up in the middle of the night with a vicious cramp in my legs. My mother would comfort me by telling me it was just my developing bones finding their feet, so to speak."

"Growing pains."

"Exactly. This feels like that, but inside my mind. Everything I know is being pushed around by unseen forces, pressing against the top of my head so that I find myself flummoxed by even the simplest task. More than that, I keep catching glimpses of something else, something that keeps trying to break through and make itself known to me."

"What do you mean, 'something?' "

"Words or sayings I have never heard before. Pictures sometimes, shimmering at the edge of my vision. Whatever it is, it comes from beyond me, I know that. Maybe from beyond this world. And I fear the effect it is having on my work. I am past my threescore years, I am reaching the end of my working life."

"Rubbish."

"But I do not fear the effect of it, half as much as I fear the thing itself. I do not want it. I will not have it. I will master it, Beaumains. It will not beat me."

I realised to my shame that I was shaking, my hands clenched into tight fists, my back hunched and stiff. Beaumains put her hands over mine.

"Then, that settles it. You must go with them," she said. Her touch was warm and soft and light.

"I cannot leave Camelot. Not after today. After I have prepared the ship, I will beg the King's leave to stay here."

"But you said it yourself. The solution to what troubles you may lie beyond this world," she said. I nodded weakly.

"But Mordred —"

"I am more than a match for Mordred. Come on. I will help you make a start with your packing." Beaumains began to arrange a pile of my things on the bed.

I suddenly knew what had made me pause on stepping through the door, at the very start of our evening meeting. It was not the feeling that I was witnessing such moments of domestic tranquillity for the first time. But that I was seeing them for the last.

# Day Five

# I

I stood on the edge of the collapsed cliff, the immense vortex churning at my feet. I reckoned the time to be well past midnight, perhaps even approaching dawn, but the colour of the sky was now so unnatural it was hard to say with any degree of accuracy. Neither was my trusty pocket watch of any use; its face bruised and broken, damage undoubtedly sustained during my many recent exertions. My hands were wet, and I noticed for the first time that they were covered with blood. More to stop their incessant shaking than anything else, I wiped them on my shirt, thinking that the stains would be a devil to get out. The spectral forms within the vortex swirling up out of the Otherworld resembled clothes in a giant washing machine. This small image of normality calmed me down enough to check again for a pulse in the motionless body at my feet. Nothing. My hands started shaking again, and this time I clasped them tightly together, sending a sharp tang of blood up to my nostrils.

I tried to think of something else I could have done. Something that I could still do. But what? What could I do for any of them anymore? More to the point, what did I even *want* to do for them anymore? *Perhaps the Grail*, I kept thinking, *perhaps the Grail*. Then, remembering where the Grail had gone, I dismissed it from my mind. But there it stubbornly remained, printed across my thoughts as indelibly as the bloody stains on my shirt.

Time was running out. What was I thinking — time *had* run out. Even now, back in the stadium, the last of the Master's life-blood was draining from his body, and only one person could save him. Even now, the gap between this world and the next yawned fully open, and only one person could stop the destructive forces his own return had unleashed. But Merlin was nowhere to be seen.

I stared into the swirling abyss of the portal. For the moment it was calm and quiet, as if it were drawing one last long breath before disgorging the last of its contents into the world. When we had first opened it, the magical vortex had possessed all the wild unpredictability of a tornado. Now, however, although awesome in circumference, it nestled against the remains of the cliff, a domesticated apocalypse challenging you to think of it as the end of all things.

Then I saw him. Standing on the shore below me, at the base of the breach where the rift disappeared underground. Cloaked and hooded and beckoning. Very well, then. I picked up the body in my arms and stumbled down the crumbling remains of the cliff to where the wizard Merlin waited.

# II

Immediately following the triumph of Sir Lancelot's troops with 'Operation: Hostile Takedown,' I had returned to Camelot. It was my hope that the Master would have witnessed the victory himself on television, or at least been told the news by Megan and her colleagues. By now I was highly concerned to see him, it being several hours since I had left him in their care. So I teleported first to Lower Camelot, the better to arrive in the Royal Tower unannounced.

Materialising in my old quarters, I was surprised to find myself in a room full of people. Several soldiers were hacking chunks of stone out of the wall and passing them to men and women in white coats, who sat in front of a vast array of test tubes, microscopes and computers. One of them looked up abruptly at the sudden arrival of a stranger in their midst. "Who are you?" she said. "Where's your pass?" A soldier dropped the stone he was carrying and reached for his revolver, which I took as a cue to try my luck elsewhere. The Lower Great Hall was the first place to enter my mind, and that is where I went.

The place in which I arrived bore little resemblance to everything I had previously known. Huge chunks of the roof and its covering of floorstones had been removed between the crossbeams, giving strange jigsaw shaped views of the Great Hall one floor above me. My intricate winch and pulley system was being dismantled; the sturdy ropes of a thousand conveyances hacked down, iron counterweights whose ballast had delivered dishes to many a feast passed along a line of soldiers and heaped carelessly in a corner. I wondered why they had not used my water-powered conveyor belt for this purpose, until I saw water seeping from where the pipe network had been wrenched out of the wall. Everywhere, people in military garb bustled around me, heedless of my presence, their sole purpose apparently to destroy every last trace of my subterranean invention. Steel ladders lined the empty lift shafts, and via one of these I climbed upwards, parting the tattered remnants of a tapestry and stepping into the Great Hall.

Here it was the same story as below. The north wall had been entirely knocked down, as had the room behind it, which we had once called the Green Room. The space ahead of me stretched out into the open air and as far as the courtyard, the ground becoming steadily more impassable the closer I got to the Royal Tower. Radar dishes, machinery and power generators blocked my way. Men and women scurried about, speaking incomprehensible words into their headsets. Thick cables snaked to and fro in such profusion it was a miracle nobody tripped over them. Nobody but myself, I should say, for with my very next step I caught my foot under one of these electrical vines and went sprawling to my knees.

I was about to teleport up to the Royal Chambers when Megan appeared in front of me. So swift and sudden was her arrival that it was almost as if she had an amulet of her own.

"Megan, thank goodness I have found you," I said, getting to my feet. "What on earth is going on here?"

"What do you mean?" she said.

"The dismantling of Lower Camelot. Had I known it would result in so much disarray, I would never have allowed you access in such numbers."

"Correct me if I'm wrong, but this time two days ago, none of this —" she circled her hand airily "— existed."

"Well, no, not as such —"

"And as far as everybody was aware, none of you existed, either."

"Indeed, but —"

"Then what did you expect? The world has been turned upside down, and for all they know, it's about to end." She smiled a smile as black as a raven's wing. "People want explanations. And I for one think they deserve them."

"Yes, well. Put like that, I suppose I can understand," I said. I understood nothing of the sort, but her words were having a curious effect on me, which I tried to ignore by addressing the purpose of my return. "I take it you know of Sir Lancelot's success in quelling the dragon menace?" I said.

"Yes."

"Then the Master also knows of it?"

"No."

"May I ask why?"

"He's got other things to deal with."

"In that case, I would like to inform him of it; as well as speaking to him about other matters."

"Not possible," she said.

"Excuse me?"

"I told you. He's busy."

"Busy in what respect?"

"He's about to be interviewed," said Megan.

"I see. Well, I suppose that is a positive move, but I would still like to talk with him. I only require a moment or two."

"His interview is with the military. The reason King Arthur's not allowed to see anyone at the moment is because he's under arrest."

"Under what charge?" I said.

"Charges. There are lots of them. But to save time, let's group them under the general heading of 'threat to national security.' "

"But, this is preposterous!"

"No, this is the *Official Secrets Act*."

"I do not follow you."

" 'I do not follow you,' " she mimicked, in a self-pitying whine. "Don't worry. You will, soon enough." There was that smile again. Megan walked back to the Royal Tower, where two guards flanked the only entrance from ground level, blocking the door with rifles that parted as she approached. "Oh, and by the way," she added, turning back to me, "if you're thinking of scurrying in through any of your pathetic secret passages, don't bother. They're either guarded or blocked off." The rifles crossed again behind her.

I was, to put it mildly, incensed, more determined than ever to reach the Master, and to get to him before she did. But when I touched the amulet, to my surprise, nothing happened. I touched it again. Still nothing. The confounded magical item had chosen the very worst moment to break! When I started to think of the Master, it was the same as when I had tried to teleport to Sir Perceval and the Grail, or attempted to picture Merlin. His form was shrouded in a thick mist, with only the vaguest visible outline. The more I tried, the deeper the fog became, billowing out and threatening to fill every corner of my mind. The mist dissipated as soon as I stopped trying, leaving me to consider clearer thoughts.

Chief among them was the realisation that the walls of Camelot had fallen. And I was the one who had let the invaders in. But a modicum of hope remained. There was every chance the marauders had passed over an element of the architecture easily overlooked; even by eyes as thoroughly prying as theirs. Indeed, once upon a time, I had overlooked it myself.

I closed my eyes and thought of laundry.

✝

The laundry room was the only place that existed on a level beneath Lower Camelot. This 'Lower Lower Camelot,' if you like, was constructed as something of a hasty afterthought — a salutary lesson in the potential pitfalls of castle planning. For it was only after the last stone of Lower Camelot had been laid that I realised I had made absolutely no provision for the collection and cleaning of dirty washing. But a fortuitous solution presented itself. Beneath my own quarters, directly below the Master's Royal Tower, was a small natural cave, a discovery which had been the cause of much consternation when laying the castle foundations. It would have been a very costly exercise to fill in all that space, so after much deliberation I had decided merely to seal it off, trusting my chief builder's assertion that there was enough foundation work already in place to ensure a solid structure above.

In the event, this cave provided the perfect location for a laundry room. It was central. It was clean and dry. And, with only a minor diversion of the underground stream, it had its own water supply. So it was that, when the Royal Tower was constructed, I included a small chute running up through a chimney-sized gap in the wall. Other similar chutes were positioned at regular intervals throughout the highest points of Upper Camelot. These corresponded to collection points in the Lower levels, where staff would gather the laundry and deposit it into the main chute through an access hatch in its side. The final destination of all soiled garments was a large walk-in earthenware pot in the middle of the laundry room, the size and shape of a small hut, where they awaited the weekly arrival of wash day.

As efficient as this was, however, it was only ever meant to be a one way system, as I now realised, lighting a wall-mounted torch with a match and peering up the long cobwebbed shaft. A test with the amulet confirmed what I strongly suspected: the malfunction concerning the Master formed a barrier around the whole of the Royal Tower. But three factors were in my favour. The first was a draught of air coming down the shaft, hinting that the laundry chute had escaped the invaders' attention and remained unblocked. The second was that by climbing up and balancing on the rim of the central pot, I could reach into the opening of the chute above and pull myself up inside. The third was that, by a combined effort of wedging my feet against the wall and using gaps in the masonry as foot-and-hand-holds, I could slowly but surely make my way up to the very top of the chute, which came out into a false-bottomed laundry chest in the Master's room. This I now proceeded to do, stone by awkward stone.

# III

If the climb was all discomfort, it was luxury compared to the cramped conditions awaiting me above. I pushed up the bottom panel of the laundry chest and pulled myself through, closing it behind me, and arranging my limbs into as pleasant a position as possible without making any noise. This was not easy. Crouched on my haunches inside that small space, my every movement generated a symphony of sound, from banging my head on the wooden lid, to the creaking that each shift of my buckled legs produced from the floor panel below. At any moment I expected the lid to be thrown back, exposing me on my knees like a shamefaced penitent.

But as my ears grew more accustomed, I realised that any noises I made within would be lost in the general hubbub without. The Royal Chamber reverberated to a multitude of voices, muffled, as though I were hearing them from under water. I raised myself up from a low crouch into a half-stoop and pushed my head slowly but firmly against the lid, creating a slim letterbox view of the room outside.

It was as if someone had taken all the chaos occurring in the rest of Camelot and attempted to cram it into one room. The Master's four-poster bed had been overturned and shoved up against the wall, kept in place by a row of soldiers. Where the dressing table used to stand, a bank of television monitors had been erected, twelve of them stacked three screens high, all of them, for the moment, blank. Small cameras on brackets were bolted or hammered into the walls. Slightly bigger cameras were in the hands of people arguing over the best position in which to stand and point them. Enormous lamps of the kind used on a theatre stage were set up high on poles and filled the room with a harsh unnatural light, as if to catch in their pitiless beam anything that the all-seeing cameras might have missed. And every remaining inch was filled with the swaggering members of this curious coalition of the media and the military.

Together with the cumbersome tools of their trade, these people obscured from my view the place at which all this industry was directed — the middle of the wall opposite my hiding place. There was currently no sign of Megan herself, but I was in little doubt that the Master, whatever his current state, was the focus of attention. I had arrived just in time, as this burst of frantic activity turned out to be a last minute rush before the event that Megan had ominously referred to as the Master's interview. The television screens I could see to my left flickered into life. I suddenly saw the Master, and wished with all my heart that I had not.

He sat in a wooden chair, secured by means of ropes tied around his waist, pinioning his arms behind his back. I knew this because one of the cameras offered a view from directly behind him; just one of the dozens of angles from which he was being observed. One zoomed close enough to show the individual drops of sweat on his brow, multiplying like germs under a microscope. Another showed only his eyes, pupils shrunk to pinheads against the lights' unforgiving glare. He breathed in and out, and the sound of it filled the room, amplified by an invisible microphone. In front of the Master were several anonymous military figures, and among their number stood Megan. By some tacit agreement she was in charge of the entire enterprise, as if she outranked even the most highly decorated generals in the room.

"Why don't you start by telling us about the Eternal Quest, Arthur?" she said.

The Master looked up, as if hearing his name called from a far-off place. For a moment his eyes flickered at the corners, a tiny gesture writ large on screen. Then he spoke, his voice no higher than a whisper.

"You know nothing of the Eternal Quest," he said, and lowered his head again. Megan laughed at this, and the room joined her in a wave of sycophantic giggling, as if the Master had made some witty attempt to break the ice.

"I think you'll find that we know everything. Are we ready?" she asked a technician at the control desk.

The man nodded. "They've just gone live."

"Then show him," said Megan. The screens changed, the images of the Master all replaced by the same picture revealing the room at the stadium in Cardiff, where Sir Gawain had made his call to arms. And it showed an interviewer, sat opposite a man in late middle-age.

Sir Lancelot took every question the interviewer threw at him without flinching. But Megan was right.

They knew everything.

Contrary to orders, Sir Kay had kept on writing his *Chronicles*; a story I thought he had destroyed long ago, for I had watched him do so with my own eyes. The authorities had found it in his study, which they had searched after discovering the body of the intruder in his garden. Countless manuscripts, pages upon pages, all telling the same story. A story of books written and books burned. A story of kingdoms lost and treasures found, and what it meant to find them. A story of a hidden glade in a forest; of a road taken, and a road not taken. Our story.

As with the earlier press conference, I was struck again by what Sir Lancelot did not say. He did not speak of decisions being made out of necessity, in pursuit of a higher cause; decisions that called for sacrifice in the name of a greater good. He did not speak of the things we could not go back for, however much we might have wanted to; for to go back would mean sacrificing something far greater. He did not speak of the cost of following a noble dream, of dedicating everything you have to a working life in the service of such a quest. No. Sir Lancelot merely nodded his head, confirming everything that the interviewer said with a weary sense of resignation.

"But if all this is true," said the interrogator, "why did you do it? Why go along with something you didn't agree with?"

Sir Lancelot shrugged. "For love," he said.

And then Sir Lancelot told another story. A story I had always believed belonged to the world of hints and allegations, whispers and rumours. A story I would have denied unto death before believing it to be true. Sir Lancelot and Queen Guinevere as lovers. Behind the Master's back, while all of Camelot laughed and smirked and revelled in the squalid detail, like pigs wallowing in mud. Sir Lancelot finished his story with another shrug, as if that gesture were a closing quotation mark.

With that, the interview ended and the monitor screens in the Royal Chamber returned to the Master. Sitting up straight now, a fire in his eyes that I had not seen for over a thousand years.

"To think," said Megan. "All this for love."

"What did you say?" said the Master, looking at Megan properly for the first time.

"Was the Eternal Quest for her, Arthur? Is that why you did it? For Guinevere? A funny kind of love, don't you think? One that condemns the beloved to death."

In one movement the Master tore free of his bonds. He snatched an assault rifle from a soldier and fired around the room in a wild burst. The monitors exploded in a shower of sparks. Everywhere, people ran or dived for cover. The captors drew their pistols, but the Master grabbed Megan before she could move, pulling his arm around her neck and holding the gun to her head.

"Take me to Lancelot," he said.

"Take me...

"to him...

"now."

Time ground to a standstill. But on this occasion, I was ready for the anomaly, wishing for it with every atom of my being. I was so deeply grateful when it occurred that I almost burst into tears. It was not too late! I could do something! I willed my cramped legs into life and stood up in the laundry chest.

Everything in the Royal Chamber had stopped in a tableau of pure pandemonium. I started to step out of the chest, uttering a prayer of thanks that the invisible force had chosen this moment to manifest again. But when I looked up I realised that this time, I was not the source of it.

Megan clapped her hands in languorous applause and removed herself from the Master's frozen embrace. "In the nick of time, the trusty butler appears to save the day." She flicked her hand at me as if batting away a fly. My leg jerked back into the chest like a puppet under her control. When I tried to move it again, I found myself completely rooted to the spot.

"Morgan Le Fay," I said.

"You might have known?"

"Yes. Well I might."

"But you didn't, did you? And now it's too late."

The screens flickered on again to show various shots of evacuated Cardiff. The city centre stood empty beneath a black sky. The only movement came from the main road, where hundreds of dirty white bumps pushed up through the asphalt like carbuncular cauliflowers. On another monitor a group of civilians, a ragtag band of fifty or so men presumably enlisted by Sir Gawain, nervously patrolled the streets, perhaps searching for their leader, who did not seem to be among their number. As they marched past a row of shops, the garden of skulls grew ever riper ahead of them, domed heads and empty eyes protruding through the cracked tarmac.

"The dead will rise," I said.

"The *damned* dead. Those who died with their minds mired in pain and frustration. Bring them to life, and they form an army who seek only to destroy everything they find. A useful tool."

"To bring about the end of the world?"

"Probably. To tell you the truth, I don't really care. As long as I destroy *him*." She walked back to where the Master was frozen in his escape bid. "The final humiliation of my dear half-brother. All debts repaid in full, and with interest. His father's debt, for killing my father. His own debt, for the audacity of taking the Grail. I will see him broken. I will see everything he stands for in ruin. The legend of Arthur reduced to a laughing stock." She cast him a long look of utter disgust and then turned back to me, her revulsion undiminished. "Of course, he's done a pretty good job of that already. But I shall enjoy watching him and Lancelot tear each other limb-from-limb." She ducked under the Master's stationary arm and placed the muzzle of the gun back against her head. "Goodbye."

She clicked her fingers and the room came back to life again. The snap of her fingers resonated with a dry splintering sound under my feet. The bottom of the chest gave way and I dropped down into the darkness of the laundry chute, pitching backwards and then upside down, banging my head as I fell. Thick cobwebs slapped past my face, and something else, something round and hard — the amulet, falling from my neck before I could catch hold of it. Most of the air was knocked out of me as I rebounded from side-to-side in the narrow blackness. In vain I reached out for any kind of holdfast, receiving sharp jabs of pain as the rough stone planed my hands and knees, causing me to gasp out the last of the air in my lungs.

The darkness became dappled with bright specks of colour, and I knew I had only a few seconds before losing consciousness. One of the colours, in all that dark rushing confusion, seemed to be the size and shape of the amulet, a falling orb that glistered amber. I pulled my arms up tight to my chest. I placed my hands together, as if in prayer. Then I stretched them out above my head like a high-diver. With the last of my strength I reached out, my hand closing around the orb, my last thought of row upon row of sprouting skulls. The narrow chute opened out into the wide space of the laundry room, and the hard earthen floor rose up to meet my plummeting form.

# IV

I landed on my back. Hard and fast, like a carcass slapped down on a butcher's block. A light wind caressed my face, and I realised that I was not in the laundry room. I had teleported, to quote Morgan, 'in the nick of time.' But where was I? My last thought had been of the skulls protruding from the ground. That was it; the amulet had returned me to Cardiff.

As I lay there I was struck by a wave of physical pain, of an intensity I had not experienced since my long-ago mortal years. Perhaps this was the absence of the Grail, starting to take its toll? Or perhaps there was simply a limit to the amount of punishment even an immortal body could take. Scarcely an inch of me was un-afflicted by one hurt or another. However, I reasoned that I could bear my burden of bruises long enough to find Sir Gawain and his men and alert them to the invasion of the dead. Or to come to their aid, if such a warning proved to be too late.

Concerning Sir Lancelot and the impending arrival of Morgan and the Master, my thoughts were in a state of jumbled anguish. Everything I had just seen and heard reasserted itself in my mind, like a nightmare from which one believes one has awoken, only to feel the bogeyman's dread tap on one's shoulder. I felt naked and fully exposed to the world, as if I had been divested not merely of my clothing but of my very flesh, stripped down to my bare bones.

Very much, in fact, like the skull that suddenly loomed into view above me like a gibbous moon in the dark sky. The face was upside down, held in place by a skeletal spine, and it fixed me with its hollow-socket stare. As strange as it may sound, this gaunt apparition seemed like the only one who understood how it felt to be me at that precise moment. The skeleton smiled at me. I was about to return his goodwill when I realised, of course, that it was nothing of the sort; merely the permanent rictus grin of the dead.

In a flash he jabbed a sword of jagged black down towards my heart. Such was my state of utter desolation that I had a good mind to just lie there and receive it. Instead, I rolled to the left and jumped to my feet, inches beyond the range of his second swipe. Now that I was up, I saw that only the head, arms and torso of my attacker were visible. Everything below waist level was in the process of emerging, slowly but surely, but as yet still stuck in the ground. I persuaded him against taking a third swipe at me with a well-aimed kick to the cranium. The skull flew off the neck with a loud crack. It bounced on the ground behind him, rolled around in a semi-circle and sprang straight back up onto the neck joint, as if attached by an invisible cord of elastic. The skeleton shook his head, flexed his shoulders, and returned to his assault with renewed vigour.

I took a step backwards and felt a tearing in my left trouser leg. Looking down, I saw another skeleton, similarly half-emerged and just within range. He was one of a great horde that stretched up the road as far as I could see, all straining towards me and slicing frantically at the air. I turned back to my original attacker. He was the nearest of a large group that sprouted up in front of the pedestrianised shopping area, and I realised that I had teleported to the main road that circled the city centre. Ahead of me on the black horizon stood the stadium and, somewhere in the city's streets, Sir Gawain and his men. Behind me, on the other side of the road, a bus had been abandoned at its stop, cast adrift in a skeletal sea. Thunder rumbled and heavy drops of rain began to fall. My first attacker had now emerged to his pelvic bone. Once again he bestowed upon me his grim grin of the grave.

This time, I smiled back.

✝

One might expect a skull to be smooth and slippery, ill-suited to providing the kind of purchase required underfoot, should circumstances force one to use it as a stepping stone. In reality they provide a gratifying amount of traction, their surface pitted and knobbled, just the thing for gaining a foothold when one's progress is imbued with the kind of haste that only comes from having an army of skeletons whirling swords at one's legs. It was by no means a perfect causeway, however, as I discovered when, thrown off step by a particularly vicious swipe, I lost my balance and found myself on my hands and knees, surrounded by five torsos keen to take full advantage of my slip. Two swords whistled towards either side of my neck. I threw myself down flat, as three more swords clashed above me. I was up on my feet as soon as they all withdrew their blades. Their eagerness to skewer me was to my advantage, for their second strike was even more uncoordinated than the first. By jumping up and dodging the blades, I was able to use the mesh of criss-crossed swords as a spring board and resume my skull-stepping progress to the abandoned bus. I dived inside the open doors, black blades scything at my heels.

Several swords hit the front window, thrown in fury at my brazen route through their midst. Well, my next move would do nothing to alleviate their outrage. The bus key had been left in the ignition. I turned it, and the engine spluttered into life. At the sound of the bus, the skeletons directly ahead of me pushed at the ground in a desperate attempt to lever out their legs. The vehicle juddered as I ground it into gear and pressed my foot down hard on the accelerator.

The bus lurched forwards. The first skeletons I hit bent and snapped with the slight resistance of a wishbone. The next group yielded with an immediate, full crack as I picked up speed. Then the vehicle hit its stride, a flurry of skulls flying up and splintering the windscreen as I ploughed across the road and into the pedestrianised town centre. In the rear view mirror, I saw that no sooner were the bones strewn in my wake than they started to move, skittering back into their respective skeletons and reforming once more.

What with the darkness of the evening, the thick sheets of rain, and skulls flying like giant hailstones, it was some task to navigate my way without driving into a shop window or hitting one of the numerous trees and streetlights in my path. The skeletons were now fully emerged and providing much greater resistance to the severely battered bus. Some of them were clinging to the side, smashing their bony fists against the windows. My driver's door was relatively clear, and to the right of the street the going seemed a little easier. I swung the bus over and picked up speed.

Now that the front of the bus was less obstructed, I could see what lay ahead. A battalion of skeletons had surrounded the band of men I presumed to be Sir Gawain's civilian recruits. They were outnumbered and outperformed, and had closed ranks around a smashed-up shop front. I coaxed a fresh burst of speed from the bus and drove it into the rear guard of the skeletons. Their ranks temporarily scattered, and I ran from the bus and into their midst.

†

In less apocalyptic times, the shop had sold electronic goods. Most of the contents had been destroyed by whatever had shattered the glass frontage, but a few television screens remained intact, both in the window display and inside the shop itself. And there, standing in the smouldering ruins, stood Sir Gawain. He had his back to the entrance and was gazing at a looped replay of Sir Lancelot's interview. His sword hung limply by his side. Outside, his recruits had been reduced to a dozen or so survivors. I picked up a blade and evened out the odds as best I could, but here it was the same story — as soon as one of the skeletons fell, it restored itself to fighting fitness in a matter of seconds. These men were in dire need of their distracted leader. Entreating them to hold off the horde as best as they could, I stepped through the broken glass of the window and walked over to him.

"Sir Gawain," I said, placing my hand on his shoulder. "I take it you have seen Sir Lancelot's interview?" He turned to me, and it was as if he were experiencing one of the Master's trance-like episodes. "What was it all for, Lucas?" he said vacantly. "What was it all *for*, if we could have gone back?"

"I am struggling to make sense of recent events myself, Sir Gawain, but now is not... now is not the time. For such reflection."

"They died for nothing. All of them. We sentenced them to death! And for this? *This* is what the Eternal Quest comes down to, at the end of it all?"

"It is a lot to take in, Sir Gawain, but unless we muster our forces, the day will be lost." Several screams and the dull clank of jagged swords from outside did not bode well.

Sir Gawain's eyes filled with tears. "The day is already lost. It was lost when he lied through his teeth. What kind of a man does that to his friends?"

"The Master had our best interests at heart, Sir Gawain."

"Arthur? Oh, I'm long past caring about Arthur. Lancelot's the one I blame for all this. He's the one I listened to. He's the one I trusted."

The sounds of battle outside ceased, suddenly and ominously. Two skull heads, their footsteps crunching in the glass, peered through the broken window and looked at us.

"We must get to Sir Lancelot before the Master does," I said.

Sir Gawain wiped his eyes and sniffed. "You said it, Lucas."

The first skeleton attacked, swinging back his sword. Sir Gawain's fist punched through its rib cage and yanked out the spine with the startled head still attached. With three mighty strokes, Sir Gawain used it to smash the second skeleton to pieces, then jammed the head and spine of the first skeleton into a wide-screen television in a shower of sparks. He picked up the smoking television set and slammed it down onto the bones of the second skeleton, before they could reassemble.

"Let's go," he said.

# V

Back inside the stadium, the roof had been damaged beyond repair. It remained open to the supernatural elements, rain sweeping down in veil-like sheets that drenched any remaining dryness out of my clothes. I stood in the centre of the pitch and looked up to the interview room where Sir Lancelot had recently delivered his crushing revelation. A great number of people still stood within. It seemed like the best place to start looking for him. Yes, I really should go there, *poste haste*. I should tell him of Sir Gawain's chagrin. I should tell him of the Master's approaching wrath. I should tell him of the skeleton army of the dead and the return of Morgan Le Fay.

Yet this word 'should' was like a sledge-hammer, striking repeated blows on the ground in front of me, until a small crack opened up beneath my feet. The crack became a fissure, like the very first movement of a tectonic split dividing a continent, and I felt as if I were standing with my feet placed in two separate lands. My right foot stood in the place of service. Honour, duty and knighthood; the Master and the Eternal Quest. My left was in the new domain created by Sir Lancelot's revelation. So I stood there awhile, shifting my weight from either side, wondering which territory would receive my next step and claim my allegiance.

Five soldiers stumbled past me, dragging the carcass of a dragon across the muddy pitch. One of them lost his grip on the scaly wet wing, stumbled, and went down head-first towards the mire. Instinctively, I grabbed his arm and pulled him up before he hit the ground. He gave me a brief nod of thanks, and I realised that in performing this action I had stepped back into the territory of service, in which I had once felt so at home. Very well, then. As I seemed to be incapable of doing anything else, that was where I would remain for now.

Some way behind me, Sir Gawain had been waylaid by a group of late-comers to his civilian recruitment drive. Upon our arrival at the stadium in the remains of the bus, he had barged his way through the military barricade outside, hell bent on getting to Sir Lancelot, when some faintly familiar faces had caught up with him. At first I did not recognise them, and neither did Sir Gawain, which is why they had followed him inside the stadium with increasing persistence, until they had collared him in the tunnel used by the players to emerge onto the field. These men were kitted out with swords, which they now swung at Sir Gawain with slow menace, trying to provoke a reaction with blows and taunts. But his step was resolute and their goading fell on deaf ears, like a father late for work shrugging off whining pleas from his restless children to stop and play.

Then I realised where I had seen these men before. They were the patrons of Jennifer's Nightclub we had encountered in what seemed like another century, but must have been only — what, four days ago? I recognised them by their colourful bruises and even more colourful language. Sir Gawain's eyes were fixed firmly beyond them on the pitch, his physical progress stopped only when the gang surrounded him and made it impossible for him to pass. This development spurred me on to find Sir Lancelot. If nothing else, it was something to be getting on with.

†

Sir Lancelot was indeed still in the interview room, and no less surrounded than Sir Gawain, by a mixture of high-ranking generals and several of the soldiers who had done so well in taking down the dragons. The last time I had seen him, the tone of those around him had been one of mutual respect and self-congratulation. Now their mood had turned decidedly sour. Some of the screens in the room showed pictures of the advancing skeleton army, tearing up the city, killing all those unfortunate enough to stand in their way. Others depicted dragons in different cities, some as far away as the continent, all suffering similar assaults to Cardiff.

"We need to deploy more trained men straight away," said one general. "Damn dragons just keep coming, hitting every major city on the planet."

"Never mind that, what about *those*?" said another, indicating footage of the skeleton army. "Where the hell did they come from?"

"Annwn, I presume," muttered Sir Lancelot. He had his back to the door where I was standing, looking down out of the window towards the group around Sir Gawain, who had now spilled out of the players' corridor and onto the pitch.

"Why didn't you tell us about those things, Lancelot?"

"They were something of a surprise to me, too."

"How many more of the buggers are there?"

"I honestly don't know. Hundreds?"

"So what in God's name are you going to do about it?"

Out on the pitch Sir Gawain was now fully engaged in fighting off the group. They had not reckoned with the head of steam he had built up for Sir Lancelot's benefit, and were already halved in number. That still left ten against one, however. "I'm going to help my friend," said Sir Lancelot, drawing his sword.

"Sir Lancelot. Wait," I said, as he passed me in the doorway.

"What is it, Lucas?" he said, not the least bit surprised at my return.

"I would like a quick word," I said.

"We are past the point of words." Sir Lancelot barged out onto the tiered seating of the stadium.

"Indeed, but there are matters to appraise you of," I said.

"Butler to the last, huh? Still clinging to the tatters of duty. So what is it now, Lucas? 'Matters' to appraise me of? What matters?"

His voice sounded how I felt. He sounded his age.

"Nothing," I said. "Nothing at all."

The noise of an approaching helicopter filled the air. I needed no sight of it to tell me it came from the west. I required no amulet to show me who it contained. Sir Lancelot jumped down the steps, four apiece, and ran across the rain-logged pitch. I took the steps leisurely, one at a time. When I reached the last one I walked to the centre of the bottom row, pushed down a plastic seat, sat down, and watched.

# VI

Sir Gawain's remaining opponents had gained the upper hand. What they lacked in art they made up for in relentless rage, and by such a pummelling he was pushed up against the siding surrounding the far side of the pitch, opposite to where I was positioned on the tiered seating. From my direction, Sir Lancelot ran over the soggy grass, his sword drawn. Sir Gawain shouted out his name and the approaching knight mistook his exclamation as a cry for help, increasing his speed despite the slippery ground. The sight of Sir Lancelot galvanised Sir Gawain, and with one neat head-butt he floored his leading opponent, taking the sword from him as he fell.

So it was that, when Sir Lancelot engaged his nearest man, he was surprised to find himself also fending off a twin-sword assault from Sir Gawain within the fray. This naturally demanded that Sir Lancelot respond in kind, and the battle took up a strange formation. The duelling knights were surrounded by an attacking circle, maintaining a joint defence only to better accomplish the other's destruction. The stalemate was a temporary one. Both were forced to look to their flanks with increasing frequency, as they found themselves steadily backed against the siding. Their attackers took full advantage of their waning stamina. Sir Lancelot took a gash across his torso. Sir Gawain received a pommel blow on the head. Their wounds became marked and many. The fight was nearly over.

While the three sides played out their curious conflict, the sound of the helicopter had grown ever closer. Now it descended on the pitch, whirling rotor blades rippling the puddled earth. Before it touched down, the Master dropped from within and hit the ground running, stopping only to snatch up a sword from the battlefield. Sir Lancelot pushed his way out of the mêlée and ran to meet him. As soon as Sir Lancelot's support was removed from the equation, the tide turned against Sir Gawain, and he disappeared beneath the blows of his remaining foes.

Sir Lancelot and the Master sprinted towards each other with the speed of jousters on horseback. When there was still a lance-length between them, Sir Lancelot took a flying leap and spun towards Master with a twisted grace. The Master brought his sword up to block his move. Sir Lancelot brought his sword down. Their blades met with a clash that made the very air resound. Both men fell back at the impact, as if at the force of an explosion. The Master was first up. He hacked down at Sir Lancelot, chopping up so many clods of turf that they filled the air like a flock of blackbirds. Each blow was accompanied by a hail of recriminations, hurled at Sir Lancelot with no less fury than the sword, their content lost in the wind and rain.

Sir Lancelot parried and rolled, countering the verbal and physical strikes with his own. But no sooner was he up on his feet than the Master delivered a kick to the stomach, doubling him over, followed by an upper cut to Sir Lancelot's jaw that sent him aquaplaning backwards along the sodden turf.

Morgan Le Fay emerged from the landed helicopter and hovered a foot above the mud, holding her arms wide, basking in the scene before her. There was a hubbub behind me as the military and media men left their booth, gawping slack-jawed at the scene. Many of them had their weapons drawn. But their attention was not focused on the fight. For some reason they were looking over to the far siding, where Sir Gawain lay buried somewhere beneath his still furious attackers.

As for me, I could not take my eyes from the centre of the pitch where the Master and Sir Lancelot were locked in close combat. Each successive sword stroke threatened to be the last, dolorous blow. So hard and so fast did they fight that their movements became a blur, until at last they slowed down in the strange manner to which I was now wearily accustomed. I looked at Morgan. She was conducting their drawn out movements in slow motion, head tipped back and laughing, determined to stretch out the final instant and savour every last drop of her revenge.

In such half-speed, the Master swung his sword at Sir Lancelot's shoulder. Sir Lancelot deflected it, and with his next move the Master aimed for Sir Lancelot's neck. Again, the block came to meet it. But this time Sir Lancelot's defensive stroke skimmed the Master's sword belt around his waist. The point of Sir Lancelot's blade sliced through the fastening of Excalibur's scabbard, which came loose and fell to the ground.

I stood up, the plastic seat beneath me flipping back with a dead *thunk*. The Master dropped his sword. He touched his hand to his neck and looked at the blood on his fingers. I ran down the steps and vaulted over the siding, slipping and slithering across the pitch. Morgan must have overlooked my presence, or else did not consider me a threat, for I found that I was able to move at a normal pace. I willed myself to run faster, urging my tired and aching legs onwards.

I was now close enough to hear the Master cough. To see blood spill out through the sides of his mouth. Close enough to see the slashes on his face, and a large bite mark appear on his neck — the jaw print of a werewolf. To see the bite widen, and turn crimson, as if an invisible animal were tearing at him anew, though the wound was received a long, long time ago.

Sir Lancelot was down on the ground, clawing at the mud and grass for the Master's scabbard. He was about to pick it up when a skeletal foot stamped down hard on his hand. He cried out in pain as the sharp bone pinned him to the ground. The skeleton stooped down, picked up the scabbard and threw it through the air towards Morgan Le Fay's outstretched arms. Over on the opposite siding, I realised too late what the military men behind me had been staring at. The army of the dead had breached the stadium walls. They were tearing through Sir Gawain's attackers in horrible half-speed, revealing his immobile form, curled up like a foetus in the mud.

Dozens of skeletons poured onto the pitch and surrounded us. They looked to Morgan, awaiting her final command. Sir Lancelot pulled in vain at his pinioned hand. The Master fell face-forward into a widening pool of his own blood.

I closed my eyes and teleported to the only knight I could think of.

# VII

I ran down the collapsed cliff-side, stumbling and staggering. The amulet had taken me directly to Sir Pellinore. Down on the beach below, not far from the Otherworld portal, I saw his inert figure, splayed out on his back. The sand around him was churned up, heavily marked with the signs of a recent skirmish. I knelt beside him and rested his head on my knees. He had lost his jacket, and his T-shirt was soaked in blood.

"Sir Pellinore," I said, and shook him gently but firmly. I could find only the weakest of pulses. "If you have the strength, the Master needs you."

"Herne?" said Sir Pellinore, opening an eye.

"It is Sir Lucas," I said. "We must hurry. We have to go and get Sir Kay, and bring aid to our fellow knights in the field." But even before I spoke the words, I knew how empty they were.

"The Beast turned the tables on me, butler. Got me on the chest — see?"

He pulled up his T-shirt to reveal two large bloody puncture marks from a snake's teeth. "The quest mastered the man, in the end." Sir Pellinore chuckled.

Then he closed his eyes and breathed out his last rattling breath.

✝

Sir Pellinore was a lot heavier than I expected. I had carried him up the cliff from the beach, not knowing where I was going or what to do next, lost in a numb, grief-struck daze. Then I saw Merlin, and had stumbled half way back down the cliff-side towards the cowled wizard when I dropped Sir Pellinore's body. He slid down the scree and came to rest by a rock on the shore. Merlin did not lift a finger to help me. He merely stayed there like a standing stone. It was this more than anything that made me quake with anger and want to throttle him with my bare hands.

"The Eternal Quest is over!" I called to the wizard. "The Master lies on the brink of death."

Merlin nodded.

"I hope you are pleased with yourself," I said.

He nodded again.

"All this is your fault."

He shook his head.

"Do not try to deny it. You knew this would happen if you came back."

He nodded. I laughed, mirthlessly.

"Is there any point in even asking for your help?"

Merlin pointed at the inert body of Sir Pellinore, and then to me, to my bloodstained chest. "This is no time for riddles, damn you!" I shouted, my voice echoing around the rocks. Merlin pointed to his own chest, to the place where an amulet would have hung, had he been wearing one beneath his cloak. His finger traced the outline of a necklace. My hand reached up to my chest. There was nothing there. I was no longer wearing the amulet. Exactly when and where I had lost it, I could not say. But now that I thought about it, I was not sure it had been with me ever since falling off my neck during my tumble down the Camelot laundry chute.

So how on earth had I teleported? This and a hundred other thoughts were vying for utterance when Merlin stepped into the vortex of the Otherworld portal, swirled around a few times, and vanished.

I picked up the body of Sir Pellinore, this time hoisting him over my shoulder more securely in a fireman's lift. I walked towards the portal. The hairs on my head stood up as I approached. My face tingled with what felt like static electricity.

I stepped over the edge, and followed Merlin into the Otherworld.

# Yesterday Three

# I

"We meet at last, Sir Guy of Gisbourne," said Robin Hood. His bow was drawn, the tip of an arrow aimed directly at my heart.

"The pleasure is all mine, so-called Robin of the Hood," I replied.

"You are a good deal shorter than I expected, Sir Guy."

"Your insolence, however, is of precisely the stature I anticipated. Did you really think you could steal from the Sheriff's purse without reaping the full harvest of his wrath?"

"Be that as it may, I have you at an advantage."

"Indeed? How so?"

"Surely even one as distant from the life of the working man as you has heard of my skill with the bow? I could fell you and your lackeys in half a breath," said Robin.

"Though it pains me to admit it, you are correct."

"So give me one good reason not to pierce your black heart and leave your corpse for the crows?"

"I will give you two." A second squad of my men emerged from their hiding place in the greenwood, leading two captives at sword-point. "Friar Tuck and Little John."

"Hello, Robin," grinned the Friar. "What a thing to happen, eh?"

"Came out of nowhere. Had no choice but to surrender," said John, less amused than his companion. "Give the word, Robbie, an' we fight to the death."

"Nobody dies today, John," said Robin Hood. "Sir Guy knows that full well."

"Do I?"

"Yes. You do." Robin Hood seemed to have something in his right eye, for it closed and opened in a sudden spasm.

"Do not be so confident about that," I said. "If you ask me, Robin Hood, you look far from hale and hearty."

"Oh... Do I?"

"Yes, I am afraid that you do. Guards, seize him! Bring him to the castle."

†

"The charges laid against the outlaw Robin Hood are as follows," said the Sheriff of Nottingham. "That in the year of our Lord eleven hundred and ninety eight, he did knowingly steal property of the Crown, namely: five hundred gold marks, fifteen hundred silver marks, thirty pigs, twenty two swords —"

"Twenty six," said Robin Hood, picking his nails.

"Twenty six swords and shields, fifty barrels of mead —"

"Fifty five."

"Suffice to say," I interjected, lest the Sheriff burst a blood vessel, "that the outlaw is guilty of crimes numerous and grievous against the Sheriff of Nottingham, wise and generous administrator of this county."

"Aye, generous to him and his own, while the poor starve to death!"

"Peace, John," said Robin Hood.

"What is the punishment to fit such a list of crimes, Gisbourne?"

"I believe that would be death, Sheriff," I said. "To be more precise, death by firing squad."

"Firing squad?" said the Sheriff. "What the devil is that?"

"I meant archers, Sheriff. My apologies."

"No, don't apologise, I like it. 'Firing squad.' I shall use it again."

"Does the prisoner have any last words?" I said.

"Yes I have actually, Sir Guy," said Robin Hood. "You are *quite sure* that I look far from hale and hearty?"

"Indeed, Robin."

"Not as much as he's about to look, eh, Gisbourne?"

"Most amusingly put, Sheriff."

"Sir Guy, you can't do this," said Friar Tuck. "Not now." He looked at me beseechingly. "Not yet," he added, so that only I could hear.

"The law is the law," I said. "An example must be made. Archers at the ready!" Ten archers drew their bows taut with a sound like the stretching of a great muscle.

"Take aim!"

Robin Hood looked at me without fear or regret. Indeed, if I had to describe his expression in one word, it would be 'peeved.'

"Fire!"

Ten arrows were loosed from their bows. Eight struck him in the torso; two hit wide of the mark. Crimson bloomed on Lincoln green. Robin Hood staggered but did not fall.

"Is that the best you can do?" he laughed.

"Reload," I said.

"No!" said Friar Tuck, attempting to rush forwards. My men held him back. Little John merely watched in silence.

"Fire!"

Another ten arrows, this time all of them hitting their target. Robin Hood fell to his knees and fixed the Sheriff with an unblinking stare. "Now I come to think of it, it wasn't five hundred gold marks at all," said Robin, and spat out a mouthful of blood. "It was a thousand."

"Fire!" screamed the Sheriff. Another ten arrows loosed. Three of them hit Robin Hood in the face; one in each eye, and one in the middle of his forehead.

"That tickled," he said, and lurched backwards into the wall.

"One more round, just to make sure" I said, as Robin Hood slumped to the floor and died.

"Good job, Gisbourne," said the Sheriff.

"Thank you, Sheriff," I replied. "Now cut the throats of those other two, and we shall see about a spot of lunch."

†

The cart bumped and bounced along the pitted track. I tried for the third time to get a suitable grip on the arrow. "Aaaaah!" said Sir Lancelot. "By all the Treasures, be careful, Lucas!"

"I am sorry, Sir Lancelot, but these are far from ideal conditions."

"So stop the bloody cart!"

"We daren't risk it till we clear the district," said Sir Gawain with a grin, the scar already fading on his freshly-renewed throat.

"It would take the edge off the advantage of being dead if we were recognised," said Sir Perceval, taking off his friar's cassock. "By God, this stuff itches."

"Alright, alright," sighed Sir Lancelot. "Just get on with it."

"Aye, Lucas. Lancelot gets the point."

"Shut up, Gawain."

"Sorry, King Harold."

"I mean it!"

I waited until the cart stopped rattling and tried once more to pull the final arrow out of Sir Lancelot's face. The eyeball stretched and quivered around the edges of the arrowhead. Sir Lancelot took another gulp from the flagon of Grail potion.

"Not too much, Sir Lancelot, until I have got it all out."

"Hurry up then!"

The punctured organ yielded the arrow. The elements of Sir Lancelot's eye rearranged themselves as the eyeball resumed its natural shape. Sir Lancelot blinked hard, taking a deep glug from his flagon. "What was that 'one more round, just to make sure' business?"

"I am sorry, Sir Lancelot," I said, turning my attention to the many arrows still sticking out of his chest. "The Master instructed me to make your death appear as convincing as possible."

"*That* I would call over-convincing."

"Fine one you are," said Sir Gawain. " 'That tickled' indeed. Serves ya right. Glory hog."

"Glory hedgehog, more like."

"Ha, good one, Percy."

"Glory's got nothing to do with it. The least I could do was give the people something to remember me by. Five years was the agreement, Lucas, not five months! What the hell happened?"

"A change of plan, Sir Lancelot."

"You don't — ow, watch my nipple! — say."

"The Master is becoming increasingly anxious at the rumours in circulation, concerning his return," I said.

"He's been officially dead for 600 years. Surely no-one believes he's coming back now?" said Sir Gawain.

"The Master pays a great deal of attention to what he refers to as 'tavern talk.' He also feels that Sir Lancelot's current interpretation of the Eternal Quest is, how can I put this —"

"Bloody showing off?"

"I was going to say, a little on the colourful side, Sir Gawain."

"So tell me, Lucas," said Sir Lancelot, "where was this expert on the outlaw tradition today? Why didn't he grace us with a personal appearance? Maybe then he could see some of the 'colourful side' for himself. Like the colour in the cheeks of the villagers, who face a well-fed winter thanks to our hard work."

"As I say, the aforementioned tavern talk has given the Master much cause for concern. He feels it is best that the Eternal Quest enter another period of quietude —"

"What?!"

"— until he can put in place certain measures, to ensure these rumours are dealt with once and for all. To that end, you are to head to France, establish a new identity and lodgings, and await further instructions," I said.

"And what if I say no?" said Sir Lancelot, pulling out the final arrow from his chest with a hard yank. "What if I refuse to twiddle my thumbs for yet another hundred years? Has he got 'certain measures' in place to deal with that?"

"No, Sir Lancelot."

"No, I thought not."

"The Master merely said he was *sure Knight X would do whatever was required to further the greater interests of the Eternal Quest.*"

We all left our seats as the cart took a particularly deep rut. Sir Lancelot had been pressing an arrow tip against his thumb. The force of the jolt broke the skin, the blood congealing as soon as it appeared. He flicked away the scabrous husk.

"Alright then, fine. But tell me one thing, Lucas. Exactly what do you mean by 'tavern talk'?"

# II

*All gentlemen and yeomen bold*
*All drinking men come listen*
*To hear a shining story told*
*With lustre it doth glisten!*

Flagons clashed, sending a sousing of ale down onto my head. The drinkers marked the rhythm of the ballad by stamping their feet on the ground, so that the floorboards of the tavern creaked and see-sawed. This, combined with the falling spray and raucous noise, gave me the fleeting but vivid impression of standing on the deck of a ship in the middle of a wild sea.

*A man so brave and strong and bright*
*That none may share his name-o!*
*The doom of evil in the night,*
*Let villains run in shame-o!*

I tried to banish such thoughts by concentrating on the matter at hand. If, for example, I were to tear up these wooden floorboards, they would serve as an effective means of escape from a disintegrating boat.

No. What was I thinking?

That was not the matter at hand; that was not it at all.

I shook my head to clear the image, and ducked a flying puddle of beer. Sir Pellinore! Yes, that was it. I was here to find Sir Pellinore. I stepped further into the fug of mead and masculinity.

*It is a tale of a knight so fair*
*From whence he came no man can say*

I tapped the shoulder of a stout fellow in front of me. The parts of his face not covered by a wiry black beard were blotched and ruddy, giving him the appearance of a wild boar.

"Excuse me," I said, "I wonder if you have seen a certain fellow I happen to be seeking?"

"Maybe," he replied. "Whasse look like?"

"He is of my approximate age and height, though somewhat more dishevelled in appearance."

"Whassis name?"

*But yet he is beyond compare*
*This noble man we call Sir Kay!*
*Kay! Kay! His name is Kay!*
*His legend grows with every day*

"He does not often have cause to give his name," I said, conscious of aggressive scrutiny from porcine eyes.

*So raise a cup and drink with me...*
*To the greatest man in history!*

"But if he had, you may know him by the title of Sir Pellinore."

At this the music stopped, as if the name had ordered me one awkward silence, instantly delivered. The hog-man grunted into the quiet. "Garr!" he said. "The devil is among us!" Before I could say 'no, he is not,' rough hands were pulling me through the angry throng and out into the sharp night air.

In the field behind the tavern, a large pile of dry wood was stacked around a central stake. Some distance away from this, a small outhouse stood by the fringe of a forest next to a makeshift gallows, created from the nearest tree, a length of rope, and a barrel. The motley band of locals spilled out of the pub and gathered around me. Some of them held flaming torches. Others brandished sharp agricultural tools with an enthusiasm that suggested they were not about to be used for the purpose for which they were designed.

"Ho, Tom! We've got another one!" said the hog-man.

"Have we now," said Tom. "Best be getting on with it, then." At his signal, several drinkers walked to the outhouse while another brought a second barrel and length of rope over to the tree.

"Another one of whom, may I ask?" I said, trying and failing to loosen my shoulders from the tight grip of trotter hands.

"As if you don't know!" said Tom, clearly the master of whatever unsavoury ceremony was about to transpire. "In the last days, before the return of King Arthur (his name be praised) and the start of his new Golden Age, certain false knights will walk among us. Only one man is worthy to pave the way for King Arthur (his name be praised) and that is Sir Kay, who even now fights in disguise for the cause of the common folk, with his brave band of merry men."

"He robs from the rich and gives to the poor!" said one fellow, still ballad-minded.

"Any other knights claiming to be of his court are demons in disguise," hog-face hissed in my ear. "Sent from Hell to deceive the hearts of men. Like this 'Sir' Pellinore. Ain't that right, Tom?"

"I saw it with me own eyes. Found him in the forest half dead, gored by a wild animal. Took him to the village, and by sundown his wounds had gone! Babbling, he was; full of talk of dragons. Claims he can speak their language. And *I* says, them that talks with dragons, is like to be warlocks!"

"And them that looks for warlocks, is of that same warlock company!"

Tom's lackeys returned from the outhouse with the pinioned person of Sir Pellinore. It was fruitless to attempt to unravel such a tangle of supposition and superstition. Clearly, a more direct approach was required.

"Did I say Sir Pellinore?" I said. "A simple mistake on my part, easily explained. My name is William Rees of Dyfed, a wandering tailor. I was searching for a Lord *Palomides*, by whom I am commissioned to fashion a garment for his forthcoming nuptials to Lady —"

"What ho, Sir Lucas!" said Sir Pellinore.

"Liar!" shouted the hog-man. "He's of the warlock's company an' all!"

"There's only one thing to do with warlocks," said Tom, "And that's hang 'em, draw 'em and quarter 'em!"

"Then burn 'em!"

"Aye, then burn 'em! So that the name of our once and future King Arthur (his name be praised) should be... praised." The trotters tightened and I was shoved towards the gallows alongside Sir Pellinore.

"Evening, footman," he whispered. "Between you and me, I seem to have mislaid my Grail snifter in all this kerfuffle."

I felt in my pocket for my own Grail flask. There was a small amount of fluid remaining, but I doubted it would be enough for the two of us. Still less when one factored in the effects of hanging, drawing, quartering and burning. None of our company had experienced such a thorough execution before. I was not at all sure how well we might recover, not to mention who would administer the required dosage.

My hands were tied behind my back and a coarse noose pulled over my head. As it scraped against my nose I inhaled a whiff of damp rope that sent my stomach lurching as if it were trying to climb up through my insides.

"I must say, you are brave men indeed," I said, trying not to let my voice quiver.

"Thankee," said Tom.

"Brave; but mistaken."

"Oh?"

"This Sir Pellinore is no warlock."

"Ha! Says you!"

Hog-man spat on the ground. "An' what makes you so sure?"

"Because *I* am a warlock." The noose was pulled tight around my neck. It imbued my voice with a strangulated pitch that did little to give my words the desired degree of menace.

"We knows that!" The crowd roared with laughter.

"That's why we're hanging, drawing and quartering you!"

"*Then* burning you!"

"But I am no ordinary warlock," I said. "I am Herne the Hunter."

"Ha, ha!"

"Herne!"

"Hark at him!"

"Set us free immediately, or I will use my magic on you."

The crowd laughed even harder, imagining the spectacle, which was exactly what I wanted them to do.

"Do not force me to demonstrate my powers by further provoking my wrath." I waited for the fresh hilarity this generated to pass.

"What's all this, footman?" said Sir Pellinore.

"A ruse, Sir Pellinore," I whispered from the corner of my mouth. "This is your last chance!" I shouted. "Let us go, or suffer the consequences!"

As I hoped, my words were having the desired effect on highly impressionable minds. Already some of the mob had lost their mirth and replaced it with a nervous sense of expectation.

"I've had enough of these games," said Tom. "We're wasting precious drinking time! Remove the barrels!" Our hangman took a step towards me, but I was gratified to see him pause for a moment before doing so.

"Stay your hand, and I shall spare you," I said to him. He looked to Tom and the hog-man.

"What are you waiting for?" roared Tom. "Move!" The hangman still hesitated. A cloud covered the moon. A gust of wind guttered the torches and sent a whispering rustle through the trees.

The perfect moment.

I drew myself up to full height, teetering on tip-toe on top of the barrel, and deepened my voice. The effect of the tight noose changed my tone from comical to sinister.

"Foul creatures from the deep places. Harken to the summons of Herne! Dread demons that dwell in the dark. Answer my call and come to my aid!"

The hangman took a couple of steps backwards, bumping into the man behind him.

"From the depths of Annwn, I summon thee, Glatisant, the Questing Beast!"

The wind whipped up a treat and my confidence in the charade increased a hundredfold. A breaking storm at this moment would be of great benefit to my plan.

"Let the noise of your arrival fill the air! The sound of sixty hounds baying for blood!"

"Whassat?" said one, dropping his cudgel. "Was that dogs barking?"

"Yes! I hear it too, Herne!" said Sir Pellinore beside me.

"Mighty Beast of Herne! Head of a snake, with fangs like knives! Body of a beast to bear down on your prey! Feet of a stag, no man may out-run! Sweep out of the forest and devour my foes!"

Lightning split the sky directly above, a flash of inverted antlers over my head. The first drops of rain fell, hissing as they hit the torches. The crowd started to split into smaller groups, wavering, uncertain. "Ah hell, I'll do it myself," said Tom, but he was knocked over by the hog-man, who ran squealing for the tavern.

"Behold, the Beast! Behind you and before you! Around you and about you! See its forked tongue flicker! Hear its ravening roar!"

Thunder rolled. The rest of the crowd screamed and scattered.

"Yell hound, yelper, hound of doom! Heed the Hunter's call! Destroy these people, destroy them all!"

Tom got back on his feet and froze, a look of utter terror in his eyes as he saw something move in the trees. "Call it off! Call it off! I was about to set you free!" With shaking hands, Tom cut my bonds and removed the noose from my neck. I took his knife and released Sir Pellinore, and we stepped down from the barrels. "Herne, I beg you," quailed Tom, "keep your foul Beast at bay!"

Seeing as the ruse had served its purpose, I was about to do just that when a mighty gust of wind shook the forest, as if my 'Questing Beast' were about to burst forth from the branches. Tom screamed and looked above him. Whatever he imagined he saw passed over his head, blocking the way back into the tavern. He uttered another chilling cry and ran headlong into the woods, the Beast apparently at his heels.

"That was decidedly more effective than I hoped," I said, rather pleased with myself. "It is always gratifying when one can escape from a tight spot without resorting to swords and fisticuffs. Would you not agree, Sir Pellinore?"

Sir Pellinore was rubbing his chafed wrists, his eyes glazed over with a film of wonder. "Such quarry as I have never seen... Never dreamed to see, not in all my years of beast lore. A monster of many parts. What greater quest can there be for Pellinore?"

"Surely you did not — come now, Sir Pellinore, you jest! There was no actual beast, it was merely the power of my suggestion. A conjuring trick, if you will."

Sir Pellinore ignored me. He started to jog towards the forest.

"Sir Pellinore, where are you going?"

"To hunt that Questing Beast," he shouted. "I will master it. Or else I shall bleed of the best blood of my body!"

In a last flash of lightning, Sir Pellinore was absorbed by the trees.

✝

"Stay where you are!" said Sir Kay. One step closer — just one step, Lucas — and I throw the whole damn lot into the fire!"

The storm was in full swing now, trying with all its might to get inside the small cottage. Lightning illuminated a trapped nerve pulsing in Sir Kay's temple, as if a maggot were trying to force its way out from under his skin. I shivered at the image, and then from the cold, for the storm had soaked me to the marrow. The thought of Sir Pellinore running wild in such weather was most disturbing, but there was little I could do for the moment, especially when other pressing matters were at hand. I leaned forward into the roaring warmth of the fire.

"Keep back!" A strip of parchment slipped from the rope-tied bundle in Sir Kay's arms, inches away from the hungry flames.

"Please, Sir Kay, if you would only move away from the fireplace and sit down, I will explain the reason for my visit."

"No! I've had enough, Lucas. I'm at my wit's end."

"Then at least step forward a small pace. Your tunic is starting to smoulder."

"Good! I shall burn myself, along with these infernal pages!"

"Come now, Sir Kay. You and I both know that would achieve little more than a temporary unpleasantness you would only regret in the morning. Along with your hangover."

"Don't care. And I'll have you know I've had very drink to little. To drink. Very little to drink."

Lightning flashed again, and I noticed that the room was in dire need of a thorough clean. Mercifully, Sir Kay took half a step down from the hearth, still holding the bundle of parchment close to his chest.

"I appreciate the enormous strain you are under," I said. "If you would only take a seat —"

"There's just no pleasing him! Never. I've spent years trying to get it right. Adding this and removing that. Tweaking here, revising there. And for what? Who ever hears *The Chronicles of Sir Kay*? No-one, because they're secret! I'm the laughing stock of every tale-teller and minstrel from here to France."

"I have been meaning to talk to you on this whole matter of minstrels. It seems that several of your songs are in wide circulation."

"Really? Are they?" Sir Kay perked up a touch. "I have been dabbling in ditties lately. More of a side-line, really, seeing as how I'm not allowed to tell any of my proper stories."

"That is partly the reason for my visit, Sir Kay. Your ballads are creating an unhealthy atmosphere of tavern talk, in which the activities of the Eternal Quest are attracting undue attention."

"And we can't have that, can we?" said Sir Kay, but his smile spoke otherwise.

"The common mind is very impressionable on the matter of the Master's return; even now, all these years later. I myself have had first hand experience of it, this very night."

"You can't blame me for the pot-valiant prattling of mead-muddled morons."

"Perhaps not, but there is also the matter of verity."

"I don't know what you mean."

"I think Sir Lancelot would have a few things to say about the content of some of your ballads," I said.

"I'm sure he would. But the preening of Lance Hood is no concern of mine, and it doesn't make my complaint any less valid. The only person who ever pays any attention to my work is Arthur, and even then it's only so he can pick holes in it. What's the point of it all?"

"It is funny you should ask, Sir Kay —"

"I won't make any more changes. I refuse. I'd sooner burn the whole lot of it."

"Please, Sir Kay, if you would only sit —"

"*And stop telling me to sit down!*" Sir Kay stepped back up onto the hearth again. "It's alright for you! You're out there with the rest of the gang, having adventures, and, and, larks!"

"Larks?"

"*Jolly* larks! And all this so-called 'Secret Historian' gets to do is write about it. And even then, Arthur's not happy! Well *you* can sit down for once, Lucas. Sit down and listen to my latest instalment. And after you've listened, you can go back and tell him it's not changing. Not by one single word."

I sighed, pulling up a chair and sitting down at the table.

"That's better," he said. "Now, pour yourself some wine."

"I would really rather —"

"Pour it!"

I managed to find enough dregs in the several flagons on the table to passably fill a goblet. Sir Kay perched on the hearth, placing the pile of parchment beside him. He sniffed, and rubbed his red-rimmed eyes with a sleeve. "Now. Where did we get up to last time?"

"Your last rewrite concerned the Master seizing the Grail."

"Ah yes. 'The Escape from the Otherworld.' Are you sitting comfortably?"

I pulled my chair closer to the fire. My clothes started to gently steam dry.

"Yes."

Sir Kay picked up a squashed scroll from the top of the bundle and unrolled it. "Then I shall begin:

# III

...and no sooner had King Arthur seized the Grail, than the air was rent by a piercing cry.

"Hark! Mermaidens!" said Pellinore.

Lancelot shook his head. "Le Fay. Sire, we must not tarry." But though King Arthur knelt within an arm's reach of Sir Lancelot, it was as if a vast distance stood between them.

"Sire, please," said Sir Lucas the butler.

"Haste!" said Pellinore, laying a hand upon the King's shoulder and breaking the spell.

"Yes, of course, we must fly," said Arthur, getting to his feet. "To the Prydwen!" Whereupon the Grail did rise up into the air and follow behind King Arthur like a faithful hound.

They had scarcely gone ten paces when the cry of Morgan Le Fay rose to a shriek. As if at the bidding of this foul scream, the walls of the Glass Fortress splintered like winter ice pressed by a boot. The cracks widened, revealing soldiers made entirely of glass and with the heads of dogs (these heads were *also* made of glass, should any man have cause to wonder). These strange warriors blocked the way ahead and behind. Death most certain stared the four knights full in the face, as the dog soldiers advanced with their swords of crystal, snarling as if they had never been fed. "Now we are done for!" cried Sir Lancelot, with damsel-like distress.

But just then, when all hope seemed lost, the heads of a dozen of the dogs shattered into smithereens! With a mighty battle cry, Sir Kay arrived on the scene, felling twelve of the monsters in a single stroke. So thoroughly did he set upon them that Sir Gawain, who was following behind, was forced to cry, "Save some for me, Sir Kay!" Thanks to the timely inspiration afforded by this brave and bold hero, the six-strong company fought their way back into the entrance hall of the Glass Fortress.

Her warriors defeated, the unseen Morgan howled with rage. The shining walls darkened. The roof above the knights cracked and fell in a swift sharp blizzard. The company ran for the doorway, jumping and rolling and leaping through the raining shards, and not a single cut upon their heads did this deadly ice sustain. Once outside, the six and the Grail found themselves upon the coast, where a blessed sight met their eyes. King Arthur's ship the Prydwen, moored beyond the surf with Sir Perceval standing on the deck, their small landing boat still beached and waiting on the shore. "Raise anchor!" King Arthur cried out to Perceval, as twelve hands pushed the landing boat into the waves, the Grail alighting in its stern.

The evil enchantress rose up from out of her dark castle, in the land of Annwn that lies behind the Glass Fortress. Full wroth was she at the raiding of the Otherworld's greatest treasure. "Do not look back!" said Sir Lancelot. Only the heart of Sir Kay was stout enough not to heed his warning. Glancing o'er his manly shoulder, he saw the form of Le Fay filling the sky, tall as a tower, churning up the earth as if the land itself had turned to ocean. A torrent of rocks and sand crashed into the sea. But fortune smiled upon the fleeing knights, for instead of capsizing their small vessel, the rising wave carried them past the breakers and out to the waiting Prydwen, where Perceval pulled them safely aboard.

Seeing the advantage her rash rage had afforded her foes, Le Fay's mood blackened a hundredfold. Mustering all her magic, she summoned forth a wild tempest that tore up the water around the Prydwen. The sea writhed as if it were a nest of angry serpents, and lo, it was indeed full of serpents, and angry ones at that. They champed their pin-like teeth in the ship's wake, crunching up the wooden deck of the boat beneath the knights' feet. The elements united in the service of the Dark Queen, pouring down on the seven with all their might. The blasting wind battered mast and sail. Rods of rain beat down on the deck. The Prydwen rolled on a gathering wave, pitching up a mountain of water into the death-dark sky.

"Secure the Grail!" said King Arthur, and Perceval and Lucas lashed it fast to the mast, while the rest of the knights turned their hands to tiller and sail.

"The ship will be torn apart!" howled Perceval.

"Sturdy is the vessel that brought us to the Otherworld shore," said King Arthur. "And sound the sail that outran the Flying Squids of Atlantis. By my soul, *she will not fail us now!*"

The Prydwen bared its teeth into the eye of the storm, the gigantic wave rising ever higher, until the ship sat near upright on its rear. Barrels slid down the deck and down into the sea, swallowed up by the champing serpents. The knights grabbed for hand-holds, hanging tight with all their might. All save Perceval, who could not secure a grip fast enough, pawing and clutching in vain at the slippery deck. A serpent bit through the stern and opened wide its jaws to welcome him. With a desperate cry, Perceval fell head-first down the length of the ship. But swift and strong was the arm of Sir Kay, who caught the plummeting Perceval by the foot and held him fast, a hair's breadth from the snapping teeth, until the serpent slid back into the deep.

Up and up the Prydwen climbed, till it seemed as if her prow would puncture the roof of the world. Then, with a sad groan, the deck of the ship began to break apart. At this, King Arthur at the mast fell to his knees before his new-won treasure.

"Deliver us," he said to the Grail, and his voice, though still and small, came clear to the ears of every knight in the midst of that squall. "Deliver us back to our own sweet shore." At his words the Grail did seem to glow like the first light of dawn. All turned their eyes to the heavens and lo, there indeed was the dawn — shining down over the crest of the wave, a small patch of blessed light caressing the blighted deck.

Morgan Le Fay poured the last of her powers into the seething sea, which snatched at the ship with watery fingers, pulling at its sides, ripping down the sail and sousing the deck so that the knights knew not if they were on the water or under it. But the Prydwen heeded her not, pressing on to the peak of the wave, where it seemed to pass briefly through a doorway. There, all of a sudden, the foul malevolence of the maelstrom fell away. And Morgan Le Fay was no longer in the water and the air, but somewhere back in the depths of her realm. There was a sound like a door being slammed with a thooming thud. The scream of the witch was replaced by the keening cry of sea birds. The Prydwen, still atop the giant wave, was thrust out into the cold fresh air of a summer morn.

Bold now was the light, bold and bright, warming each knight to his bones and causing him to laugh aloud with the brimming joy in his breast. The Prydwen soared high above the wide green meadows of the sea, like a swan, like a ship of the sky. And it seemed to all seven souls as if they were sailing a course into the very heart of the sun...

✝

...Well? What do you think?" said Sir Kay.

The front of my tunic had dried out nicely but my cloak still clung to my back, cold and clammy. "Most entertaining, Sir Kay," I said.

"As requested, I've toned down my own role a *lot* since the last draft," he said.

"It is much improved in that respect, Sir Kay. Though, if memory serves, was it not the Master who saved Sir Perceval from the sea serpent's jaws?"

"That's what I said, wasn't it?"

"I believe in the current draft it was you who performed that heroic function."

Sir Kay cast his eye back over the scroll. "You're right. Hang on, though. It couldn't have been Arthur. He was next to the Grail at the mast. He *had* to be, in order to speak to it, remember?" I tried to cast my mind back to the episode in question, but found, as I often did, that my own memory of events was overlaid by the many subsequent revisions of Sir Kay's story.

"I shall make the necessary changes," he said.

"Before you do, perhaps I might come to the reason —"

"Hold your horses, Lucas. I've not finished the story yet:

# IV

Not forever could the brave knights be born aloft on the wings of their escape. And so it was, that the mountain of water upon which the Prydwen perched came foaming down, as all waves must, into the sea.

The ship gave up her ghost and began to split from stern to prow. "Land ahoy!" shouted Perceval, and lo, white cliffs filled the horizon. But the falling wave was full and mighty and would surely dash them onto the rocks without mercy.

"I have not been to Hell and back to be smashed and strewn like driftwood!" said King Arthur. It was then that Sir Kay had another of his justly famous great ideas. This being that each knight should tear up a plank from the disintegrating deck, and by means of balancing upon it, traverse the surf to the safety of the shore.

"As fine a plan as any I've heard!" said Sir Gawain, and with his axe he cleaved seven boards from the deck, while the King unlashed the Grail from the mast, at which the cauldron hovered amidst the splintering chaos, awaiting the event.

And so from out of the shipwreck of the Prydwen there passed a sight most strange. Seven knights balanced on boards of wood, sliding down the tumult of surf as it curled and broke on the shore, the Grail flying ahead like a stone skimming the surface. The wave snatched the dragon-headed prow of the Prydwen from out of the wreckage and threw it after them, like some last remnant of the Otherworld still snapping at their heels. In this manner did the seven pass through the deep and crashing waters and into the shallows, where the prow ran aground. The knights rode the surf until they could ride no more, wading out of the water and flinging themselves down upon the sand.

King Arthur coughed so mightily that Sir Lucas began to beat upon his back to dislodge the brine blocking his breath. But the King pushed the old fuss-pot away, and all then realised that he was seized by a fit of mirth. Tears of laughter mingled with the salt water still running down his cheeks. "Riding the back of the surf! Like mermaidens!" he wheezed.

"Speak for yourself, sire," smiled Lancelot, "I felt like a flying fish."

"But you looked like a mermaiden," said Gawain.

"Nonsense," said Pellinore. "We haven't got the right bits."

"Oh I dunno, Perceval's developing quite a bosom."

"All I need now are your long ginger locks, Gawain, and I'll be quite a catch."

"Stop, stop," said the King, laughing so hard he really did seem on the brink of suffocation.

"I was merely making the basic anatomical observation that we have no tails," said Pellinore, shaking his head as Lucas helped the King to his feet.

"I appreciate the importance of such banter in releasing the accumulated tension of our recent perils, and am loath to bring it to an end," said Sir Lucas.

"Well don't do it, then," said Sir Kay, which set the King off again.

"However, we do not appear to have arrived back at the same shore from whence we departed."

"Thanks for that, Sir Laughsalot."

"What I mean, Sir Gawain, is that the rock type does not resemble the coastline in the vicinity of Camelot."

"Lucas is wise where he is not witty."

"Thank you, Sir Lancelot."

"These white cliffs do not resemble our own."

"Whereas *that*," said Sir Kay, pointing to a veil of smoke besmirching the summer sky above the headland, "does indeed resemble trouble."

†

Wise Sir Kay had put his finger on it yet again. Trouble it certainly was, and of the troll-shaped variety. The seven knights lay hidden in the tall reeds by the side of a stream and watched the beast rampage through a small village. Several dwellings were alight, and many more flattened, some with lifeless limbs protruding from within.

"Well, Pellinore?" said the King.

"Adult male. Mountain species. A grey-back. But there's something about him that's not quite right."

"Apart from the smashing and the killing and the smell?" said Perceval.

Sir Pellinore scratched his chin. "I don't like the look of this."

"Good. Because you're not taking it home," said Lancelot.

"Grey-backs are rare enough in the mountain regions. They keep to caves and crannies, cool dark places where they can stay out of sight. Can't think for the life of me what one would be doing on the coast."

"Visiting relatives?"

"Hush, Perceval. What do you suggest, Pellinore?" said the King.

"Ach, leave this to me," said Sir Gawain. "All I need is my trusty sling."

Sir Gawain selected a pebble from the stream. Striding towards the troll, he set his sling a-whirling, loosing a stone that hit the creature full in the forehead. Whereupon the troll did set his arm a-whirling, loosing a fist which hit Sir Gawain full in the face. By such means did Sir Gawain return to the stream, in a much less dignified manner to that in which he left. At his splashdown the knights made great mirth, save for Sir Lucas, who fished him out, and Sir Pellinore, who stared at the troll, deep in thought.

"I'm alright, Lucas. I thought that might happen," said Gawain. "Just gives me the chance to pick out pebbles for you lot, that's all."

"Us lot?" said Perceval.

"Aye. We hit him with seven stones at the same time. That'll change his tune!"

"To what? *The Ballad of Pulling Our Limbs Off?*"

"Pellinore has it under control," said King Arthur.

Sir Pellinore was indeed walking towards the troll, slowly and quietly, as if approaching a frightened horse. The giant creature snorted and grunted and beat upon its chest, then flung a handful of mud and stones at Sir Pellinore, who calmly dodged aside. He untied his sword belt and made a great show of casting it away. The rest of the knights emerged from their cover, ready to spring into action should their comrade's plan go awry, save for Sir Perceval, who was instructed to remain hidden and guard the Grail.

Sir Pellinore uttered a series of soft clucks and coos. The troll stood very still. Only when Sir Pellinore came up close to the creature did it move, lowering its head so that the knight could whisper something into its ear. Then Sir Pellinore stepped quickly aside as the troll toppled over, hitting the ground with a slam big enough to make the trees jump. At the sound of its falling, several villagers emerged from their dwellings. The man foremost amongst them threw his arms around Sir Pellinore.

"Thank the good Lord, we are saved! You killed the beast!"

"No," said Pellinore. "He wanted to die. All I did was tell him he could."

"I do not understand," said the King.

"Neither do I. It is hard to put into words. More of a feeling I got. As if the creature no longer had any place in this world."

"Whatever the means of its downfall, I beg you to tell us to whom we owe our lives," said the man, finally releasing Pellinore from his embrace.

"Do you not know us, sir? We are —" began Sir Lancelot.

"Travellers," said the King, swiftly. "Concerned passers-by. Tell me, friend, why do no knights patrol this district?"

"Knights?" The man's mood soured. "A knight brought this beast upon us! The good-for-nothing knight who owns this land and keeps putting the rent up, then unleashing his troll when we cannot pay."

"But this land is free land," said the King.

"Not according to Camelot."

"Sir, mind your tongue," said Sir Lancelot. "The name of Camelot shines like a beacon, lighting up every corner of this country."

"You truly have travelled far," said the man in wonder.

"Far enough at that," said Arthur. "If there is trouble in this part of the kingdom, why did you not send word to Camelot? I promise you, the King would see to such an injustice personally."

The man started to laugh. "The *King*? I spit on the King's name, and I don't care who knows it."

Sir Lancelot drew his sword. "I will not warn you a third time."

"Peace, Lancelot," said the King. "What manner of grievance have you and your kinsmen against King Arthur?"

"Arthur? Good sir, King Arthur has been gone for seven years."

"Seven *years*?"

"Dead, most men say. Perished on a quest, along with his best knights. And if he isn't dead, he might as well be. There's a price on his head no man would turn down in such lean times. A bounty — by order of King Mordred."

# V

King Arthur stood in silence, weighed down with thought. The Grail, as if sensing its master's mood, hovered low to the ground and hid beneath the King's horse. In gratitude for their deliverance, the villagers had provided the knights with steeds, a thankfulness that only deepened when the King announced that Gawain, Pellinore and Perceval would be staying to help them rebuild their homes, while the rest of the company went on to the west.

"A difficult road lies ahead. We must proceed with caution," said King Arthur.

"Caution my arse! We should ride like the wind to Camelot and kick that snake to kingdom come!" said Gawain.

"Mordred has had seven years to build up his army, to strengthen his position."

"Seven years riding roughshod over our home, you mean. Over all we hold dear," said Lancelot.

"Aye, Lancelot's right! Who knows what's become of them?"

"All the more reason not to go charging in. I will not forfeit our advantage for the sake of letting off steam."

"Letting off steam?!"

"That is an end to it, Gawain. You three will wait here. If we do not return or send word by dawn the day after tomorrow, then ride west. But before then, you do not move by so much as a furlong. Is that clear?"

Sir Gawain walked off, muttering and shaking his head, picking up the stones from a collapsed wall with demented gusto.

"I agree with you, sire," said Perceval. "I will see to it that we wait."

†

And so King Arthur, Sir Lancelot, Sir Kay and Sir Lucas the Butler rode westward. As they travelled, it was as if they were back in the most forsaken plains of Annwn. The fields were untilled and overgrown, choked with brambles. Those few dwellings that were not run down and ramshackle showed no signs of life. A shroud had fallen upon the bright hues of summer, obscuring all their vitality. Not a soul did they meet upon the road, and not a breath of breeze refreshed the stifling air of that blighted wasteland.

Then Kay, who was in the lead, saw a sight most curious in a passing paddock. "What manner of demon is this?" he said. Demon was the word, for the animal foamed at the mouth and fixed them with glowing red eyes.

"That is no demon," said Lancelot. "That's a unicorn. Or rather, it *was*." He drew his sword to put the creature out of its misery. But no sooner had Sir Lancelot alighted from his horse than a long shadow spread out on the ground around the knights, and the sound of a mighty falling object filled their ears. "Move!" said Lancelot, and all scattered as a large dragon dropped out of the sky. The beast hit the ground and burst open, showering its innards over the road. The knights recoiled, choking at the stench of rotten flesh. In the paddock, the unicorn went out of its mind with fear at the sight, legs splaying out in a skittering run. Lancelot took out his bow and delivered a single arrow to its head, whereupon it tumbled to an ungainly rest.

"Like the troll," said Kay. "As if it no longer had any place in this world."

"I am beginning to understand how they feel," said King Arthur, to no-one but himself.

Moving across country they picked up their pace. By nightfall they had reached a vast forest, and here they made camp, in a glade hidden by a thicket of trees from a crossroads.

"My bones ache fit to snap," said Lancelot. "I feel like I've ridden for years without a minute's rest."

"That may not be so fanciful a notion," said Sir Lucas. "I have been observing us closely as we travelled. It is as if we have taken on the seven years of our absence within the space of a single day." And each knight looked at his reflection in his shield, counting off new wrinkles and grey hairs.

The night was sultry with no need for a fire, but Kay lit one anyway against the dark, and made a pot of the few vegetables they had been given by the villagers that morning. The Grail hovered by his side, watching him prepare the meagre meal. Before Kay could place the pot over the fire, the Grail nudged him aside and settled itself upon the flames. At this a most wonderful smell filled the nostrils of every man, causing their stomachs to gurgle in unison. The cauldron of the Grail was filled to the brim with a rich and wondrous stew. Upon eating it, each knight tasted whatever food it was that he loved the most.

"So this is what the Grail does?" said Lancelot, when he had eaten his fill.

"Something of its power, yes," said King Arthur.

"A treasure indeed," said Kay. "But I am loathe to think we quested so hard for a glorified cooking pot."

"It is more than that. Much more."

For the first time since returning from the Otherworld, the King was all vigour. He leaned into the firelight and his eyes shone with zeal. The other three knights moved in closer. "When I knelt before it in the Glass Fortress, I asked the Grail how it could serve me. It told me something of its power."

"And?" said Lancelot.

The King lay back on the grass and the light left him. "And I would sooner die than see such a treasure fall into the wrong hands. Which is why I think we need to modify our plan a little."

✝

So it was that dawn saw Sir Kay and Sir Lucas the Butler on horseback, riding cross-country towards Camelot, attempting to fashion two disguises from a leaf and a clump of moss. Of this Sir Kay made a fine example by tying the leaf around his head with horsehair, creating a patch over his left eye.

"Well, Lucas? How do I look?"

"The very model of a modern knight errant, Sir Kay."

"I'm surprised you can see me, with your head tilted back like that. Anyone we meet will think you've broken your neck."

"I take your point, Sir Kay, but if I lean forward any more, it will dislodge my false beard."

"You're being too ambitious. Try tearing off a piece of the moss and clenching it between your nose and lip as a moustache."

"I shall endeavour to do so, Sir Kay."

"Now then, here's the road. We need new names and a cover story, for anyone we happen to meet. I shall be Sir Howard, seasoned traveller and lover of women. No, beloved *by* women. Returning to the place of his birth... his family seat, perhaps... yes, yes... in... Tenby. And you can be my dogsbody, Culver."

"Very good, Sir Howard."

"For a moment back there, I thought Sir Lancelot would insist on coming with us."

"As did I. But I am glad he saw reason. His concern is understandable, but the Master's circumspection is wise, not least because of the bounty on his own head."

"I suppose. Let's just find out how the land lays and get back to them. For one thing, I want some more of that Grail food. Nothing but a simple stew to look at, yet it tasted like roast suckling pig, with apples and onions and fresh spring greens."

"My own repast was strongly reminiscent of a boiled egg with bread and butter," said Sir Lucas.

"You are a funny old bird, Lucas," said Kay. "Look sharp! Someone's coming." Sure enough, Sir Kay's gimlet eyes were not mistaken. A cloud of dust cleared to reveal a galloping knight coming up the road towards them.

"Greetings, Sir Knight!" shouted Sir Kay.

The approaching knight drew his sword and held them both at its point. But the hearts of Sir Kay and Sir Lucas lightened with joy, for this was none other than Sir Gareth — kinsman of Sir Gawain, and as dear as a brother to them both.

"Names?" said Sir Gareth.

Kay turned to Lucas. "A warm welcome for visitors to a new land."

"Forgive me, sir," he replied. "These are cold times."

"If cold be the times, then shiver we must. I am Sir Howard, and this is my servant Culver," said Sir Kay.

"You're a knight?" Fear creased Sir Gareth's eyes at the corners. "Of the old King's company?"

"I could hardly claim to be. I have not been in this realm since I was a mewling whelp."

"Then, if I were you, I would turn your horse around and seek your welcome elsewhere," said Sir Gareth.

"Why so?"

"This is a country on the verge of war."

"With whom, may I ask?" said Lucas.

"With itself," said Sir Gareth. "This land was once ruled by King Arthur, the most noble King who ever lived."

"I have heard legend of his name," said Sir Kay.

"A legend is all that remains. He went away on quest seven years ago with six of his best knights, my own brother among them, and never returned. Arthur's half-brother Mordred wasted no time in securing his advantage. Within half a year, he proclaimed Arthur dead and took Queen Guinevere as his wife."

"But what of the Knights of the Round Table? The legends I've heard speak of good men, steadfast and true. How could they let this happen?"

"For every knight loyal to the King, there were ten who served Mordred. Those barons who despised Arthur from the very first days of his coronation were suddenly among us, like wolves in the fold. Before we knew it, Mordred's rot had spread deep into the Round Table. All it took for it to crumble was the slightest pressure from his boot. Those who opposed him were quickly silenced, or found life at court unbearable and fled."

"Including you," said Kay.

"We are a small band of knights in exile, supported by our servants."

"Forgive me, but what do you mean by 'servants?' " interrupted Sir Lucas.

"Kitchen staff and the like. Their acting leader has proved herself skilful with a sword. The rest of them... less so."

"Forgive me again, but what is her n —"

"Damn it, Culver, let the man talk! I apologise for my servant's rudeness, I shall thrash him later. Continue, Sir Knight."

"Our numbers are swelled by those of our fellow folk sick of seeing their land fall into ruin. But we are no more than a hundred. Gathered in a valley known as Camlann, a day's ride over yonder hill. At noon tomorrow, Midsummer's Day, we ride against Mordred for one last battle. We are sorely outnumbered, but we intend to take many of his men down with us. You find me out on a final sortie, seeking any still loyal to the name of King Arthur."

"With stout souls like you fighting for her, perhaps all is not lost at Camelot," said Sir Kay.

"You know the name of Camelot, then?" said Sir Gareth.

"Indeed I do," said Sir Kay.

"Perhaps from some of those legends you have heard."

"That'll be it."

"*Chronicles*, one might call them," said Sir Gareth, raising his eyebrows.

"One might," said Sir Kay.

"Tell me, Sir Howard. How did you lose your eye?" asked Sir Gareth.

"Duelling. Nasty business. But you should see the other fellow, eh Culver?"

"He came off the worst, Sir Howard," said Sir Lucas.

"Sir, would you think me rude if I were to ask you to remove your eye patch?" Sir Gareth said. "You seem passing familiar, and it would satisfy my curiosity."

"I can't, I'm afraid. It, er —"

"Your request goes against Sir Howard's strict religious beliefs, and will have to be declined," said Sir Lucas.

"Yes, that's right. It would not do to anger my gods and suchlike."

"Well, I must ride on," said Sir Gareth. "If you have a heart for lost causes, perhaps you may join us tomorrow."

"Perhaps we may," said Sir Kay.

"You, and… anyone else you may bump into on the road."

"Till we meet again," said Sir Lucas.

"In this life or the next," said Sir Gareth, urging his horse on. "By the way Culver, you have some moss on your lip."

# VI

"That settles it," said Sir Lancelot. "We go, and we go now."

Sir Lucas and Sir Kay had returned to find him in a state of frenzied activity, his horse saddled and ready to leave, even before they had delivered the news that sent them back to the hidden glade with all haste. Throughout the imparting of their tidings, King Arthur had remained a picture of serenity. He sat cross-legged by the unlit fire, using the edge of Excalibur to whittle on a stick, carving it into a small sculpture of a woman's head.

"We go nowhere without Gawain, Pellinore and Perceval," he said, gathering up a handful of wood shavings and setting them aside for kindling.

"Then, Lucas should remain here until they arrive. With luck and a fair wind they may also make the battle while there is still time."

"No, Lancelot."

"But we have no choice!"

"There is always a choice."

"Didn't you hear a single word Kay said? This time tomorrow, it will all be over! If we ride now, there is a chance, a good chance, that we can turn the tide. Mordred will not be so cocksure when King Arthur returns to reclaim Camelot."

"Do you think?"

"Every second we wait, we risk losing our loved ones."

"*Our* loved ones?"

Sir Lancelot paused before replying. "Yes," he said.

"Now who might that be, I wonder?" The King dropped his stick and stood up. "I know, Lancelot," he said. "I know it all."

"Know what?"

"You may think me blind. You may think me deaf. But at least do me the honour of not thinking me stupid," said the King.

"I — sire, no. It was never..."

King Arthur's voice took on the light tone of one delivering a delightful anecdote. "As for me, Lancelot, my 'loved one' was lost to me a long time ago. And as for Camelot; if Mordred wants it so badly, let him have it. I have no use for it. I have found something better. Something time can never tarnish."

"Sire? What do you mean?" said Sir Kay.

"Let me show you," said King Arthur.

Sir Lancelot walked towards his horse. "You have lost your mind," he said.

"No, Lancelot," said the King.

Lancelot turned back to find the point of Excalibur pressed against his heart. The last few rays of the sun caught the blade, tracing its outline in gold.

"I have found it."

King Arthur thrust Excalibur through Sir Lancelot's breast and did not stop until the hilt lay flush to his chest.

"Now tell me," said the King, pulling Sir Lancelot close to him, as if in an embrace. "How does it feel?"

Sir Lancelot held the King's gaze, even as he drew in what was surely his last breath.

"Hurts."

"That's a sundered heart for you. Hurts like the devil. But beyond that. In your *soul*. What does it feel like?"

"Like... the end."

The King nodded, as if that was the very response he had been seeking. "Again, you are wrong."

King Arthur pulled out Excalibur lightly and fiercely from Sir Lancelot's chest. Sir Lancelot gasped in agony as the sword point came free in a wellspring of blood. Sir Lucas and Sir Kay cried out to see such a dolorous stroke delivered. They moved to help the dying knight, but the King blocked their way with the dripping blade. Lancelot teetered on his feet, first to the left, then to the right, as if deciding on the best spot to fall and breathe his last. From beneath the King's horse, the Grail hovered up to its master's side. "No-one ever died of a broken heart. No matter what the minstrels say," said the King.

Of its own accord, the Grail moved up to Sir Lancelot's face. The cauldron had filled with a dark liquid, a rich and heady brew. It tilted itself to his lips, and Sir Lancelot drank. And no sooner did he swallow, than the blood ceased to bubble from his wound and the light of life returned to his eyes.

"Do you see?" said the King. "The Grail can restore life, preserve life, sustain life. Eternally. That is why we will not be going back to Camelot. For there is nothing there but death."

King Arthur lowered Excalibur. But as he did so, his hand began to shake, as if the sword were being struck by many hammers at the same time. The King held tight to the hilt and trembled mightily until, with a crack like the pulling of a rotten tooth, Excalibur split down the middle in a jagged break, shattering into a thousand tiny pieces. The smithereens of the sword, hilt and all, burnt and hissed as they fell upon the grass, dissolving back to that place deep in the Otherworld where Excalibur was first forged.

Then it was King Arthur's turn to bleed, and most freely, from many places all over his body. Not least from his neck, where the old bite mark of a werewolf bloomed across his skin. At the sight of this Sir Lucas and Sir Kay, frozen to the spot by all they had just seen, came to life again and rushed to the King's aid. But so great in number were his ailments that they knew not where to direct their assistance first. Just as it had done for Sir Lancelot, the Grail came unbidden to the maimed King. He drank from it, a long deep draught, but it provided no healing for his many wounds. Then Sir Lucas ran to King Arthur's horse, and took from his saddlebag the scabbard of Excalibur, and fastened it about the King's sword belt. Only then did the bleeding stop; only then did the wounds close and miraculously heal.

Thus King Arthur brought upon himself the curse of Excalibur, because he used the sword against another who had also wielded that enchanted blade. And thus he was fated to retain the scabbard about his person for the rest of his days, on pain of death from the thousand cuts the magical covering had ever saved him from.

† 

True to their word, it was noon on the following day when Perceval, Gawain and Pellinore came riding down the road from the east. Sir Lucas met them at the crossroads, and accompanied them to the hidden glade.

Many words had passed between King Arthur and Sir Lancelot that previous night, after their confrontation. Sir Kay and Sir Lucas sat apart from them, their hearts full anxious, so that the first light of day fell upon a company of tired and sleepless knights. Kay and Lucas had not been party to their parleying, but were addressed by Arthur and Lancelot before they broke their fast. The King gave his orders. They would not be joining the last battle, for that would be futile. Instead, the company were shortly to embark upon a new quest; one made possible thanks to the bountiful Grail. To spare the heartbreak of their fellow knights, not a word was to be said to Gawain, Perceval or Pellinore, of Kay and Lucas's meeting with Sir Gareth on the road, and of all he had told them. Lucas and Kay looked to Lancelot, who nodded his consent, and so both men swore a solemn oath of secrecy.

So it was that when their three companions arrived, they were told that, during the seven years of their absence, Camelot had fallen into a long and terrible decline. Not a single soul remained alive within her walls. All they had once known and loved had fallen into wrack and ruin, utterly destroyed by civil war. On hearing this, each knight bowed his head, his heart heavy with sorrow and his eyes full of tears.

Suddenly Sir Gawain became so wonderfully wroth that he took up his axe and hewed in frenzy at a tree. Then he vowed, amid heavy cursing, to find Sir Mordred and tear him apart. Only Sir Lancelot succeeded in calming his savage fury. He told Gawain that he had seen the smithereens of Camelot with his own eyes, but of Mordred there was no sign. And Sir Gawain threw himself upon Sir Lancelot's shoulder and wept nigh out of his mind.

The King left each knight to his own grief for a time. Then at last he spoke. "This is not a time for sorrow," he said, and at his words the Grail rose up above him like a crown. "My knights, today is a glorious day. We have been given that rarest of gifts. The chance to start again. Today is the first day of the quest of our lives. The Eternal Quest. The noble dream of Camelot will never die, while we seven are still alive to uphold it. And thanks to the Grail, we shall uphold it forever."

The Grail shone in the glade, and all seven felt themselves transported back to those sweet heavens glimpsed from the Prydwen in flight, as if a second sun were rising in the east. And King Arthur's voice rang out like a bell, saying...

# VII

"...where the bloody hell did I put the last page?"

Sir Kay tossed the thick bundle of manuscript onto the table and looked frantically around him. The fire had burned down to embers and my clothes were fully dry. The storm had passed, along with most of the night. "Bloody typical. Well, you know how it ends. The King gets the Grail to freeze our physical growth from that day forth, providing, of course we meet every year on the same day to drink again. We start our secret freelance life of truth, justice and the Arthurian way, also known as the Glorious and Eternal Quest. And away we trot to France to lay low until we're forgotten about, riding off into the sunset. Or sunrise. I forget which. It was definitely sunny. Anyway, what do you think?"

"This new draft is a vast improvement, Sir Kay, but —"

"You hated it, didn't you."

"No, not at all."

"The corners of your mouth are twitching like they always do when you don't like something. It's the writing style, isn't it? You hate my style."

"No, Sir Kay. The problem —"

"So there is a problem, then! I knew it."

"The problem is one of content. Specifically, in relation to our 'lying low in France,' as you put it, and its effect on the aforementioned tavern talk."

"Go on..."

"The Master feels that the very existence of your *Chronicles* is a threat to the continuation of the Eternal Quest. Until now, he has found it useful, even necessary, to maintain our secret history. Recently, as I have said, he has had cause to revise that opinion."

"But that's crazy! How can my stories be a threat when no bugger will ever read them, apart from you and the King? It's not as if anybody *can* read on this island, aside from us and about eight monks."

"Be that as it may, the Master envisions a time when far more primacy is placed upon the written word."

"So what are you saying?"

"He wants you to start again. To write a brand new history. One that ends by stating that King Arthur and his knights did *not* go off to seek the Grail, but remained at Camelot, where they died in a last battle against the usurper Mordred."

"Died?"

"Unequivocally. And permanently."

"Blimey. Talk about a downbeat ending."

"The Master even has a title and a pen name in mind. *The History of King Arthur and His Noble Knights* by Godfrey of Wales."

"That's... actually not bad."

"Then, having written this definitive history, you are to circulate it amongst monks and clerics schooled in the art of penmanship. So that it might be copied, and eventually filter down to the common people, to become the accepted version of things."

"I see. So, all of this," Sir Kay waved a hand over the heap of parchment, "just stays between us?"

"No, Sir Kay. The Master wishes you to destroy all your existing *Chronicles*."

"When you say 'wishes'..."

"I am under express instructions to consign every last piece of parchment to the flames," I said.

"Oh."

"I am sorry, Sir Kay."

"The very thing I was threatening to do when you first arrived. Talk about dramatic irony."

"Indeed, Sir Kay."

"Right then. Best make a start, I suppose. I shall see to it the moment you leave."

"My orders are to witness the book's destruction with my own eyes. I really am sorry, Sir Kay."

"Stop apologising Lucas, for God's sake." Sir Kay sighed and sat down. He picked up a flagon, but not a drop of wine remained. "Official History, you say?"

"Yes."

"Big potential readership, there. Something like that could last for a long time."

"That is the intention, Sir Kay."

"Right then. Put the kettle on the fire, Lucas."

"The fire is almost out, Sir Kay."

"We'll soon sort that, won't we?"

Sir Kay dropped the first pile of his *Chronicles* onto the embers and stirred them up with the poker. The cottage filled with the smell of burning parchment. A single page lay at my feet. I picked it up and glanced at the last line. 'And they rode off into the sunrise, into the dawn of the Eternal Quest.' I added it to the fire. Sir Kay selected a clean page, cut a fresh quill, and started to write as the flames licked higher.

# The Otherday

# I

As I swished and spun in the Otherworld vortex, I offered up a prayer of repentance for every spider I had mistakenly washed down a drain. I soon lost all sense of my bearings as I was buffeted in every direction, and sometimes in several directions at once. The sound was like a torrent of water thundering in my ears. And all I could see were dazzling swirls of colour, as if a child were scribbling on my retina with a handful of crayons. It therefore came as no surprise that I could make out nothing at all of Merlin within this supernatural whirlpool.

Just when I could not endure the experience for a second longer, my feet touched solid ground. My senses gradually steadied and reset themselves. Sir Pellinore's lifeless body lay heavy on my shoulder, but I was reluctant to put him down until I had gathered my bearings. I blinked a few times.

No Merlin. Nobody at all.

I was in a large, gloomy room, its true size obscured by endless tables piled with teetering towers of dirty plates, bowls and serving dishes. My hands itched at such vast dereliction of domestic duty. But it was difficult to know where to begin, not least because everything beyond my immediate surroundings was obscured with a dingy haze. I was also still burdened with Sir Pellinore, so I lowered him as gently as I could to the floor. Something crunched beneath his body. I looked down and saw that the vortex had delivered me knee-deep into the middle of a graveyard of unburied carcasses.

My first thought was that the room was the site of a battle, even a massacre, but I breathed slightly easier when I realised the remains belonged to various species of animal. The glowing eyes of a large rat, very much alive, stared at me from inside a boar skull, on which half of the flesh still hung like a loose hood. The rodent was competing for the stinking meat with a swarm of flies, and small pulsing forms I was happy to assume without closer inspection to be maggots. Disturbed mid-meal, the rat dived for cover. His departure alerted his unseen dining companions, and the putrid bones around me shook with secret scurrying.

This sudden movement jolted the nearest table. A stack of plates, poised on the edge like coins in an amusement park machine, crashed down onto the floor, the sound strangely muffled in the room's heavy atmosphere. This sound in turn provoked a different kind of movement, coming from the darkness over to my right.

"Hello?" I called, my voice feeble in that vast expanse. The commotion was coming from a large empty alcove. A thumping sound, as of something hard knocking against stone. The wide space of the alcove was festooned in thick cobwebs. I brushed them away and leaned my head inside. The pounding came again, making me jump and bang my head, dislodging a cloud of black dust.

A heavy *thud, thud, thud* was coming from under the stone floor.

"Merlin?" I whispered.

An arm shot up out of the stone, and I fell backwards onto a bed of sharp bones. The arm snatched at my foot, grabbing my ankle and pulling me towards the hole from which it had appeared. I flailed about for a hand-hold, my palms sliding on the greasy floor, the phantom arm dragging me ever closer. I changed my tactic and faced the creature head on. I caught a glimpse of green eyes and yellow teeth, before I smashed a serving platter into its monstrous face. The creature released its grip with a low groan. Then another hand pulled me up onto my feet. "Run!" said a male voice, its owner turning away before I could see his face.

"No, wait," I said, intending to go back for Sir Pellinore. But several other creatures had now emerged from various sides of the room and were dragging his body away like incompetent pall-bearers.

"Leave him! There's nothing you can do!" cried the voice of my rescuer, and I reluctantly ran alongside him as he sped between row-upon-row of the laden tables.

Several of the creatures gave chase. My saviour pushed over stacks of plates as we ran past. I followed his example, sending cascades of crockery into the creatures' path. At the end of the room, we flung ourselves against a pair of heavy wooden doors, pushing open a gap just big enough for us to squeeze through. The creatures had almost caught up with us. I could see their livid faces and caught the warm stench of rotting flesh as they loped out of the gloom. I shoved the doors shut and my rescuer wedged a timber of wood through the thick outer handles, forming a barrier that held fast as the doors buckled. The creatures' pounding gradually ceased as they abandoned their thwarted chase.

I gulped in a lungful of the cold outside air, only to immediately expel it again in an exclamation of surprise.

"Sir Perceval!"

"Lucas," he said, flatly. I was disappointed my delight at seeing him was not mutual. But before I could say another word, I realised where I was standing. "That was the Great Hall!" I said.

"Yes."

"This is Camelot?"

"Yes."

"My heavens."

"There's no Heaven about it," said Sir Perceval. "Welcome to Hell."

# II

We did not remain overlong in the ruins of Camelot and made our way out through the dilapidated rear gates. The road was uneven and unkempt, strewn with rubbish and clumps of weed. The light was failing, but enough of the surroundings were visible for me to see that the land surrounding Camelot had fallen into a similar state of barren neglect. A cold mist seeped up out of the ground and seemed to grasp at our feet.

"Those creatures will come for you again. You can be sure of that," said Sir Perceval. "What happened to you, Lucas? How did you die?"

"I am not sure that I did, Sir Perceval."

"You must have. Those things go for all the dead, when they first arrive. They came for me. Showed me what I had to do. Lucky I found you when I did. I was only at Camelot because that's where the Grail led me."

"The Grail! Then it is safe?"

"As safe as anything can be, here. I've been seeking it since the moment I arrived."

"Where did it go?"

"This way. I was about to follow it out of Camelot, and then I found you."

"What manner of creature are those things?" I said. Something about them reminded me of Morgan's skeletal army, for they seemed to be neither living nor dead.

"Whatever they are, they're part of this place. Part of Hell. Part of Annwn."

"That cannot be so, Sir Perceval. Annwn is only one part of the Otherworld. It does not account for this wasteland. And in any case, it does not explain what Camelot is doing here. I do not understand."

"I don't either, Lucas, and Lord knows I've had enough time to try."

"But you have only just arrived."

Sir Perceval shook his head. "It's hard to keep track, but it feels like I've been here for years. And every day is the same. I catch a glimpse of the Grail, soon after I wake. I chase it for miles, until I can run no more, and sleep where I fall. Then I wake up cold and bone weary, see the Grail, and off I go again. Like I said: 'Hell.' "

"Come, Sir Perceval, there is hope yet. I came here in search of Merlin, and I intend to find him. To get him to put everything right, once and for all. And while there is strength left in my body, dead or otherwise, that is what I intend to do. Are you with me?"

"There!" said Sir Perceval, pointing into the mist. "Did you see it?"

"I saw nothing, Sir Perceval."

"Are you blind? The Grail was right there! Floating between the weeds, low to the ground." He fixed me with a cold glare. "Don't you dare follow me. It's my quest this time. Mine!" And off he sprinted into the fog, leaving me alone on the path.

†

The track took me down to the outskirts of the Enchanted Forest. Here, too, the desolation had spread its curse. I quickly lost the path and became surrounded by a conspiracy of trees, hampering my progress with thick branches as if the forest were folding its arms against me. I wanted to call out for Sir Perceval, but had no desire to attract any more of those monsters from the Great Hall. In any case I was reluctant to disturb the complete silence of the forest; the kind of silence so intense it very nearly shouts.

So I pushed on as best as I could, the brush of every branch like the grasping half-dead fingers of those pitiful creatures. But the more I struggled forwards, the more the forest seemed to tighten its grip. I stopped and forced myself to breathe deeply. What was I doing? A butler does not panic, no matter what the circumstances; and I *was* still a butler, even in Hell. I would just have to start thinking like one, for I was damned if I was going to be thwarted by foliage, infernal or otherwise.

I lifted the branch directly blocking my face. Another dropped down to take its place. I lifted that one with my other hand, and yet another replaced it. But I found that by holding up the two branches, and ducking under a third, I could pass through, and by stepping over the low branches beyond these, I was on my way. By such methodical means my progress soon became, if not smooth, then certainly steady going. The fog started to thin out and so did the forest, my stride growing more confident. Until, that is, I took a step forward and lost my footing, tumbling down a steep bank and through several clumps of brambles before coming to a winded standstill.

I had fallen into a small valley with a stream running through it. On the opposite bank was the beginning of a large camp. Tents and marquees, men, women and horses, lights and voices. And fire. The sight of it reminded me how cold I was. Such a camp did not seem to be the kind of gathering the creatures would make, and so I crossed the stream to take a closer look.

†

It was not merely a camp, but an encampment. And one I well recognised, for half of Camelot were among its number! I walked towards them in a daze, but still keeping to the shadows, not yet daring to make my presence known. In a large main marquee, a group of knights talked of tactics. I glimpsed Sir Palomides holding up one of his maps and arguing with Sir Dagonet over lines of attack. Sir Accolon and Sir Marhalt stood in the awning, issuing instructions to Owen the armourer as he sharpened their swords outside. I could not fathom it. Had my passage through the forest taken me out of the Otherworld, and back in time? Did this explain what Camelot was doing here? But the explanation did not suffice, for the main marquee did not fly the Master's emblem — the red flag of Pendragon which signified his residence. But of course, that was it. He was not here; none of us were. This was the valley of Camlann. I stroked my upper lip, recalling a moss moustache and the words of Sir Gareth. So this was the eve of battle. Or at least, not far from it.

It was then that I heard a woman's voice, soft and low, coming from a small tent to the side of the main marquee. A voice that was passing familiar, giving instructions to a young man outside her tent. My spirits lifted. It was a voice I had given up hope of ever hearing again. Beaumains bid the page *adieu* and went back inside. I sank into despair. What on earth was I going to say to her? There were so many things to speak of. It would take me a lifetime to give voice to them all. If this was indeed the time and place I thought it was, then I had been away on the Grail Quest for seven years. I could not simply walk back in there with nothing but a wave and a 'how was your day?'

Perhaps I would ask the young man walking towards me. As he came closer I saw that he was none other than young Gwion. Why, this was a homecoming and a half! "Gwion!" I said, but he heard me not. Indeed, before I could move out of his way, he passed straight through me as if I were a ghost. Emboldened by the shock, I ran into the tent after Beaumains.

She was making her bed with those deft swift movements I knew so well. "Beaumains," I said. Then again, louder this time. But just like Gwion she carried on, unheeding. I dithered in the tent as she went about her work, torn between the desire to make her see me and guilt at invading her privacy. I was loath to leave her, for now that I had found her again there was nowhere else I would rather be. More than anything, I wanted to hear her voice. Perhaps she talked to herself when she was alone. Perhaps she talked in her sleep. I had no right to such intimate details, yet somehow that only deepened my desire to know them. I turned my back as she undressed, then sat by her bedside. As she lay there, restless and full of care, I had the fanciful notion that, although she could not tell me about her day, there was nothing to stop me telling her about mine. And so I started to talk.

After a while she seemed to relax, for all the world as if she were being soothed by my voice. So I kept going, thinking that perhaps my story might mingle with her dreams and cause her to mumble back some words of her own. I told her about my week; of all that had transpired since first setting off from the cottage with the Master on Ritual Day. And, as she eventually drifted into a deep sleep, I told her of the Eternal Quest. Of the sacrifices one must make in the service of one's master. Of a working life without her by my side. Of how such a life, and such sacrifices, might stretch tight the skin of a man's heart and hollow out its insides like a drum, so that its every beat strikes out a deep thud of resounding solitude.

She did not make a sound all night, but I kept my vigil into the small hours, maintaining my ghostly monologue, just in case. Eventually, crushed into silence by the weight of my one-sided conversation, I thought about how right Sir Perceval had been: in stumbling away from that cursed Great Hall and into this time and place, I had not left Hell behind me at all, only fallen deeper into its depths.

# III

At some point I must have drifted off myself, for I awoke to find Beaumains up and about, her bed put away and the tent full of familiar faces. About fifty of my former domestic staff were gathered in exactly the same manner as they would have been for a team briefing at Camelot. Upon waking, I instinctively cleared my throat and, in my befuddled state, was preparing to address them, when Beaumains spoke.

"Good morning everybody, thank you for your attendance," she said. To hear that voice say even such commonplace words gave me the sustenance of a thousand breakfasts. Fortified and curious, I took advantage of my invisibility to walk among my old friends and colleagues.

They were dressed in armour, most of it old and ill-fitting. Likewise their hands, accustomed to wielding mops and platters, looked clumsy and awkward holding swords and shields. Again, the words of Sir Gareth came back to me, and I saw the full reality of the situation. My staff were going to war.

"I would like to start with a reminder that you are under no obligation to stay," said Beaumains. "Nobody would think any worse of you, if you wanted to leave."

"Never," said Bedwyr.

"I'll stand and fight as long as I can grip me sword, ma'am," said Enid.

"Thank you, Enid. But in that case, please belt it to your left side, not the right. Like we practised, remember?"

"Oops. Silly me. Forget my head if it wasn't screwed on."

"Mordred's the one who'll be missing a head, if I've got anything to do with it," said Owen. "When I think of all the hours I've wasted sharpening and smelting for the likes of him... well, it's payback time." He swiped his sword, narrowly missing Bedwyr's ear.

"Owen, be careful," said Beaumains. "And Bedwyr, for heaven's sake, look to your reflexes! You did not bat an eyelid just then."

"I like that, Owen, 'It's payback time'. Might use that as a battle cry," said Bedwyr.

"Get your own."

"Aw, go on."

"Alright. But don't wear it out."

"Bedwyr," said Beaumains, her smooth voice wrinkling with exasperation, "you will not last five minutes on the battlefield if you do not pay attention to what is happening around you."

"Sorry, ma'am, I was distracted by Geraint."

The former Gatekeeper was engaged in a separate huddle with Gwion, who was highly amused at the demonstration of a coin trick that Geraint kept getting wrong, then insisting his mistake was intentional.

"Geraint?"

"Yes, Miss B!"

"Am I keeping you from some important conjuring engagement?"

"No, Miss B. Just showing Gwion how to do the old three-coin-switcheroo."

"Badly," grinned Gwion.

"Watch it, lad."

"Can you imagine any situation where the demonstration of a coin trick would help in combat?" sighed Beaumains.

"Could come in handy as a spot of misdirection? Someone comes charging at you with an axe, it's the last thing they'd expect."

"Please, Geraint, be serious. This might well be our last stand. Don't you want to make it one they will remember?"

"I dunno, Miss B, if you ask me all these so-called Last Stands are getting to be a bit much. Seems like you can't have so much as a small scuffle these days without it being Final Battle this or Overwhelming Odds that. It's the all or nothing of it that narks me."

Beaumains ran a hand through her hair, the black flecked with grey. It would have suited her, had she not looked so tired. She sighed with her whole body and seemed on the verge of a colourful outburst, when Sir Gareth entered the tent and beckoned in her direction. I followed her outside, leaving the infantry, such as they were, to their preparations.

✝

Back outside, most of the camp had been packed away. Armoured knights circled on horseback, arranging men into fighting units. Some practised sword moves on foot, while others kneeled and prayed. Dark clouds gathered in the west, but above the camp and over to the east it was a bright midsummer's day. Sir Gareth drew Beaumains as far away from the army as possible, over to the stream that ran through the valley. I followed them, fast becoming accustomed to my role of impotent eavesdropper.

"Any news?" she said, when Sir Gareth was confident it was safe to stop.

"A curious encounter. I dare not think of it as news of either good or ill, but I cannot help wondering."

"Go on."

"The only men I met on the eastern road were a wandering knight who gave his name as Sir Howard, and his manservant. 'Strangers to this land,' or so they said. And a strange sight they were, the pair of them, for they had made an attempt to hide their features."

"But you recognised them?"

"Take away seven years, and a disguise that would shame a child, and I would swear they were Sir Kay and Sir Lucas."

Beaumains swayed as if Sir Gareth had just struck her across the cheek. "You are sure?"

"Yes. Especially Lucas. He had a bit of moss stuck to his lip. I think he was hoping it might pass for a moustache."

"But, this means that King Arthur —"

"I don't know what it means. And neither do you. That is why it must go no further."

"But if there is hope, why should we let our comrades think there is none?"

"Because false hope can be worse than no hope at all."

Beaumains shook her head.

"Listen to me," said Sir Gareth. "If they are coming, they will return from the east. I told them the place and the hour of our fight. The rest is up to them. Take such inspiration from that as you can, let it give you strength to lead your staff. I have seen them train. They need every advantage they can get." Sir Gareth smiled, not unkindly.

"A moss moustache," said Beaumains, and tried to smile back. "Without their aid, it will be a massacre."

"No," I said, pointlessly.

"I have to get back," said Sir Gareth. "It is almost noon. Take heart Beaumains. We may yet —"

The sudden blast of a horn rang out through the valley, shattering the stillness of the battle-ready camp. A single horseman came galloping down the hill to the south west, not far from the forest through which I had travelled. The knights jumped to arms and all eyes were fixed on the valley slope, for this was the approach from Camelot. But the rider was alone and bore only a white flag that flowed out behind him like the plume of a jet plane.

"A peace offering? From Mordred?" said Beaumains.

"I doubt it. Go to your staff. Prepare to ride." Beaumains hurried back to the camp. I longed to follow her, but knew there was nothing to be gained from it. Whereas learning the nature of this stranger's arrival might at least provide me with more information. I took a last look at my deputy running across the grass, and followed Sir Gareth to intercept the horseman.

†

At the bottom of the valley slope, Sir Gareth and his invisible shadow were met by a most surprising sight. The rider removed a helmet to reveal the long black hair of Queen Guinevere.

"My lady," said Sir Gareth, kneeling.

"Don't kneel for me," she said, dismounting. "I lost the right to that courtesy a long time ago."

"Not as far as I'm concerned, ma'am," said Sir Gareth.

"I doubt King Mordred would agree. Especially after I stabbed him in the leg."

"My lady?"

"One drunken grope too many," she said. "The straw that broke the donkey's back, and caused it to sever its master's tendon."

"You should not have come here. We are about to march on Camelot."

"I know. And so does Mordred.

"Spies?"

"Scouts, most likely. He marches against you with an army that outnumbers yours ten to one. I rode with them in disguise, then broke free during the night."

"Thank you, my lady. I will arrange a consort to convey you to a monastery or holy haven, where you can claim sanctuary."

The Queen snorted and her horse harrumphed, as if in agreement. "What? You think I'm going to leave it at one tendon? No, Sir Gareth. I intend to give my so-called husband a thoroughly good seeing-to, and I don't mean the kind he's been sniffing after these past seven years."

I smiled at the spirit I was hearing. I wondered if King Mordred had reckoned on so many people vying for a piece of him, and whether an advantage of ten to one would be enough to save him from their collective wrath. Sir Gareth smiled too. "Then find Owen, and arm yourself."

"Where is Beaumains?"

"Leading the servants."

"The servants are fighting too?"

"If you could call it that, ma'am."

"Good. Then we shall make a last stand to make the minstrels sing."

"Perhaps sooner than we think," said Sir Gareth. "Look." He pointed up to the top of the hillside.

"I was followed. God's teeth!"

The Queen mounted her horse, pulling Sir Gareth up behind her, and they galloped over to their comrades. Stood at the foot of the slope, I looked up to where Mordred's army gathered in their hundreds beneath the flag of a white dragon, stark against the storm-brewing sky.

# IV

Despite the surprise attack, the forces loyal to King Arthur mustered with lightning speed and did not suffer any disadvantage from being found in disarray. Straightaway, Sir Palomides moved the garrisons into position. Then, with a great spurring and plucking up of horses, they charged uphill. Mordred's army waited, stretching out the psychological advantage of the higher ground for as long as possible. Then they too charged, the armies clashing with a terrible force at the brow of the hill.

Stuck on foot as I was, I lacked the bigger picture I would have had on horseback, but from the little I could gather the usurper King was nowhere to be seen. His absence had been noted by Guinevere, who fought alongside the knights in the vanguard. "The coward is not among them!" she said, hacking and hewing past the first attacking wave, and I remembered with a glow of pride who had taught her to fight with such skill.

But my place was among my people. I found them fighting on foot, taking up the middle guard, for combat on horseback is a skill not easily mastered. On foot, however, they proved themselves a force to be reckoned with. Gumption and elbow grease gave their fighting a workmanlike quality that served them well against their opponents. These were barons or knights who had known only the tournament ground for many years. As a result, many of their moves had a showy, superfluous quality that allowed, for example, Enid to dispatch men twice her size with simple but swift work from her sword, and Gwion to find a chink in many a breastplate.

But alas, this was a failing that extended to both sides. Too many good knights were laid low for lack of focus and an excess of flamboyance. Sir Bors, Sir Ector and Sir Dagonet all fell before my eyes, struck by blows that would never have hit home in the days when they kept a leaner sword-arm. With almost unbearable sorrow, I watched as these knights of the Golden Age gave up their ghost. As the first of them died, I looked out for their shade-selves, thinking they might appear to me in death, as one of my own kind. But they did not, and I remembered that I was still somewhere in Hell, and perhaps not yet truly dead myself. I wondered if this battle, as real as it seemed, was only a re-enactment of one that had been fought long ago, its outcome already known to the mind of history.

The vanguard made a brave uphill struggle but were soon pushed back down to the valley floor by the sheer force of opposing numbers, so that they were now fighting alongside my old team. Gradually, they were forced still further back to the opposite, northern side of the valley, where they dug in and stood firm.

And then there was Beaumains.

I knew that she had received a martial training in her youth, but to see her fight was a sight most astounding. Side-by-side with Sir Gareth, Sir Marhalt and Sir Palomides, she and Guinevere smote a good many upon the brainpans. Not only that, but she encouraged all those around her, spurring them on to fight faster, harder, better. Such as Geraint and Gwion, who had developed a tactic whereby the younger man would use his smallness and speed to position himself behind an enemy, who Geraint would push over and then finish off on the ground.

"Where is Mordred?" said the Queen again. "I won't fall until he does."

"They are retreating," said Sir Gareth. "Look!"

Sure enough, the tide was turning in their favour. I had scarcely noticed it, but this brave company had evened up the odds and were now on the offensive. I cheered with elation, regardless of the fact that nobody could hear me.

It is hard to convey how frustrated I had felt, watching that battle play out. To see men fight and fall, to stand in the midst of all that chaos and be so utterly powerless, was a furtherance of this Hell indeed. However, my primary instinct was not to take up arms and fight myself. It was hard to define, but something about the battle's management offended my professional sensibility. Not so much where the army was concerned, in spite of all their rusty, fussy moves, but among my own staff. A feeling that for all their stamina and pluck, they were somehow not getting the job done properly. I can put it no clearer than that.

Sir Gareth and Guinevere dispatched the last man before them, and the surviving warriors, no more than fifty now, stopped to rest. Beaumains looked to the east, where the sun still shone. "A bright light," she said. "Like a second sunrise. A good omen?"

"I wonder," said Sir Gareth.

"In my experience, it's one of the best," said Geraint. "You can't get any better sign than a bright light in the east."

A gust of wind swept down on the small band. They turned their eyes up to the north hill behind them. There, at the summit, a second army gathered, as numerous as the first, while up on the opposite hillside, the first army had regrouped, their numbers refreshed, awaiting orders.

"That was not a retreat," said Sir Gareth. "It was to prevent one of our own."

Now Mordred appeared, among the number to the north.

"Hemming us in on both sides," said Guinevere. "A coward, but a cunning one."

"On the other hand," said Geraint, his voice faint and wavering, "maybe it's a bright light in the *west* that's a good omen..."

"Curious to say," said Sir Gareth, "this does not feel like the end."

"They have archers!" said Sir Palomides. "To your shields!" Shields were raised, too late for some, and beneath that thick and deadly barrage the second army of the white dragon roared down the north hill and into the crooked enclosure of Camlann. From the opposite side, the other forces advanced, at a pace that was almost leisurely.

Sir Palomides led his comrades back to the middle of the valley again; his last act before succumbing to a trident of arrows. The Queen took an arrow to the side and swooned, sore-wounded. The survivors formed a tight circle around her. Dear Geraint was among the first to go, hit by another hail of arrows. As he fell, I realised the extent to which the Grail had desensitised me to the reality of death; immunised me against its sharp sting. How many times had we cheated it, over the years? Stretching the fabric of our mortality until it had been pulled out of all recognition? Here at Camlann there was no such reprieve. Here, Gwion fell, never to rise again with a cheery quip. Here, Enid would not sit up to have arrows pulled from a healing heart. Here, the spear that did for Bedwyr would remain like a lever in his chest. Of course, the Grail could have saved them, too. But as I knew full well, the Grail was not here. It did not belong to Camelot in smithereens, but to King Arthur's bright new hope of the Eternal Quest. All the Grail meant to these fine few was a tantalising glimpse of a gleam on the horizon; a cruel flicker of false hope before the final failing of the light.

And then there were none left standing, save for Sir Gareth and Beaumains and the wounded Queen. "Ma'am, with your leave," said Sir Gareth. "Since we are to die anyway, I would consider it rude to depart this earth unaccompanied."

"Godspeed," said Guinevere. Raising his sword aloft, Sir Gareth charged towards the enemy on the southern bank. They made much mockery at his approach. Some of them were still mocking as their limbs were severed from their bodies, as that good knight did not go gentle, but hacked and hewed until the angry mob closed in upon him for the last time.

Beaumains stood alone in the middle of the valley, the dying Queen slumped by her side. I was some distance away and could bear to see no more. Yet I could not simply stand idly by, and so I ran towards her. At Mordred's command, the spear-throwers readied their arms. I reached Beaumains in the nick of time, jumping in front of her as they let fly their missiles. Painlessly, the spears pierced my spectral form. Painfully, I heard them hit their target. I fell to the ground, blood seeping from somewhere behind me, a patina of crimson on the battle-churned grass. Slowly it disappeared, as if soaked up by the earth, and with it the sights and sounds faded too, all the triumphant clamour of King Mordred's army advancing, victorious.

† 

There was a certain story told about Merlin, perhaps one of Sir Kay's old *Chronicles*, dating back to before the time of Arthur's father, King Uther. Merlin witnessed a battle, so the story goes, in which many dear to him died, and the sight of it drove the wizard mad. I resolved there and then on the field of Camlann that I would indulge in no such breaking of the barriers. All this was in the past. There was nothing to be gained by wringing one's hands in regret and recrimination. There was nothing we could have done. There was nothing *I* could have done. All this was a distraction, another hellish device employed by this place to keep me from my goal of finding Merlin. I had to keep telling myself that I was not dead. Hell had no claim on me. I would not let it beat me with this tawdry emotional blackmail.

All the same, it was one thing to know this, quite another to feel it. I therefore forced myself to focus on practical matters. There was no sign of the wizard in this particular field, now completely deserted, and nothing save my own testimony to differentiate it from a thousand others. The only sound was the faint gurgling of the valley stream.

A shadow fell over me, accompanied by a harrumphing and a wet nose pushing my cheek. I looked up into a familiar long face. "Plum!" I said, and he whinnied in reply. Whatever he was doing here, he was evidently as real as I was. I threw my arms around his neck and pulled myself up. Thankfully, Plum had a mind to leave that place, and seemed eager for me to do likewise. I mounted, surprised but grateful to find him saddled, and he started to canter up the northern slope, out of the fateful valley. And there, at the crest of the hill, I saw the very man I had been seeking since arriving through the vortex: Merlin, still hooded, riding a grey mare. He was not going to get away from me this time. Plum struck up a full gallop and we were away, speeding after the wayward wizard.

The fields and trees withered and died as we travelled, turning by degrees into a landscape of endless sand dunes that bore no resemblance to anywhere I had ever been. Nothing grew here save for those plants native to desert places, the only signs of life the occasional bones of long-dead beasts, bleached to bright ivory by the sun. The featureless monotony was a comfort to my eyes, for every furlong put more distance between us and the horrors of Camlann.

Suddenly, up ahead and shimmering like a mirage, I saw the form of a large beast galumphing across the arid plain — a beast that was chasing Sir Pellinore! It was the very creature he had dubbed the Questing Beast, and here it was, as real as the hoof-prints it left in the sand. This Questing Beast was being ridden with expert skill, by one of those foul creatures who had dragged Sir Pellinore away upon our arrival in the decrepit Great Hall.

It was remarkable to observe, but the Beast was rendered in the flesh exactly as I had imagined it all those years ago. The feet and legs of a stag propelled a streamlined leopard body, with all the pouncing power of its lion hindquarters. All this served as the engine for a long snake-head, which snapped its fangs after the frantically fleeing knight. The Beast and its rider were toying with Sir Pellinore, letting him run until he reached a sand dune, which he would scramble up as fast as he could. Once at the top, the Beast would whack Sir Pellinore with its snout and send him rolling down the other side, waiting for him to get up and start running across the flat ground. Then the rider would send the Beast bounding after him again with a flick of the reins.

"Sir Pellinore!" I cried, and tried to urge Plum over to lend aid to the helpless knight. But Plum only increased his speed, intent on chasing Merlin. The desert flew past us, until Sir Pellinore and his grim hunters were no bigger than specks of sand.

# V

It was not long before we lost all sight of the wizard. The relentless glare of the landscape induced in me a sort of blindness. So when the desert rose up before me in a wild sandstorm, I took it for an optical illusion and received an eye full of grit for my complacency. Plum did not falter, but pressed ever onwards, and I clung tight to his neck, narrowing my eyes against the stinging tornado. At last the storm fell away and we found ourselves on a green path, Merlin once more in our sights, approaching a palace that glittered like ice.

As I wiped away the worst of the sand, I saw that this castle was constructed entirely from glass, and looked vaguely familiar. Then I recognised it as the Glass Fortress, located on the Otherworld coastline where the Master had found the Grail. On the hills in the distance away to my right stood another very different castle, that of Morgan Le Fay, guarding the part of the Otherworld known as Annwn.

Plum slowed to a trot as we approached the rear entrance. Ahead of us was a wide, deep ravine with access to the gleaming fortress only possible via a single, tunnel-like bridge. The floor of the tunnel bridge was covered with a close arrangement of crystal swords, slicing back and forth at irregular intervals. Above this walkway of doom, twelve semi-circular axe blades swung like pendulums. The single doorway at the far end of the tunnel was revolving with such great speed that anyone stepping into it would surely be flung back out onto the fatal bridge. But all this was nothing to Merlin. He had apparently gained access with ease, and stood for a moment beyond the revolving blur of the doorway, just long enough for me to see him before he moved inside. Very well. If that was the way he wanted to play it, he was not going to stop me now.

But what was I thinking? I was a ghost here in the Otherworld, yet I was approaching this obstacle like a man of flesh and blood! I took a step towards the nearest sword, then hesitated. It would be wise to check that the rules of the Otherworld applied universally. I removed a handkerchief from my pocket and dropped it onto the bridge. It was instantly shredded to confetti, along with my bright idea.

Perhaps I would make better progress by thinking like a butler again. The smooth operation of this bridge-of-certain-death suggested a rigidly-observed maintenance schedule. Presumably, whenever anyone was unsuccessful in their crossing, the bridge was thoroughly cleaned of the hapless quester's remains. There had to be some way of stopping the various mechanisms, in order for such work to be carried out. If I were in charge, my first concern would be to enable my staff to do their job with the bare minimum of faff. I would also count on the approaching adventurer being so preoccupied with the deadly challenge, that he would fail to notice anything beyond his immediate, quest-dazzled eye line.

I was therefore looking for something close at hand, but perhaps not immediately visible. I knelt down and took a good look at the left hand glass pillar where the bridge began. A square compartment no bigger than my hand was concealed by an arrangement of four crystals, reflecting back a smooth surface to anyone not crouching directly in front of it. I reached inside and touched what felt like a lever. I pulled it down. There was a soft clink, followed by a whine like the sound produced by circling a wet finger on the rim of a wine glass. The apparatus on the bridge and the revolving door beyond it slowed and came to a smooth stop. Plum gave me a snort of approval. "Wait here old boy," I said, and entered the Fortress of Glass.

†

The revolving door led to a long passageway stretching up in a series of gentle steps. Inside the fortress it was cool and quiet, the silence and the glass creating an atmosphere of reverence, like a museum after closing time. Various doors were spaced at intervals to the left and right, but here the glass was like pearl, allowing no sight of the rooms within. Not that I could have entered them anyway, for the doors had no handles and did not yield to an experimental push. So I forged ever upwards, my footsteps echoing around me. Occasionally I would stop, the footfalls continuing on the stairs ahead, but whether this was an acoustic illusion or the progress of Merlin, I could not tell.

Eventually the corridor opened out into a wide room, and here the walls afforded a more transparent view. There, behind a vast screen of glass, was the hall where we had first found the Grail. I had just enough time to see Merlin before he passed through the screen to the other side. I pressed my hands up against it, but to me the glass presented a solid barrier. The Grail was positioned on a small low table, as before. Behind the Grail were twelve other tables, all empty, save for one which, as before, displayed an old tattered cloak. Merlin stood within an arm's reach of the Grail, watching and waiting. But for what, and for whom? Was this the Grail as it was now — the Grail the Otherworld had reclaimed, along with Sir Perceval? Or was it the Grail as it was back then, *before* we had taken it? A commotion on the other side of the glass screen answered my question. King Arthur, Sir Lancelot, Sir Pellinore and, most alarmingly, a younger version of myself, came running into the hall.

The Master made straight for the Grail and knelt before it. The sound was clear enough for me to make out their words if I pressed my ear to the transparent wall between us.

"Hurry, sire," said Sir Lancelot.

The King, lost in wonder, seemed almost coy. "Do I just... take it?"

The other knights were similarly bashful. "Don't ask me," shrugged Sir Pellinore.

"Presumably," said Sir Lancelot.

Why do they not ask Merlin? I thought. From this angle, the wizard looked as if he was standing next to me — that is, the earlier me — as I watched over the Master, although Merlin had certainly not been present back then.

The Grail moved, as if it were looking at us all. Or looking *to* us, perhaps; hopeful and expectant.

"Tell me of your power," said the King. "Tell me what can you do." And he listened, as the Grail spoke to him alone. Through the glass I saw that by some trick of the light Merlin grew in stature for a brief moment, his body outlined with a spectrum of prism-cast light.

"Then, you will serve me?" said the King. In answer the Grail lifted itself up off the table. As it did so, I heard a scream, painfully loud and clear on my side of the glass, coming from outside the walls of the city.

"Hark! Mermaidens!" said Sir Pellinore.

Sir Lancelot shook his head. "Le Fay. Sire, we must not tarry."

"Sire, please," said the earlier me, on the other side of the glass.

"Haste!" said Sir Pellinore.

"Yes, of course, we must fly," said the Master, getting to his feet. "To the Prydwen!" The knights turned and ran, the Grail following its new master. I watched them go, the scream rising to a shriek.

Merlin stood with his head bowed, a forlorn curator mourning the theft of his prize exhibit. I pounded on the glass wall between us with my fists, desperately trying to break through. The wizard glided quickly out of the hall. Then the walls of the Glass Fortress cracked and shattered, plunging me into a world of flying particles. Shielding my eyes with my arm, I ran back down the disintegrating corridor.

Volcanoes of glass erupted in my wake. A wide fissure snaked after me down the centre of the quaking stairway and out through the revolving door. The sword bridge collapsed beneath my feet as I ran across it, and with one last stumbling leap I made it back to the other side.

# VI

Faithful Plum was waiting, impatient for the off, his hooves crunching in the raining glass. Merlin was also back on his grey mare, galloping away towards Annwn and the fortress of Morgan Le Fay. The Dark Queen's billowing form rose up into the clouds, preparing to bring down her reckoning on the fleeing knights. Behind me, through the still-collapsing ruins of the Glass Fortress, I could see the shoreline and the storm-tossed shape of the Prydwen striving against the waves.

Plum sped across the flat fields. The spirit of Morgan left her hilltop castle and passed above us. The remains of the Glass Fortress fell. As they did, a gust of wind swept out from the fresh ruins, a warm wave that ruffled the grass around me. At its touch, every living thing fell into instant decay. Leaves turned to a dead autumnal brown. The grass withered as if at a dragon's breath, and the green hills ahead became black and cankerous. I looked at my hands and was relieved to see that I was not affected. Plum shivered at the sudden drop in temperature, so I geed him forwards on Merlin's trail.

†

Merlin's route took us through the dead fields and along the bottom of a valley. On I followed, weary of the chase now, hoping against hope this was the last leg of the journey. The valley narrowed and came to an end in an opening in a wall of rock — the start of a cave leading into the hillside, under Morgan's castle. Plum reluctantly stepped inside. I shared his hesitation, regretting my fervent hope that this was the end of our quest. For that is how it felt, going into the hillside. Like stepping into the end of something.

No sooner had Plum entered the cave than he collapsed beneath me with a whinny of pain. I had thought him immune to the ill wind that decomposed the landscape outside, but I was mistaken. His legs had turned a ghastly green, bones visible beneath the skin. His coat was cold to the touch and felt loose and limp on his body, a thin blanket that the slightest tug would pull free. Plum sank down with a shudder, head bowed and tongue lolling, flecks of foam collecting in the corners of his mouth. "Come on old boy," I said. "Let's get you back outside." But even as I tried to move his equine bulk, he fell still and silent.

I gripped his reins until they cut into my palms. "Merlin!" I shouted, my voice echoing in the cave. "Show yourself!"

Shapes moved in the dark. Low moans, like a whispered curse. In the dim light I suddenly saw that the cave was teeming with the creatures from the ruins of Camelot. They swarmed over poor Plum's body, tearing at him with their hands, dragging him off somewhere underground. One of them lunged at me. His hand did not pass through me, but gripped me around the throat with bony fingers half covered in flesh. "Merlin is my master," it said, with a wheeze of rancid breath.

I pushed it away, gagging and choking, running back to the cave entrance. From outside, away over the dead plain and from out to sea, there came a sound like a door being slammed with a great thooming thud. Just as I reached the way out, the exit closed in front of me and everything went dark.

†

I experienced the sensation of being pressed among a large number of the putrefying creatures, pulled along by their forward momentum and powerless to resist. The ground sloped beneath my dragging feet, sometimes falling away completely as if we had entered a shaft. At such moments I felt the creatures' hands passing me down like a piece of baggage, going to great pains to manoeuvre me past various obstacles in the total blackness. As soon as the ground levelled out, a small amount of light met my eyes, growing brighter until we emerged into an empty torch-lit cave no bigger than a broom cupboard. I was deposited there without formality as the creatures went about their business, leaving me to gather the few of my wits still worthy of the name.

My first impression was an accurate one. This was indeed a broom cupboard, or at least, its infernal equivalent. All manner of tools lined the walls, fashioned from the bones of the dead and in a state of poor repair. Behind me was the way I had come in, a door of rock closed tight on my arrival. In front of me was another closed door, through which my escorts had departed. As I was inspecting it for a handle, this door swung smoothly open.

Two of the creatures entered, taking down spade-like implements from a long rack chiselled out of the rock. Their previous manic intensity had left them upon arriving in the depths, and they walked with the methodical shuffle of a slow-moving queue. All I received by way of acknowledgement was a simple look from their bloodshot eyes, as if the onus were on me to speak, and when I did not they simply left in order to carry on with their work.

Merlin's work, I should say, for I had surely arrived in his true realm. I wondered how he had come to this, what he had done to deserve an afterlife so far from everything fresh and fine. But I was clearly not going to find the answer in a broom cupboard. This time, the creatures had made no attempt to close the door as they left, and so I ventured cautiously out behind them.

# VII

The creatures were working in a long room, poorly lit and low-ceilinged, with a conveyor belt running down the centre. Two of them stood either side at the far end, operating the belt by turning a winch. Above them, through a hole or chute in the rock, a large object slumped down onto the conveyor. At the halfway point, the conveyor stopped long enough for another creature to remove items from this object and drop them into a wooden wheelbarrow, which another creature trundled away. Coming closer, I saw that these items were weapons — a knife, a sword and a shield. Curious, I went to inspect the large object on the conveyor belt.

I stepped back in horror when I realised that this was the dead body of Sir Gareth.

He was dressed as he had been at Camlann, bearing the fresh wounds of one recently slain in battle. I picked him up and tried to remove him from the conveyor belt, but one of the creatures pulled him away from me and put him back into place, while another held me back until the belt started moving again.

"What are you doing?" I said, struggling against its iron grip. "This knight is of King Arthur's court!" But the creatures only looked at me with dismay. As soon as the body had moved into the next room the creature let go of me, and I followed after Sir Gareth's corpse.

A blast of heat and light and noise greeted me. I was standing on a broad outcrop of rock looking out over a vast cavern. The heat and the noise came from my right, where a group of the creatures were working in an armoury, smelting and re-forging Sir Gareth's weapons into new blades, black and jagged. These were dropped over the precipice, creating a curious fizzing sound. The conveyor belt stopped just over the end of the crag. I was just in time to see Sir Gareth tip over, and I ran to the edge.

The end of the conveyor was positioned directly above a large underground pool that steamed and simmered with sulphurous vapours. Here was the source of the light that filled the cavern with a luminous intensity, which increased when the fresh-forged weapons passed into the water. Sir Gareth's body hit the surface with a similar fizz, creating a small geyser that bubbled and broiled as he sank below the lake. The surface of the pool grew calm. Moments later, the waters broke at the other side. A round oval shape emerged, gleaming white. A skull.

"The damned dead, brought to life," I said. *Those who died with their minds mired in pain and frustration.* The skeleton that used to be Sir Gareth gripped his new jagged blade and marched off out of the cavern. So *this* was the occupation of these poor creatures! This was the industry overseen by Merlin: clearing the field of Camlann, creating an army that served Morgan Le Fay! But I would save at least one soul from this dark destiny.

I ran alongside the conveyor belt into the low room again, all the way back to the chute. But she was not there; none of them were. There were no more bodies left. Back into the cavern I went, frantically searching for answers in the blank stares of the pitiful creatures, for someone to tell me that I was not too late, that her fate was not already sealed.

"Sir Gareth was the last of them," said a voice. "The one you seek is not among the skeleton army of the dead. She was not a knight."

I turned to where the voice was coming from. Just above the armoury, on a chair cut into the rock, sat the overseer of all this demonic industry. I approached his throne, a bold petitioner with nothing left to lose.

"Merlin," I said, my voice wavering as tears rolled down my cheeks. "If this is indeed your realm, then please. Release her. Keep the rest, keep all of them. Just give me back Beaumains."

"I cannot."

"Then take me instead."

He laughed. "You cannot offer what you have already given."

"I did not come here as one of the dead. These creatures have no claim on me."

"They might not agree with that."

"But this has nothing to do with me!"

"Ah, Sir Lucas the butler. It has everything to do with you."

"Lies do not become you, Merlin."

"I did not create any of this. You did."

"No."

"Master?" said the nearest creature, tugging at my arm.

"I am here to welcome you to your kingdom, Sir Lucas. To conduct you through your realm. To show you how its foundations were laid in the decision you made."

"Master?" said the creature again.

"All this belongs to you," said Merlin. "Take up your rightful place. Head Butler to the domestic damned, the service staff of Hell."

"Lucas?" said the creature, and I pulled my arm away angrily from its fetid grasp. Then saw its hands, jaundiced and rotten, but still with patches of their old pale skin. The strong supple hand of a kitchen worker.

"Beaumains," I said.

And Merlin smiled.

Taking up a freshly forged blade still hot from the fire I ran at Merlin and attacked him with all my might. Lightly, he jumped down from his throne and met my onslaught with ease, blocking every blow. The harder I attacked, the easier time he seemed to have of it, shifting his sword from left hand to right, then holding one hand behind his back, laughing at my efforts. The more he laughed, the harder I attacked, and on it went. Not once did he strike any blow, but simply waited for me to wear myself out.

When at last his patience had expired, Merlin employed a light offensive, pushing me back to the very brink of the outcrop. I quickly expended my remaining energy in maintaining a feeble defence, until every movement of my sword felt like trying to lift a tree trunk with one hand.

"You can never defeat me, Lucas," said Merlin.

The blade started to slip from my numb fingers. "Nevertheless, I will die trying," I said.

"Yes," said Merlin. He pulled down his hood. "You will."

I looked fully into the face of Merlin. I dropped my blade and stumbled backwards to the edge of the outcrop. The noxious fumes wafting up from the pool were like a draught of smelling salts, bringing me to my senses. For at last, deep in the bowels of the earth and at the end of all things, I understood.

I understood everything.

And it was too late.

I accepted my fate, and stepped off the edge of the precipice.

# The Last Day

# I

Today being Initiation Day, I rose an hour earlier than usual, to pay particular attention to the preparations for my successor. I was up to meet the sunrise, and sat in the study window seat with my morning cup, the wash of the waves below the cottage a pleasant soundtrack to the reviewing of yesterday's final amendments. I took a sip of tea, noting that, as ever, she had brewed it to perfection, and considered my speech.

It was true that my words did not possess the narrative sweep of a *Chronicles*, or the authoritative clout of a *History*. But what my address lacked in literary flourishes, it more than made up for in practical application. Plus, as I knew better than anyone, in our line of work practical application is everything. With that in mind, I decided to heed the advice my dearest had given me only last night, and get it to the person it was intended for. I finished my tea, picked up the first page, and sent my mind strolling through time and space.

Every human consciousness that has ever existed spread out before me like stars in the night sky. I needed no map to guide me, for only a handful of souls in every generation gleam as brightly as ours. Stepping softly, lest I tread on his dreams, I stood in the corner of his consciousness and uttered a small cough — just enough to make him aware of my presence. Then I spoke the following words:

Gwion. Gwion? Do not be alarmed. This is indeed the voice of Sir Lucas, your old employer. Speaking into your head. Hello there. Please, calm down, you are not possessed. No no, do not get Geraint, he will only add to your confusion. Just lie back and take a deep breath.

There.

Better?

Good.

Now, I want you to do something for me. I want you to remember all those times recently when you've heard my voice in your head, and put it down to a trick of the imagination. 'It cannot be him,' you have told yourself. 'He is long gone.' Well, yes and no, but more of that later.

You will, I know, have heard me speaking to you, either in fragments, or as if from a very great distance. You will have heard my voice during moments of high stress. Or perhaps on those absent-minded occasions when you entered a room and forgot what you came in for. Maybe you have heard me in the hinterland between sleeping and waking, a still small voice in the corner of your consciousness. Such moments were often accompanied by certain episodes, weren't they? Alarming occurrences, such as the ability to manipulate the minds of others, or of time slowing down and even stopping around you for apparently random intervals.

Well, I am here to tell you that there is nothing alarming or indeed random about any of this. My voice is speaking within you now as a sort of welcome address, to help you find your feet and take those first steps over the threshold of a new life. I will explain everything that you need to know, in a way that it was never explained to me. This was partly the fault of my predecessor, who preferred puzzles and tests, such as so-called amulets of teleportation, which have no power in themselves, but serve as a means of focusing and honing our latent abilities. But a great deal of the blame also lies with me, for misunderstanding the true nature of my life's work.

True service, as practised by the best in our profession, is about fluctuation and change. So much of the business of butlery and housekeeping has to do with maintenance and preservation that it is very easy to overlook this fact. Indeed, once such a truth is overlooked, avoiding it can become something of a life's work. When that happens, you risk destroying the very thing you are seeking to preserve. It was in such a way that I turned my back on magic, as on a black sheep of the family, little realising (as I should have done from the example of my then-Master, who had some experience in the matter of troublesome family members) that a black sheep shunned only bleats louder.

But I digress. I have promised myself that I will be a better mentor than I was a novice, and to that end I have composed this address to help you along the way. Not to do all the work for you, you understand. The quest — and it *is* a quest, make no mistake about that — is yours alone. Think of these as guidelines. With that in mind, the best way to guide you is to tell you about the end of my own working life and the start of my new one, so that you might learn from my mistakes. For I made a lot of them, Gwion, enough to fill a thousand years with their telling. But we are butlers, to the end and beyond. And as you shall see, butlers always find a way of getting the job done, often in the most trying of circumstances, and with precious little time for a sit down.

So, without further ado, let's get started, shall we?

# II

In the bottommost point of the lowest pit of Hell, I hit the water with a crack that felt like the breaking of every bone in my body. As I sank beneath the scalding waters, I saw that the pool itself was also breaking, water pouring out and flooding the cavern as the rocky bed beneath me split wide open. The water level subsided around me, and I had a brief moment in which to gasp for air. In that split second the entire cavern was filled with a mighty rumble, before the cracks in the bottom of the pool opened wide and I fell through them, swallowed up by the earth. I was surrounded by detritus, small rocks, big rocks, earth and rubble, worms and mulch, and me no more than a speck among all that thundering firmament, a single mote of dust in a vacuum cleaner bag.

Then came the settling. The swift accumulation of an incredible weight. Squeezing my lungs empty, pressing down on me with immense power, a pure push of pain on every inch of my body. And with the settling of the earth came the realisation of what was actually happening.

I was being buried alive.

This sent me into a flurry of panic, pushing against a load I could never hope to lift, hands flailing and fingers digging even as they became stuck fast. It did not last long; it could not. It was time to gasp my last. Time to give up the ghost in a Hell of my own making. My final thoughts were of Beaumains. Of how I would like to see her just one more time, back as she was, not the foul travesty I had just confronted.

My body shuddered with a final burst of life. The dying spasm reached my right hand. My index finger found a little pocket of space, a tiny recess in which to stretch itself out, as my mind narrowed to a single dark point, towards death, towards nothingness.

But not quite yet. For there was still something remaining. Something within me, but also without. My finger touched that something. It was cold and hard. It was not made of earth. In those last fleeting seconds of my life, the feel of it reminded me of the Grail, and I felt a rush of empathy for that magical artefact. A lifetime of unquestioning service. I wondered if it had ever felt tired. I wondered if anybody had ever thought to ask the Grail what it wanted out of all this. If it could choose, who did it really *want* to serve? I even tried to say it aloud, but my mouth filled with soil even as I spoke the words:

"Whom does the Grail serve?"

Well, Gwion my boy, as it turned out, that was quite the question.

✝

I felt myself being pulled up towards a bright light. Not softly and in spirit as I have heard it said of the soul at the moment of death, but physically *hoiked* up, the weight of all that earth no greater than a clump of soil on a gardener's trowel. The light was all around me, and next to me was the Grail. There it had been, awaiting my arrival at the lowest point of Hell, just as it had been awaiting my arrival back then, all those years ago in the Glass Fortress when I had failed to claim it. But the light was not coming from the Grail, as it had done when Arthur first instructed it with the terms and conditions of the Eternal Quest. The light was coming from me. Pouring off me like water, as I forged upstream on my unstoppable journey towards new life.

I held out both my hands, a sunrise in each palm. And as I raised my arms, all the earth of Lower Annwn rose up and separated, scattering around me. I ascended into the cavern and back up to the outcrop, stopping in mid-air so that I was facing the spot where the wizard Merlin still waited for me. Still with his hood down, and still with the same face that had so surprised me only moments ago, but now seemed as natural as my own reflection. For that is exactly what it was.

"Whom does the Grail serve, Sir Lucas?" said the Merlin me. "That is the question. The Grail serves a servant. A butler like you. A butler like me."

"Hello, Sir Lucas," I said.

"Hello, Sir Lucas," he said. "I expect that there are some matters that need clarifying at this point."

"There is nothing worse than a loose end," I agreed.

"I would be happy to answer any questions you may have," he said.

"Thank you, Sir Lucas. Firstly, you are not the previous Merlin, are you?"

"No, Sir Lucas. I am you. A foreshadow of you, sent by the old Merlin to help you achieve your somewhat delayed destiny."

"So when the Master summoned Merlin back from the Otherworld, he was actually summoning forth you. That is to say, me."

"That is correct. Your predecessor 'Merlin' is now in retirement and could not be recalled for love nor money. He keeps bees, I believe."

"Was my predecessor also a butler, before he became Merlin?"

"Yes. You even worked under him, briefly, in the household of King Uther, Arthur's father."

"Master Blaise? But he went away."

"On his own Grail Quest to the Otherworld, to the Glass Fortress. He came back as Merlin, just in time to arrange Arthur's conception and help him with the early days of his reign."

"His *own* Grail Quest?"

"Different to yours, but in essence the same. A magical object, a catalyst for a coming of age. For him it was a rather fine hamper. The Grail cauldron was yours. For your successor, the last of the butler-magicians, it will be something else."

"So King Arthur was never meant to take the Grail?"

"Good gracious me, no! Treasures as powerful as that should never be removed from the Otherworld by the uninitiated. If anyone else takes a magical object away, it upsets the balance and seals off the Otherworld, allowing the likes of Le Fay to turn it into Hell. No, King Arthur's destiny was at Camelot."

"And at the Last Battle," I said, shuddering at the memory of Camlann.

"Well, it's difficult to say for sure. If you'd got the Grail when you were supposed to, and then returned as a wizard to advise Arthur, perhaps there never would have been a Last Battle. Then again, maybe it was for the best that there was. That's the funny thing about Golden Ages: they only really work when they never last. No quest was ever meant to be eternal."

"I must say, all this seems rather a lot of information for someone to figure out on their own."

"You were never supposed to. Every magician has his other half. They become part of his transition, eventually passing on with him to live beyond the Otherworld, on a far flung shore."

"Beaumains," I said. "Am I too late to save her?" I gestured to her monstrous form, still standing on the outcrop with the other living dead, my loyal staff of Lower Camelot who fought and died so bravely.

"That I cannot say. Certainly, now that you are a butler-magician, nothing is ever too late. Or too early."

"Well, as pleasant as this interval has been, I can't stay here talking forever," I said.

"No," said Sir Lucas. "You certainly can't."

And with that, he passed into me. Or rather, *I* passed into me; my destined Merlin-self, followed by the ever-obedient Grail. And as I absorbed the Grail, it unlocked the full extent of its power, next to which the uses Arthur had put it to on the Eternal Quest were mere sundries.

And so Sir Lucas the Butler became Lucas the Magician, Lucas the Merlin. Transfigured and suspended in Lower Annwn, the manifestation of all the power at my disposal blazed with the light of a thousand stars. I knew that I had only to desire it, and all knowledge, all of space and time, was mine for the taking. And frankly, it was all a bit much. All that radiance and omnipotence is suitably impressive, no doubt, but something of a distraction when trying to focus one's mind on the tasks in hand. No, what I really needed was to concentrate all that power, to pour it into a manageable mould. Something that I could work with.

With that thought, the light fractured into fragments, each the size of a small pane of glass. The pieces arranged themselves in a circle around me, then multiplied, spreading out into three dimensions like the seeds on a dandelion clock. Words appeared on each piece, written in my own hand. Lists and routines, items and itineraries; all the stuff of the first working day of a butler-magician.

I gathered all the gleaming fragments together, piling them up in a stack in my palm until they condensed into a whole. The light faded, and in its place was a small leather-bound notebook edged with gold, which flipped open to the first page. I read it and nodded, satisfied. It told me everything I needed to do next, and exactly how to do it, and that was more than enough to be going on with.

And so I set to work.

# III

"Master?"

"Good morning, staff," I said to the living dead of Lower Annwn. At the sudden manifestation of my Merlin-self, their jaws dropped. Which, seeing as most of them were barely attached to their faces anyway, was quite a sight. "Item one on the agenda. Cancelling curses and de-damning the damned." The creatures moaned and groaned, but from habit rather than complaint. Indeed, I detected a certain lightness to their tone, my magical ear picking up a faint anticipation of job satisfaction. As they gathered together in a group, they seemed to stand a little taller, their flesh slightly less decomposed. Restoration had begun.

While they were assembling (for down here they shuffled somewhat slowly) I closed my eyes and sent my mind off deep into the Otherworld for a good rummage around. I was looking for the place where lost legends go, waiting to be claimed by their rightful owners. When I found what I was looking for, I gathered together all the broken pieces and pulled them up out of the depths. I opened my eyes. In the air before me were many shards of metal. "Owen," I said to the creature who had once been the finest armourer in the land. At the sound of his old name, he cocked his head like a near-deaf dog. "Take these shards to your smithy. Re-forge me a sword fit for a King.

"As for the rest of you," I continued, "item two."

I drew an arc in the air and peeled back the earth above our heads like the skin of a satsuma. The gloom of Annwn seeped down from above. Tools and implements flew out from the store room in which I had first arrived, distributing themselves among the creatures so that no-one was without a mop, bucket, brush or broom. "Time to give Hell a thorough spring clean," I said. They murmured in the affirmative, and off they all went, crawling up the rock face. The one who had been Beaumains I kept by my side. "For my next task, a mode of transportation is in order," I said.

"Stables," she said, a brightness returning to her eyes. It was joyous to see, but I restrained myself from celebrating prematurely. She pointed down the precipice, past the now-dry pool and the pit into which I had passed, over to where Sir Gareth's skeleton had marched. At her signal, a stone rolled away to reveal a hidden cave. With one step I passed over the edge and floated down to the lower level, taking her with me.

The stables were full of skeleton horses, stamping and whinnying as the once-Beaumains and I walked among them. I soon found the one I was looking for. To my eyes he stood out from all the others, for although most of his flesh had fallen away, he was not a knight's horse, and had not died at Camlann. Plum recognised me too, staring back at me from empty eye sockets, pushing at my arm with his long white skull.

I felt like I should give him something, and accordingly a lump of sugar appeared in my hand. Yellow teeth took it from my palm. As he crunched it in his jaws, the sinews quickly knitted back into place around his mouth. Flesh reformed on his flanks. Bright eyes and a glossy coat glowed with healthy radiance. The other horses stamped their skeletal feet in jealousy. "Hush. Your time will come. Take these horses up for your fellow creatures," I said to Beaumains. "When they have finished their work, have them ready to ride at my command." I mounted Plum and looked up at the rocky ceiling. "Let's raise the roof, Plum old thing," I said. "Full gallop."

Up we flew, Plum's hooves pounding at the earth, out from the depths of Hell, smashing up through Morgan's castle, then higher still, into the dark skies of Annwn. Here one could see the full extent to which her realm had extended. But my staff were already hard at work, pushing the power of Annwn back to where it belonged, restoring the Otherworld that still lay beneath, like the dormant ground of winter awaiting the first touch of spring.

Plum galloped on through the sky. Down below us I saw Perceval, stumbling through a forest that was blooming into life all around him. Yet wherever he stepped, the wasteland still held sway, as if he were enclosed in his own black bubble of desolation. I set Plum down on the path amid a blossoming patch of bluebells. Ahead of Perceval, there moved an object not unlike the Grail. But from this angle I could see it was just a model, a wooden replica carried by two living dead creatures, gleefully leading Sir Perceval on a wild goose chase. I stood in their path and they stopped in their tracks, caught in the act.

"Well?" I said. "What have you got to say for yourselves?"

"Master," said one, looking at his feet.

"Master," said the other, shrugging rotting shoulders. Aspects of their appearance were familiar, and I knew that these culprits had once been Geraint the Gatekeeper, and you, Gwion, although you will thankfully have no memory of it.

"Get yourselves to Lower Annwn, and we'll say no more about it," I said.

The two of them sank apologetically down through the forest floor, just as Perceval, worn and weary, fell upon the false Grail like a pauper on a crust. At his embrace the dead wood broke apart, and the look in his eyes spoke of a heart about to do likewise.

"Please, Merlin," he said. "If you have the real Grail, take me to it."

"Why?"

"It's my quest. It always has been, yet I'm cursed to be its keeper, or its seeker, never its achiever."

"The Grail is not the quest of a knight, Perceval. The Grail serves a servant."

Perceval squinted at me. "Lucas? Is that you?"

"In a manner of speaking," I said. And in that moment my true self was revealed to him, and the black bubble surrounding him burst, flowers flourishing at his feet.

"Come along," I said. "There is work to be done."

"The Eternal Quest?" he said.

"The end of it," I said. "You might call it the Quest to end all Quests."

"Count me in," said Perceval, and he got up onto Plum behind me. "Where are the others?"

"One thing at a time, Perceval," I said.

†

Spring had not yet reached the desert where the Questing Beast chivvied Sir Pellinore up and down the endless sands. I set Plum down at the foot of a dune and alighted. Pellinore skidded down from the top and came to a stop. Behind him, the Beast and its rider did likewise. "Herne the Hunter," said Pellinore, his voice parched and panting. "You summoned this Questing Beast of burden. End it now. Destroy it, before it destroys me."

"The man is master of the quest; the quest is not master of the man," I said.

"Sounds very quotable. Who said that?"

"You did."

"All the same, a vow is a vow. And I swore to master this Beast."

"Then master it. Look behind you." Pellinore turned. "The Beast stopped running when you did."

Pellinore walked towards the Questing Beast. It squared up to him, hissing through its snake jaws, poised pounce-ready on lion haunches. But Pellinore hissed right back at it, holding its serpentine stare. The Beast retreated, cowed and submissive. The creature riding it dismounted and scurried to my side. In one bound Pellinore was up on the Beast's back.

"Ha! You're right, Herne!" he said. "You haven't seen a butler round about these parts, have you? Goes by the name of Lucas. Seem to remember seeing him just before I came to this place. What *is* this place, by the way?"

"Hell. Though not for much longer, I am pleased to say. But as for Sir Lucas the butler, I regret to inform you that he is no longer with us."

"Pity," said Pellinore. "Splendid fellow. You two would've got on."

"I'm sure we would, Pellinore."

"So what now?" said Perceval. "Plum here is champing at the bit."

"We're almost ready," I said.

Spreading over the horizon, shimmering like an oasis, the regeneration of the Otherworld swept across the desert, returning it to the fertile land of legend. Almost. But not quite. The restoration would not be complete until everything that had passed through the portal between worlds had been returned, and the door sealed up once more. Or, as I preferred to call it, item three on the agenda.

I stretched out with my mind for the breach between the Otherworld and the real world beyond, pulling it towards me until the vortex spun before us like a horizontal funnel. "Staff!" I said. The creatures rose up out of the earth at my command, mounted on the skeleton horses of the army of the dead. Since I had left them, my staff's appearance had improved even more, the balance of their condition tipping away from the dead and towards the living. Someone who now looked a lot more like Owen rode up to my side and presented me with a sword, shining and new, sheathed in a temporary scabbard. I hid it inside my cloak, and inspected my strange companions. What a sight we made. A newly minted magician and a knight sharing a steed, leading an army of fifty of the living-dead on skeleton horses, accompanied by a knight riding a Beast that could not decide if it were snake, leopard, lion or stag. Such a rag-tag band of the broken and the mended were entirely appropriate for the work ahead.

"Follow me," I said, and led them out of the Otherworld.

# IV

We emerged from the breach between worlds on the West Wales coast, precisely one second after I had stepped into it with the body of Sir Pellinore. I consulted my notebook. The next page informed me that Morgan was still savouring her triumph over King Arthur back at the stadium. Well, let her enjoy it while she may. It would give me just enough time to make my preparations.

I divided my domestic army into two equal units. The first, under the leadership of Pellinore, were tasked with rounding up all the dragons, demons, and chaotic creatures of the Otherworld and herding them back into the portal. "Consider it done, Herne," said Pellinore, sending the Questing Beast springing up over the headland. "Now, the first rule of beast herding is, always work as a team. Remember, there's no 'I' in dragon." The rest of his words were lost in the yelping and baying coming from the belly of his steed as Pellinore led his crew of skeletal horses and living-dead horsemen in a wild hunt across the sky.

The second unit would follow Perceval and myself. The magical energy that streamed up out of the portal had changed in colour with our return. It now possessed a light freshness that took the edge of apocalypse out of the air, the effects of my staff's spring clean of Hell following in our wake. As we flew, I could see the difference it made to the ground below. The recreated Camelot was rubbling gently back into the earth. The town of Cardigan reassembled in the right place, the enchanted, sleeping people sitting up and rubbing their eyes. Everywhere the devastation wrought by the outpourings of the Otherworld was being undone, reversing the end of the world. Ahead of us, to the east, the darkness still held sway over Cardiff. I spurred Plum onwards.

I have no idea what history Cardiff prison has known in the subject of escaped convicts. But I think it is safe to assume it has never held any fugitive quite like the one known only as Sir Kay. I instructed Perceval and the others to wait for me while I teleported directly into his cell, along with Plum and a spare skeletal steed.

Kay was sitting at a small desk, working in longhand on a great sheaf, the floor covered with balls of scrunched-up paper. Piles of prison library books covered both the upper and lower bunks of his bed, and possibly his cellmate. He was so engrossed in his work that he did not notice my sudden visitation.

"Kay," I said. "I am here to end your incarceration."

"You've completely interrupted my stream of thought," he said, pausing his pen. "My prison diary, *Sentence by Sentence*. Only a working title."

"Very droll."

Kay turned to face me and his mouth opened in amazement. "Lucas?"

"Yes," I said. "But I've been promoted. It's time to go."

Kay looked around, taking in myself, Plum, and the skeleton horse in his cell.

"I can't," he said. "I'm better off here. They found that dead body, Lucas, as well as my *Chronicles*. They know what really happened."

"Yes, they do."

"I never meant to disobey Arthur's orders. But after I'd finished the *History* cover-story, I had nothing left to write. So I went back to the *Chronicles* and started again." He smiled, weakly. "Yet another draft. Arthur's going to kill me."

"King Arthur has other things on his mind," I said. "Besides, I have an idea for a new story. One with a better ending to any we have known."

"Why don't you write it?" said Kay, but without malice.

"It requires an expert hand."

Kay picked up his pen and tucked it behind his ear. He pushed back the chair and stood up. "Better stop distracting me so I can make a start then, eh?"

"Your steed awaits," I said.

"What, *that* steed?"

"Yes, Kay."

Using the bed as a mounting block, Kay got on the horse, wincing a little. "Bit bony."

"Its gaunt aspect is compensated for by other qualities," I said.

"Such as?"

"Teleportation, and flight."

I clicked my tongue, Plum whinnied, and we vanished from the cell.

†

Of course, young Gwion, the situations I am describing to you are not normal working conditions. Your own transition from butler to magician will, I'm sure, be an altogether smoother one. I doubt, for example, if you will ever have cause to open a Nick in Time, as I did. But, as for the whole matter of Service Time, that is something that could do with explaining. It is a butler-magician's greatest asset, and the foundation on which his working practise rests. You experienced it shortly before I left you for the last time. But once again, I am getting ahead of myself. In order to illustrate the full application of Service Time, I must first tell you about the Nick in Time, and a picture as hopeless as any painted by even the most morose of myth-makers.

Arriving at the stadium, I alighted from Plum and told him and the others to await my signal, for the matter of a Fay was a wizard's work. Everything was more or less as I had left it. Morgan had her arms spread wide in triumph, holding the scabbard and now standing directly over King Arthur as he bled his last from the curse of Excalibur. Lancelot was still skewered to the ground by a skeleton foot. Gawain remained in a bloody heap on the ground, lying ominously still. And the skeletons themselves surrounded the scene like spectral spectators. But now they looked wholly different to my eyes. They were no longer an anonymous threat, the marauding horde of the damned dead. Each and every one of them was a knight I had once called a brother.

"Merlin," she said, blankly, at my arrival. "Tardy, as usual. Well, you are too late this time."

"I come to make peace," I said. I held out my hand, flat and open, offering it for her to shake. "I give you one last chance for redemption. End this, and return to Annwn of your own free will. Or reap the destiny you have sown."

Morgan curled her lip in disgust and spat into my hand. The spit landed in the middle of my palm. I transformed it into a miniature lake, its waters lapping tiny reeds at my wrist.

"Pathetic games and parlour tricks," she said. "You are going soft in your old age."

"Actually, I have only just been born," I said.

The sword Excalibur, fresh-formed and full-sized, rose up from the lake in my palm. Morgan shrieked, as was her wont, but it was to no avail, for in the twinkling of an eye the magical scabbard flew out of her hands to be reunited with the sword. I fastened them to the waist of the fallen maimed King, as I had first done all those years ago.

At the return of Excalibur the curse was lifted. Blood flowed back up out of the ground and into King Arthur. He rose to his feet as his flesh meshed together. Morgan flew up into the air, howling with rage. "Army of the Dead! Destroy them!" she cried. The skeletons moved forwards at her command. But I had a command of my own at the ready. "Staff!" I shouted.

The entire sky above the Millennium Stadium was filled with the massed ranks of the domestic living-dead and their horses, led by Kay, Perceval and Pellinore upon the Questing Beast. They descended to the pitch and dismounted, surrounding the skeleton army. The sight of their old horses, as bereft of skin as they, awakened the memory of the skeletons' old knightly selves. They dropped their jagged black swords on the ground, scratching their skulls, as if trying to puzzle out how they had got there. The one pinning down Lancelot pulled his foot from out of the fallen knight's hand. Perceval and Kay helped Gawain to his feet.

Morgan drew on all her powers, focusing them into one last mustering of black magic. She threw it with all her might at King Arthur, a beam of bile that crackled through the air. King Arthur drew Excalibur to meet it. The blast struck the sword with a sizzle, like hot fat hitting cold water. Gaining more strength with every step, Arthur pushed the beam back until he stood level with his half-sister.

"Curse you," she said.

"Not anymore," said King Arthur, and chopped off her head.

The nearest skeleton caught it before it hit the ground, jumping onto a horse and taking off into the air. The other skeletons followed him, plucking up Morgan's decapitated body and riding back to the Otherworld portal, a hundred of them in a flying stampede, until only my living-dead staff remained.

Except that they were no longer the living-dead, but now fully returned to the people I remembered. You, Gwion, shook your head woozily. Geraint looked around himself in wonder, while Enid, Bedwyr and Owen embraced each other. And Beaumains walked towards me, the light of recognition in her bright eyes, her full, reinstated mouth breaking into a wonderful smile. I smiled back, but not without sadness, for with this restoration her work was done, and I knew what would happen now that the curse was broken. Beaumains got to within an arm's reach of me and dissolved into the air. Her departure, like all the passing away of my old staff, was no more than a breath of breeze on my cheek.

"Well, Herne," said Pellinore, slapping me on the back, hard. "That's every last critter back in the hole. Except for this one." Pellinore patted the Questing Beast's flank. It wagged its tail. At least, I think it did, for my vision was temporarily blurred.

"I am afraid you can't keep it, Pellinore," I said, wiping my eyes.

"Damn. Thought you were going to say that. Well, I can't say I won't miss it after all these years. Gave me quite the run-around, all told. But, you're the hunter, huntsman." I clicked my fingers and sent the Questing Beast back to the Otherworld.

"Lucas?" said Arthur. "What happened to you?"

I ignored him for a moment and shut my eyes, stretching my mind out to the West Wales coast, sealing up the portal between this world and the Otherworld forever. When I opened my eyes again, the dark skies had been replaced by bright June sunshine. The media and military people, who had remained on the tiered seating throughout the finalé,

*The Last Day* / **391**

still held their distance, not yet trusting the evidence of their senses against everything they had seen over the past few days.

Arthur and Lancelot stood side-by-side, looking at me, their expression one of curiosity mingled with surprise, pushing aside all their recent enmity. Even Gawain's rage at Lancelot seemed to have left him.

"You have some explaining to do, Lucas," Arthur said to me. Of course, I had to do nothing of the sort. But old habits die hard, even when one has just started a new life.

And loose ends have always bothered my eye.

# V

The first thing you need to know about a Nick in Time, Gwion, is what it is not. It is categorically *not* time travel. Such things are, to my knowledge, highly unwise, even for magicians as powerful as we. There are, however, certain points in time that possess rare qualities, setting them apart from the more common moments in the endless procession of days. In order to make effective use of such nuggets, you first have to ask yourself some searching questions. I suppose what it all boils down to, is this:

*Do you really want the way back to be the way forwards?*

And that is something that I could not answer, as I stood there among the knights I had served for so long, after telling them the story of how Lucas the butler achieved the Quest for the Grail and became Lucas the Merlin. Certainly, my notebook offered no clues. The next page remained stubbornly blank, as did all the pages after that. So we stood there, the seven of us, while the world returned to normal. The ranks of the media had increased up on the seating. Cameras were pointing down at us. With a familiar yawn of clatter and clamour, the world once more woke up to our presence among them.

"I must say," said Kay, "all this has a whiff of anti-climax. I mean, it's all well and good you being a wizard,

Lucas — congratulations, by the way — but what about the rest of us?"

"Aye. And don't think my grievance is done," said Gawain. "Magic Pants Lucas is all well and good, but it doesn't alter the fact that we're only here 'cos both of you lied." He pointed to Lancelot, and to Arthur. "So don't go pretending everything's all mead and honey. Gareth still died for nothing. They all did."

"The question is," said Perceval. "What do we do next? Wait around to get arrested?"

"No thanks, not again," said Kay.

"Like we'll have any choice in the matter!" said Gawain. "We'll be freaks. They'll put us in cages an' prod us with sticks. If we're lucky."

"And now that there's no Grail — well, now that *you're* the Grail, Lucas — I suppose there's nothing left for us to do but... what? Wait around to wither and die?" said Kay.

"Not so Eternal a Quest after all, it would seem," said Lancelot.

King Arthur remained silent, drawing a circle in the mud with the point of Excalibur.

"If we are to die as mortal men, then I would sooner have done so back when such a death meant something," said Lancelot to the King. The King cut the circle in half, forming two semi-circular shapes.

The notebook trembled in my hand like a timorous mouse.

"To have the world remember us at our best," agreed King Arthur, "not as tarnished and sullied knights past their prime."

"Returning with the Grail to save the day," said Lancelot.

"Back in the nick of time," said Arthur.

The notebook gave a sudden jolt. Words started to write themselves on the open page. Aha. So that was it.

"I might be able to do something about that," I said. "Or rather, you might, Arthur." King Arthur looked at me expectantly, as the pitch started to fill with running men and women. I stretched out my hands and pressed my palms against the air in front of me.

"Whatever are you doing, Lucas?" said the King at my side.

"Looking for a loose end," I said. "The tiniest tear; a Nick in Time. Arthur, when I give the word, take Excalibur and draw a slow, wide arc in the air, starting from the exact point that I show you." The King unsheathed his sword and stood ready.

Wherever the Nick was, it would be near me. It was only *because* of me that it was there in the first place. I pressed again with my hands. The air to my left felt a little looser, like a wobbly floorboard. I brought my eye up close to the spot — a tiny point of light, no bigger than a pin-hole. I looked into it and saw, with the distorted magnification of a fisheye lens, seven men standing in a hidden glade. I turned my ear to the pin-hole, and listened. The clamour of the approaching crowd grew ever louder, but I tuned them out easily, for I knew exactly what I was listening for.

"This is not a time for sorrow," said a voice.

Bright light shone through the pin-hole as the Grail, as it was back then, rose up in the glade, hovering above the head of the old King Arthur like a large and clumsy crown.

"My knights," said the voice through the hole, "today is a glorious day."

The military pounded towards us, a crowd of cameras and microphones following after them like reinforcements.

"There," I said to King Arthur, pointing at the seam. "Cut there."

The King raised Excalibur. He tucked the tip of the sword into the pin-hole, and sliced through the air in a wide arc to his right. At the sword's passing there was a loud ripping sound, like a thick material being torn in two. The stadium was suddenly filled with light, as if the sun were rising in front of us. The crowd dropped back, blinded and awestruck. The radiance increased, until the King had sliced away a full semicircular section. The air in the stadium dropped down like a fold of cut cloth, revealing a perfectly formed archway, a door between today and yesterday.

A bridge between Grails.

"The noble dream of Camelot will never die while we seven are still alive to uphold it," said the old King in the glade.

"Amen to that," said the King in the stadium.

He stepped through the archway and into the glade, back into the moment when the power of the Grail had first been unleashed at his command. King Arthur walked over to his old self, frozen in the transfigured moment. He passed into his own body, settling into its outline, the once and future king united. The rest of the knights followed him back to their past selves and did likewise.

I stood for a moment on the torn seam between worlds, on the frayed edges of a Nick in Time, and signalled for Plum to follow me through. Then I too stepped into the hidden glade. And for the second time, I achieved the Grail, and at last I knew everything else I had to do — the full knowledge of Service Time, my final destiny as butler-magician. The old Grail passed into me, and I passed into my old self, and I closed up the Nick in Time behind us as easy as pulling up a zip.

And King Arthur and the Knights of the Round Table left the modern world, forever.

# VI

The phenomenon we butler-magicians call 'Service Time,' Gwion, has its origin in situations of high domestic crisis — moments when one has a hundred things to do and not enough hours in the day in which to do them. It is not that time itself slows down. It is more that you yourself speed up, in such a way that you catch time unawares, giving it no choice but to follow *your* schedule for a change. I left King Arthur and the knights behind in the glade, to make their return on horseback, and took Plum and myself to Camlann the very instant we returned, for there were things I had to do first, in order for our return to have the maximum effect. We teleported into the valley of Camlann, and I tethered him to a tree out of sight before setting out across the battlefield.

I strode through the mêlée, ducking axes and avoiding swords with no more inconvenience as if they were platters of food being conveyed to a feast along a busy corridor. Mordred's forces had mounted their first attack, down the southern slope into the valley. Sir Gareth and the garrisons had been pushed back down to the valley floor and over towards the opposite, northern side. There were my staff, in the middle guard, acquitting themselves admirably against Mordred's forces. Enid, Bedwyr and Geraint, all grit and determination. And you, Gwion, brave and resourceful; I smiled at the thought of what a worthy successor you will make. Sir Bors, Sir Ector and Sir Dagonet had fallen, but this time my heart was light at their passing, for I knew that the Otherworld they were going to was now an afterlife fit for heroes.

And there was Beaumains. Not yet dead. Better still, not yet the living-dead. Full of life and fighting fit. I walked up to her, dodging a falling horse.

"Beaumains," I said.

At the sound of my voice she turned, her opponent falling dead at her feet.

"Lucas?" she cried in disbelief. "What are you — where the hell have you been? Are you out of your mind?"

"I'm glad to see you," I said. *With all your flesh intact,* I almost added, but felt it might ruin the moment. I took her free left hand, and held it in mine.

"You must be deranged to act like this in the middle of a battle — look out!" A knight hurled an axe at my head.

"What? Oh yes, that. Of course." I held up my other hand.

The axe stopped. So did the rest of the battle. Every spear stood still and every arrow paused mid-flight. Every sword thrust ceased as every heartbeat froze, save for mine and the woman I loved, standing together centre stage in the theatre of war. Beaumains looked around us at the arrested conflict, amazed.

"What just happened?"

"It's magic."

"You have changed."

"Yes. It's rather difficult to explain. It involves the Grail."

"No, I mean: you are holding my hand. You don't seriously mean to tell me you have strolled back into my life after seven years, slap bang into the middle of a war, and stopped the world turning, just to hold my hand?" She seemed more irritated than I had been expecting.

"Beaumains. I have spanned centuries, killed dragons and defeated witches, journeyed to Hell and back, died, been reborn, and torn apart the very seams of time. And all to get back to the deepest enchantment I have ever known on the good green earth."

"On it, under it, above it, beyond it," she said, testily. But then she smiled. "Well, better late than never, I suppose." And she pulled me towards her, and kissed me.

Knowing that, if I wanted to, I could make such a kiss last forever, it took a supreme effort of will not to simply make it so. But, as soul-soaringly wonderful as the moment was, sooner or later we had a Last Battle to be getting on with. Still in each other's arms, we took in the scene around us. I told her how I had felt witnessing the conflict replayed in Hell; that indefinable offence to my professional sensibility, an inkling that the battle could somehow have been better managed.

"They are doing their best," she said. "But they are not soldiers."

"Of course. That's it!" I said, looking at the next page of my notebook. "They were never meant to be."

I unfroze my staff. And I briefed them in the Last Staff Meeting.

†

So it was that when the Last Battle of Camlann recommenced, it was fought on decidedly different lines. Sir Gareth and his remaining forces found their numbers suddenly and mysteriously depleted, as those service staff who had fought alongside them only a moment ago appeared to have vanished. Of course, they hadn't really gone anywhere. They were still *in* the battle. They were just not *of* the battle. Indeed, if they were to be noticed by anyone, it would mean that they were not doing their job properly. When in the midst of a fray, a servant must remain all but invisible until the precise moment their services are required.

As for the nature of such services, there is no challenge war can throw up that one has not already faced in the course of one's duties. A good butler has an eye fine-tuned to detail, down to the last speck of dust in a room. To this can be added his skill at drawing-up lists, plans and itineraries of every description. I have organised feasts more physically demanding than any military campaign. Likewise, I have experienced hospitality just as damaging to body and soul as any conflict. More importantly, a butler can keep his head while all around him are losing theirs, be it literally or metaphorically.

Consider: Sir Gareth fighting Sir Sagramour. Gareth drops his dagger, but soon it appears again at his side, freshly sharpened and cleaned of blood. He sustains a cut to the leg; moments later, a dollop of healing ointment stems the wound. Sir Marhalt is unhorsed; his steed is conveyed to a safe distance, fed, watered, re-saddled, and sent back to his master, who is still marvelling at the sudden appearance of a cup of water to soothe his own parched throat.

It has often been said that an army marches on its stomach. But it wins wars on its service industry.

And all of this occurred in the full application of Service Time. Each member of my staff found that they had exactly the right amount of time to complete their tasks. No sword was fast enough to catch us the slightest nick, no spear provided any occupational hazard. Thus did the remaining knights find themselves in a perpetual state of replenishment and refreshment, while their opponents, tired and wounded and confounded by the sight of the enemy's self-bandaging wounds and freshly polished shields, were soon on the retreat. Beaumains looked up to the east where the residual light loosed from our return to the glade still blazed in the sky.

"Like a second sunrise," she said. "A good omen?"

"I wonder," said Sir Gareth, then noticed my presence for the first time. "Lucas!" he cried, clasping my shoulders. "So it *was* you I met on the road!"

"Indeed it was, Sir Gareth."

A gust of wind swept down on us. We turned our eyes up to the north hill. There at the summit stood a second army, as numerous as the first, while up on the opposing hillside the first army had regrouped.

"That was not a retreat," said Sir Gareth. "It was to prevent one of our own."

Now Mordred appeared, among the number to the north. "Hemming us in on both sides," said Guinevere. "A coward, but a cunning one."

"Lucas," whispered Sir Gareth. "What about the others? What about the King?"

"On their way. But though they move on swift hooves, we need to buy them a little more time."

"What do you suggest?"

"With the support of my staff, you will last a good while longer. But when the enemy's numbers overwhelm us, we should lay down our weapons," I said.

"Surrender?"

"Only a temporary one. In that, you will have to trust me."

"Only a fool doesn't listen to his butler," said Sir Gareth. "Curious to say," he added, "this does not feel like the end."

†

"They have archers!" said Sir Palomides.

"Prepare your bows!" ordered Sir Gareth. A hail of arrows sped towards the knights, slowed, and then stopped, suspended in Service Time. My staff quickly plucked them out of the air and placed them in the taut bows of the very men they were aimed at. Time resumed its normal flow. Astonishment filled the minds of the archers at the top of the north slope, shortly before their own arrows filled their bodies. At a signal from Mordred, the forces on the southern side of the valley charged down, but we held our ground and forced them back until not one of them was left standing. Mordred advanced to the very crest of the north hill, an army of hundreds still behind him.

He was about to order his final attack when he saw a man approaching him from within the ranks of the rebels, a single emissary limping up the valley slope, waving a white flag. Flanked by two guards, Mordred spurred his horse forwards to speak with him.

"Hello there," said Geraint.

"Is that... the Gatekeeper?" said Mordred.

"That's me, buddy."

"That's me, *sire*," corrected one guard, darkly.

"You will address the King in the proper manner, rebel scum," said the other.

"See now, there's a logical flaw to that. It doesn't make me much of a rebel if I acknowledge him as King, does it?"

"Do not bandy riddles with me, porter," said Mordred.

"How about a coin trick, then?"

"What?"

"Never mind. I've come to announce our unconditional surrender." Geraint waved his white flag to his comrades below. Every last one of them dropped their weapons. Mordred smiled a reedy smile.

"That," he said, "was a mistake."

"No," said Geraint. "*That* was misdirection."

A horn blast reverberated around the valley. From the eastern end, six knights on horseback galloped through the stream and into Camlann, flying the banner of King Arthur. A cheer went up from the knights below and they took up their weapons again. Mordred's forces shifted uneasily, as news of King Arthur's return swept through their ranks like wildfire. Many at the back turned tail and fled, while those at the front broke ranks in fear and disarray.

"Yes," said Geraint to Mordred, "in my experience, there's no better sign than a bright light in the east." And I teleported him back to our side for the end of the Last Battle.

# VII

Well Gwion, the sun is shining and breakfast beckons, and I do not intend to start such a splendid day with eggs over-boiled. Besides, that was about all I can give to you by way of an introduction. The rest of it you will have to work out for yourself. I'm sorry I left in such a hurry. But, having instructed my staff and returned King Arthur and his greatest knights to their place in the Last Battle, I consulted my To Do list for the last time, and saw that my only remaining task was to leave them to work out the finer points of their destiny for themselves.

I do, however, keep up with my reading, and occasionally some volume of history or folklore will find its way out here, to the very back of beyond. My current favourite is a large tome called *The Chronicles of Godfrey of Wales*. It speaks of the Last Battle of Camlann as a time of heroes, but also as the inevitable end of the noble dream of Camelot. It says that such a Golden Age was never meant to be eternal. That to draw it out past its natural end would only diminish its potential to inspire all the generations to follow.

It tells of how Sir Gawain gave his life to save Sir Lancelot, of how Sir Lancelot died to save Guinevere, and how Guinevere died for her King. Of how King Arthur finally faced the traitor Mordred, and how they struck each other down at the last. Of how the King, sore-wounded, was taken away by his surviving knights, his body and the sword Excalibur borne across the Enchanted Lake in the Enchanted Forest, off to the Otherworld, so some men say. And of how, of those six knights in shining armour who returned in the nick of time that day, none fought so finely or so fiercely as the brave and noble Sir Kay.

Of course, I know from experience not to take such tales on face value, for there have been many books written on the subject, and there will be many more, for as long as the world keeps turning. However, there is one matter on which this book and others like it remain curiously silent. And that concerns the fate of Sir Lucas the butler; or Sir Lucas the Merlin, as he was latterly known to only a few.

On that matter I might shed some light, but only a little, and for you alone, Gwion, for the destiny of wizards is not for the ears of all and sundry. But I can tell you at least of how Sir Lucas slipped away from the skirmish and returned to where he had tethered his trusty steed, hand-in-hand with the woman to whom his fate was so irresistibly bound. Of how they made their way down to the coast together, and from there set out at a full gallop for the Otherworld. Away into the west with the setting sun, across the wide green meadows of the sea.

# Acknowledgements

The feedback, inspiration and advice provided by the following people was invaluable throughout the writing of *Sleepless Knights*. To detail the breadth and variety of their encouragement would require a new Eternal Quest. I hope this Round Table roll-call of knights and ladies of legend will suffice.

At the High Table: thanks to Laura Cotton for love and support in every adventure.

Hearty toasts of gratitude are due to the company of Camelot: Dinos Aristidou, Kym Bartlett, Rachel Benbow, Joanna Burnett, Phil Clark, Neil Cocker, Angharad Devonald, Charlotte Geeves, Emma & Simon Gough, Richard Hall, Llinos Harries, Sharlene Harvard-Young, James Hodgkins, Sue & Dave Hutchings, Mark Jones, Sarah Kent, Stephen Knight, Tim Lebbon, Lisa, Damien & Erin Murphy, Jessica Naish, Richard Nichols, Richard Parker, Kate Perridge, Pam & Mike Pickford, Ben Potter, William Rees, Jane Rawson, Derek Ritchie, Adam Strange, Granville Swan, Annabel Tremlett, Gareth & Hannah Williams, and Juliette Wood.

And last but by no means least, ballads and bumpers aplenty to Ian Alexander Martin, for his unending enthusiasm for this Chronicle.

# About the Author

**Mark H Williams** is a playwright and scriptwriter. His work includes *Here Be Monsters* (Theatr Iolo, 2013) and a stage adaptation of *Jason & The Argonauts* (Courtyard Hereford, 2013).

He has written two UK-touring stage adaptations of Scholastic's "Horrible" series for The Birmingham Stage Company: *Horrible Histories: The Frightful First World War* (2009; nominated for a *"Manchester Evening News* Award") and *Horrible Science* (2010 & 2013).

Mark has written extensively for BBC Wales radio and TV, and is currently developing new projects with National Theatre Wales and the Torch Theatre.

*Sleepless Knights* is his first published work in any form. He is working on his second book, a fantasy novel about magic, bards and monsters.

He can be found on Twitter as @MarkHWilliams and at www.MarkHWilliams.WordPress.com.

# ATOMIC FEZ PUBLISHING

*Eclectic, Genre-Busting Fiction*

www.AtomicFez.com